Under Suspicion

THE MULGRAY TWINS

ISIS
LARGE PRINT
Oxford

First published in Great Britain 2008
by
Allison & Busby Limited

Published in Large Print 2008 by ISIS Publishing Ltd.,
7 Centremead, Osney Mead, Oxford OX2 0ES
by arrangement with
Allison & Busby

British Library Cataloguing in Publication Data
Mulgray, Helen
Under suspicion. – Large print ed.
1. Customs administration – Scotland – Officials and
employees – Fiction
2. Money laundering investigation – Fiction
3. Undercover operations – Fiction
4. Persian cat – Fiction
5. Detective and mystery stories
6. Large type books
I. Title II. Mulgray, Morna
823.9'2 [F]

ISBN 978–0–7531–8216–1 (hb)
ISBN 978–0–7531–8217–8 (pb)

Printed and bound in Great Britain by
T. J. International Ltd., Padstow, Cornwall

To Norman,

*whose mastery of words
we cannot hope to emulate.*

Acknowledgements

Our thanks to Alanna Knight for her advice, support and friendship.

In research matters we are indebted to the following:
   Cherry and Ray Legg, whose expertise in windsurfing contributed a vital element of the plot.
   The Maritime and Coastguard Agency for advice on International Maritime Regulations.
   Norrie Wilson for electrical know-how essential to the plot.
   Elizabeth Scott who continues to keep us right on matters feline.

For those readers interested in the phenomenon of cats that paint (or find the idea totally incredible), we refer you to the works of art in *Why Cats Paint — a theory of feline aesthetics* by Burton Silver and Heather Busch, published by Ten Speed Press, Toronto.

And thanks as always to our agent, Frances Hanna of Acacia House Publishing, Brantford, Ontario, for her ongoing endeavours for DJ Smith and Gorgonzola.

Prologue

12.30p.m. Playa de las Américas, Tenerife, Canary Islands. In five minutes Bill Gardener, undercover agent for Her Majesty's Revenue & Customs, would be dead. The order had been given. At this very moment the killer was purposefully making his way towards him along the pink-tiled pavement of Geranium Walk.

Bill Gardener sipped thoughtfully at his beer. He'd taken quite a chance this morning in snatching a look at the files in Devereux's office. It'd been a bit of a scary moment when Security had burst in, checking to find out why, on a holiday, somebody was in the office. He'd expected it, had his story ready. And he'd got away with it. But what he'd found had been disappointing, nothing out of the ordinary, just photos of sold properties, contracts, that sort of thing. It hadn't been worth the risk of blowing his cover.

He finished his beer and watched the foam slide slowly down the empty glass. It was a couple of minutes after 12.30, and it must be 28°C out there on the exposed pontoons of the marina. He hitched his chair further back into the shade. The sun danced on the ruffled blue water, flashed off windows in the serried ranks of moored cruisers and spotlighted the white hulls of bobbing powerboats.

Seagulls screeched and squabbled over pickings thrown from one of the deep-sea game-fishing boats tied up at its berth. He'd always fancied going after big fish like marlin — or Ambrose Vanheusen, if it came to that. Of course, it wasn't just a case of dangling a baited hook. That's what drew him. It was a battle of wits, the outguessing your opponent's twists and turns — in other words, the thrill of the chase. When the team had cracked this case, he'd book himself on a game boat, have his photo taken with his catch, just like that lucky guy over there.

It was by sheer chance, a combination of his angle of view and the harsh lighting of the midday sun, that he connected the T-shirted crewman with the photos he'd seen in the files. The pieces of the puzzle clicked into place. He knew now how the money-laundering scam operated. He had to hand it to Vanheusen. That scheme of his was pretty neat, could have run for years without detection. It had taken months of planning for HMRC to set up the operation and plant him undercover in Vanheusen's HQ. Now he, Bill Gardener, was about to bring home the goods. He reached out his hand for his camera phone, eyes still on the figure in the white T-shirt.

The thin blade of the spring-loaded knife reached its target. 12.35p.m.

CHAPTER
ONE

Jim Orr, senior investigating officer in Her Majesty's Revenue & Customs, for once looked ruffled. Nothing too obvious, but the signs were there in the way he fussily aligned and realigned the papers on his desk.

"Sorry about the short notice, Deborah." He sounded weary. "Bit of an emergency in our Tenerife office. We're sending you and your cat to help them out."

"So, it's undercover in the sun for me, and a specialist drug-detection job for Gorgonzola, eh?" I quipped. After my previous chilly assignment in the cold and mist of a Scottish summer, that sounded a bit of all right.

There was no answering smile. He broke the news about the murder of Bill Gardener. I opened my mouth to speak, but he hurried on. "With our carefully planted mole suddenly taken out, Operation Canary Creeper has ground to a halt. Many months of careful planning are about to go down the drain." He fell silent, mulling over the seriousness of the situation, softening me up for the request he was about to make. "Then I thought of your cat Gorgonzola. You see, Ambrose Vanheusen, the target of this money-laundering investigation, has an Achilles heel." His thumb riffled the corner of the stack of papers. "To be more exact, he has an obsession with that pedigree Persian cat of his. And that's where your cat will come in."

"Well," I laughed, "G's definitely a Persian, but as far as *appearance* goes . . ."

A short silence fell as we both called up a vision of the decidedly moth-eaten Gorgonzola.

"Yes, well . . ." He gave the stack of papers another quick riffle. "After Bill Gardener's unfortunate er . . . we're going to need a replacement mole inside Vanheusen's organisation. In his last report, Gardener said that he was on the verge of being able to prove that large amounts of cash were being couriered to this man Vanheusen by clients on inspection visits to his various properties in Tenerife. So his company, Exclusive, is almost certainly a front for money-laundering. By happy coincidence, Exclusive has just advertised for an assistant PA Leisure. I'm hoping that your ownership of a Persian cat, together with your experience in client hospitality, will convince Vanheusen that you're the one for the job. Interviews are set for the end of the month. How do you feel about it?"

"Well, er . . ."

"In view of Bill Gardener's murder, we're not instructing you to take this assignment in Tenerife, Deborah." His grey eyes regarded me steadily. "It's entirely voluntary."

A week later, as the plane made its final approach to Reina Sofia airport I looked down on Tenerife, the scenario for Operation Canary Creeper. White fluffy clouds left their negative images on the surface of a sea rippled and silvered like frosted glass. Through the small window I could see the snow-capped peak of Mount Teide, the browns and greens of its jagged foothills, and nearer the coast, the shiny rectangles and rhomboids of plastic-roofed banana and tomato plantations. It seemed a paradise of year-round sunshine, warm seas, subtropical rainforest and savage lava moonscapes, all presided over by the dramatic cone of Teide.

But Eden had its serpent. That's why Bill Gardener had come here. That was why I was here. Vanheusen's current venture, the sale of luxury properties to wealthy clients, was almost certainly a money-laundering front for heroin and cocaine profits. On several occasions HM Revenue & Customs had come close to nailing him. And each time, fancy manoeuvres by his lawyers had got him off the hook. The Department had moved fast with the application for the post of assistant PA Leisure, complete with armour-plated CV. Now it was all up to me.

In a last-minute attempt to find something that would give me the edge at that all-important interview, I flicked once more through the dossier on Vanheusen — police reports, newspaper cuttings, pages from a Sunday supplement. I pulled out the Lifestyle article and browsed through it for inspiration . . . All the usual stuff about the successful businessman . . . and a double-page photo captioned *Ambrose Vanheusen relaxes in his Orangery.* There was no sign of potted oranges, but the place was a jungle of exotic passionflowers, pale blue plumbago and assorted unfamiliar tropical plants. The lacy fronds of a magnificent clump of tree ferns shaded a mass display of white moth orchids in antique pots — and a large black Persian cat lounging on a white velvet cushion. My prospective employer was sitting at a wrought-iron table. He was in his early thirties, mid-brown hair flecked with gold, beard and moustache closely trimmed. Except for those eyes, astute, calculating, pale against the tan of his skin, there was no sign that he was a twenty-first-century Al Capone, a smooth operator who'd run rings round both the Drug Enforcement Agency and the Fraud Squad.

Vanheusen's obsession with his pedigree Persian cat was his weak pointt. . . How to bring up at the interview that I was a lover not only of cats but, in particular, of Persian cats? It would have to be done so subtly . . . I studied the picture again, seeking inspiration . . . The cat's coat was thick, shiny and luxuriant, and against the white of the cushion very, very black. I glanced over to where Gorgonzola was lolling in post-breakfast slumber. Pure Persians come in a limited range of colours, a good red being one of the rarest. G scored there, but the texture of *her* coat left much to be desired. To be honest, *everything* to be desired. She'd inherited the characteristic Persian face, but her coat was fluffy only in patches. One of her parents had been a full-pedigreed Persian, no doubt about that. The other must have been a scruffy gingery

creature. Even as a kitten she had looked moth-eaten —
no amount of brushing had made any difference.

Which reminded me . . . I put aside the dossier and
retrieved the grooming comb from the drawer. "C'mon,
G, time for your morning brush."

Before I'd finished speaking, she yawned, stretched
and leapt lightly onto my knee. At the first stroke of the
brush, her eyes closed. A slow rumbling purr vibrated
in her throat. Perhaps at this very moment Ambrose
Vanheusen's cat was undergoing the same pleasurable
ritual. While I worked on G's tangles, my mind was
teasing away at how I could plausibly introduce the
subject of cats at the interview, but ten minutes later all
I'd achieved was a brush clogged with ginger fluff.

I scratched her gently behind an ear. "OK, that's
your lot."

No response. She sat there swaying gently as in a
hypnotic trance, the opening gambit in what could
often be a lengthy battle of wits. Something I wasn't in
the mood for today.

"Gerroff, G." Before she could dig in her claws, I
stood up.

She surrendered to the force of gravity with a
half-hearted *miaow* of protest.

Game, set and match to DJ Smith. All very well, but
the interview was getting close and I *still* hadn't
thought of anything. Abstractedly I picked at some
stray fluff on my jeans. Fluff. Hairs, cat *hairs*. The very
answer I'd been looking for. If there happened to be a
few hairs from a red Persian on my jacket at the

interview . . . long, silky, red hairs, guaranteed to make the owner of a black Persian salivate . . .

Gorgonzola's reddest hairs — distinctively long and silky — were to be found at the end of her moth-eaten tail. Through narrowed eyes I gazed speculatively at her already recumbent form. Always a mind-reader, she twitched her whiskers, curled her tail round her and rested her chin proprietorially on its tip. Those hairs would have to be plucked. Cutting them would not give the natural effect I needed. Sensing my continued scrutiny, she opened one eye and shifted uneasily. The eye closed to a thin slit. A clear *Do Not Disturb* notice had been put up.

I tried bribery. I tried blandishments. All failed, even tuna chunks, her favourite. She merely sniffed suspiciously at the saucer and clasped her tail even more firmly to her. I'm ashamed to admit it, but it was then that I resorted to Unscrupulous Underhand Means, re-enactment of that eighteenth-century poem *The Rape of the Lock*, or in twenty-first-century parlance, *The Snatching of the Hairs*. I fetched G's on-duty collar with its miniaturised transmitter. Once I'd fastened it round her neck, she stood expectantly, tail erect. I pounced. One quick yank and I'd got my hairs.

I'd expected the ear-piercing *yo-ow-l* of outrage. What I wasn't prepared for was the stunned look of betrayal in her wide-open eyes. In a gingery blur she disappeared under the bed.

"Sacrifice in the Line of Duty. Sorry, G," I muttered, overcome with guilt.

Long and silky and red, the stolen hairs clung tenaciously to the sleeve of my green linen jacket as if they'd been glued there. If the smiling man lounging on the black hide sofa realised that I'd planted them as part of the HMRC operation to infiltrate his organisation, it would undoubtedly cost me my life. Bill Gardener had come under suspicion and . . .

Everything about him and the room murmured wealth. From his expensive Armani suit and heavy gold watch-strap, to the white alpaca skins draping the two black hide sofas, from the brushed-steel chamber of a striking hole-in-the-wall fire where pale flames flickered over grey ceramic pebbles, to the dramatic red, blue and gold Howard Hodgson abstract, spectacular against black silk wall coverings. On a black lacquered table beside him, an ethereal white moth orchid floated out of an authentic Lucie Rie ceramic pot. Beside it, neatly arranged, were a laptop, a telephone and a leather-bound appointment diary, the only evidence that this room was an office rather than an art-lover's salon.

"As you must be aware," he flicked a microscopic speck of dust from a dark silk tie shot with muted iridescent colours, "the clients of Exclusive (Tenerife) are aristocratic, privileged, moneyed — the elite of society. So those who work for us must have special qualities too." After a stage-managed pause: "There have been many applicants for the position. But you, Ms Smith, have the X-factor, something which gives me confidence that you are indeed the right person to be personal assistant to my PA Leisure."

"Why, thank you, Mr Vanheusen." I was jubilant. Phase One of Operation Canary Creeper had been initiated. *These people don't play around*, a cautionary voice said. *One slip and . . .*

"All the applicants on the short list are intelligent, personable and experienced in the travel and holiday trade. However . . ." His thumb caressed his upper lip. A moment's silence hung between us.

I replaced a warm smile with a raised eyebrow.

"However, only *you* have demonstrated that you are a lover of that prince of animals — *felis catus persica*, the Persian cat."

"How . . . how on earth do you know *that*?" I widened my eyes in astonishment, careful not to overdo the surprise.

He grinned. "The evidence is there on your sleeve."

Remember to look at the wrong arm. I studied my jacket, frowning as if in bewilderment.

A glint of amusement surfaced in those pale eyes. "I haven't got psychic powers, Ms Smith."

Thank God for that. From my repertoire of appropriate expressions I selected an uncertain smile.

"Try the other sleeve."

"Ohhh . . ." With a suitable intake of breath I brushed frantically in a doomed-to-failure attempt to remove the long red hairs.

"I shouldn't worry about it. Those cat hairs singled you out for the job."

Things were going exactly as I had hoped. It had been a near certainty that he'd home in on those cat hairs. I summoned up an embarrassed little smile. "Do

I take it, Mr Vanheusen, that you yourself are the owner of a Persian cat?"

"His picture's on the wall behind you, Ms Smith."

I swivelled round to look. Glowering down at me with malevolent orange eyes from a satinised steel-framed oil painting was the fluffy black Persian cat featured in the dossier. A disagreeable bad-tempered mouth indicated that The Prince, like his owner, was nothing more or less than a beautifully groomed thug.

"Samarkand Black Prince. Champion of Champions." Pride of ownership warmed his voice.

"He's wonderful!" I breathed. "So *sweet!*"

I'd said just the right thing.

"Most valuable — and most valued — cat in Tenerife," purred the owner of the Brute of Samarkand. He leant back. "And now, Ms Smith, tell me about *your* cat."

I visualised moth-eaten Gorgonzola. She too was a Champion of Champions — as drug-detector for Her Majesty's Revenue & Customs in their war against heroin and cocaine.

"I have to admit that she is not at all in the same league as The Prince." My voice carried a ring of unmistakable sincerity that I couldn't have counterfeited if I'd tried. "Her name's Persepolis Desert Sandstorm."

He ran a finger thoughtfully over his lip, calculation lurking under those lowered lids. He reached over and pressed a keypad on the lacquered table. "Well, I think I've heard enough. Your background in travel and client hospitality is just what we're looking for. I'd like you to start next week, if that's convenient."

I nodded, outwardly cool, inwardly elated. The couple of carefully arranged cat hairs had clinched it.

"That's settled then." He rose to his feet. "Monique, my PA Leisure, will set you right."

The door opened. Tall, slim, elegant, Monique Devereux would not have been out of place in the salon of one of the leading European fashion houses. Jacket and skirt were impeccably cut, shoes manufactured from the softest leather, jewellery understated and expensive. It was power-dressing with an ultra-feminine slant. Her dark hair swept smoothly upwards in a stylish French roll, accentuating large brown eyes and perfect facial bone structure.

The hand-shake was cool, the smile perfunctory. "Welcome to Exclusive (Tenerife), Deborah."

Was there a faint note of hostility? I didn't care. I'd surmounted the first hurdle. I was in.

Half an hour later, as the electric gates to the grounds of the Vanheusen estate swung silently shut behind my car, I hummed a little tune. Operation Canary Creeper was up and running. The groundwork of the past couple of weeks had paid off — those dawn-to-dusk explorations on foot and in 4×4 of the island's most spectacular locations, tucked away, unvisited, unseen, unknown to the madding tourist crowd in their air-conditioned coaches. I'd been able to enthuse from first-hand experience when Vanheusen had asked me what ideas I had for the entertainment of clients between their scheduled inspections of his luxury properties. But it was that last-minute inspiration of the cat hairs which had proved to be the trump card. I was returning to report success.

A flicker of unease pricked the bubble of my self-satisfaction. The hum triumphant faltered and died, withered on the date palm, so to speak. "You must show me a picture of Persepolis sometime, Ms Smith," Vanheusen had said. At the time it had seemed a polite response to my compliments, one cat owner to another, but now I could detect a hidden agenda. A good red Persian is extremely rare, a female even rarer. I'd glimpsed the covetous gleam in his eyes. Had I introduced a wild card, a factor I couldn't control?

Pooooop pooooooooop. An impatient blare from a tour coach with protruding mirrors like the eye-stalks of a gigantic insect interrupted this rather unpleasant train of thought. Oh well, sufficient unto the day. *Qué sera sera.* Negotiating the rush hour traffic clogging the main route through Las Américas was enough to think about.

The Control Centre for Operation Canary Creeper was tucked away in one of the back streets of the old town. Perhaps "old town" was a bit of a misnomer. Gone the fishermen's cottages, elbowed aside by hotels and balconied apartments. Gone, too, the evocative plaintive mewing of seagulls on the lookout for edible scraps, drowned now by the roar of the ride-on street vacuum hoovering up cigarette ends, drink cans and leaflets.

HM Revenue & Customs in the guise of Extreme Travel Agency was sandwiched between a laundry and a solicitor's office, one of three nondescript shops in a slightly seedy back street of drab entryphone doorways. So it wasn't exactly hidden away. It wasn't exactly conspicuous either, just another tourist agency among the many in Los Cristianos. An agency specialising in exotic holidays and personalised packages. Few stopped to look in the windows at the posters of emerald paddy fields in Vietnam, the eternal snows of Everest and K2, or a sailing ship battling its way through icy mast-high seas in the Straits of Magellan. Even fewer pushed open the door and made enquiries. Which gave Her Majesty's Revenue & Customs ample time to carry out their clandestine activities. It was perfect cover for their investigations into British national Vanheusen's undercover activities.

In the chic minimal outer office — desk, telephone, fax machine, neatly stacked brochures — there was nothing to excite curiosity in even the most suspicious of minds. But there were those who would have been very interested indeed in what lay behind that plain white door at the back of the room. Stored behind the steel frontage of innocent-looking grey filing cabinets were the latest satellite communication systems and surveillance devices.

Parking at this time of day was not a problem, and I drew into the kerb right outside. The small notice on the outer door of Extreme Travel announced *Closed 1300 till 1700*. Untrue. HM Revenue & Customs never closes. Indeed, we're at our most active when others sleep. As I inserted my key in the lock and opened the door, the muted sound of a buzzer gave warning of my arrival, but I knew I'd been on camera from the moment my car had nosed into the street. In our line of work there can never be too much security. I dumped the bulky Exclusive folder on a chair and idly studied myself in the large rectangular mirror covering most of the wall behind the desk. That mirror was in fact a window fitted with one-way glass. I brushed my jacket, tweaked my collar and ran a hand through my hair. Finally I gave myself a small approving smile. It signalled that I was sure I hadn't been followed, was not under observation; in other words, that I was clean. Any doubts about security and I'd have frowned, and the door would have remained locked.

When I heard the distinctive click of levered locks being activated, I gathered up the Exclusive folder and took it with me into the secret domain behind the plain white door.

"Operation Canary Creeper up and running," I said. "Thanks to Gorgonzola."

"So the cat hairs did the trick, then." Case officer Gerry Burnside nodded approvingly, "Clever of you. Now that you've sneaked your foot inside the door, let's hear your first impressions."

"Cosy little set-up Vanheusen's got." I sat down and pushed the folder across the desk. "Luxury villa, all marble and exotic hardwoods. Extensive grounds — palm trees, exotic plants, manicured lawns and bougainvillea everywhere. High security throughout, of course — multiple locks on his office door, electronic gates and video surveillance of the corridors and grounds. According to Monique Devereux, his PA Leisure, dogs are loose at night."

"How far is she in Vanheusen's confidence, would you say?"

"I'll be able to tell you after Monday. I'm to report for a week's training in company methods." I flipped open the folder. "The Exclusive approach is simple really. It's an appeal to vanity by flattering clients that they are part of a very select bunch. Look at this." I stabbed a finger down on the Exclusive marketing catchphrase in bold centimetre-high type, repeated on every page. *If you have to ask who we are, you're not one of us!* "It's The Emperor's clothes story — vanity clouds the judgement. Stops awkward questions. Interesting, eh?"

Gerry took the folder from me and thumbed through the pages.

"The guy's spent millions on this set-up, most of it drug money. Has to be." He looked up. "For the first time we've a good chance of nailing him. But now you've become 'one of them', Deborah, you'll have to tread very carefully. I don't have to tell you that, do I?"

CHAPTER
TWO

I let myself out through the plain white door and drove back home with something more pressing on my mind than Gerry's warning — this morning's confrontation with my feline colleague Gorgonzola, alias Persepolis Desert Sandstorm.

How did a cat come to be on the payroll of HM Revenue & Customs? Late one autumn afternoon several years ago I found her as a kitten clinging to an old log in the river, the only survivor of a drowned litter. I couldn't just abandon her and leave her to die. The combination of round-the-clock intensive care and her stubborn fighting spirit cemented the bond between us.

"You can stay here, Kitten, till I find you a good home," I told her.

At that time I worked from home for HM Revenue & Customs, training young dogs to assess their potential to sniff out drugs. I kept her out of the way of the dogs at first, but she soon showed she could take care of herself. Kitten stayed.

Kitten's career with Revenue & Customs began the day I chose a few crumbs of smelly ripe cheese as my lure to train the dogs. While I was collecting the dogs

17

from their kennels, she sneaked into the lounge, tracked down the crumbs and ate them. All that was left of my test was a single crumb on her whiskers. I changed her name to Gorgonzola, an allusion to the cheese, and allowed her to join the dogs in their sniffing games. Her sense of smell and intelligence were outstanding. She passed the training with flying colours. Later, when I began undercover work for Revenue & Customs, she made the ideal undercover drug-detector.

As I said, I was feeling guilty about what I'd done this morning. A trust betrayed is not easily forgiven. I wasn't looking forward to meeting Gorgonzola's reproachful gaze. In an attempt to postpone the inevitable, I drove home by the most roundabout way.

Home, for the duration of Operation Canary Creeper, was a rented house in the little village of La Caleta. Alas, the tentacles of Las Américas had crept westward along the pink granite promenade, slithered over the intervening headlands and a couple of ravine *barrancos* to lay siege to the quaint old houses, narrow alleys and the picturesque micro harbour.

The Department had installed me in Calle Rafael Alberti, numero 2, in a smart cream bungalow accessorised with olive wood Canarian-style balcony, motorised louvred shutters and elegant double-tiered pantiled roof. Stylish, comfortable, soulless. In my planter window-boxes the red poinsettias drooped, shamefaced that the developers had grafted this modern structure onto the end of a row of traditional fishermen's cottages. Their white walls, simple dark green shutters, white-painted flat corrugated roofs and

18

tapering smoke-blackened chimneys had a naïve stylishness of their own. All had heavy wooden doors with a centrally placed door handle in the shape of a large bronze ball. My neighbour, old Jesús Domingo, had added his own personal touch. His shutters were the same dark green as the rest of the terrace, but his walls were washed a faded salmon pink. His sun-bleached front door of rough wooden boards and diagonal bracing strut had not been upgraded to "fancy" panelling. It remained as it always had been.

Would Gorgonzola have forgiven me for this morning's sneaky snatch 'n' grab? If she was there to welcome me, I'd know she had. Her favourite spot was under the shade of the magenta bougainvillea that climbed one cream-washed wall and sent exploratory fingers over a shaky wooden framework that in my more grandiose moments I referred to as my pergola.

At the rear, all our houses had a patch of ground enclosed by a neat lava wall. "Garden" might be too complimentary a term for these plots. They ranged from a free-for-all of euphorbia and prickly pear, to neighbour Jesús's colourful oil can garden. His scarlet and pink geraniums were potted up in old olive oil cans painted a cheerful vivid blue. Flowerpot cans were perched on every surface — window ledges, back step, even hanging from the rickety fence itself. There was barely room for the old wooden seat on which he sat in the warm evenings crooning the plaintive melancholy notes of a haunting *madrelena*. Under the impression that a male suitor was serenading her, Gorgonzola would stretch out in a seductive manner and lie there purring softly to herself.

Tonight I'd make a point of sending in a special request for one of Jesús's *madrelenas*. That and a plateful of her favourite tuna chunks should help to erase the painful memories. I unlatched the back gate. When you know you're in the wrong, body language is important. So no hung head, dragging feet or faltering step. Honeyed tones, simpering smiles were also out. G would treat all that with the contempt it deserved. I paused at the rickety fence separating my plot from Jesús's garden and made a show of sniffing at the scentless geranium flowers in their oil can pots, while taking the opportunity to slide a covert sideways glance at the shade under the magenta bougainvillea.

No cat purring in welcome. No cat with lips drawn into a thin line of displeasure. But on the old cushion that she'd commandeered as her day-bed, I detected a shallow depression and a drool mark, still wet. I'd been blackballed, cold-shouldered, handed the frozen furry mitt, given the stiff-legged brush-off. In a word, scorned. It was time to grovel. Outside the open pantry window I rummaged in my bag for the house keys and prepared to raise the white flag of surrender. Total abasement would be the order of the day.

For three days after the "rape of the hair" episode, I was subjected to accusing looks and tail clamped firmly round her feet, Oscar-winning performances every one. Usually Gorgonzola didn't bear a grudge for long, but on this occasion I had to abase myself for a record length of time. I could tell that her heart was gradually softening, however, and that she'd soon relent and give me that toothy Cheshire Cat grin. I'd soon be restored to favour. Just as well. Those last three days I'd had enough critical glances and disapproving mutters from Monique Devereux.

Vanheusen's PA in charge of Leisure had not one, but two spacious rooms in her office suite. The outer office, my domain, was large and airy and furnished in modern minimalist style, all matt black leather furniture with skinny chrome tubular legs. Three walls were white, with white ceiling and white marble floor. The facing wall was a vivid red, inset with a huge yellow rectangle enclosing a smaller blue one. When I was at my desk I felt I was working inside a Mondrian painting. The desk itself stood on a large rug of the same bright red. The only other patches of colour were a yellow desk lamp and blue telephone. Adjustable blinds screened the large picture window, filtering the strong sunlight and imparting a shady coolness. An unobtrusive door gave access to the PA Leisure's office, antechamber to Vanheusen's inner sanctum with all its secrets. Was she part and parcel of Vanheusen's money-laundering set-up? I wasn't sure.

One thing I *was* sure of by the middle of week one — she and I would never get along. That faint antagonism towards me that I had detected at our first meeting had become more noticeable, a complication I hadn't foreseen. The tension between us wasn't just a case of two people not hitting it off. There was something else behind it. And if I didn't suss it out soon, it could well jeopardise the success of Operation Canary Creeper.

I made the decision to bring things to a head, lance the boil, so to speak. I took the opportunity to tackle her when she summoned me to go over Exclusive's procedure for meeting and greeting new clients at the airport.

As she handed me a sheaf of instructions, I said, "I'm really anxious to do well, but I've a feeling that something about my work isn't pleasing you, Monique."

I wasn't prepared for the dam to break. She suddenly burst out with, "I've *no* idea why Mr Vanheusen chose *you*. He had as good as promised my cousin Ashley the post, you know." One of the photographs on her desk showed herself and another woman sitting on the patio of a smart-looking villa. She turned it so I could see it better. "That's Ashley. To be frank, I'd *much* prefer her to be my assistant."

I'd unwittingly given her cause to dislike me, and that was worrying.

Next morning, I sat on the edge of the bed and covertly studied Gorgonzola as she prepared to launch into her wake-up exercises. Her tail, only a trifle more moth-eaten than before, swung lazily back and forth. I'd been forgiven.

I spelt out what was in my mind. "I feel she's keeping tabs on me. But it's only because Monique's looking for an excuse to sack me and make way for Cousin Ashley, don't you think, G?"

22

The joint and muscle-loosening stretches of her front legs came to a momentary halt. An ear twitched in my direction.

Encouraged, I added, "Is that all it is, eh?"

The wake-up exercises recommenced. G dug her claws into the bedroom rug and, eyes closed, slowly and thoughtfully hollowed her back in an arch.

"Or have I aroused her suspicions in some way?"

Back legs stre-e-tched out in turn.

"Well, what *do* you think, G?"

Her eyes narrowed to a slit. I was treated to a long ya-a-wn. The jury was out. It's not the right moment to ask questions when a cat is in the middle of its limbering-up routine.

"We'll just have to wait and see. Is that what you're saying?" I gave her a quick caress and locked the apartment door.

Meeting and greeting, it seemed, was an important part of the Exclusive softening-up experience. My first assignment was to collect new clients from the airport and install them in the Alhambra, a newly opened five-star hotel, designed as a Moorish palace — plashing fountains, marble floors, mosaic tiles, white lattice-work and minarets, all that sort of thing.

A white chauffeur-driven limousine was waiting for me beside the designer grove of palm trees in the Alhambra's Moroccan-themed car park. I leant back against the mint green leather upholstery and ran through the meeting and greeting routine. The countryside swept past. This morning, the scattering of mountain villages on the foothills of Teide were wrapped in a blanket of low cloud, but ahead and to my left, the sun rising over the sea fingered the little houses of the fishing village of Los Abrigos, just visible beyond the white radar dome at the end of the runway.

Clutching the Exclusive logo, I took up position at the Arrivals barrier. While I waited, I thought about Bill Gardener. I hadn't even met him. Too cocky by half, they said. Was that why he'd slipped up? Just how had Vanheusen's mob got onto him? He'd met his death two days after he'd reported he was on the verge of a breakthrough for Operation Canary Creeper. Had his cover already been blown, the information, whatever it was, planted solely to mislead him? I didn't need warnings to be careful . . .

First a trickle, then a mass of people surged towards me through the Arrivals door. I scanned the faces as I held aloft the clipboard with its silvered Exclusive lettering. According to Gardener, cash was being couriered to Vanheusen by clients coming on inspection visits. I had no way of knowing if I was about to meet and greet one of those couriers. Victoria Knight, Millie Prentice, Rudyard Scott, Herbert G Wainwright. Just a list of names. Could be any of them. Or none. There was nothing to help me.

A man in his early forties carrying an airline cabin case broke away from the stream of people and headed purposefully in my direction. A large black suitcase on a strap trailed at his heels like an obedient retriever. They came to a halt in front of me.

"Welcome to Tenerife, Mr . . . ?"

"The name's Scott. Rudyard Finbar Scott. Writer."
He paused expectantly, ready to field the cry of
recognition.

The pause lengthened as I searched for a suitable
phrase that would convey a "Gosh! Wow! Can I have
your autograph?" reaction — and yet cover up the fact
that I'd never heard of him. That thin face with its
high-domed forehead had not featured in any of the
publicity photographs I'd come across.

"Wonderful to meet you at last, Mr Scott. I —"

I was saved from floundering on by the sudden
arrival of a flustered lady pushing a laden airport trolley
that seemed to have a mind of its own. "I'm Victoria
Knight." She held out a perspiring hand.

Beautifully permed grey hair streaked with white
swept back from a plump, homely face unadorned with
make-up. Though her necklace of large pearls perfectly
matched in size looked decidedly pricey, the engage-
ment ring and wedding band on rough work-worn
hands were simple and inexpensive. The cashmere
cardigan that hung round her shoulders suggested
wealth and class, but her manner was more favourite
granny than haughty *grande dame*. Victoria Knight was
a lady of intriguing contradictions.

"It won't take us long to get to the hotel, will it, love?
I'm just longing for a cup of tea. That awful stuff they
serve you on the plane may be brown, but it's not tea, is
it?" The accent was northern, possibly Lancashire.

I reassured her and directed both of them to the
waiting limousine. Two down, two to go.

"Hi there!" The woman's voice came from behind me.

I turned round.

"I saw your notice." She parked her trolley case. Friendly brown eyes smiled at me through round tortoiseshell glasses. "I'm Millie. Millie Prentice."

She was in her late twenties, about the same age as myself. Shoulder-length auburn hair curling into unruly ringlets framed the freckled face with its pert upturned nose.

"I'm really looking forward to seeing Exclusive in action — going round all those luxury villas, I mean. You know —"

She chattered on, but I was listening not to the words but to the subtext. Something about her body language didn't quite tally with that casual breezy manner. I looked after her speculatively as she walked towards the waiting car.

The last name on my list, Herbert G Wainwright, had an American ring to it. I scanned the crowded concourse. A tall man was homing in on me. Rimless glasses flashed like little warning beacons as he elbowed his way through the milling tourists.

"The name's Wainwright. Herbert G Wainwright III. Where the heck's the promised service?" Magnified by the pebble lenses, his eyes were two huge question marks of irritation. I put him down immediately as a troublemaker.

I stared at the balding figure in front of me. "What exactly do you mean, Mr Wainwright?"

"My bags. I've had to tote them from the baggage conveyor way back there." The thick lenses flashed impatiently. "I thought you guys collected them as part of the service." He unzipped a pocket in the back of a case, and pulled out the glossy **Exclusive** brochure. "Let me quote: *Have your every need catered for while you search for your dream property in Tenerife. Leave everything to us.*" His eyes, now a twin-barrelled shotgun of accusation, had me lined up in their sights. "Guess I'm a victim of misrepresentation, ma'am."

I glued a smile to my lips. "I'm so sorry, Mr Wainwright. I'll phone the driver to come and help me with your luggage."

Operation Canary Creeper was going to demand a *lot* in the way of self-control, I thought to myself as I trailed after the driver with one of Herbert G Wainwright III's heavy suitcases.

I left the abominable Wainwright III and the other guests ensconced in their suites at the Alhambra and made my way back to Extreme Travel. Professionals like myself don't make many mistakes. Those who do, end up dead. I should have been checking the rearview mirror. Instead, I was fuming over the spoilt, childish behaviour all too often indulged in by the ultra-rich, and I must admit that I allowed my guard to slip.

I parked on a vacant lot, a piece of about-to-become real estate, probably time-share, switched off the ignition and half-opened the door. On autopilot I glanced in the wing mirror. In my line of business you develop an instinct for when you're under observation, though it's nothing you can quite put your finger on or explain. That blue Peugeot with the star-shaped dent in its radiator, I'd seen it before, at the airport less than an hour ago, when I was trailing back to the limousine with Wainwright's case. One of the case wheels had hit the raised corner of a paving slab. The heavy piece of luggage had almost wrenched itself out of my hand. I'd just managed to prevent it toppling onto the road right in front of the same Peugeot that was now parked two doors down from the Extreme Travel office. Coincidence? I didn't think so. It was careless of them to deploy something so distinctive, but then I expect they'd counted on me driving straight off with the newly arrived clients, not lugging a bag around Arrivals.

I'd had the door half-open a fraction too long. A dead giveaway if there were hostile eyes in the blue Peugeot. I turned the hesitation into a sudden remembrance of something I needed from the glove compartment. Reaching over to the passenger seat, I flicked down the flap and rummaged for a moment or so. I pulled out a sheet of paper, and with it in one hand and the Exclusive folder in the other, clambered awkwardly out of the car. I balanced the folder on the car roof while I stuffed the piece of paper into my bag. Then I locked the car, and without even a glance at the Peugeot, walked briskly across the road and let myself into Extreme Travel.

I'd hit the office at siesta hours, so Jayne, the dumb-looking blonde who warded off any prospective client, was no longer on duty. From the other side of the mirror, I'd often admired her in action as the hidden microphone relayed her wide-ranging and inventive excuses for being unable to take a booking — floods in the Amazon basin, landslips in the Himalayas, border closings, termites causing sudden collapse of a Rest House — all little difficulties in far-flung places no one had heard of or cared about. There could be no checking up. For a particularly persistent client, she'd make a provisional booking, a booking that later had most regrettably to be cancelled.

On this occasion I had no coast-is-clear smiles for the mirror. Those behind the one-way glass would pick up the warning. Innocent activity is the best camouflage. I deposited the folder on the desk and busied myself finalising the details for my first Exclusive excursion. I had to make sure that everything ran like clockwork, for Monique would take a positive delight in reporting any incompetence to Vanheusen. And if he sacked me, Operation Canary Creeper would be back to square one.

Sunlight streamed through the rainbow logo on the plate-glass window, tinting the papers spread across the desk. I studied the checklist for tomorrow. *Transport, Pick-up time, Journey time, Reservations at restaurants, Photo* . . . A shadow fell across the papers. Someone had paused outside the window, but I didn't look up. Whoever it was would be caught on camera. The shadow lingered, and moved past.

For another five minutes I continued to work on the wording for my Exclusive excursion. Monique had harped on ad infinitum that Exclusive's leisure activities had to be *seen* to be different. So the term

Excursion wouldn't do at all. *Trek* sounded too physically demanding, and *Expedition* ditto. *Jaunt?* Cheap and nasty. I settled on *Outing*. That should give the right nuance — something special, something to look forward to ... Finally satisfied, I stretched, yawned and tidied all the papers into a neat bundle. I slipped them inside the Exclusive folder and gathered up my bag.

As a signal to those in the inner office to run a check on the street outside, I frowningly inspected my lipstick in the big mirror and glanced at my watch.

"That's me for today. I'm off," I muttered as if to myself.

Then I let myself out.

CHAPTER
THREE

Next morning, I arrived early at Exclusive to finalise the details for my first Outing. To protect me from a takeover bid by Cousin Ashley, it was important to impress Vanheusen with my capabilities, so I'd put a lot of time into the planning. Hence the zappy title *Outing to the Moon*, in reality an excursion to the lava landscape of Mount Teide. Thanks to a bit of string-pulling by HM Revenue & Customs liaising at the highest levels with GRECO, the special unit set up by the Spanish authorities to combat big-money organised crime, I'd obtained special permission to cross the volcanic caldera on a route normally strictly off-limits to public vehicles.

The door to Monique's office was ajar. From inside, silence. I took the folder containing the schedule from a drawer in my desk. I'd left nothing to chance, but perhaps I should skim over it again . . .

The blue telephone at my elbow buzzed. "I'm with Mr Vanheusen just now," Monique's brisk voice announced. "Have those excursion details ready. I'll be with you in about ten minutes."

Ten minutes . . . at last the opportunity I'd been waiting for. In half that time I'd be able to have a good poke round her office. I'd passed through it, of course, on the way to my first interview with Vanheusen, but since then I'd caught only tantalising glimpses on the occasions when the PA Leisure had issued imperiously forth to deliver her latest instructions. I gathered up the Outing folder — a feeble excuse if I was caught, but better than nothing — and pushed open the door.

In complete contrast to the stark modernism of my office, hers could be described as stylish French Classical with the ambience of a drawing room. The desk was a spindly antique table, the filing cabinet hidden behind the gilded wooden doors of an armoire. At each of the two tall windows, pale eau-de-Nil curtaining swept down to floor and spread across the white marble in green pools. Her elegant chair upholstered in green suede leather was pushed back from her vacated desk/table. Neatly lined up on the top were intercom, green onyx telephone with matching onyx desk calendar and a couple of silver-framed photographs — Monique and Ashley, and Monique and Vanheusen, champagne glass in hand at some reception.

I laid down my folder on the chair, and picked up the Vanheusen photo. What interested me were the faces in the background. I didn't recognise any of them, but it would be worth running them through Extreme Travel's computer. From an inner pocket I whipped out a slim mirror-and-lipstick case; in fact, it was a mini all-singing, all-dancing camera supplied by the Department for just such golden opportunities. Seconds later, a digital copy was nestling on the camera's memory card in my pocket. I repositioned the photo frame exactly as I had found it.

I made a quick survey of the other items on the tabletop, but saw nothing else of interest. No papers; drawers were locked. It was tempting, but too dangerous to plant a surveillance bug and risk its discovery in the regular security sweep. Was there anything else snoop-worthy? I nipped across to the armoire in the corner of the room. Its doors stood invitingly open, revealing cardboard box files labelled *Brochures, Contacts, Contracts, Members, Properties, Promotions*. Reluctantly I decided there wasn't enough time even for a skim-through. Better to be safe than sorry. I turned away . . . Ten seconds later I was back in my own office, interconnecting door once more ajar.

From my desk I could see sprinklers sending their fine mists in whirling spirals over the manicured lawns of Vanheusen's spare-no-expense exotic garden. A gardener was chopping at the yellowing frond of a palm tree, the wicker basket at his feet already overflowing with trimmings. I fingered the camera in my pocket. I'd definitely struck gold with that photograph. If our computer came up with a match for even one of those smudgy background faces, that could be the break the Department needed . . . I *should* have taken another couple of minutes to delve into that armoire, though. That was definitely a missed opportunity. The box labelled *Members (Potential)* would have contained the names of other targeted purchasers of Vanheusen properties, people like Wainwright, Scott, Prentice and

Knight, who had first to be softened up by an Exclusive Outing.

The gardener flung the pieces of palm frond into his basket and began sweeping up stray clippings . . . I'd better get on with *my* tasks. I reached for the Outing folder. *It wasn't there.* I'd taken it in with me to Monique's office. I'd laid it down on her chair to take out the camera . . . Sick disbelief swept over me, followed by beads of sweat on the brow and an icy boulder in the pit of the stomach. All clichés, but that's how it felt when I realised I'd just made the careless slip that would jeopardise months of careful planning. I'd spent barely four minutes checking out the room, but how long had I been sitting here gazing out the window like a fool? It might only be seconds before . . .

I flung myself through the interconnecting door, darted across the expanse of marble, snatched up the incriminating folder, and whirled on my heel. One, two, three strides. I was going to make it —

Behind me, I heard the click of the security lock on Vanheusen's office door. No time to escape to the safety of my own office. To reach it would take three more strides, three more seconds, but I didn't have them. A fleeing figure is obviously guilty of something. Vanheusen's whole set-up showed that he was paranoid about security. When they searched me and found the camera . . .

There was only one option left. I must appear to be entering, not leaving. I whirled round, and stood a couple of metres into the room, folder held prominently in front of me. As the door to Vanheusen's

34

office opened, I was moving slowly in the direction of Monique's desk. In the widening gap appeared the edge of a box file followed by a silk-clad shoulder, a pigskin shoe and Monique's startled face.

"Who gave you permission to enter my office?" Her expression was glacial, her tone icy.

"I've brought you the finalised itinerary for the Outing, Monique. I thought . . . I thought . . ." I faltered, "that you wanted to see it in ten minutes. I hope that you'll find —" Was I injecting the right blend of uncertainty and apology? "I thought . . ." My voice trailed away into silence. Tentatively, I held out the folder.

She made no move to take it from me. "That's one of your faults, Deborah. You don't listen. I said I'd be *with you* in ten minutes. Something *entirely* different." Her lips compressed into a thin line. "Go back to your office. I'll be *with you* shortly."

Like a reprimanded schoolgirl I crept out, closing the interconnecting door softly behind me. I sat down at my desk and, with hands that trembled slightly, spread out the contents of the Outing folder ready for Monique's inspection. Had my act been convincing enough? Was she even now summoning Security? Would burly uniformed men burst through the door? Was I about to be thrown to the ground, handcuffed, body-searched? I dropped the lipstick/camera into the wastebasket and crumpled some paper on top of it.

I heard the sound of the interconnecting door opening quietly, the leisurely brush of feet on carpeting, the rustle of paper. Not Security. I didn't look up.

"*If* I could have your attention, Deborah."

There was still a degree of frost in Monique's voice, but I had obviously prostrated myself enough to appease her. As I hoped, she was putting down my intrusion to misplaced zeal.

"I'm sorry, Monique, I didn't hear you come in." I indicated the papers on the desk. "I was just rechecking all the details for the Outing. I do *so* want my first one to be a success."

A long red fingernail rested on the last name on the Outing list. "Take that Mr J Hambleton off. *He's* not one of Exclusive's new arrivals. Miguel at reception put him on the list because he rang from the Alhambra, but he's *definitely* not one of us. Rules are rules, and necessary for the efficient running of an organisation — only *our* guests on *our* excursions, otherwise they wouldn't be *exclusive*. See to it now." She swept back into her lair, leaving me staring at the closed door.

Monique in pompous mode was a nasty sight and I felt a sneaking sympathy for Mr Hambleton, whoever he was. There would have been plenty of room in the people-carrier for him. Why had she been so angry when she'd found me in her office? It seemed a bit over the top. Was there something she didn't want me to see? It made me all the more determined to have another rake round when I got the opportunity. Thoughtfully, I fished in the wastebasket and retrieved the lipstick/camera.

The Exclusive schedule had been carefully designed to soften up clients before they were exposed to the hard sell of the villas in Vanheusen's portfolio.

When I asked Victoria Knight if she would like to come on the Outing, she was certainly in receptive mood. "*Outing to the Moon* with champagne breakfast? How intriguing! Where *could* we be going?"

"The car will pick you up outside the Alhambra at eight o'clock tomorrow morning for the trip to —"

She held up a hand. "Now, don't tell me any more details. I love surprises. But, just one thing — will I need my cardigan?"

When I tracked down Millie Prentice on a sun-lounger beside the pool, she was just as enthusiastic. "*Outing to the Moon.* Sounds great. Where are we really going? I take it we don't need spacesuits."

Even grouchy Herbert G Wainwright said, though somewhat grudgingly, that he'd give it a go. He probably felt that otherwise he would be missing out on what he'd paid for. So it was somewhat of a surprise that when I buttonholed Rudyard Finbar Scott in the Café Bar Oasis he turned me down flat.

"I'm a writer. This is a working holiday for me. We writers can't afford to indulge in frivolous distractions." He barely glanced up from the sheaf of papers on the table. "It's essential to focus, you know, on the task in hand."

That presented me with the opportunity for a little gentle probing as most people like to talk about themselves. "And what exactly are you working on just now, Mr Scott?"

To my surprise, the reply was brusque to the point of rudeness. "We writers prefer not to talk about work in progress. Now, if you'll forgive me, I'll get back to my notes." He started thumbing through his papers.

"I quite understand, Mr Scott," I said. "I'll take your name off the list."

While my hand was drawing a line through his name, my eyes were squinting over the top of my clipboard to decipher the upside-down handwriting. I've found this skill invaluable on many occasions.

He looked up impatiently. "Yes, was there anything else?"

I'd only had a moment, but it was enough. At the bottom of the page he was reading was the unmistakable flamboyant signature of Ambrose Vanheusen. It might mean nothing, but Rudyard Finbar Scott would merit further investigation. I'd ask the office to dig into his background.

When the 4×4 people-carrier drew up punctually at the Alhambra next morning, I put Monique's training into practice and launched into the approved Exclusive meeting and greeting routine.

"Welcome aboard your shuttle to the moon, or rather, to the National Park of Mount Teide, the nearest likeness on earth to a lunar landscape." Hammer home the exclusivity, Monique had said, so I did, positively bludgeoning them with it. "We'll be driving on a road normally closed to tourist vehicles, a concession granted by the National Park authorities *only* to Exclusive clients."

I got the reactions I'd expected from two of them — a sceptical sniff from Wainwright, a clap of the hands and an exclamation of delight from Victoria. But Millie's abstracted, "Beam me up, Debbie!" with an accompanying wave of her tortoiseshell glasses was just a little too delayed, as if her mind had been on something else — a little odd in view of her enthusiasm yesterday. It pays to take note of little things like that.

The road to Teide climbed slowly through the sprawl of new-build Italian-style terracotta villas complete with white balustrades and classical pediments, a sprawl that oozed out from the core of Las Américas and Los Cristianos as relentlessly as molten lava. Where the new-build ended, infrastructure for the next phase — tarmac, pavements, lamp standards — lay ready, cutting a brutal swathe through the toasted brown landscape of volcanic outcrops, cinders, cactus and euphorbia scrub.

The road twisted and turned up through villages with whitewashed walls and red pantiled roofs. Here, a roofless sandy-walled *finca* crumbled back into a landscape of prickly pear and grey-green spiky aloes. There, low dry-stone walls enclosed small fields of tiny Canarian potatoes and rows of gnarled, arthritic vines hugged the stony ground seeking shelter against the elements.

Above the village of Vilaflor, the air and vegetation became suddenly alpine. The road clawed its way up through pine trees with deeply fissured grey trunks and long, silky needles tufted like chimney sweeps' brushes. A thin metal barrier was the only protection against a drop of a thousand metres to the hazy coastal plain below.

The road twisted for the last time, and suddenly the cone of Teide rose majestically out of a dark choppy sea of chocolate, russet and hazel-brown lava, fuzzed here and there with the dusty eau-de-Nil green of *retama* bushes. Straight ahead, a jagged ridge of lava broke the skyline.

Though Millie Prentice muttered, "Gosh, isn't that just something," I had the distinct impression that the scenery held no real interest for her. In unguarded moments she'd looked decidedly bored. Why had she come? Why had she not made her excuses like Rudyard Scott?

After a private champagne breakfast at the Parador, we drove into the protected zone of the Cañadas and stopped in a patch of shade cast by a tortured outcrop peppered with rounded cavities like a gigantic chunk of Emmental cheese. From it a dark sea of lava rippled out till it washed against the distant wall of the encircling caldera at Teide's base. Above us towered yellow, ochre and brown cliffs spiking a cobalt blue sky. Undercover work sometimes has its compensations . . .

Wainwright's jaded yawn was true to form. "Our Grand Canyon beats the hell out of this. Now *that's* sure something you . . ."

I didn't hear any more, for I'd just caught a snatch of Millie's conversation with Victoria.

". . . so," Millie was saying, "Rudyard Scott's definitely going to buy a Vanheusen property?"

"Oh yes," Victoria lowered her voice, "he's got an airline cabin case positively stuffed with notes. I don't think that's *at all* wise, do you? I mean —" She broke off to point at a clump of spiky silver plants shimmering in the haze of heat amid the hedgehog mounds of dusty green *retama*. "Ooh, what's that over there, Deborah? They look just like giant quill pens."

While I launched into a description of the life cycle of the *tajinaste* flower, my mind was working on how I could reopen that most interesting conversation . . . It would have to be on another occasion. Some instinct deterred me from revealing any interest in Rudyard Scott in the presence of Millie Prentice. I was more convinced than ever that there was something that didn't quite add up about that young woman.

CHAPTER
FOUR

As I drove home, I was still trying to work out the best way of asking Victoria about Rudyard Scott's case of cash. Where the road dips down to La Caleta, it passes close to the sea. On impulse, I parked the car at the top of the path that slopes down to the pebble beach and its little bar, El Chiringuito. I'd watch the sunset and down a *barraquito*, a layer of condensed milk followed by a dash of liqueur topped with coffee and a froth of milk, the concoction served in a tiny glass, with an optional twist of sugar and a biscuit. It was a favourite way for me to relax after work.

At this time of day the rows of white sun-loungers on the artificial beach were unoccupied. Only a handful of people stood at the bar or sat under sea-grass parasols at the small tables. I ordered my *barraquito*, carried it to the table at the end of the boardwalk where the pebble bank shelved steeply into the sea, and sat idly watching a ship sail silently and imperceptibly along the tightrope of the horizon towards La Gomera, this evening a faint grey smudge through the haze. I found it surprisingly calming to contemplate the vast emptiness of the Atlantic Ocean stretching unbroken to the far shores of America.

As light faded from the sky, I sat there sipping the warm sweet liquid and listening to the murmur of *Blanca Navidad* from the sound system set on the roof of the bar. I let my mind mull over the problems facing Operation Canary Creeper and the possible significance of Rudyard Finbar Scott's stash of cash, and what lay behind Millie Prentice's behaviour . . . in the background the rhythmic *slursh* of the waves and the soft *rrrrr* of pebbles as large as ostrich eggs rumbling in the undertow like distant thunder. The amber rays of sunset brushed the surface of the stones at the top of the pebble bank, gilding them and throwing them into sharp relief. It caught the tops of the waves, turning the sea into a sheet of rippling molten glass. The lights of the fish restaurants began to twinkle on the dark headland behind La Caleta . . .

A burst of laughter from the bar broke the spell. I spooned up the last trace of the *barraquito*, pushed back my chair and stood up. A rainbow of colour now washed the horizon where the sun had vanished — terracotta melting to ochre, yellow, pale green. The sky overhead was an inverted indigo bowl. Gomera had gone, hidden behind a band of cloud. The tensions of Operation Canary Creeper, too, had faded . . .

But that mental rosy glow vanished the instant I inserted my key in the lock of my front door and realised I'd had an uninvited visitor. He or she had been somewhat amateurish, for the lock had only been turned once. Something I never do. For extra security I always make a point of locking *à double clef*.

If someone *was* still inside, I didn't want to be stabbed or bludgeoned. To give the intruder a chance to get out, I rattled the key noisily in the lock, and as I pushed the door open, launched into the opening bars of "*Viva España*". "*Oh, I'm off to sunny Spain . . .*" I listened for the sound of anyone legging it out the back door. Nothing.

But it didn't mean that there wasn't someone there. In my line of business you never take anything for granted. So, for the ears of anyone still lurking inside, I gave an exclamation of annoyance and said loudly, "Damn, I've left the cat food in the car."

Leaving the door ajar, I retreated along the polished stone pavements of Calle Rafael Alberti to where I'd parked. I didn't look round. If anyone wanted to exit by my front door, he or she was welcome. I'd rather that than be attacked by a panicking intruder who didn't know enough to make an escape via the rear of the house.

I opened the boot and emptied a stack of tourist maps out of a carrier bag, replacing them with the heavy car jack, a useful weapon to whack into an attacker's guts. Swinging the makeshift weapon casually from one hand, I made my way back to my front door.

I crashed the door back against the wall with a violence calculated to flatten anyone standing behind it. No bashed body, only cracked and broken plaster. Sunlight poured through the open door and sent my shadow ahead of me as I crept down the hall, car jack at the ready. The door to the bedroom was closed. I flung it open with my left hand, thrusting the carrier bag viciously forward with my right. Nobody behind that door either. Feeling more than a little foolish, I returned to the hall

It was only then that I noticed the position of the bathroom door. I always leave both it and the small grilled window wide open to clear any condensation after my morning shower. Now the door was barely ajar. Could a gust of wind have caught it and blown it shut? But today had been particularly hot and airless — there'd been no wind of any kind, let alone gusts strong enough to move a heavy door. Perhaps Gorgonzola prowling round the empty house had pushed it shut? No way. She was quite capable of pushing *open* a door with one meaty paw, but she couldn't have closed it behind her.

The hairs on the back of my neck prickled. Some primitive instinct told me that I was not alone, that there was someone else in the house. I held my breath, listening for the scrape of foot on floor, the noisy breathing of someone as jittery as myself . . . Not a sound. But then, an intruder wouldn't be jittery. Professional intruders never were. *His* breathing would be calm, measured, under control.

I took a firmer grip on the car jack in the carrier bag and moved silently forward. I'd put out my hand to slam the bathroom door back on its hinges, when common sense belatedly kicked in. Though I'd completed the obligatory course in unarmed combat and had a good chance of holding my own against a violent assailant, there was always the possibility of serious injury. The person who had broken in might merely be a common thief, but if he *was* one of Vanheusen's heavies, my expertise in unarmed combat would only lead to further questions and confirm their suspicions. The best course of action would be to beat a strategic retreat, pretending that I hadn't noticed anything amiss. After all, a lot of care had been taken to leave no sign of entry. Whoever was behind this hadn't wanted me to know that I was under investigation.

But was it too late, had I already blown it? Crashing the doors against the walls would have signalled to the intruder that I knew someone was there, and now, after this lengthy silence, he'd know for certain. Perhaps it wasn't too late to give the impression that I had no suspicions. But if I was going to think of something, it would have to be fast. Nothing came to mind. Heart pounding, palms sweating, I started to edge back down the hall. I'd just have to make a bolt for it and let the intruder make a getaway. I took another step backward.

A shadow joined mine on the terracotta tiles of my hall floor. Somebody was standing in the doorway blocking my escape. *Trapped.* I whirled round, car jack at the ready to ward off the anticipated blow.

I let my arm fall to my side. No hoodlum. Only my neighbour Jesús inspecting the chunks of plaster broken off the wall by the door handle.

"*Qué pasa, señora?* I hear big noise and I think something is wrong."

I put my finger to my lips miming silence, and pointed at the bathroom door.

"Oh hello, Jesús," I said loudly. "Sorry if that banging of the doors disturbed you. What a *hell* of a

46

day I've had. Rude clients, unreasonable demands from the boss, and then I was held up in a traffic jam. By the time I got home, I was in such a bad mood that I took it out on the doors."

All the time I was speaking, I was moving down the hall to safety. I grabbed his arm and steered him out onto the doorstep.

"Someone has broken in, and I think he's still here," I hissed into his ear.

"*Un ladrón!*" he breathed, eyes bright with excitement.

I mouthed, "We get the *policía.*"

He nodded.

For the benefit of the listener in the bathroom, I said loudly, "What I need now is a drink, Jesús. Make me one of your famous *barraquitos*, and I'll tell you all about my terrible day."

I slammed the front door hard enough to indicate to the intruder that we had gone. Judging by the patter of falling plaster, the Department was in for an expensive bill.

"But, señora," Jesús whispered anxiously, "you forget that I no have *teléfono.* You have *teléfono móvil* to call *policía?*"

I nodded, again miming silence, and we scurried into his house. When Jesús's door had closed behind us, I flattened myself against the wall next to the window.

"The man will not just sit there waiting for the police to come and arrest him, Jesús. He'll leave very quickly. What we need for the police is a good description."

"I look at back, señora." He scuttled away.

From this angle I had a clear view of the street and a partial view of my doorway. I was banking on the fact that the intruder would want to make a quick escape instead of wasting precious time picking the secure lock on the back door. Anyone leaving would pass into my field of vision.

I waited ... I pictured the intruder listening, listening, then slowly, slowly pushing open the bathroom door. Just when I'd decided I must have got it all wrong, I saw my front door open. Someone walked confidently past Jesús's window, a thin-faced man, beard and moustache trimmed to a neat O round his lips, hair cropped so short as to be a mere shadow on his scalp. He didn't draw attention to himself by moving quickly. A professional. I lost sight of him as he turned in the direction of the harbour. But I'd know him again.

"He's gone, Jesús," I called, "but I got a good look at him. It's safe for me to go back now."

There was a loud *clang* from the kitchen, and my neighbour appeared in the doorway brandishing an enormous fire-blackened paella pan.

"I will come with you, señora. Perhaps you have another *ladrón* in the *cocina*."

I didn't think it likely that there'd be anyone else still lurking in the kitchen, but it was somehow reassuring to have moral support from the paella pan and its wiry owner.

"If there is anyone there, Señora Smith," he flourished the pan, "I will seek him out and deal with him. Have no fear. I will save you."

I hid a smile. I owed him his moment of glory.

Together we entered my house and moved along the hall. The kitchen door was closed, indicating that the clandestine visitor had been there too. Like the bathroom door, that door was always left open so that Gorgonzola could make her way to the cool bathroom for her siesta if the kitchen became too hot. G *should* be all right, I told myself. She knew to make a quick exit through the barred pantry window if there were any unauthorised callers.

"I go first, señora." Slowly, slowly, he turned the handle. Then he flung the door open. "*Te pillé,* gotcha!"

BOING. The flat of the pan crashed down on the wooden table.

"If you hiding in here, you better come out," he quavered, "or it be the worse for you!"

"No one's here now," I said to forestall another deafening assault on the kitchen furniture.

With some reluctance, he let his arm drop to his side. "I have frighten the trouser off him!" He showed his two remaining teeth in a gummy grin of triumph.

"You are a hero, Jesús," I said putting an arm round his bony shoulders. "*Muchas gracias.*" I planted a kiss on his leathery cheek.

"*De nada, señora.*" His thin chest swelled with pride. "You have more trouble, I come again and —" The paella pan scythed through the air, narrowly missing the overhead light.

He shuffled briskly down the hall to the front door. A farewell flourish of the culinary anti-burglar device gouged a large chip out of the woodwork. The paella pan had notched up its first victory against crime.

The back door was still securely locked. I inserted the key and went out onto the patio. A break-in is an occupational hazard in my line of work, but I always find it disturbing because I have the secret fear of coming home to find Gorgonzola brutally battered. This time, though, there was no nightmare scenario, no bloodied ginger body lying on the kitchen floor. The odds were that this had been a routine security check on a new employee. I wasn't too worried. The intruder wouldn't have found anything to connect me to my undercover work. That was kept safely behind the white door in the Extreme Travel office. And G's working collar with its radio transmitter didn't look anything out of the ordinary. I stretched out on the bench beneath my pergola. Gorgonzola would show up soon. When she saw me, she would know it was safe to return. Now I had time to relax.

CHAPTER
FIVE

The palms of the Café Bar Oasis soared five metres up towards a green-tinted cupola. As the rays of the sun angled through the curved glass, their branches swayed in the cool, temperature-controlled air, casting restful green shadows on the starched white tablecloths below. In the centre, under the cupola, a huge gilded cage was home to tiny songbirds twittering and chirping a musical accompaniment to the muted hum of conversation.

Victoria Knight selected a strawberry tart and handed me the plate of cakes. "I did so enjoy yesterday's Outing. I do hope there's going to be another one before Christmas."

"That's what I've come to discuss with you." Untrue. I'd really come to find out more about Rudyard Scott's hoard of cash. I bit into my choice, a squishy chocolate éclair. "Delicious," I murmured.

After a pause while we demolished our respective cakes, I brought the conversation neatly round to villas and their purchase. "With the villa visits there won't be enough time to fit in another Outing before Christmas. I just want to check that you'll be free on the 27th."

"Let me see." She produced her diary and flicked through it. "Miss Devereux will be taking me to the first villa tomorrow, and to another one on the 21st. Then there's a gap over Christmas." She turned the page. "The next villa appointment is on Friday the 28th."

Just the opening I'd been angling for. "Tell me, Mrs Knight, did you come to Tenerife with the firm intention of buying a villa, price no object?"

"Oh no, dear." She poured out another cup of strong English Breakfast tea. "At the money he's asking, the property will have to be just right. I'll know it if I see it." A faraway look came into her eyes as she sipped her tea. Just as I was pondering the best way to ask her directly about Rudyard Scott, she put down her cup and added, "But Mr Scott definitely made up *his* mind before he came."

"Really?" I said, injecting surprise with that subtle underlying hint of doubt that makes the speaker rush to expand on what has just been said.

"Yes, he's got the cash ready to hand over."

"Well, it's a good idea to have your finances in place if you intend to purchase property. Banks can take ages to transfer money." That should bring out what I wanted to hear. It did.

"I mean cash as in 'cash in hand'." Though the competition of the birdsong from the gilded cage made it unnecessary, she lowered her voice. "He's come with *bundles* of notes."

"No! I can't believe anyone would be so —"

"That's exactly what I think, but I've seen the money. When we arrived at the Alhambra, Mr Scott — he's such an impatient person, you know — couldn't wait for the luggage to be put on a trolley. He grabbed his small airline case from the porter's hands and marched off to reception, leaving us all standing. So rude."

Mustn't interrupt the flow. I sipped my tea.

She eyed me over the rim of the cup. "I didn't realise — and neither did he, obviously — that *my* case looked exactly the same as his. And who actually bothers to check labels on cabin baggage, dear?" Victoria was enjoying telling her tale to a receptive listener. "When I got to my room and couldn't open the combination lock of my airline case, I took it down to reception. They were *so* helpful when I told them that my heart pills were inside. The maintenance man came with lopper things that just sliced through the padlock. And off I went back to my room. And then, and then," her eyes grew round with recollected wonder, "I opened the case and saw all that money."

It's a common money-laundering practice for a network of couriers to make frequent transfers of cash between Europe and the UK to avoid using the banking system with its restrictive financial controls. If Scott's cash was in pounds sterling, he could be Vanheusen's courier. I leant forward. "You mean it was full of *euros*?"

"Oh no, dear. English notes! Definitely English notes. And definitely not mine! There was a label on the case, but the name was just a squiggle. I knew, though, it must belong to somebody staying at the hotel. 'What a panic that poor person will be in,' I thought."

I nodded. I could well visualise Rudyard Scott's panic when he realised he'd picked up the wrong case.

"So I took the case straight back down to reception, and we were all standing looking at the money when the lift doors opened and Mr Scott came rushing out carrying an identical piece of luggage. Quite red-faced he was. He shouted, 'That's *my* case! Thank God you've found it!'"

I raised a sceptical eyebrow. "With all that money on view, just how did he prove that?"

"That's exactly what the receptionist asked — in a polite way, of course. So Mr Scott picked up the combination lock lying on the desk, fiddled with the numbers, and the hasp opened." She frowned. "I hope he's put all that money in the hotel safe. I didn't see what he did, I was only interested in rushing up to my room and getting out my heart pills."

We chatted on, but all I could really think of was the brownie points I'd earn from Gerry when I in turn told the story of Rudyard Finbar Scott and his bundles of notes.

Gerry Burnside looked up from the tangle of papers on his desk. With his thin tanned face, straight black hair and brown eyes, he could pass for a Spaniard, and in fact when working on a case, often did.

I flopped into the seat opposite him. "Anything new on writer Rudyard Finbar Scott?"

He shook his head. "I've been making enquiries. There's no record of him in the British Library, or with the Society of Authors. That only means, of course, that he's not a *published* author."

"Well, I think it's worth continuing to check him out," I said, feeling somewhat smug. "It seems he's carrying a case full of money about with him." Like a dog that has deposited a slipper at his master's feet, I sat back waiting for the pat on the head.

Gerry didn't appear to be quite as impressed as I'd expected. He leant back in his chair, clasped his fingers and slowly rotated his thumbs. "It's probably to pay for that villa he's going to buy from Vanheusen. In Spain it's quite usual for people purchasing property to tote large sums of euros around in carrier bags. It's a favoured way of beating the taxman."

He knew I'd wanted him to be impressed. I ground my teeth and counted to ten.

I let the silence lengthen. Then I added, "In pounds sterling."

The thumbs stopped in mid-twiddle. "Well, now. *That* might make a difference." He leant forward, giving me his full attention. "Tell me what you've found out."

I told him about the mix-up with the suitcases, and had just congratulated myself on winning those brownie points, when he said, "There's one big snag about your theory, I'm afraid, Deborah. If he's a courier, why is he still hanging around here? Why hasn't he just handed over the dough and scarpered?"

He must have detected my chagrin — Gerry can read me like a book — for he switched on Mr Nice Guy. "But perhaps you'd like to know that the reception photo you spotted on Devereux's desk has opened up a new line of enquiry. Jayne keeps our newspaper files and recognised one of the background faces as Jonathan Mansell, the owner of the Alhambra Hotel."

Gerry normally operated on a strict need-to-know basis as far as we operatives were concerned, so I recognised this piece of info as the dog's pat on the head for delivering the slipper.

From a folder on his desk he deftly extracted a page of newsprint and pushed it across the desk. Under the headline FIVE-STAR HOTEL TO OPEN FOR BUSINESS was a picture of white minarets and turrets against an impossibly blue sky, and an interior shot of soaring reception hall with its intricate lacy plasterwork, marble floor, gleaming brass urns and squashy sofas. Alongside a lengthy interview was a photograph of the owner, Jonathan Mansell.

Gerry ran a hand through his hair. "So now we know that there's social contact between Vanheusen and Mansell. And they also have business contacts because . . ."

"Because Exclusive installs its clients in his hotel as part of the softening-up process . . ." I said, feeling my way.

He took off his glasses. "But is there also an *illegal* business connection between Vanheusen and Mansell?

That's what we have to find out." He chewed thoughtfully on one gold-edged earpiece.

The opportunity presented itself two days later among the morning mail on my desk.

Mr Jonathan Mansell has great pleasure in inviting Ms Deborah Smith of Exclusive Properties to the Official Grand Opening of the Alhambra Hotel on Thursday 20th December at 19.30.

I traced the embossed black letters with a thoughtful finger. This might be the perfect chance to do a little digging. With that in mind, I got Gerry to issue me with a natty little device to deal with hotel electronic door locks.

I was late for my rendezvous at the Alhambra. Best-laid schemes and all that. I'd had it all planned — give Gerry my daily report, go home in plenty of time to change, transform myself from ugly duckling into swan, as Gerry so flatteringly put it. But I'd reckoned without the persistent — suspiciously persistent — would-be traveller who came into the front shop.

Jayne, our dumb-looking front-person, bored with the current window display, had that very morning swept it all away. Gone were the paddy fields in Vietnam. Gone the snows of Everest and K2, and the sailing ship battling its way through the Straits of Magellan. She'd replaced them with exhortations to suffer in more esoteric freezing hell-holes. *Trek to the South Pole in the footsteps of Scott. Relive Shackleton's Epic Winter Crossing of South Georgia.*

Spend the Winter Months in a Siberian Gulag.
Cardboard models of icebergs sailed the windows of
Extreme Travel amid huge heaps of polystyrene beads
mimicking the snows of the Antarctic.

Just as I was about to leave the inner office for home,
the buzzer signalled someone coming into the shop
from the street. Through the one-way mirror we
watched a thin-faced man advance to Jayne's desk. His
beard and moustache were trimmed to a neat O, his
hair cropped to be a mere shadow on his scalp.

"Just a minute," I said to Gerry, "that's the guy who
broke into my apartment."

We sat back and watched with interest, confident
that Jayne was well able to handle the situation. But this
time she had to pull out all the stops. The hidden
microphone relayed every gambit and counter-gambit
in the battle of wits. It would have been most diverting
if I hadn't been desperate to get home to change into
my glad rags for the Official Grand Opening.

From the moment that he'd come in, his eyes had
been making a thorough inspection of the office. He sat
down on a chair and hitched it closer to Jayne's desk.
"Hi, doll, you're looking at the twenty-first-century
Shackleton of South Georgia. I want to book right now.
How do I go about it?"

"Just a minute, sir." Gunfire rattle of keyboard keys.
"There's a cruise that includes the opportunity of a
crossing of South Georgia following Shackleton's route,
starting from Argentina in — oh, November. I'm sorry
but you've missed it by a couple of weeks. It's summer

58

down there now and the ice has begun to melt, so I *could* try to book you on a supply ship."

"OK." His eyes swept the office again, scanning, assessing.

Jayne was unfazed. "Right. Exactly how much time do you have at your disposal?"

"Two months." He was now staring directly into the mirror.

"Oh dear!" She sounded genuinely disappointed. "The voyage by supply ship takes six weeks. The trek itself another . . . You *do* realise that the expedition is on foot, hauling your own supplies? And that you will be required to carry a 40 lb pack, pull a 200 lb sled, and be familiar with roped glacier travel, crevasse rescue, snow camping and usage of ice-axe and crampon?"

"Oh." A perceptible lessening of enthusiasm.

Jayne again consulted the screen. "The minimum number in the party is four, including the leader." A few more taps on the computer keys, then, "No one else has booked so far."

"I can't believe that!" He seized the monitor and whirled it round towards him. "Lemme see."

We tensed. Jayne smiled. We'd glimpsed an expertly designed web page. She had done her homework, left nothing to chance. Which, in our business, can mean the difference between life and death.

"You see, no one." Jayne swivelled the monitor back towards herself. "But I can certainly put your name down. To ensure commitment, there is quite a large deposit, twenty per cent of the total. Non-returnable,

I'm afraid. I suppose if they had just the minimum number and someone pulled out, it *would* be a bit of a disaster. Now the deadline for bookings is . . . in about three weeks, to allow the supply ship to return before the ice pack refreezes." She whirled the screen round towards him so that he could see. "Shall I put your name down?" Another big bright smile.

"Well . . . er . . ." His eyes seemed to be appraising the locks on the white door. "How about the Scott trip then?"

We were treated to a repeat performance of Jayne in action. The Scott trip was stymied by the discovery, in the small print, of a requirement for the possession of certificates in dog-sled handling and winter survival techniques such as igloo building.

Edgily I looked at my watch. I might just make it to the Alhambra in time if I left in the next five minutes . . .

Jayne was saying, "The Siberian Gulag? Yes, I'm *sure* we'll be able to fix you up with that." She rummaged in a drawer and produced a form. "There's just the visa to complete. We'll have to send it off to the Embassy. But I'm afraid the Russians are a bit slow in processing them, four weeks is standard, so you might not get it back in time. The last application I sent in got lost, would you believe it? As there was no time to reapply, the unfortunate lady had to cancel her holiday." She poised the pen invitingly. "Now what was the name?"

"Er . . . I'm running a bit late. I'll fill in the form at home and bring it back tomorrow."

We all sensed victory.

"Well, perhaps you might like to book for something shorter and warmer, like *The Smoke that Thunders*. It's a four-day journey in a *mokoro* dug-out down the Zambezi to the Victoria Falls, sleeping rough under the stars." She reached for the booklet *Health for Travellers* and flicked through the pages. "Let me see . . . U . . . V . . . W . . . Z. Zambia, Zimbabwe. Hmm . . . I have to warn you that there's the risk of dengue haemorrhagic fever and —"

"OK. As I said, I'm running late. I'll let you know tomorrow." He stuffed the visa form into a pocket and hurried out.

We awarded her a spontaneous burst of applause. Gerry leant over and switched on the intercom. "Star performance there, Jayne."

I picked up my bag and made for the door.

"Hold it a minute, Deborah." His voice was unexpectedly sharp.

I stopped.

"That *tipo* had his eyes everywhere." He took off his glasses and polished the lenses. "He's definitely a professional and dangerous. They're checking you out. Let's hope they're satisfied. Be careful."

Gerry's warnings were to be taken very seriously indeed. I let myself out by the unobtrusive back door.

CHAPTER
SIX

Of course, it's always the same when you're in a hurry. Lights at red, pedestrians surging over crossings, unusually heavy evening traffic . . . but at last I drove into the car park of the Alhambra. Dramatically spot-lit towers and minarets reared whiter than white against the dark night sky, floodlights probed fingers of colour skyward and soft blue lighting along the façade created mysterious pools of shadow.

By now I was far too late for the opening ceremony. *No problema*. My main objective was to seek out Vanheusen, see who his chums were tonight and engage in a little ferreting . . . I hurried across the marble floor of the foyer with its soaring arches, pillars, and jungle of greenery. An expanse of blue water shimmered in the rectangle formed at the meeting point of four interior courtyards. Other establishments might have their swim-up bars. The Alhambra's pool went one step further. It was dotted with tiny "islands", each with its clump of palm trees, fringe of sand and a "feature" such as a hammock or a driftwood shack.

If I found Mansell, I might find Vanheusen. No sign of either of them in the Casablanca courtyard, a place of plashing fountains, cascades spilling smoothly over mosaic ledges, and potted orange trees hung with tiny fairy lights. A few guests were conversing, wineglasses in hand, and a small orchestra was busily unpacking its instruments.

I collared a waiter in kaftan and fez who was arranging forks in precision lines on the buffet tables. "Excuse me. I'm looking for Señor Mansell."

He repositioned a fork by a couple of millimetres. "Try the Marrakesh courtyard, señora."

The Marrakesh was set out with open-sided tent pavilions. In each hung a pierced and fretted pottery oil lamp casting flickering shadows on little round tables and spindly chairs.

Ha ha ha haaaah. A woman's laugh, honed and practised, the tinkle of ice cubes in a crystal glass. Above the sounds of the orchestra tuning up in the adjoining courtyard, the musical notes of the designer laugh soared, hung for a moment, and fell to earth. It was elegant, stylish and totally artificial. I'd heard it before. Monique.

Like a retriever on the grouse moors, I homed in. Monique, Mansell and Vanheusen were seated, heads together in one of the tent pavilions, little oases of light in the encircling shadows. The links on Vanheusen's expensive wristwatch gleamed in the dim light of the oil lamps as he reached into his dinner jacket and drew out a folded sheaf of papers. What Gerry wanted was the exact nature of the connection between Mansell and Vanheusen, so a bit of casual eavesdropping might be very informative. They seemed pretty much engrossed. It should be safe enough for me to stroll by.

The pavilions nearest the group were as yet unoccupied by any of the couples drifting in from the Casablanca. A discreet flanking movement, tagging along behind a small group of new arrivals, and a couple of minutes later I was sitting in an adjacent pavilion, back turned, sipping a drink. On the way I'd seized a couple of champagne flutes from a passing waiter's tray. An extra glass on the table would suggest an absent companion. Mission accomplished, I toasted the Alhambra in its own rather fine champagne and tuned in to the conversation going on next door.

Vanheusen was saying decisively, ". . . well, that's agreed then."

". . . need . . . we don't want . . ." Because of the background murmur, few words of Mansell's reply were audible.

"Yes, yes, I'll see to it. Don't worry. Monique will . . ." The scrape of chairs being pushed back drowned out the rest.

Well, I hadn't learnt much there, except that they were definitely discussing some kind of business deal. Allowing them time to move away, I took a leisurely sip of my champagne. Couples wandered by, the men in dinner jackets or white tuxedos, the women in long gowns, the more daring in fashionable see-through dresses or diaphanous harem pants. I placed myself in the not-so-daring pants category, mazarine-blue silk with matching long-sleeved chemise.

Where was Vanheusen now? I stood up and caught a glimpse of him forging through the crowd in the direction of the Casablanca courtyard, but the other two were no longer with him. I scanned the shadowy figures promenading round the lake/pool to admire the ingenious islands with their sandy shores. Opposite the island with the shack, I could see Monique talking to Mansell, listening intently to him, apparently hanging on every word. I had to admit that the emerald green gown fitted her to perfection, emphasising her slender waist and ample curves. Green opals threaded through her piled-up hair complemented an opal choker necklace and a thin gold circlet round her wrist.

Using the crowd as cover I drifted closer, angling my approach so that I'd come up behind them. It would be worth eavesdropping for a couple of minutes. After that, I'd snoop around Vanheusen and see what he was up to . . .

They were four metres or so ahead of me now, but I didn't dare close the gap. Their conversation — light conversation, nothing of interest — came in snatches, drowned intermittently by the chatter of passing groups.

They stopped.

Half-turning away, I rummaged in my bag, making a show of glancing impatiently at my watch and staring in the direction of the Casablanca courtyard as if searching for somebody. When I looked again, they'd moved off, and were some distance ahead. I hurried to catch up.

". . . I quite understand your reservations. It's all a matter of presentation, isn't it? Exclusive will provide most of the funding, and you provide . . ." Monique's words faded frustratingly.

"Risky. If it came out . . ." Mansell put out a hand to steady her as she teetered close to the sparkling waters on those precariously high heels.

Her elegantly manicured hand rested lightly on his arm. "You're right, it's absolutely vital that *nobody* finds out about it . . ."

If they looked back and saw me . . . I was taking a risk, a calculated gamble, by moving up so close.

". . . On the plus side, this new venture of Vanheusen's is a real gold mine. If the deal comes off, I'll be able to afford another place like this. I'd make a few changes, of course. Back there, for instance —"

I sensed he was about to swing round. I turned on my heel and melted into the strolling crowds.

I took up my stance in the shadows of the Casablanca courtyard sipping a glass of champagne. What I'd just heard was interesting, but I didn't have time to think it over as I'd just caught sight of Rudyard Scott. Only this morning, he had informed me rather brusquely that he wouldn't be present at the official opening. The Grand Opening, like the Outing to the Moon, was apparently a frivolity that he didn't have time for. But now here he was in close conversation with Vanheusen. Like myself, they were standing in the shadows, and I wouldn't have noticed them if it hadn't been for a sudden movement. Interesting to see his reaction if I went over to them and called out a breezy greeting on the lines of, "So you've made it, after all, Mr Scott".

Nursing my half-full glass against the jutting elbows and suddenly turning shoulders of chatting groups, I weaved past the fountains and the potted orange trees hung with tiny fairy lights. Progress was slow, and I had just wormed my way into reasonable hailing distance, when someone clutched my arm.

"Great atmosphere, isn't it?" Millie Prentice brushed back her tangle of auburn curls. "Just a mo." She lunged at a passing waiter's tray of drinks. "This is my third glass of champers," she giggled, "and it won't be my last. I must hand it to Mr V. He arranged all this, didn't he? He's not looking for a lady-love, trouble-and-strife wife, by any chance, is he?" Another giggle, more inebriated than the last.

"No, he didn't, and no, he's not," I said. "Jonathan Mansell, who owns the hotel, arranged all this. And as far as I know, Mr Vanheusen's not looking for a partner, permanent or not." I didn't add, "and certainly not an unsophisticated young woman who can't hold her drink."

"Jon-a-than Man-sell," she rolled the syllables round her tongue, as if savouring a particularly tasty canapé. "No harm in getting acquainted, though." She stood on tiptoe to crane over the heads of the surrounding throng. "Can you see him?" She teetered, threatening to slop the contents of her glass onto my expensive hired silk outfit.

I put out a supporting hand and steered her towards a currently unoccupied chaise longue. "Why don't you lie in wait over here?" And she would indeed soon be assuming a horizontal position if her champagne input continued at the same reckless rate. "I saw him down by the lake. He'll be circulating among his guests all evening."

That had given me an idea. With Mansell circulating for the next couple of hours, I could have a rake around his office — perhaps unearth something of interest. And since I knew the present whereabouts of Prentice and Scott, I could kill three birds with one stone and pay their rooms a visit too. I left Millie Prentice draped tipsily over the chaise longue and headed for the administrative wing.

The cool marbled expanse of the reception area with its lacy plasterwork was almost deserted, apart from a courting couple in their own small world gazing dreamily into each other's eyes, a porter loading the luggage of some new arrivals onto a large brass trolley, and an elegantly dressed woman walking towards the elevator. High-stepping behind her on twiggy legs was a tiny poodle, jet-black, pom-pom cut, lollipop tail perkily erect.

"Cute," I thought. "Gorgonzola would have him for lunch."

Gorgonzola . . . Her drug-detecting talent would be useful if I had her with me when I made that search of Mansell's office. I was unlikely to get such a good opportunity again. I made some mental calculations. In ten minutes I could nip back to La Caleta, and hopefully there'd not be too much trouble getting her into the hated cat-carrier once I'd buckled on her working collar, training overcoming reluctance.

Gorgonzola had wined and dined, so to speak, and was in cooperative mood. Barely thirty minutes later I was once again walking across the foyer, the carrier half-concealed under a pashmina wrap, draped toga-style loosely over one shoulder and allowed to slide down my arm. The lovers on the enveloping sofa still had eyes only for each other, the porter was nowhere in sight and the staff behind the reception desk were chatting to each other or busy with paperwork and spared me hardly a glance.

I made my way to the ladies' room beside one of the first-floor lounges and released the catch on the carrier. G emerged yawning and, knowing it would annoy me, made a token display of independence by using one of the wooden legs of the two-seater chaise as an upmarket scratching post.

If one lady could lead a prancing poodle around the corridors, another could lead a creative cat. I was counting on the fact that in a five-star hotel, guests' eccentric little foibles go unremarked. Trusting that Gorgonzola's collar would look like some fancy pet accessory, I snapped on the lead, stowed the carrier discreetly under the chaise and together we sallied forth ready for action.

G enjoyed duty walks with her collar, and tail erect, tip twitching, she paraded along a corridor designed as an open-sided Moorish cloister. On my left, a wall of arches overlooked the Casablanca courtyard. On my right, electric candle sconces shed a soft light on the terracotta plaster and elongated the shadows of dwarf palms in gleaming brass pots.

In the elevator I pressed the button for floor four so there'd be no tell-tale 5 illuminated down in the foyer.

From there, I took the stairs to the administration offices on the floor above. G and I ran lightly up the steps — underhand activity can usually be disguised by bold and confident actions, so no furtive tiptoeing. At the top I paused. The public corridors and the stairs had been comfortably, even brightly, lit, but up here at this time of night, there was only subdued stand-by lighting separating pools of darkness. No candle sconces, no leafy palms in brass pots, no decorative windows, no windows at all, just a wide corridor lined with solid wooden doors. Last week when I'd engineered a daytime visit to the administration floor, the corridors had been well lit and anything but silent. A constant stream of people had moved between the various offices. There had been a buzz of activity — people talking, telephones ringing, photocopiers and printers chattering and humming. Now only the muted hum of the air-con broke the silence.

I wasn't expecting to see the thin line of light beneath the door third along to my left, Mansell's office. I wouldn't have seen it at all if the corridor illumination had been brighter. Someone was working late, probably updating the files on the computers. Just my luck, best-laid schemes and all that . . .

G and I walked softly along and stopped outside Mansell's office. On the other side of the door, I heard the rumble of a filing drawer being pulled open, the *clunk* as it shut, another rumble, another *clunk*. Then *click-click-click*, the sharp sound of heels crossing the office's marble floor.

70

As a shadow broke the line of light at the foot of the door, I scooped G up and took half a dozen strides along the corridor. Putting her down, I took up position close to the wall in the pocket of darkness between the dim lights, a shadow amid the shadows in my darkish blue outfit. As the door opened, I crouched down and half-turned away to conceal the white blob of my face. If the late-working employee came my way, I could pass myself off as a guest fussing over her pet. I heard the door close softly. The heels clicked their way towards the elevator and the stairs. I risked a look.

Millie Prentice. As she passed under one of the lights there was no mistaking those unruly curls or that skimpy dress. In her brisk walk there was not a trace of the tipsy young woman that I'd left sprawled on the divan in the courtyard, no sign of intoxication at all.

The elevator doors closed silently behind her, and Gorgonzola and I were left alone. 5-4-3 the floor indicator flickered down, 2-1-0. I waited a few minutes to make sure that she wasn't going to return. Then, courtesy of Gerry's natty electronic device, Mansell's office received its second unauthorised visitor of the evening. How had innocent-seeming Millie managed to gain entry? Something else to ponder.

I left G to do her own ferreting while I tackled the desk and filing cabinet. Millie might have got something out of her little rummage-around, but I drew a blank. The papers I could access seemed to be above board. I hadn't really expected anything else. Unless he was a very careless man, he'd have stowed away any obviously incriminating documents in that fireproof safe in the corner.

"Time for us to make ourselves scarce, G," I said.

Taking the elevator from the fifth floor had been careless of Millie. We professionals once again used the stairs, then took the lift down from the fourth floor to the ladies' room. There was no trouble getting Gorgonzola into the cat-carrier, perhaps because she knew she was going home, and it wasn't long before I was looking down into the Casablanca courtyard from the first floor arches. If Millie had returned to the chaise longue, I could take the chance of paying a visit to her room. I was in luck, she had. No longer the lolling, squiffy figure, she was now soberly upright in earnest conversation with Rudyard Scott. More food for thought, but not now. Gorgonzola, the natty device and I had those visits to make.

In 307, Rudyard Scott's room, I stuck a telephone card into the slot to operate the lights, and released G for an investigative roam-around while I did some snooping myself. On the floor of the wardrobe, sporting a shiny new padlock, lay the black airline case. Empty by the feel of it, but I'd take a look anyway. I reached into my pocket for my set of picklocks. *Shit*. They weren't there. I'd discarded them in favour of that all-singing, all-dancing natty device of Gerry's. If the money wasn't in the airline case, was it stashed inside the safe? I pulled out my lipstick/camera. The close-up I took of the safe's lock and the maker's name might be useful if Gerry decided to send somebody to have a peek inside. We spent a few more minutes looking round, but as far as drugs or incriminating papers were concerned, G and I again drew a blank.

"Nothing more for us here," I said ushering G ahead of me, and off we went along the corridor to 323, Millie's room.

With that laid-back attitude of hers, I'd somehow expected to find the room a bit of a tip — clothes, make-up items, tourist bumf, bits and bobs scattered about. To my surprise, there were few personal items on display — beside the bed an alarm clock displaying world times, on a small table an open book face down, a few toiletries neatly arranged on the bathroom shelf and a laptop plugged into the wall. That last item would be worth investigating — once I'd had a rummage through the suitcase wedged between the bedside table and the wall.

I watched G stroll around for a moment, then swung the suitcase up onto the bed. If it was locked, I'd be scuppered again. But this time I was in luck, the open padlock hung loose. Any great expectations were soon dashed, however. The suitcase held only a plastic carrier bag of laundry and a sealed carton of cigarettes. Didn't look promising, but I summoned Gorgonzola for a second opinion.

"Anything, G?"

Gorgonzola peered in, yawned, then headed for the cat-carrier in a pointed reminder that it was late and she wanted to go home.

I was closing the case when a laminated card slithered out of a pocket in the lid. The word PRESS, the green NUJ logo, and Millie's photo, name and membership number stared up at me. My heart sank. The last thing Operation Canary Creeper needed was a journalist stirring up murky waters, alerting Vanheusen and his mob that they were under investigation. Just how deep had she dug? If she hadn't set a password on that laptop . . . I flipped it open, pressed the On button and waited.

As I'd hoped, Millie had been careless. Without the security of a password, the machine powered straight up to the Windows desktop. I scanned the folder icons in *My Documents. Vanheusen Dossier,* now *that* was interesting . . . One click opened it. *Drug Dealing, Exclusive Properties, Money Laundering, Tax Evasion, VAT Fraud.* Millie's investigations were spot on. I scented Trouble with a capital T. Gerry would not be happy.

On the way back to La Caleta, I pondered the night's interesting developments. I'd seen Rudyard Finbar Scott and Vanheusen in close conversation, though that was no *proof* that Scott's money was for anything other than purchasing a property. We'd have our work cut out to prevent Millie Prentice from throwing a spanner into the works, but at least we could now remove her from our list of suspects. Best of all, I'd confirmed there was indeed a business connection between Vanheusen and Mansell. And that connection, from what I'd overheard, could very well be illegal.

All in all, Operation Canary Creeper had made some progress. Yes, with a clear conscience I could submit an expenses chit for the hire of my mazarine blue silk outfit with its matching long-sleeved chemise.

CHAPTER
SEVEN

Two days later, Vanheusen summoned me to his office on the pretext of finalising the details of the Donkey Safari Outing — and made the move I'd hoped he'd never make.

"Before you go," he handed me back the folder, "there's something I've been meaning to discuss with you, Deborah." He leant back on the black hide sofa, his gaze wandering to the oil painting of Black Prince on the wall behind me. "Over the years I've amassed some interesting data on the Persian cat, *felis persicus*. Did you know that the Persians defeated the ancient Egyptians by using cats as weapons?"

"Weapons?" I had a vision of an ancestor of the Brute of Samarkand hurled from a giant sling, whizzing through the air, claws extended, to wrap himself round some hapless pharaoh's head.

His gaze switched back to me. "They tied cats to their shields, playing on the Egyptians' reverence for the creatures. Knew they wouldn't counter-attack in case they injured the animals. One of the earliest cases of psychological warfare, I suppose. Stylish, elegant, classic." He picked up the Lucie Rie pot from the black lacquered table and ran his finger round the rim. "I'm planning to write a book on *felis persicus*, so bring in a photograph of Persepolis Desert Sandstorm. I'd like to feature her." Friendly smile, scheming eyes. "When I have collected enough material, I'll . . ." He was silent for a moment, lost in thought.

I summoned up an easy smile in return. "For a book, you said?" A request of this sort had been on the cards, and I'd thought long and hard how to counter it. "My Persepolis in a book, that would be *wonderful*, Mr Vanheusen." Now for the planned regretful, "But I'm afraid I haven't got a photo of her. You see, two years ago she was so frightened by a camera flash that she had to be sedated by the vet. And ever since then," I embroidered my fictitious tale with increasing enthusiasm, disappointment oozing from every word, "whenever she sees a camera so much as *pointed* in her direction, she rushes under the sofa and refuses to come out for hours." *That* should snooker a possible counter-proposal to take her picture without flash. I sat back, confident that I'd managed to head him off.

He replaced the Lucie Rie pot on the side table and leant forward. "No problem, Deborah. We'll set up a hidden camera here, in my office. I guarantee she'll not notice a thing." He reached over to the diary on the table. "Now when can we fit her in?"

Hell. I hadn't anticipated *this*. How was I going to get out of producing moth-eaten Gorgonzola? I felt tiny beads of sweat forming on my hairline.

"Shall we say after Christmas, the 28th?" His pen poised over the entry.

I played for time by making a show of consulting my diary. "No-o, I'll be away. That's the date of the Donkey Safari Outing." I tapped the folder on my lap.

"Then, the day after?"

"Yes, that should be all right." I waited till he'd written it down, confident that I'd found a way out. "Er . . . there's one little difficulty, Mr Vanheusen. When I have to put Persepolis in her carrying box, she throws a positively diva tantrum," I said truthfully. "And it's the same when I let her out . . ."

An understanding nod. "It's the same with The Prince."

"So, no carrying box. The hidden camera's a good idea, but I'll have to take the photo myself, at home."

"Well, we'll give it a try." Reluctantly he closed the diary.

I'd bought time.

I turned into Calle Rafael Alberti and parked as usual opposite a patch of waste ground hedged by dusty oleanders. I'd overcome one hurdle but it would not be so easy to get my hands on a photo of a female red Persian that would fool Vanheusen. Top pedigree cats, like celebrities in any field, are instantly recognisable to devotees. The catch-22 of producing a photograph was that he'd be even more eager to see Persepolis Desert Sandstorm in the fur. That gleam in his eye made me certain of it.

This was the night for my weekly trudge round the *supermercado*, but I really didn't have the energy for it. I decided to treat myself instead to a cool San Miguel on the bench under my pergola listening to something soothing and classical. The plaintive notes of *"Misa Criolla"* would fit the bill. A tired brain churns out no solutions. I'd leave the problem of the photo till later in the hope that the answer might suggest itself.

After that beer, I'd continue the job I'd started yesterday. Jesús's patio was vibrant with a colourful display of blue-painted olive oil tins and red and pink geraniums. My patio was dull in comparison and this had been niggling me for some time. I'd pick up the paintbrush and continue with the therapeutic painting of my flowerpots. Yesterday I had transformed three of my once dowdy pots with a coat of vivid blue or scarlet.

I'd got out of the car, and was just reaching in for my bag when I heard Jesús calling.

"Señora-a-a, señora-a-a!" Not a cheerful shout of greeting, but the wail of a harbinger of doom.

A hundred metres away on the pavement outside my house, my elderly neighbour was doing an odd dance, his raised arms and shuffling feet a strange combination of Spanish flamenco and Scottish Highland fling. Once he had attracted my attention, he lowered his arms and commenced a hand-wringing routine guaranteed to make the blood run cold. My blood, anyway.

Something had happened to Gorgonzola. Run over? Dead, or at least severely injured. I flung myself across the road, narrowly avoiding the wheels of a speeding taxi.

"*Qué pasa*, Jesús?"

"Señora, señora, how can I sa-a-y." The hand wringing increased in intensity.

My throat constricted. "Just say it in Spanish, Jesús."

"No, no, señora. I know how to say in *Inglés*, but I do not *want* to say."

"Gorgonzola, has she been . . ." I gripped his shoulder a little more roughly than I had intended.

The hand-wringing paused briefly. "The cat she is OK. Do not have worry about her. This morning I think she is looking a little sad, so I sing her one of my songs. After that she is happy. No, no, señora, that is not the trouble . . ." His voice trailed away.

Gorgonzola was safe. That was all that mattered.

"Has someone tried to break in again?"

"*Si*, the back door . . ." Jesús reverted to his native Catalan as he did in moments of crisis.

Overwhelmed by the torrent, I could only wait. When he stopped to draw breath, I seized my opportunity. "You've lost me, Jesús. What exactly has happened?"

The bright eyes flashed in anger. "It is *los vándalos*. They have made a visit."

"Vandals?"

"I show you." He seized me by the hand and led me through his house. In the kitchen he stopped. "You must get ready for big shock." He threw open the back door and pointed dramatically over the sea of red and pink geraniums.

My two tins of acrylic paint lay on their sides on the patio. From one snaked a stream of blue, from the other a ribbon of scarlet. When I'd left this morning, my kitchen door had been a faded nondescript brown. Now streaks and splashes of red and blue splattered the lower half. Gorgonzola sat directly in front of the

80

defaced door, tail curled round feet, head on one side as if critically viewing a Jackson Pollock artwork.

I leant against Jesús's doorpost, hysterical with relief, laughing till the tears ran down my cheeks.

"Please, señora, it is not so very bad." He shifted uncomfortably from foot to foot, making sympathetic aerial patting motions. "I go to the *ferretería* and buy the paint remove. Then you see the door is good again, and if the vandals come for second time . . ." He squared his bony shoulders and made a movement towards the paella pan hanging on its hook above the stove.

"The vandal is still here," I managed to gasp out.

In a flash the pan was off the wall and being whirled dangerously close to my head. "*Dónde está*, where is he? I teach him lesson he never forget." He sprang forward.

"No, no. *There's* the vandal, Jesús." I pointed at G. "*She* painted the door."

The paella pan wobbled in its orbit and crashed to earth, delivering a death blow to an already rickety fence post. Gorgonzola didn't even turn her head. She was totally absorbed in contemplation of her masterpiece. Jesús stared at me with narrowed eyes. It was the wary look you would direct at a dangerous lunatic.

"She's done this kind of thing before, you know," I hastened to reassure him. "The first time it happened I was as shocked as you were. I was nearly in tears when I saw that she'd splashed paint all over somebody's kitchen. But the owner of the kitchen said G was a rare

Painting Cat and her Work of Art, as he called it, was worth thousands. He was *en éxtasis*, delighted, over the moon, as we say. Can you believe it, that old door is now worth —"

"Señora!" he grabbed my arm and pointed.

Gorgonzola had come to an artistic decision. She was delicately dipping a paw in the red paint. An upward leap, and *splat!* A finishing splodge was added to the masterwork.

I laughed. "In England when someone is discovered doing something wrong, we say he — or she — is caught red-handed."

The black eyes sparkled. "Not the red hand, the red foot, I think, señora."

"No gain without pain," I said later as I battled to remove the paint from G's coat. It was always the same after one of her creative episodes. She hated the aftermath, her feet being dabbled in a bowl of water. "All great artists have suffered for their art," I added as she struggled to escape from my grasp.

After that little diversion, I certainly needed my bit of quiet relaxation on the patio, but it was not to be. In the warm dusk Jesús launched into a *madrelena* in honour of Gorgonzola The Artist. She at least was going to have her bit of relaxation. She lay down on her back, paws limp, eyes closed, head turned towards the sound.

Eeeee . . . aa . . . eee . . . Aaaah . . . aaa . . . eeee . . . The notes quavered and hung in the still air.

As the sun sank into the sea beyond the harbour, I gazed at my technicolor back door and pondered the problem of her photograph. Despite what I'd said to Vanheusen, G was far from being a cameraphobe. On the contrary, when a lens was pointed in her direction, she would begin grooming herself in preparation for the Big Photo Opportunity. It would be easy enough, therefore, for me to take her picture. The problem was that in the photo her moth-eaten coat would be only too obvious. It would be evident that my grandiose pedigree name for such a disreputable-looking cat was nothing but a flagrant attempt to deceive. I'd certainly lose the job I'd taken such pains to get.

At last, Jesús's song creaked to a close. Furry paws twitched peevishly.

"That was great, Jesús," I called. "So — so Spanish. *Muchas gracias* from Gorgonzola." I advanced to the fence and held out a can of San Miguel. "Thirsty work. *Aqui tiene*, here you are."

"*Gracias*, señora. Next time I compose new words in celebration of this so-clever cat."

G signalled her appreciation with half-closed eyes and a deep reverberating purr.

He stepped over the paella-pan-felled post and peered down at her recumbent form. "It was easy to clean the feet? You not have to cut the hair?"

"No, all I had to do was —" *Cut the hair. That was it.* He had given me the solution I had been looking for.

I planted a kiss on each leathery cheek. "What you've just said has given me a wonderful idea for the Day of Tricks next week."

"El Día de los Santos Inocentes?" His eyes twinkled.

"Yes, on Holy Innocents' Day I'll play a trick on a friend of mine. I'll show him a photo of Gorgonzola sitting in front of the door, and say the tricksters have splashed paint over the door and hacked pieces out of her coat." I giggled. "He's never seen her, so it will be easy to fool him."

December 28th, *El Día de los Santos Inocentes*, April Fool's Day Spanish style, would save Operation Canary Creeper. I could stall Vanheusen till then.

CHAPTER
EIGHT

On the morning of the Donkey Safari, Monique swept into my office sporting an elegant pair of white linen slacks topped by a black silk designer shirt. Flimsy high-heeled sandals in black suede completed the outfit. An enamelled gold badge pinning down a silk neckerchief proclaimed her status as PA Leisure.

She eyed my clean, serviceable and definitely non-designer jeans and cotton shirt with undisguised disapproval.

"My dear Deborah, you'll have to smarten yourself up a bit. Our clients expect a little more class. A piece of advice. One should always dress *up* for an occasion, not *down*. However, today, *n'importe*. Ambrose has decided that I should take your place as leader on today's Outing."

"But, Monique —"

She held up a hand to silence further protest.

"It's more important that you make a start on sending out the invitations to Ambrose's Three Kings Party on the 6th. They'll have to be posted tomorrow. You'll find the boxes of invitation cards and envelopes over there."

From behind her back she produced a wide-brimmed floppy hat of the type seen at garden parties attended by the Queen and, whipping a mirror out of her shoulder bag, stared at her reflection.

She flicked the brim of the hat upwards. "Jon phoned me this morning. Now *there's* somebody who recognises experience and quality when he sees it. Ambrose has arranged for him to sample this Exclusive Outing, to see if he can recommend it to his hotel guests." She made a few minor and unnecessary adjustments to the brim. "That's the reason an experienced person such as *myself* has to be in charge." She picked up the Outing folder and glanced at the typewritten list. "I expect all our clients will be taking advantage of our free excursion."

"Well —"

"Only Victoria Knight and Herbert Wainwright are on the list. I see that you've failed to interest both Mr Scott and Miss Prentice."

I'd a good idea why Rudyard Scott was keeping himself to himself. A courier has no interest in socialising for the sake of it. "He said he's at a critical stage of his writing," I lied.

As for Millie, a journalist has a one-track mind. She hadn't bothered to show any interest in the Donkey Safari. She'd already pumped Wainwright and Mrs Knight for all the info they had on Exclusive and Vanheusen. But whatever her alternative plans had been, they'd had to be put on hold. At this very minute she was being warned off at police HQ.

"Miss Prentice told me she —"

Fortunately, Monique was not interested. A final twitch to the already perfectly arranged hat, a slight adjustment to the genuine Louis Vuitton bag on her shoulder and out she swept.

I converted a snort of laughter into a cough. The donkey ranch was situated in the hills above Santiago del Teide in the west of the island, remote from motorways, grandiose hotels and boutiques. In a landscape of gnarled almond trees, dry-stone terraces and rust-brown volcanic soil, a fashion model riding a donkey would be as bizarre a figure as Don Quixote.

I thought about what she'd said. That reference to Mansell as "Jon" suggested a degree of intimacy. Had she taken a fancy to him, or was she latching onto him as part of a Vanheusen master plan? And how was Millie reacting to being warned off? I'd a feeling *that* young lady wouldn't easily be dissuaded from pursuing her investigations. If I got stuck into the pile of invitation envelopes, I'd have time to nip down to Extreme Travel to find out.

By quarter past twelve I'd twenty envelopes left to address. I reached into the card box for the final batch of invitations and grabbed a handful. As I dumped them on the desk, a piece of paper fluttered onto the floor. I picked it up and recognised Vanheusen's flamboyant handwriting.

Monique, make sure Mansell will accept the invitation to the Three Kings fancy dress barbecue. You should be able to clinch the deal then. AV

Again mention of a deal. Associating with a crook didn't necessarily mean Mansell was one himself, so could we use him as a Trojan Horse? I'd have to find a way of attending the barbecue, invited guest or not. I tucked the note in amongst the remaining cards in the box. Monique just might come looking for it.

Jayne was turning the notice on the door to *Closed* when I arrived at the office a few minutes after one o'clock.

"Didn't expect to see you today, Debs?" She raised her eyebrows in enquiry.

"It's OK, not an emergency. Monique took over the Donkey Safari and landed me with the office chores. She won't be back till late this afternoon, so I thought I'd slip away to see how things turned out with Millie."

As she locked the door behind me, I heard her mutter, "Trouble that one. Trouble with a capital T."

Gerry looked up as I entered the inner office.

"So how did it go then?" I said, knowing the microphone had picked up my exchange with Jayne.

"The lady's not for turning. A senior officer came down from Santa Cruz and interviewed her at the Police HQ here." He slotted a disk into the machine on his desk and pressed *play*.

The screen showed Millie in a sparsely furnished interview room sitting at a table opposite two men, one a uniformed policeman, the other a civilian with an air of authority. Judging from her compressed lips, things were not going well.

The plain-clothes man leant forward. "I'm asking you once again, Señora Prentice, to cease your investigations on this island and return to England."

Millie's eyes narrowed. "Getting too near the truth, am I? You don't want anybody digging up the dirt, washing your dirty linen in public, is that it?"

88

Gerry stopped the machine. "Just a sample of how it went . . . She refused to back off. Trotted out the old catchphrases: Freedom of the Press, Public's Right to Know, and all that." He sighed.

"There's something more?" I prompted.

He leant forward. "After half an hour she flounced out. See for yourself."

A furious Millie was leaning forward across the table. "Let me get this clear, Comandante. You are telling me to pack my bags and return to England. You are asking me to bin three months of investigation and research. And what are you offering in return?" Her voice rose. "Nothing, Comandante. *Nothing*." She leapt to her feet, sending her chair toppling to the floor. "All this stinks of a cover-up. And the next copy I file will expose how you tried to gag me. Just you wait . . ."

The screen faded to grey as he switched off.

"If she plays that card, she'll torpedo the whole operation." He fell silent. It wasn't like Gerry to be at a loss.

"She *might* just think better of it," I ventured. "After all, an exposé would scupper her own investigations too."

He shook his head. "To make someone like that back down would take a miracle."

"Or a Millie-kill," I punned.

He didn't smile.

Millie wasn't the only one to fly off the handle that day. When I dropped in at the Alhambra on my way back to Exclusive, Rudyard Finbar Scott was blowing his top in a spectacular way.

"I've been robbed!" His angry shout echoed round the marble expanse of the foyer.

Heads turned, couples halted in their tracks, their conversations killed stone dead.

"I'm telling you I've been robbed, damn you, robbed!" He leant over the reception desk, and brought the flat of his hand crashing down on the leather surface with a report like a gunshot. "That safe wasn't jemmied open. Somebody had a master key and used it. It's been an inside job, no two ways about it." *Thwack*. His hand crashed down again.

Though I'd been half-prepared for it, it made me jump. The manager, hastily summoned, was making soothing noises, but I wasn't really paying much attention . . .

Had a master key been used? A week ago I'd taken that photo of the safe and its lock. And given it to Gerry. Could he have arranged . . .? Yes, that was just the way his devious mind worked. If Rudyard Scott *was* a courier, failure to deliver his cash could well be a death sentence. And there was a very good chance that in his panic he might provide the evidence we needed against Vanheusen and his organisation . . .

Unnoticed, I slipped away.

"You'll never guess what's happened," I said. "Rudyard Scott's just made one helluva scene in the foyer of the Alhambra."

Gerry raised an eyebrow. "Hmm?"

90

I eyed him narrowly. He didn't seem at all surprised. I'd been right in thinking he'd brought in a safe-cracker. There'd be a snowball's chance in hell of getting him to come clean, though. I'd have a go, anyway.

"Yes, *really* upset. 'Really' as in incandescent."

"Let me guess." He tilted his chair and frowning, inspected the ceiling. After a moment, he transferred his gaze back to me. "Upset because the room maid binned the manuscript of his latest novel. Nothing left except the title page."

Damn Gerry and his doling out of info only on a need-to-know basis. He wasn't going to tell me. I accepted defeat.

"*If*," I said, studying my fingernails, "someone *has* opened the safe and taken the money, what do you think Scott's next move will be?"

"Or Vanheusen's? We'll just have to wait and see." Gerry wandered over to the coffee machine. "Coffee, Deborah?"

I made it back to the Exclusive office barely ten minutes before a dusty and dishevelled Monique swept in.

"How was your day, Monique?" It was pretty obvious just how her day had gone, but I thought I'd ask anyway.

"It's fortunate Ambrose put *me* in charge. I had to handle one or two difficult situations, believe me. And nothing but dirt and dust. I'm flaked out. *Bloody* donkeys." She scowled and held up the Garden Party hat, now redesigned by a ragged circular bite out of the brim. "Ruined! *Shit, Shit, Shit!*"

She turned away and limped towards her office. One glance at her rigid back made me wonder if I'd get the chance to organise any more outings. The Donkey Safari had been somewhat of a disaster as far as she had been concerned. And who was going to get the blame? Me. Not Vanheusen who had ordered her to take over. I could imagine her relating the whole sorry tale to my rival, Cousin Ashley — a lady no doubt cast in the same mould as herself.

Before the door closed behind her she snapped, "On a *properly* organised Outing, Deborah, *nothing* would have gone wrong."

She'd be in a better mood tomorrow when the first of the villa inspection visits would give her the chance to launch into her hard-sell sales pitch describing the site and attributes of the properties available for purchase. Two of the four prospective purchasers had been on today's softening-up Outing. The other two obviously had no intention of buying. They might give the whole thing a miss, even though that would flout the conditions of the Exclusive holiday offer. Scott, I guessed, would be too occupied trying to track down his missing cash to go through the charade of villa tours. Freckle-faced Millie was more of an unknown quantity. She was a pain, but I didn't want to see her dead. Might she have thought better of her outburst at police HQ and been warned off — or would she turn up intent on ferreting out secrets, full of questions, and set alarm bells ringing?

The answer came almost immediately. The phone on my desk buzzed.

"Hi, it's Millie Prentice here. I'm scheduled for villa visits tomorrow. Are they morning or afternoon?"

CHAPTER
NINE

Buzzz from Monique's office. Vanheusen was ready to see me. It was the summons I had been waiting for. In preparation, I'd stood for quite a time in front of the bathroom mirror cultivating an appropriate look for the role of distraught victim of *los vándalos* — a subtle blend of anguish and suppressed rage — hand run through hair, moist eyes, judicious use of blusher, that sort of thing.

Monique was sitting at her desk/table buffing her long fingernails. She seemed to have recovered from the fraught experience of the Donkey Safari and be in a better mood, buoyed up no doubt by the prospect of cash registers ringing from yesterday's villa inspections.

Without looking up she said, "Do you know, Deborah, I think you overreached yourself organising such a gruelling Outing. Yes, it was a little *too* fatiguing."

When I didn't reply, she glanced at me curiously. "Something wrong?" She raised a cool eyebrow. "If I may say so, you're looking a *soupçon distrait* this morning."

So, I'd passed the audition.

"It's my cat. She's —" I broke off, as though overwhelmed with emotion.

"Lost, stolen, strayed —" She spread out her fingers, studying the burgundy nail enamel for almost imperceptible flaws, "— dead?"

"Oh no, Monique. Not *quite* as bad as that. But bad enough." I launched into a trial run of my tale. "I arrived home yesterday to find —" Dramatic pause. "My cat —"

"Don't tell me," she didn't try to hide a moue of distaste, "the creature sicked up all over the bed, went berserk and shredded the curtains and the place stank of cat pee. Messy, destructive beasts, cats."

On a par with donkeys, I suppose. "Oh no," I protested, "Persepolis has never done anything like that."

Always a first time, her look said.

"Yesterday, Holy Innocents' Day, practical jokers splashed paint all over my back door. And . . . and . . . then they caught Persepolis and cut lumps out of her coat. You should have seen the state they left her in. I've got a photo here somewhere." I zipped open my shoulder bag and began to rake.

Stifling a yawn that plainly said, "Don't bother," she leant across the spindly table that served her as a desk and switched on the computer. The screen lit up, *Enter password*. Automatically she began to type it in.

M-O

If I stopped talking, she'd sense my interest, be on her guard.

95

"Of course, it was all my own fault," I babbled on. "I shouldn't have left those paint tins on the patio."

N-I

"But I don't want to keep Mr Vanheusen waiting. I'll tell you about it later."

K-A

Monika.

I'm amazed how careless people are about security — even those who should know better. The musical note of the boot-up sounded behind me as I made my way across the expanse of carpet to Vanheusen's office. Would the photo of G in my bag get me off the hook?

He was standing at the huge plate-glass window overlooking the gardens. He didn't shift his gaze from the scene outside as he beckoned me over.

"You're just in time to see the finishing touches being put to the kinetic sculpture I've commissioned in honour of Black Prince."

Down below in the garden a group of workmen were removing the covering from around a three-metre-high bronze tree. In the fork of the tree crouched a life-sized black cat, paw outstretched. A mini cloud of iridescent metal butterflies shimmered and trembled just out of reach.

"Wonderful!" I breathed. "You'd think that cat was alive."

"Carved from obsidian. Without flaw. Each measurement exact. Now," he turned away from the window, "what I've been waiting for — that photograph of Persepolis. Did you —?"

I switched on my previously tested-on-Monique anguished look.

"Oh, Mr Vanheusen, something simply *awful*'s happened to her."

His smile faded.

"Yesterday," I rushed on, "when I got back from the office, my door was absolutely covered with paint. Then I found," I swallowed hard, "that — that — someone had cut lumps out of her coat. Holy Innocents' Day pranksters going too far, I think . . ." I trailed off.

"But the cat's not been injured?" The concern seemed genuine. It almost made me warm to him.

"No, she's not injured, but she had *such* a beautiful coat. So long and silky. Now just look at her."

I delved for the photo and thrust it into his hands. There she was, moth-eaten Gorgonzola, sitting in front of her work of art — namely my rainbow-splattered back door. She was staring into the camera, eyes wide with shock-horror. Out of camera shot, I had strategically placed a large basin of soapy water and the hated sponge used on the occasions she had to be subjected to the torture of a *bath*.

"*Christ!*" Vanheusen collapsed onto a sofa as if I had crept up behind him and suddenly kicked him behind the knee. "That poor cat's been traumatised. *Outrageous.*" He leapt up, strode over to the side table, and flicked the telephone-intercom. "Monique, get me Roberto."

A wave of the hand indicated that I should sit down. He propped the photo against the Lucie Rie bowl, the better to study the tortured look that G was so expert at assuming.

"After an experience like that, Persepolis needs urgent treatment. Psychological damage *ruins* show and breeding potential."

A bubble of laughter welled up inside me. I converted it into a long sigh. She certainly had potential. But not in either of those departments. Gorgonzola as Show Champion, Gorgonzola as Mother, *no way*.

The intercom buzzed. "Roberto on the line for you, Mr Vanheusen."

He picked up the photo and studied it as he spoke. "Roberto, I've a cat that needs your services. Bad case of trauma . . . No, no, thankfully not Black Prince . . . Soon as possible. This afternoon would be fine . . . Not here, familiar surroundings would be better. At . . .?" He looked at me enquiringly.

"Calle Rafael Alberti, numero 2, La Caleta."

I hid my unease. Was this Roberto a vet — and what treatment would he give a perfectly healthy cat? Treatment there would be, I was sure of it, justification for his no doubt exorbitant private charges.

"Good, that's arranged then. *Adiòs*." He regarded me with satisfaction. "Roberto will commence treatment on Persepolis this afternoon. At 3 o'clock."

"Treatment?" I panicked. Now I wasn't acting. "Injections? I don't — She'll be even more —"

"No, no, no. Nothing like that." He was grinning. "Something much more effective. What Persepolis requires is the healing hands of a Reikimaster. Roberto,

I can assure you, is one of the best in the business. Now, if you'll forgive me . . ." He wandered over to the window.

I left him in silent contemplation of his kinetic Black Prince.

And so it was that the Reikimaster came to Calle Rafael Alberti, numero 2. When I opened the door to him, I expected to see someone enveloped in an indefinable air of mystery, someone not exactly muffled in black cloak and sombrero, a Zorro-like figure as in the old ad for Sandeman's Port, but at least someone tall and commanding. Roberto was small, fat and ordinary. Unimpressive. Until he spoke to G.

"Come to me, *pequeña gata*." His voice was deep, soft, velvety, caressing.

The effect on Gorgonzola was startling. She'd been eyeing this stranger suspiciously from the top of the refrigerator. Now she took a flying leap, landed with a light thump at his feet, and twined herself round his legs, tail erect, purring loudly.

"Ca-r-r-r-issima," he purred in return, "how much you have suffered. Your so beautiful hair, it has been much despoiled."

His voice . . . so soothing, so tender, so warm . . . so hypnotic. Any minute now there'd be two besotted females wrapped dreamily round his calves.

"So now we have to relax for the treatment." He extricated himself carefully from G's clutches and made his way over to the table. "Señora, please to bring the

99

soft blanket or the small fur carpet for her to lie on when I am making the music."

It's hot in Tenerife. Not the sort of place you need thick or furry furnishings, but I did the best I could with a thin blanket from the top shelf of the wardrobe. Roberto nodded approval as I folded it into a Gorgonzola-sized rectangle and laid it on the wood of the table.

"*Aaaaah . . . ee . . . aaah . . .* " He let out a long-drawn-out *madrelena* wail.

G sprang onto the improvised bed and flopped down, eyes closed.

"*Aah . . . eee . . . eee . . . aaaah . . .*" The sound undulated, soared to the ceiling and ricocheted softly off the walls.

In *madrelena*-receiving mode she turned on her back, paws limp.

"So, *carissima*, you are ready to receive the healing power." With a quiet smile of satisfaction, he lightly clasped her face in his chubby hands.

"She doesn't like —" I stopped, my warning cut short by a loud rumbling purr. There had been no explosive reaction. No angry spitting and hissing. No frantic squirming from the hated imprisoning grasp.

From then on I kept my mouth shut, a silent and curious observer. Roberto's hands moved to her chest, then to her belly. As she lay there emitting a series of gentle ladylike snores, the *madrelena* faded to a barely audible croon.

"So now she will sleep. She will feel much better." He stepped back from the table. "The healing energy it was flowing into her. I feel the heat in my hands."

"It was very good of Mr Vanheusen to send you," I said as I prepared to show him out.

He looked at me gravely. "Mr Vanheusen always takes great care of his cats. They are to him like sons and daughters."

I gazed down at G's recumbent form. *Mr Vanheusen always takes great care of his cats.* I didn't like the implication one little bit.

I left Gorgonzola to sleep off the ministrations of the Reikimaster and headed for the Alhambra and the "office" allocated to clientele seeking information or help from Exclusive. In keeping with the exotic ambience, this was no plain desk screened off by potted palms, but a stylish table set in a striped open-sided tent modelled on the pavilions depicted in Moorish manuscripts. As I approached across the foyer, my heart sank. I'd spotted the stringy figure seated bolt upright in the client chair.

Even before I'd sat down Herbert G Wainwright launched into a long-winded tale about the villas he'd inspected. ". . . class establishments but . . . too isolated . . . not my style at all . . . none of them . . ."

I let him drone on. I nodded or *tsk tsked* at appropriate moments, but I was only half-listening. I was thinking about Millie's behaviour on her inspection tour of the villas. Had she been wise and adopted a softly-softly approach? Or had she drawn attention to herself by firing a barrage of probing questions that positively shrieked, "I'm sussing you out"? She'd probably have watched her step at first, but if she'd sensed she was onto something . . .

". . . that Millie Prentice should . . ." The name leapt out of Wainwright's tedious monologue.

Damn, what had I missed? I leant forward. "I think the point you're making deserves looking into, Mr Wainwright. Would you go over that again so I can make a note of it?" I poised my pen invitingly over my notepad.

"Sure I will. She has no interest in buying a villa, told me so herself. So how come that same young lady fixed herself an invite to that classy boat of Vanheusen's? Yep, she's pulled a fast one there."

Oh Millie, I thought, I really do hope you know what you're doing.

CHAPTER
TEN

"That photo — I think we might have turned up something."

"Photo?" I said blankly. The only one that sprang to mind was the photo of "traumatised" Gorgonzola that had so wrung Vanheusen's heart. "What? G sitting in front of her artwork door?"

Gerry shook his head impatiently. "No, no."

He shoved in front of me the photograph of Monique and Vanheusen clutching champagne glasses at some reception. Truth was, I'd pushed that little foray into Monique's sanctum to the back of my mind.

"We've run the faces in the background through the computer and come up with a match on one of them." He pulled off his glasses and gnawed at an earpiece. "A bit fuzzy, a difficult job. The lab boys had to do some enlarging and enhancing. But it's him, no mistake." He reinstalled the glasses on his nose.

"Well, just who *is* Mr X, then?" I said. Gerry could be so exasperating.

"Didn't I say? Thought I had." He leant back in his chair, knowing that little fib would irritate me even more. "It's John Sinclair. Owner of *The Saucy Nancy*."

The Saucy Nancy was perhaps one of the biggest, and undoubtedly the fastest, of the game-fishing boats based in Puerto Colon, Las Américas's expensive marina. I don't take much interest in that kind of thing, preferring the power and beauty of living tuna and marlin to dead bones and skin.

Gerry rummaged in the pile of papers on his desk, pulled out last month's copy of the *Tenerife News*, and shoved the paper across the desk in my direction.

A grainy black and white pic showed a proud angler standing beside a very dead marlin suspended by its tail from a gantry at the stern of a game-fishing boat. The caption read, *The Old Man and the Fish! Eighty-year-old hooks a big 'un on* The Saucy Nancy.

Gerry stabbed a finger down on the skipper, a stocky man in jeans and a tartan shirt. "That's Sinclair."

"So, apart from being at the same party as Vanheusen," I said, "what have we got on him?"

Gerry dumped a folder on top of the newspaper. "Plenty. Back in the UK he ran a used-car dealership that specialised in hiring out camper vans. Nothing luxurious, just a cooker, mini-fridge, seats convertible into bunks. Throw in a tent and you've got the perfect cheap family holiday. Tour the Continent, drive down to the south of France or Spain, hop over to Morocco for a couple of days. Nice little earner."

I thumbed idly through the folder. "Not much of a profit in that, by the time you take wear and tear on tyres and engine into account. Unless, of course," I looked up, "they brought back a holiday souvenir or two?"

"Getting close." He pushed back his chair and went over to the coffee machine. "Try looking at page 24."

"Oh come on, Gerry." I took the cup he was holding out. "Life's too short. Just tell me."

That was another of his annoying habits. He'd feed you dribs and drabs of information to see if you could forward-guess what he was about to reveal. He called it *exercising the brain*. "A brain workout is just as important as a body workout," he'd say piously when his victim griped about it.

He sighed in surrender. He really hated it when cheated out of the full question-answer routine. "Souvenir in the form of white powder, Class A type. The punters were dupes. They *really* thought they were getting a bargain holiday, especially when he offered an extra few days in Morocco as a freebie, see round the kasbah etc. And while they were busy haggling in the souk, the local boys would be busy stashing the dope in secret compartments in the van."

I sipped at the coffee. Not enough milk. "Nobody ever ask awkward questions?"

"Why should they?" He perched on the corner of his desk. Off came the glasses, twirl, twirl. "None so blind as those who don't *want* to see."

I took another sip and gave up on the coffee. Time to earn a few Brownie points. "Let me guess. We knew about this pretty soon — couldn't miss a stream of camper vans going from A to B. We let it run, though. All masterly inactivity to catch Mr Big."

"Right." Another twirl of the long-suffering glasses. "But last year he suddenly ups sticks and comes over here. Whether he got wind that we were breathing down his neck, or somebody made him an offer he couldn't refuse . . . Now he's doing pretty well, too well. Big boat, big car, big house, big spender. So what — or who — is bankrolling him?"

He hitched himself off the corner of the desk and slid into his seat. He peered over the bridge of his fingers, elbows planted on desk, fingers interlocked, chin supported on thumbs. Oh, oh, bad sign. I recognised the ritual. An unpleasant assignment was coming up and heading in my direction.

"That photo was taken last New Year in Vanheusen's house at a private party. So why did Sinclair get an invite? That's where —" He shot me a probing glance.

"— where I come in." I finished the sentence for him.

He nodded. "I want you to plant a bug. On that boat of his."

It all *sounded* straightforward. But the bridged-finger ritual signalled a hidden snag. Whatever it was, I knew I wasn't going to like it. I sighed heavily. Blood sports of the fishy kind went very much against the grain as far as I was concerned.

"On a game-fishing boat? You're not asking me to take rod in hand and murder a fish, are you?"

His "No, no, no" was said a little too quickly. "You can leave that to your partner." The look he gave me was decidedly shifty. "All you'll have to do is find a good position for the bug. Simple really."

"Partner?" There was an edge to my voice. He knew I liked to work alone.

106

"Someone to do the dirty work with rod and line." He spread his hands in a gesture of innocence.

"I see. So I'm to be cast in the role of empty-headed girlfriend of —?"

I sensed a quickening of interest from the operator at the communications console.

Off came the specs. Nibble, nibble on the earpiece. "— of the best man for the job. The *only* man for the job." He studiously avoided my eye.

It couldn't be. It must be.

"*Jason*. You're not trying to tell me that my partner will be Jason Weston?"

"Now don't get on your high horse, Deborah. I know you two don't get on, but we need someone who's done a bit of game-fishing. An English guy with an English girlfriend. Perfect."

Silence. I glowered. He nibbled. In a sudden flurry of activity, the console operator busied herself flicking switches and twiddling dials.

Handsome, smooth-talking Jason had been on the team in Tenerife a month or two longer than I had. His cover as a time-share tout fitted his personality like a second skin — all those golden opportunities to chat up personable young things. The fact that they were usually accompanied by husbands or boyfriends was a challenge he couldn't resist. Harmless enough perhaps, but what really set me at loggerheads with Jason Weston was his arrogant belief that males have an innate superiority in judgement and intelligence over females. Whenever our paths crossed, his *me Tarzan, you Jane* approach made me see red.

107

But Gerry was right, of course. The overbearing, arrogant Weston *was* the only one on the team that fitted the bill. I gave in.

"OK. But *only* if he keeps his opinions — and his hands — to himself."

"Atta girl. Smith and Weston, the perfect team." Gerry beamed, relieved that the expected fireworks had failed to materialise. "I'll arrange a little get-together so that you can decide how to play it."

Jason's red convertible swung into the kerb and screeched to a stop with a loud and flamboyant fanfare on the horn. One tanned arm snaked across and released the door catch.

"Really, Jason, there's no need for all *that*." I stepped primly in and snapped the seat belt closed.

"C'mon, Debs, don't be a wet. Only a bit of fun." He gunned the engine, and we shot off with a G-force that pinned me to the seat.

"Business only, Jason. No hands. That's the deal," I managed through gritted teeth.

"OK, OK, OK, Debsy. You know me. Man of my word." One hand caressed my thigh, the other spun the wheel and we executed a corner in approved racing skid.

"We won't get there if you don't slow down." Coolly, I removed the hand from my thigh and, as a forceful reminder, shoved between us the thick wad of newspaper I had brought with me for just such a purpose.

"Point taken, Debsy." He slowed to what he considered a sedate crawl. The slipstream ruffled his blond hair, James Dean style.

"This guy Sinclair. Reckon he has an eye for the girls, eh?" A calculating leer in my direction.

I heightened my newspaper Berlin Wall. "If you mean I'm to seduce him while you plant the bug, forget it. *I* plant it while *you* in your Hemingway role grab his attention." I couldn't resist a dig. "You weren't just shooting Gerry a line? You *have* actually *done* some game-fishing?"

His size-fourteen trainer stamped heavily on the brake pedal, sending me lurching forward against the restraint of the seat belt.

A muscle twitched in his jaw. "I'll have you know I've made more than my fair share of record catches."

"Girls or fish?" I murmured *sotto voce*.

Revvv. Swoosh.

"Only joking," I said hastily. I'd forgotten how touchy he was about his image. If we were to work as a team I'd have to smooth things over a bit, give him the feeling he was running the show. "OK, truce, Jase. You decide how we're going to play it."

Revvv Swoosh. He indulged in another spot of ego-bolstering cutting-in and carving-up. I closed my eyes.

"Enjoying this are you, Debs?"

"Mmmm." I hoped he'd take my soft moan of terror as an appreciative murmur.

"Now, Deborah mine, a bit of strategic thinking here — if I *act* the novice needing help, his attention will be on *me* and that will give you more time to —"

Braaaah. He blasted from his path a poor unfortunate ditherer.

From the parking lot on top of the two storeys of shops and restaurants bordering the Puerto Colon marina, an iron Columbus points tirelessly with outstretched arm to the empty horizon, and beyond it, America. We stood shoulder to shoulder with Columbus and looked down on lines of white boats moored to parallel lines of pontoons. Those *pontones* fingered their way to the centre of the basin to service the floating caravans of the rich and mega-rich. In the stiff breeze the ruffled water sparkled and glittered in the bright sunlight, and a metallic *clink clink* of rigging drifted up from a forest of masts. A powerboat was backing slowly into a narrow space between two cruisers, accompanied by much waving of arms, shouting and frenzied repositioning of fluorescent orange buffers. I was all for lingering to watch, *schadenfreude* on my part, I have to admit, but action-man Jason was already bounding down the steps to the quay.

"Right then, Debsy, just follow my lead. And remember — act the adoring girlfriend."

"Yes, master." I touched an imaginary forelock as I trailed in his wake. Any adoration from *this* girlfriend wasn't going to be much in evidence. I intended to retire into the cabin with a convenient attack of *mal de mer* soon after we hit the open sea.

At quayside level the marina is a bit of a disappointment. Turn your back on the palm trees planted in pairs along the quayside, that sparkling sea and those bobbing boats, and all you see is yet another *centro comercial* — beachwear, luggage, shoes, karaoke bars, restaurants, and since it's a marina, offices for booking water sports or excursions to spot the whales and dolphins.

The rhythmic beat of calypso music pounded from the open windows of the Club Nautico as I scurried after Jason down a long narrow pontoon, past a line of cost-an-arm-and-a-leg cabin cruisers with their glass patio doors, sun-bleached sundeck and chrome ladder up to awning-covered bridge. The long curving fishing rods jutting up either side of the cabin made *The Saucy Nancy* easy to pick out among the lines of tethered boats. The Lord and Master was pushing his way through a line of tourists filtering from the pontoon onto the gangway of a whale-watching catamaran. I'd just caught up with him when he suddenly stopped dead.

"Wowee! Getta load of that!" His eyes were devouring the vast expanse of bronzed flesh revealed by the mini shorts and a strapless top of a scantily clad girl lolling on the net slung between the two hulls of the catamaran.

I flung an arm round his shoulders, crushed him to me, and with my mouth close to his ear muttered, "True to form, Jase, but Sinclair's watching us."

Never one to waste an opportunity, Jason twisted his head to nuzzle at my cheek. *Crackkk*. Something jabbed me just above the eye as the black iridium lenses of his designer Full Metal Jacket sunglasses tangled with my chain-store Polaroids.

"Ouch!" I hissed. "Bloody well get those hormones of yours under control, Weston."

He wasn't listening. Casanova's attention had been re-routed to an anxious examination of his poser wraparound shades. "These lenses are pretty special . . ." He moistened a finger and rubbed at a lens. "*Shit!* Scratched!"

I smiled, not just for public consumption. "File them as 'injured in the course of duty'," I whispered, and linked an arm through his. "Come *on*. He's looking at us."

"Only bought them last week. They're useless now." He jammed them into his pocket. "You should really be more careful, Debsy. That's the trouble with you women . . ."

"Mr Weston?" Sinclair had stepped over the game boat's low rail and was bearing down on us. He was wearing the same outfit as in the newspaper photo Gerry had shown me, with the addition this time of a red baseball cap and a pair of dark designer glasses (unscratched). What the photo couldn't reveal was his peculiar walk — a slightly rolling gait, deck shoes planted firmly, as if clamping to a heaving deck. All part of the Old Salt act. Only a year ago those feet had been treading the concrete pavements of north London.

"Hi there, skipper," hollered Jason the Young Sporting Blade. "I'm Jase. This here's Debsy." The arm round my waist gave an affectionate squeeze, eliciting a silly giggle from me. "Dragged her along for the fun."

Sinclair's eyes swept over me and dismissed what he saw.

112

Jason clambered over the low side rail. "Marlin or tuna today, what d'you reckon?"

I'd done a little bit of research. The marlin/tuna season ended last month. Had he slipped up, or was it a carefully considered master stroke that would confirm his role as a dilettante poser?

"Never know your luck." Sinclair's reply was slick, diplomatic. "But you're more likely to hook a barracuda or a shark." Well fielded. Avoided lies *and* didn't show the client up. He put a hand on the rail and vaulted expertly onto the white plastic deck-boarding.

Time to reinforce my image. "Jaaaase, help me!" I put a tentative sandal on the low gunwale and pressed. The boat shifted and tilted under my weight. "Ooooh," I wailed.

"Honestly, Debs, you *are* a bit of a wet." Jason took my arm and heaved me on board. Boys together, a shared glance with Sinclair said it all. His ingrained attitude to females, as normal as breathing, was now being given carte blanche, in the call of duty, of course. United in their male superiority, they clambered up the short ladder to the con deck above the cockpit and went into a huddle over the bank of dials.

Abandoned to my own devices, I edged along the narrow space between shiny chrome rail and cabin wall, making for the tiny triangle of deck in front of the curtained saloon. Gingerly I lowered myself onto the smooth whiteness, settled my brightly coloured cotton bag beside me and leant back against the glass, eyes closed, face tilted to the warm rays of the sun, top buttons of shirt seductively undone *à la* Saint Tropez fashion model . . .

"Can't stay there, doll." A voice from overhead intruded on the peaceful slap of water against the hull.

Lazily I opened my eyes and lazily closed them again. "Why not?" I practised a spoilt super-model pout.

"'S a bit rough outside the land shadow," the voice continued, indifferent to my charms. "When we hit them bigger waves out there, you'll get a good soaking. Might even be washed overboard." A hoarse chuckle. "Be a bit of a bummer for your *amigo* if you turned up on the end of his line, eh?"

Let him think he'd spooked me. "*Eeek.*" With the squawk of alarm he'd anticipated, I scrambled to my feet.

Grinning down at me from the upper con deck was a chubby-faced man, close-cropped head, broad square shoulders, square shovels of hands. A jerk of his thumb indicated that I'd find a seat inside. Obediently this little lady gathered up her beach bag and scuttled to her appointed place in the main-deck cabin.

There I readopted the recumbent Saint Tropez pose against the clotted-cream-shade, smartly practical, faux leather upholstery. Set in teak woodwork with brass inlay was an impressive instrument panel, a duplicate of the one on the con deck above. With VHF radiotelephone, satellite Global Positioning equipment and radar screen, *The Saucy Nancy* was well equipped for her operations, legitimate or otherwise. Speaking of operations — that black swivel chair out on the rear deck with its straps, harness and footboard looked uncomfortably like something out of a primitive reference book for nineteenth-century surgeons. Well, I was leaving everything in that area to Jason. The epic struggle between man and fish would go unobserved by DJ Smith. I'd be below feigning seasickness and sussing out the best place to plant the bug. Not that I would escape the tedium of a virtual-reality demonstration when we were back in the office. I knew he wouldn't be able to resist using that swivel chair of Gerry's for a rerun.

Jason's voice drifted down from the con deck. "300 hp Turbo Diesels, Debsy!" The ladder creaked and his designer trainers came into view, followed by his legs, tanned with a fuzz of blond hair and his expensively casual pale blue Bermuda shorts.

He flopped down onto the cushions beside me. "Did you hear that, Debs? *300 horses*. With that power —"

"Oh, Ja-ase, stop going on about those stupid engines." I yawned theatrically. It wasn't hard. That sort of thing bored me rigid. "When are they going to serve the free drinks?"

"How should I know? Just like a woman to ask something like that." His injured look wasn't faked. "Once we get going, I suppose."

"But we *are* moving, Jase." I abruptly abandoned the Saint Tropez pose. "Ooooh, there's nobody at the controls. Where are the crew?" My voice rose in a squeak of panic. "We've been *cast adrift*."

"Don't be so *silly*, Debs." With the slightest hint of an appreciative wink, he pushed me back onto the seat. "John's up there steering from the con deck. Once

115

we're out of the harbour, Steve and Jaime will select the lures for the sea conditions and set up the outrigger and stern lines."

The male mind seems more than a little obsessed with such technicalities. I'd have to sidetrack Jason to stop him trotting out all those boring details.

A bald head poked through the hatchway leading to the lower cabin. A small diamond-shaped scar on his temple showed pink against the swarthy skin. The crewman's gaze was directed at my Lord and Master. "When we pass entrance of the marina, *el capitan* come to talk with you about the choosing of the lures." The head withdrew.

"Jaime, I presume," I muttered. "Well, Jase," I raised my voice to carrying-level, "while you're confabbing with *el capitan*, I'll have a chance to get into my book." From the depths of my striped beach bag I plucked a fat tome. Pointedly, I held it up in front of me, flicked it open and began to read.

From the other side of the book barrier came, "I get the message, Debsy."

"Great," I said, reading on.

"*Romance, glamour, seismic sex . . .*" His finger traced the words on the front cover. "If you're looking for that, Debs, I'm ready when you are."

"Oooh, Jase!" I dropped the book, snuggled up to him and pulled his head down to mine. "Fat chance, asshole," I murmured into his ear. "You're on duty, remember."

"Of course, I don't mean *now*, Debs." He lolled back against the soft leather, arms spread wide. "You'll just

116

have to control yourself." Leaning forward he nuzzled my ear . . .

When the low thrum of those 300 horsepower engines changed to a throaty roar, I knew I was going to be in trouble. We'd cleared the artificial mole that protects the marina, and *The Saucy Nancy* began to act — well, saucily. Out here, away from shelter of the land, the waves were disconcertingly large and flecked with white-caps. I eyed them uneasily. It's funny, I'm a pretty good windsurfer and waves, even big ones, are something to be enjoyed, skimmed over, treated as an exciting challenge. But it's entirely different matter when I meet these waves as a passenger on a boat. Perhaps it's something to do with not being in control. And the powerful *Saucy Nancy* was already challenging the waves head-on, with predictable effects on my stomach. But I mustn't let Jason suspect. I'd never hear the end of it. He'd always be bringing it up. Bringing it up . . . My stomach gave a queasy lurch. I closed my eyes to shut out the oscillating horizon . . .

"I can see you're beginning to relax and enjoy yourself, Debs." Jason's voice was just audible above the roar of the engines. "We're about to set the outriggers and the stern lines. Want to join us?"

"No thanks, Jase. I'm fine as I am." From my recumbent position I had a mercifully restricted view of the stern and creaming wake. Just then, *The Saucy Nancy*'s sleek bows sliced into a wave, checked, pointed skywards and, in a whirling kaleidoscope of blues and greens as sky met sea, raced on. If I *really* concentrated,

117

maybe — just maybe — I could restrain the urge to puke . . .

After what seemed an age, the roar of the engines died to a slow rumble. I opened my eyes. The boat seemed to be more or less stationary. I eased myself into a more vertical position and tested for queasiness — on the Q scale, perhaps 4. Out on deck, Jason was bent over an oil drum stirring it with a stick, while Steve and Jaime were setting out rods at intervals round the sides of the boat.

"What are you doing, Jase?" I called.

"Come and see, Debsy. I'm making dinner for our shark."

Some kind of fish stew? I really should have known better and stayed where I was, but curiosity overruled better judgement. It was cool and shady in the cabin. Out on deck, the glare and the heat delivered a knockout punch. I tottered across to where he was standing, put my arm round his waist, and peered into the drum. "Let me see —"

An overwhelming stench rocketed the Q scale to 10, triggering an unstoppable retching from my stomach muscles. This morning's breakfast enriched the fishy slurry.

"*Debsy!*" His anguished scream rose above the cry of circling seagulls.

In disgrace, I slunk off to the sanctuary of the cabin once more . . .

"Strike!" The shout percolated a queasy half-slumber.

"Go for it, *hombre!*"

"Ya-*hee!*" Jason, exultant.

Cautiously I opened an eye and levered myself upright. Through the open doorway, I could see Jason harnessed into the swivel chair, feet braced, arms straining to hold the bowed rod. The crew were grouped at the stern collecting in the other rods in well-rehearsed action.

Tick tick tick tick tick. The ratchet on Jason's giant reel whirled round with the sound of a Geiger counter gone mad. *Zwing* the line shot out as some monster of the deep made a dash for it.

Jaime stood behind the chair shouting instructions. "Let him run, Hayson!" His gloved hand reached over and locked the clutch. "Check, *now.*"

The tip of the rod arched, dipped. The harness tightened. Steve danced about camcording for posterity the titanic struggle between man and fish. None of them had eyes for me. Certainly not Jason in his Hemingway role, braced legs and straining back, grunting with the effort. Nor Jaime, gazing astern at the leaping shape glimpsed dark against the boiling water churned up by its frenzied struggles. Nor Steve, eye glued to viewfinder zooming in on Jason's gritted teeth and white-knuckled grip. That left Sinclair up on the con deck at the reins of his 300 horses, but hopefully all his attention would be on scanning the briny with that radar fish-finder for the next scaly victim.

Excited shouts. "*Cuidado!* He going to jump!"

"Wow! How big is *that!*" Jason's voice squeaky, ecstatic.

Fighting back nausea, I slid off the banquette.

"Clutch! Clutch! *Clutch!* He dive!"

Ripping *tickticktick* of line streaking out.

"Keep pressure, Hayson. When he come up, he come like bullet from gun."

A couple of tottering steps and I was at the hatch staring into the lower cabin, dim and shadowy in contrast to the glare from sun and sea. If challenged, I'd say I was looking for somewhere dark to lie down, somewhere away from that heaving horizon and blinding sunlight flashing and sparkling and stabbing at my brain.

The boat lurched violently. I grabbed at the hatch frame and half-fell down the carpeted treads. Down below, the engine noise was very loud, the air heavy with the smell of hot diesel. I stood there, hand pressed to mouth as my hyper-sensitive stomach heaved in protest. Lucky Jason, out there in the fresh air enjoying himself. My eyes slowly adjusted to the dimness. Not much headroom, hardly space to swing a cat — certainly not one of Gorgonzola's proportions. On my right was a compact galley-sink and gleaming fridge, on the left, a smart red-cushioned bench and table. Directly in front of me I could just make out a narrow white door with the letters WC in shiny brass. No pictures. No clutter. No secure hiding place for the listening device in my pocket. No hiding place at all. Not even under the table that was designed to clip against the wall. When hinged up, it would reveal the underside. Where else could I conceal the bug? I had no luck with the two cupboards, one above and one below the sink. Both were locked.

Down in the lower cabin the motion of the boat was horribly intensified, making it difficult to think. An undignified rush to that WC was on the cards . . . the smell of diesel . . . the noise . . . Precious minutes passed before it dawned that I would be wasting my time, that it would be useless to plant a bug here. We'd not pick up anything, the engine noise would drown all talk. I should have thought of that immediately. I *would* have thought of it, if I hadn't been . . . Another crippling wave of nausea swept over me. My one thought was to get out of this claustrophobic hell, escape to the fresh air, lie down and close my eyes.

I'd one foot on the lowest stair tread when the cabin above darkened. I caught a glimpse of the camcorder dangling by its strap. Steve.

"Found the heads, doll?"

Heads? In my woozy state, the word conjured up severed heads with staring eyes, dripping gore John-the-Baptist style. Vomiting imminent.

"Bogs, WC, toilet," Steve spoke slowly and kindly as to an idiot. "Steady on, doll. You look as if you need to pay them another visit."

I smiled weakly, fighting to control the nausea.

"Shame you're not enjoying yourself. Just when your lad's landed a big 'un too."

The thought of the glassy eyes and bloody gills of shark or barracuda gasping its last was the final straw. Steve moved hastily aside as I cleared the remaining steps with the agility and speed of an Olympic athlete and made it to the rail just in time.

For the next couple of hours — it felt like days — I lay on the soft cushions of the smartly practical banquette in a haze of queasiness punctuated by dry retching, only intermittently aware of shouts and cries. Jason landing another prize catch, or losing it? I didn't care.

I must have fallen asleep. A hand on my shoulder was shaking me gently. Reluctantly I opened my eyes. Steve loomed over me.

"You'll be OK now, doll. We're almost back at the marina."

The violent see-sawing *did* seem to have diminished to a skittish bobbing. Experimentally I sat up. I was definitely back in the land of the living. Through the side window I could see the palm-lined promenade and the regimented lines of sunbeds on Fañabe beach. In another five minutes I'd be able to say farewell to *The Saucy Nancy*.

Five minutes. And my mission very much unaccomplished. *Shit*.

Might there still be a chance? Sinclair was at the console speaking quietly into the radiotelephone, one hand lightly on the wheel. Out on deck, Steve was laughing and joking with Jason who was sprawled in the swivel chair, drink in hand. Jaime was sitting cross-legged at the cabin entrance chalking *30th December — Jason Weston* and *Day's catch — Shark* on a small blackboard.

I propped one elbow on the back of the seat and let my eyes roam round. Here looked no more promising for bug planting than the cabin down below. One side was open to the deck, the rest a horseshoe of windows and banquette interrupted by the control fascia and access to the lower cabin. No ventilators, projections or handy crevices broke the smooth white expanse of roof above my head. The instrument console was the only possibility, but Sinclair was standing there. All in all, pretty hopeless. I was going to have to confess to Gerry that I'd failed.

"*Fantastic* bit of action there, Debsy." Jason, hair tousled, shirt sweat-and-salt-stained, threw himself down beside me. "I hear you missed some of it. Pity. Never mind, Steve filmed it. Can't wait to play it over tonight." He pulled my head down onto his shoulder. "And after that we'll . . ." He nuzzled softly into my ear, "Great acting back there, Debs. Especially that sicking-up. Stroke of genius."

I giggled coyly. "One of my little accomplishments," I murmured.

"*Mmmmm*." The nuzzling lips inched downwards to the hollow at the base of my throat, lingered a moment, then made to continue downward.

Damn him. He knew I couldn't make a scene. Over the top of his head I could see the grey concrete blocks of the harbour mole sliding past.

"*Mmmmm*." More nuzzling from Jason.

Over his shoulder I could see Jaime and Steve opening a refrigerated cabinet and lifting out the fishy corpse, its toothy gaping mouth and glassy eye defiant even in death. With a light thump *The Saucy Nancy* nosed into her berth at the pontoon. I sat up abruptly.

"Ouch!" Lover Boy levered himself off me, fingering his lip.

"What's happening now, Jase?" I enquired in a bright girly voice. "*Get them away from the cabin,*" I hissed in his ear. "*I need a couple of minutes.*"

Give him his due, you could always count on him in an emergency. He didn't ask any questions, just shot me a quick glance and leapt to his feet.

"Get my camera out of your bag, Debs. I want photos of me holding up my shark. All-male action pictures, so keep well back."

"Huh, holding a board and a dead fish, there's not much action in that!" I flounced petulantly towards the control console.

"Don't be like that, Debsy. I'll make it up to you later."

I swung round. "Let *me* take the photo, Jase."

"No way, Debs! Last time you cut off my head, and the time before that the pic was so fuzzy it could have been taken underwater." He flung an arm round Sinclair's shoulders and turned him so that his back was to the cabin. "C'mon, John, I want you beside me, and Jaime and Steve on either side of the board. We'll find someone to take the picture."

Scowl pinned to my face, I leant against the fascia just vacated by Sinclair. I felt a pang of remorse for J's sore lip. He'd just engineered as good an opportunity as I was going to get.

He thrust the camera at a group of gawpers on the pontoon. "Anyone do me a favour? Take a few shots of me and my catch?"

"Hey, fella, give it here." A floral-shirted arm reached out.

Jason was taking a chance. This was Tenerife, not some crime-free Utopia. Floral Shirt could well make off with the camera. Now *that* would cause a handy diversion.

"Thanks, pal. Now we'll line up here, and if you can get the upper part of the boat in . . ."

Jason would be able to string things along for perhaps a couple of minutes. That's all the time I had.

As soon as the line of backs screened me from view, I turned my attention to the instrument console. Dials set into smooth plastic . . . a couple of levers with red knobs . . . a small wooden-spoke wheel . . . panelling down to the floor. No gaps.

A shout from the pontoon: "This camera working? Nothing's happening when I press the button."

"Shit," from Jason, "forgot to switch it on. It's that button on the top beside the viewfinder."

Out of the corner of my eye I could see the row of backs. Jason's arm was still round Sinclair's broad shoulders, the group's attention focused on the black staring eye of the camera. Once again I ran my fingers over the smooth plastic and metal of the console. Nothing loose. Nothing I could prise off. *Hopeless.* I turned and leant one arm nonchalantly on the wooden wheel.

"One more shot. If the guy with the board could turn a little this way . . ." Floral Shirt indicated with the wave of a brown hand. "Now the three of you grab onto that fish."

The shark was now horizontal, the end of its tail in the crook of Steve's arm, the gunmetal grey head in the firm grasp of Jason, with Sinclair supporting the middle. Jaime was still holding the board with its chalked details, weight of catch now added.

Surely there must be *somewhere* . . .

"OK, fellas. Don't move. Hold it ju-st there."

Seconds left . . .

Something soft brushed against the top of my head as *The Saucy Nancy* lifted to the swell of a passing motor yacht. Hanging from the roof was a small dark object, a rubber mascot in the shape of Tenerife's famous dragon tree.

"OK. That's it." Floral Shirt lowered the camera and held it out.

Time up.

As Sinclair released the shark and pushed back the brim of his red baseball cap, my fingers prised apart the mascot's tangle of pliable green branches and pressed the thin disk of the bug deep inside. It would have to do.

CHAPTER
ELEVEN

The debriefing session behind the white door of Extreme Travel offices lasted two hours. After Jason had waxed lyrical about my acting skills (why disabuse him?), Gerry had been fairly philosophical about the less than perfect hiding place for the bug. Bringing him up to date, my version took ten minutes; Jason's account of the morning's action, one hour. As I'd predicted, the swivel chair was commandeered for a blow-by-blow re-enactment of the epic struggle. The surreptitious doze I managed to snatch during the video replay was interrupted all too frequently by the intrepid fisherman's excited yells, "There!" "You see!" "Wait for it . . . !"

On my way home I checked my mobile's voice mail to find Victoria Knight had left a message. *I'll be in the Café Bar Oasis at the Alhambra till 4p.m. Come and join me for afternoon tea.* I was tempted to pass on it — after that nightmare boat trip this morning, a long siesta beckoned. But I'd jettisoned breakfast on *The Saucy Nancy* and lunch was long overdue, so the lure of cream scones and sticky cakes in the Café Bar Oasis was stronger than the call of siesta. Restoring one's energy levels, I reminded myself, is important after a time of stress. If I turned left and back-tracked a bit, I'd arrive at the Alhambra in about five minutes, only a little later than Victoria's 4p.m. deadline . . .

After the heat outside, the Café Bar Oasis was shady and refreshing. I pushed aside a palm frond and spotted Victoria at a table positioned to one side of the gilded cage. She was in the process of demolishing a fluffy-textured scone liberally spread with cream and strawberry jam. A waiter in uniform of white kaftan and fez was pouring tea from a large silver teapot.

She looked up and waved. "Oh there you are, dear. I do trust you don't mind me starting." The spoon plunged into the bowl of cream and adroitly transferred a dollop to the waiting scone, evidently a well-practised technique. "You see, I didn't know if you *would* be able to come. But I'm *so* glad you have. Let me order more tea and another round of cream scones." She studied me solicitously. "You're looking a trifle peaky, dear. I *do* feel guilty about intruding on your free time, but I *really* need your advice." With deft movements, she processed the remaining piece of scone.

Matching pots of cream and jam, and a plate of golden brown scones arrived. As I tucked in, she chased the last few crumbs round her plate.

"Yes, Deborah, I need your help." For a long moment she was silent.

What could be bothering her? I paused, scone halfway to mouth. "Why, of course, Mrs Knight. That's —"

"Call me Victoria, dear." She folded and unfolded her napkin nervously. "Your advice, and another pair of

128

eyes, that's what I want. You see, on Friday Miss Devereux took me to the most beautiful houses. Of course, I was tempted at once. Who wouldn't be? All so beautiful."

This didn't sound too urgent. It was nothing that wouldn't keep. The unworthy thought occurred to me that I could have been snoozing with Gorgonzola on my patio, as I'd intended. Still, the cream tea was more than adequate compensation. I munched away steadily while Victoria launched into a glowing description of the properties inspected.

She broke off, eyeing my plate, empty now except for a smear of jam and cream. "Time for cakes, dear?" She signalled to a waiter. A silver tray of cakes and pastries materialised as if by magic. "Don't stand on ceremony, Deborah." She extracted from the pile a giant profiterole oozing cream and smothered in dark chocolate.

Thou shalt not covet . . . My eyes searched the pile of assorted cakes.

Reading my thoughts, she twirled the plate round. "There's another one. Quite irresistible, aren't they?"

Further conversation went on hold.

At last, Victoria pushed away her plate with a satisfied sigh. "Now I must tell you exactly what my problem is."

I sipped my tea and waited.

"One of the villas Miss Devereux took me to today was absolutely *wonderful*. Perfect in every way. *Just* what I've been looking for. It's the one featured on the cover of Exclusive's portfolio. "Exclusive even for Exclusive", I think it said."

"But, Victoria, that little bit of real estate is priced at £1 million."

"Yes, I know, dear. You're wondering what an old woman like me will do with a place like that, and how I can afford it." She leant across the pillaged cake plate, her voice sinking to a whisper. "It's for the children and grandchildren. And I *can* afford it. We won the lottery, Jack and I. We had great plans — a new house for us, and one each for the children. Three months later he was dead. A heart attack." Her voice trembled.

I couldn't think of anything to say. I patted her hand.

"Thank you, dear." She blew her nose on an embroidered handkerchief, and smiled at me with watery eyes. "Of course, I made sure young Jack and Anne got their new houses, but I stayed on in the bungalow. No point in moving. My memories are there, and the neighbours are very good. But it's lonely, and I said to myself, 'Victoria, though money doesn't buy happiness, it can help, if you use it in the right way.' Do you agree with me, dear?"

I nodded.

"So if I purchase a big place like the one I've just seen, I can stay in Tenerife and avoid the bad weather in England. And there will be plenty of room for the children and grandchildren to join me. No, money's not the problem." Her face clouded.

"But something else is?" I prompted.

Victoria leant forward. "There's a deadline, you see. And it's the day after tomorrow."

130

"Deadline?" I was puzzled.

She ploughed on. "I was *so* excited. I told that nice Monique Devereux, 'Yes, this is the one for me. I must have it.' Well, I thought she'd be delighted, but you know how you can sense that something's wrong?"

I nodded again, unwilling to say anything that might interrupt the flow.

"It was the way she hesitated. She seemed a bit flustered. I believe in getting things out in the open, you know, so I asked her outright, 'Is something the matter?' She was very apologetic. Said she'd no idea that I'd like the place so much that I'd consider buying. She'd only shown it to me because, after I'd seen the last of the villas, I said I'd a fancy to see the star property featured in the prospectus. And then she told me —"

"Madam is finished?" The enquiry hung over the table and encompassed us both.

Silence fell between us. From the gilded cage the twitter of birdsong and the flutter of wings suddenly seemed very loud. While the waiter cleared away the plates, I thought about what she had said. Monique had seemed "flustered". I had a hunch it would be well worth finding out why.

Victoria broke into my thoughts: "I've ordered another pot of tea, dear, if that's all right."

"About the villa," I hoped I sounded suitably casual, "what were you about to say?"

"Miss Devereux told me . . ." she paused, as if she was finding it difficult to put into words, "that I wouldn't be able to buy the property."

"Why ever not?" I was genuinely astonished. What could Vanheusen be up to? I had no doubt at all that Monique had been acting under his instructions. To turn down a sale of £1 million must mean that even more was at stake.

"It seems that there's an Offer to Buy contract on it. Someone's offered to buy the property for £1 million and Mr Vanheusen is going to accept and sign the papers tomorrow." Victoria sighed. "I'm *so* disappointed. It's silly, I know, but I've set my heart on having it."

"I'd really like to help," I said slowly, "but if it's in the hands of the lawyers, I don't see —"

"But that's just it." She leant forward eagerly. "Nothing's been signed yet. I've been thinking it over every minute since I got back. I asked myself what Jack would have done. He always said, 'If you *really* want something, you've got to fight for it. Never take no for an answer.'" She fingered the plain golden band of her wedding ring as if summoning Jack's support. "I'm going to offer £1.5 million . . ."

"*£1.5 million?*" I squeaked. "But Victoria —"

"Yes," she said firmly, "that's how I'm going to get in first. You will help, won't you? I'd be *ever* so grateful." Her pleading brown eyes reminded me of a plump spaniel begging to be allowed back into favour after some misdemeanour. "I'm going to pay another visit. This evening. Just to make sure. And I'm so hoping you'll come with me as someone who's unbiased, to point out any drawbacks, any snags I might have overlooked."

The shadows were lengthening, the sun low in the sky, as I used my Exclusive security pass to gain us entry to the grounds of the villa that had so taken Victoria's fancy. I hadn't gone to Monique to request the keys. Better not to advertise my part in this attempt to thwart whatever scheme Vanheusen had in mind.

The house, a spectacular blend of neo-classical and Spanish architecture, came into view as we rounded the curve of the drive. Even the magnificent picture in the glossy prospectus had failed to do it justice. A vision of white marble pillars, filigree iron balconies, and apricot-washed walls, it seemed to stretch out for ever. *El Sueño*, proclaimed the brass plaque beside the beautifully carved entrance door.

"El Soo-enno." Victoria traced the engraved letters with a plump forefinger. "What does it mean, Deborah?"

"It's Spanish for The Dream. Quite appropriate, isn't it?"

"Just wait till you see the back of the house." Beckoning me to follow, she darted through an archway in the left-hand colonnade.

Victoria's fingers had left smears on the pristine surface of the brass plaque. As I rubbed at the marks with the cuff of my shirt, a raised screw missing its domed cover snagged my sleeve. I picked off the tiny thread of cotton caught in the screw head. It might attract attention in these millionaire-immaculate surroundings. Something that wouldn't do at all.

"Thi-is wa-ay, Deborah."

I gave the plaque a final polish and went to join her.

From the rear, the house was spectacular. On either side of the centre block the colonnades curved to enclose an expanse of sparkling jade-green water, more lake than swimming pool. Floor-to-ceiling french windows accessed garden or balcony on each of the two-storeys. Whatever Vanheusen was up to, he certainly wasn't selling a cheap and shoddy build.

"Well, what do you think of *this*?"

"Victoria, it's wonderful," I said truthfully.

"Now I want you to be absolutely honest, dear. Do you think it's too big for me?"

I studied the prospectus she had whipped from her handbag. *El Sueño, magnificent residence in idyllic location . . . six luxurious bedrooms, all with en suite and balcony. Master bedroom and guest bedrooms open out onto terraced balcony with views of mountain or sea.*

"Six bedrooms aren't excessive, if you're having grandchildren and their parents, and perhaps a couple of friends. Those colonnades make it *look* enormous, but the main building itself is reasonably compact."

Her anxious frown changed to a beaming smile. "You're so right, dear. And when the grandchildren aren't here, I'll invite a friend or two. I've been so lonely without Jack, you see . . ."

I consulted the prospectus again. *". . . a house designed for enjoying the Tenerife climate with air-conditioning, fireplaces . . . spacious lounge and dining room . . . fully fitted kitchen . . . home-entertainment suite . . ."*

134

With Victoria trailing behind, I skirted round the end of the pool and advanced on the nearest set of french windows. Like naughty children, we pressed our noses against the glass.

"That chrome and glass dining table is stunning. This would make a great breakfast and supper room. You could throw open the doors to the garden, or —" I beetled across to the colonnaded terrace with its tasteful white furniture, "— eat alfresco out here." I sank into one of the loungers and lay back against the cushions. "Oh dear, I'm sounding just like an estate agent. But I wish *I* had enough money to buy the place. I do think you'll be very happy here, Victoria."

She gazed dreamily across the landscaped garden. "Yes, I think so too."

We sat in companionable silence as the slanting rays of the setting sun fringed palms and citrus trees with gold. Vanheusen had cut no corners in developing this piece of real estate, had spared no expense. And yet it seemed that he didn't want to recoup this expenditure by selling. So what part did El Sueño play in his money-laundering scheme? Just what would happen tomorrow when Mrs Knight arrived at Exclusive's offices with her cheque for £1.5 million?

Whirrrr. Startled, I turned to see a flock of tiny birds diving into their quarters for the night, the inverted bowl of a neatly topiarised ornamental tree. As the sun dipped behind the distant foothills of snow-capped Teide, a leaf of the tree trembled and all was still.

CHAPTER
TWELVE

Next morning, Gerry summoned me for a so-called brainstorming meeting, its real purpose to tell me the course of action he'd already decided on, and I was feeling decidedly peeved. Best-laid plans . . . I had intended to hang around in my office at Exclusive to be at hand while Mrs Knight was making her pre-emptive bid for El Sueño. I wanted, of course, to share in any rejoicing, but if the bid failed, as it undoubtedly would if there was some scam involved, perhaps I could learn something from the flurry of excuses.

Gerry smoothed out the crumpled piece of paper on the desk. "Re this note of Vanheusens to Devereux, time for a little brainstorming session, Deborah.

Monique, Important you clinch the deal with Mansell at my fancy dress barbecue for the Feast of the Three Kings. Make sure he'll accept the invitation. Keep it between the two of us."

He chewed his lip thoughtfully, "Important, eh? What we need is . . ."

". . . to find out *why* it's important," I supplied unhelpfully. I knew he would find this irritating, so I couldn't resist.

When my response was met with a withering look, I creased my brows in a faux-puzzled frown. "What we need is . . ." I allowed the pause to lengthen . . .

His chair creaked as he planted his elbows on his desk and peered at me over the bridge of his fingers. "What *I* need," Gerry's voice oozed patience, "is for you to gatecrash Vanheusen's barbecue and eavesdrop on Mansell and Monique's little tête-à-tête."

"You mean, as uninvited guest, break through the tight security and creep up on them *unseen*?"

"Exactly." He plucked off his glasses and waved them airily.

Gerry had set me a Mission Impossible, but there had been no point in protesting. He'd only have told me I'd soon think of something. And I had. That is why, on the afternoon of New Year's Eve, when everybody else seemed to be heading home for the holiday, I was on the Titsa bus speeding along the *autopista*, on a shopping expedition to Santa Cruz, eighty kilometres from Las Américas. My objective was Calle Rosa and the fancy-dress hire shop La Fiesta.

I stared out at the tufa landscape, its flatness broken only by mini *barranco* ravines winding their way to a sea hazy with fine brown dust blown from the Sahara. As the bus passed the airport, a plane was floating down towards the end of the runway. Just over a month ago, I'd been up there looking down on the *autopista* . . .

Truth to tell, I was quite enjoying being a passenger rather than a driver. I'd been to Santa Cruz once

137

before, but the *autopista* can be like a racetrack, and when you're behind the wheel, your eyes are on the road or the mirror. There's little opportunity to take more than the most cursory of glances at the fishing villages huddled above little coves of grey pebbles . . . the barren badlands . . . the silhouettes of banana leaves behind tracts of translucent white plastic . . . across a bay, pink and yellow high-rise apartments stacked up one on top of the other clinging to a cliff face.

At last the road curved down to Santa Cruz. In Gerry's opinion it was a fine city with an interesting mix of buildings, but that was hard to believe as the bus sped past factory blocks, the gasometer-like Cepsa oil tanks, the ugly grey refinery and, barricading off the seafront, a wall of cargo containers straddled by loading-gantries.

As the bus waited for the lights to change before swinging into the bus station, I had a close-up view of the Auditorium, Calatrava's architectural masterpiece, a gleaming white blend of the shells of Sydney Opera House and the curving, drooping nose of Concorde. From this low viewpoint the drooping Concorde beak was a huge curving wave frozen in mid-descent. Sunlight glinted off the white ceramic surfaces intensifying the illusion. In a rainstorm, water would stream off those curves and pour off the end of that beak in a torrential cascade. After my little bit of shopping, I'd come back and inspect The Wave at closer quarters. I might even wait till dark and see it floodlit.

The lights turned to green, the bus moved forward and swung into the bus station. I consulted my map. Every capital city has a famous location — Piccadilly Circus, Times Square, Place de la Concorde — and in the case of Santa Cruz it's the Plaza España. Nearby, off one of the pedestrianised *avenidas*, was Calle Rosa and La Fiesta dress hire. It wasn't very far to walk, only about a kilometre, but the shops, normally open till late, would be closing early tonight — just how early would depend on the shopkeeper's inclination. I folded the map and boarded one of the circulation buses that would take me to my objective in less than five minutes.

Narrow streets, tall buildings and lines of shady trees make for a welcome coolness in the height of summer. On a late afternoon in winter, when the sun is low in the sky, not much light can filter down, but La Fiesta was easy to spot. Its brightly lit windows were spilling pools of yellow over the surrounding pavement. Behind the glass, the Three Kings, richly attired, knelt in homage to a slightly bored Christ Child. In other tableaux, a couple of pirates sat on a treasure chest, a matador flourished his pink cape and a Mexican bandit twirled magnificent mustachios at a group of gypsy flamenco dancers. *Costumes And Fancy Dress For All Occasions*. What I needed was an impenetrable disguise. I'd find it here . . .

Inside was an Aladdin's cave of costumes — hanging from the ceiling, pinned to the walls, crammed on tightly packed rails.

"Señora?" A turbaned figure in flowing robes detached itself from a group of models and advanced towards me.

"I'm not sure what I want . . ."

"No problem." The Turban waved an expansive hand, "Here, we have costumes for the fiesta. And here," he gestured flamboyantly in the other direction, "we have costumes for all the times." His hand hovered over a virulent green frog. "The señora likes this? Or this?" He held up a belly dancer's costume complete with yashmak.

"Er . . . nothing too eye-catching," I muttered.

"Perhaps the señora will find something to suit among these." He indicated the fiesta rails. "I will leave you to look." He bustled off and merged once more with his stock.

I inspected the packed rail. Not the snowman, and certainly *not* that reindeer with the red nose. How about the Santa Claus outfit? I'd swelter a bit in the heat, but the beard would be a good disguise, and there'd be sure to be other Santas, so I'd blend in nicely.

I looked round for the assistant, spied the turban, and carried over the Santa suit. "I think this might do. Can I try it on?"

He paused in his struggles to fold a bulky costume into a small box. "*Probadores?*" He inclined his head towards changing rooms at the back of the shop.

I lugged the voluminous red robes into a cubicle and closed the curtain. The jolly figure of Father Christmas has a distinctively rounded silhouette. What had not

140

occurred to me was that it would necessitate much blowing up of an enormous inflatable cushion and a good deal of poking and fiddling to secure it in the supplied harness.

Jangled and sweaty, I struggled into the webbing. Encumbered by all that bulk, I felt like a grotesquely inflated Michelin Man. I bent down to pick up the red robe that had slithered to the floor during my combat with the cushions.

It was then that I discovered a truth about the human anatomy — increase in circumference of waist equals decrease in reach of arm. My fingers scrabbled in mid-air, brushed tantalisingly close to the floor, but not close enough. I paused for a tactical overview. Should I lean forward at risk of toppling over? If I went down on my knees, I'd never get up again. After a moment's thought, I sat on the flimsy stool, performed a nifty pincer movement on the robe with my feet, str-e-e-tched forward over the bulge and — *success*. I pulled on the robe, fastened the broad black belt round my waist, and studied my reflection in the small wall mirror at the rear of the cubicle.

Ho, ho, ho! Not quite what I had envisaged. My exertions had caused the harness to work itself up. The round Father Christmas paunch had now transformed itself into a mound that outrivalled the fabled bosom of Mae West. In an outfit like this, I wouldn't exactly go unnoticed, and in the unlikely event of getting close enough to Monique and Mansell to eavesdrop, I'd probably ruin everything by toppling over at their feet in a flurry of red and white. No, I'd have to —

A woman's voice rang out from the front of the shop, "I've called to collect my outfit. You *have* completed the alterations?"

Murmur from sales assistant.

Monique. There was no mistaking those assured, self-possessed tones. She mustn't see me. I wanted no association between fancy dress and myself. People with secrets are more than a touch paranoid. What was she saying? I strained to hear.

"I'll just try it on . . . the changing rooms?"

Clack clack clack of heels on the tiled floor. I snatched up the Father Christmas beard, hooked it firmly in position and was pulling down the inflated bosom to its proper position when Monique flung aside the cubicle curtains.

"Ho, ho, ho!" I chortled in the deepest tones I could muster. "*Feliz Navidad*, señora!"

"Oh," she gave a startled squeak, "excuse me, señor." And with a muttered, "Can't be doing with this unisex changing-room nonsense," she swished the curtains closed.

I could hear sounds of movement from the next cubicle. *Whump. Rustle. Clunk* of the stool. I'd better make a few dressing/undressing noises myself. I struggled out of the robe with accompanying grunts. What next? I pulled the rubber stopper out of the Santa cushion. *Ppfrrzzzzzz.* It deflated in an explosive fart.

I heard a scandalised, "Well *really!*" The curtain rings rattled as Monique pulled them roughly aside.

In the process of tugging off the Santa beard, I stopped. What if she or Mansell chose costumes that hid their faces? How could I creep up on them if — ? I jammed the beard firmly back into position and cautiously twitched aside the curtains.

In a long white dress that sparkled from head to foot, The Snow Queen was gazing appraisingly into a huge mirror on the end wall of the changing room. As she turned her head from side to side, her crown and earrings, crystal icicles, glittered and flashed sparks of light. In the outfit Monique looked devastatingly beautiful. Jonathan Mansell would be an easy prey, a pushover for any plans Vanheusen had for him. Slowly I let the cubicle curtain drop back into place. I sat there listening to the rustle of clothing as she changed out of the costume. I heard her cubicle curtain swish open and the *clack clack clack* of receding footsteps.

"The señora has a problem?" the Turban's voice called.

I jumped up from the rickety stool and flung aside the curtains. "I'm sorry to have taken so long," I mumbled indistinctly through the thick whiskers still firmly fixed behind my ears. "I was trying to make this costume fit me, but it is far too big. You have a smaller size?"

He shook his head. "That is the last one we have. It is very popular nowadays for *fiestas de niños*. Perhaps the señora would like to look again?" With a sweep of the arm worthy of a conductor inviting the audience to applaud his orchestra, he indicated the rows of racks.

I deposited Santa's paunch and whiskers in his arms and went off to rummage through the remaining costumes. Twenty . . . thirty . . . fifty . . . I lost count of the costumes I examined and rejected.

"Nothing suitable. Nothing at all," I sighed to the hovering assistant. "I'm afraid I'll —"

Behind his head, pinned to the back wall, was a palm tree, its trunk topped by a mass of thick green fronds. "Just a minute." I pointed at it. "How about that?"

His eyebrows rose in mild surprise. "The señora doesn't think that will be too eye-catching?"

"Not at all," I said with conviction.

This morning Monique had been quite specific. "New Year's Eve is no excuse for abandoning clients who might have a problem, so I expect you to be on duty as usual in the foyer."

Clutching my bulky carrier bag I arrived back in Las Américas at quarter to eight. The Alhambra was only a short taxi ride away. Exactly on time I settled myself in the striped pavilion, ready for action, or more likely, inaction. The minutes ticked by . . .

What was Millie up to? Had she taken a break from digging up the dirt on Vanheusen? Was she at this moment dolling herself up for the hotel's dinner-dance? More minutes plodded by . . .

I sat there twiddling my thumbs and casting covert glances at my carrier bag. I couldn't wait to try on that palm tree costume. "One size fits all peoples," Turban had assured me, and I'd had to take that on trust as there'd been barely enough time to leg it back to the bus station. How difficult was it going to be to fasten the damn thing up? Was the trunk closed with zip, studs or Velcro strips? Hardly professional to be examining shopping if someone did turn up to consult me, and if the person happened to be Millie, something that would set that investigative nose of hers twitching.

But by the end of the hour, no one had turned up with a problem, pressing or otherwise — not even Herbert G Wainwright with a grouse or two.

Gradually I became aware of a flurry of activity at reception. Behind the marble counter a room maid, white-faced and shaking, was clutching at the lapels of one of the receptionists. I shifted my chair for a better look. He was making an awkward attempt to calm her, but she buried her face in her hands sobbing hysterically. It was pretty obvious that something serious had happened. I saw him snatch up the telephone and speak rapidly into it.

Whatever was going on, it was a lot more interesting than staring at an almost deserted foyer or a carrier bag of shopping. The other receptionist darted into the office to emerge with a rather flustered night manager. The first inkling that the incident might be of more than a passing interest came when manager Pablo looked over to where I was sitting, said something to one of the receptionists, then hurried across the expanse of marble towards me. His body language spelt Trouble. It was the last thing I needed when I was looking forward to a bit of R&R. It *was* New Year's Eve, after all. As I've said, HM Revenue & Customs never takes a holiday, but . . .

He stopped beside my table and stood there, one hand resting on the bright blue and white canvas of the pavilion. He cleared his throat, "Señora Smith, I have to tell you that one of your guests —" He paused, seemingly at a loss for words.

It would be Wainwright, of course. He'd probably been abominably rude to the maid over some minor dereliction of duty, everything blown up out of all proportion.

Pablo cleared his throat again, "One of your guests — the maid has just reported that . . ." He tailed off and stood there in awkward silence.

Oh dear, a lot more serious than rudeness. Assault? Attempted rape? Somehow I couldn't envisage Herbert G Wainwright as a lecherous Don Juan.

"It is with heavy heart, señora," Pablo fiddled with his gold cufflinks, "that I give you the news. The maid has discovered one of your clients dead in the bedroom."

Millie. He must mean Millie. She'd asked one question too many, got onto something really important. A knife between the ribs like Bill Gardener — was that how it had been done?

"Dead?" I half-rose to my feet, mouth dry.

"Unhappily so, señora. A heart attack, it appears."

Unlikely to be Millie, then. Could it be Victoria Knight? At the time of the cabin case mix-up, she'd mentioned heart pills. Yes, must be her. I sank down into my seat again. Poor Victoria, the excitement of managing to buy El Sueño, or come to that, the disappointment of losing it, had been too much for her. All those dreams . . .

Pablo was looking at me, waiting for my response.

146

"I'm sorry, the shock . . . I didn't take in what you were saying just now."

"I quite understand, señora. The police will want a formal identification. I am asking if you will come to his room for this purpose."

"*His.* Did you say 'his'? But I thought —"

"*Perdón* that I do not make it clear. It is Señor Rudyard Scott that has sadly died in his room. We have sent for the doctor but, alas, there is nothing . . . *nada.* And as the death is not at all expected, the police will be coming also. They will come by the service stairs, so the guests are not made nervous."

"Of course, señor, if I can help in any way . . ."

I would shed no tears over the sudden demise of RF Scott, but the news of his death had given me a jolt nevertheless. Uppermost in my mind was the question: would the verdict be natural causes or not?

A stout dark-haired man carrying a metal attaché case came into the foyer and hurried towards the reception desk. After a brief consultation with a receptionist, he headed towards the lifts. The doors closed behind him.

"*Gracias,* señora. The doctor has just arrived. Now, if you will be so good as to come with me, we will go up to Mr Scott."

There was no sign of a police presence outside number 307, only a hotel employee standing beside the closed door.

"*Un momento,* señora." Pablo tapped on the door and went in, closing it behind him.

I waited, mulling over the possibilities. Assuming Scott's death was not natural — he's always appeared to be in rude health (in every sense) — how and why had he been killed? The maid had reported he'd died of a heart attack, but she hadn't actually witnessed it. So cause of death was just a presumption . . . Obviously there were no outward signs of violence, but that didn't rule out force being used.

The door opened and Pablo beckoned me forward. "There is nothing too upsetting, señora. Just take a look from the doorway to confirm that the man you see is Señor Scott."

Rudyard Finbar Scott was stretched out in an armchair, legs crossed at the ankle, hands lightly clasped across his stomach. His eyes were closed, mouth slightly open. He could have been asleep. The doctor looked up from folding his stethoscope into his attaché case and gave me a nod of greeting.

"Yes, this is Mr Scott," I said. "Can you tell me, doctor, when it happened? Er, how long has he been —?"

He snapped shut the clasps of the attaché case. "It is not possible to tell with certainty at this moment, señora, but rigor mortis is just beginning in the face and neck, so I would say between two and three hours."

"And he died of a heart attack? It's all so unexpected, I just can't believe it." And I didn't.

Back in the corridor, out of earshot of the employee guarding the door, I phoned Gerry with the news.

"Understood." His voice was matter-of-fact, deadpan. "Come in tomorrow." He ended the call.

I made my way slowly towards the lift, troubled that Rudyard Scott's sudden demise seemed to have come as no surprise to Gerry whose moves were planned to the nth degree, every possibility considered. To think of him as a spider sitting at the centre of a web of intrigue might not be too fanciful. Had the photo I'd taken of the lock on Scott's safe enabled Gerry to arrange the disappearance of the money? Had I been instrumental in bringing about a murder, if that's what it was? It was not a comfortable feeling.

I paused with my finger on the lift button, recollecting last Saturday's office hour in the striped pavilion, and Wainwright's voice, querulous, petulant, as he leant towards me. "So how come the same young lady fixed herself an invite to that classy boat?" If Vanheusen had arranged Scott's death, Millie could be in similar danger. I had to find some way of stopping her from boarding the yacht. Out at sea, there would be no witnesses, or none that would break silence. I'd check up on Millie now, and somehow work a warning into the conversation.

I rounded the curve of the corridor and pressed the bell outside the door of 323. There was no response. I rang again, longer. I tried knocking. I pressed my ear to the door. No muted sound of television or CD player, no sound at all. A quick glance both ways to make sure the coast was clear, a zap of Gerry's electronic picklock and I closed the door quietly behind me.

The room was in darkness. I slipped my telephone card into the empty lighting-key slot and flicked a light switch. The room had been stripped of all personal items. Gone was the alarm clock, the book, the laptop, the suitcase. I slid open the wardrobe door. No clothes. On the rail, only a cluster of wooden hangers. I pulled open the drawers, though I knew I wouldn't find anything. Empty. Nothing of hers in the bathroom either, no toilet bag, no toothbrush, no shower gel.

The only evidence that Millie Prentice had ever been here was a bar of soap, its Alhambra crest smooth with use.

CHAPTER
THIRTEEN

New Year's Day, but Victoria Knight was not in festive mood. She stirred her coffee glumly. "I'm afraid my offer yesterday to Miss Devereux was turned down, dear," she sighed. "You see, they'd taken the house off the market less than half an hour before I arrived. A Reservation Contract I think Miss Devereux called it." Her spoon clinked on the cup as it made another couple of slow circuits.

So that's how Vanheusen had wriggled out of accepting £1.5 million. Very neat.

"She was most apologetic." Victoria gazed unseeingly at the Café Bar Oasis's gilded cage with its twittering birds. "She explained it all, but, you know, I couldn't really take it in. All I could think about was that lovely house. My House of Dreams, I'd called it. And now . . ." She trailed off miserably and absent-mindedly dropped another sugar lump into her cup.

"Did Monique say how long the house was to be off the market?"

"How long?" Victoria looked blank. "It won't come back on sale again now." Her voice was dull and defeated.

She *was* taking it badly.

I couldn't leave her feeling like that. "Probably not, Victoria, but things aren't *completely* cut and dried." I dug the teaspoon into the mound of cream topping my cappuccino. "A Reservation Contract means that a prospective buyer pays a fee to take a house off the market for a set period, in order to have time to make legal searches etc. The sale doesn't necessarily go ahead, you know."

"You mean," a catch in her voice, "there's still a chance?"

A chance in a million, I thought. For reasons yet to be discovered, Vanheusen had no intention of selling. I was sure of it.

"I don't want to give you false hopes, Victoria. The sale *might* not go ahead, but that would only be if there's something wrong with the property, or if there's a legal difficulty involving ownership of the land."

"I suppose that's a tiny ray of hope, dear. It was foolish at my age to get so carried away, to set my heart on something before finding out if it was possible." Her tone was resigned, but her sigh was evidence that she was finding it very hard indeed to accept that El Sueño would never be hers.

The silence between us lengthened.

Then she roused herself to take a sip of her lukewarm coffee. "Happy New Year, Deborah."

I murmured a reply but there was nothing I could say that would bring comfort. Outside, the sun blazed down from the bluest of blue skies. It sashayed through the green glass cupola, boogied on the waters of the central fountain, capered on the gilded birdcage. But at our table, the outlook was grey, despondency reigned.

The war against crime is waged 365 days a year, and for me this New Year's Day was no exception. No lying on the beach for me. I left a dejected Victoria Knight at the Café Bar Oasis and drove to Los Cristianos. After a second visit this morning to Millie's room, this time accompanied by the manager, I'd another piece of disquieting news for Gerry.

Extreme Travel was outwardly deserted, slatted blinds down, staff still partying or recovering from last night's festivities. Hung on the door was a typed notice, slightly askew:

Cerrado por la fiesta. Closed for the holiday.

Feliz y Prospero Año. Happy New Year.

Jayne did like her little touches. In the inner office, behind the white door, she'd be beavering away planning a new window display and researching appropriate pretexts for cancellation of dodgy bookings.

Always assume hidden eyes are watching. Slowly and morosely, as if a bit hung-over and disgruntled at having to report for work on a holiday, I fished clumsily in my bag for the key, unlocked the outer door and locked it behind me. Dust motes danced in the bars of sunlight filtering through the blinds. On Jayne's desk three pens were neatly arranged, the dust cover had been placed over the computer and the calendar left at December 31st. Good practice, good reminder — eyes can peer through gaps in blinds. I flung my bag onto her chair, walked over to the mirror and squinted at my reflection. With one finger I pulled down a lower eyelid as if inspecting it for dissipation red-eye. Fat chance of that. With a relieved smile, I scooped up my bag and turned the handle of the white door.

I was met with "Happy New Year, Debs", the *braaah* of party kazoos, the *pop* of a champagne cork. They were all wearing paper hats.

I reeled back. "*You bastards*. Carousing away while I was working."

A howl of laughter.

I blinked. It was only then that I took in that in spite of the silly paper hats, there were no drinks in the hands of Gerry, Jason, Jayne and assorted others. No bottles, no champagne, no wine.

Pop. Grinning, Jason removed a finger from his mouth.

"Caught you there, Deb-or-ah." Jayne lassoed me with a paper streamer and blew a triumphant *braaah* on her kazoo.

Gerry took off his crumpled paper hat, folded it into a neat triangle and stuffed it into his shirt pocket.

"Bastards," I repeated, flinging myself into the seat in front of Gerry's desk. "While you've been smart-arsing here, I've been putting my *life* at risk in the course of duty." I had their full attention now.

Startled, Jayne dropped the kazoo.

"Killers. At the Café Bar Oasis." I paused, allowing the tension to build. "Their Blue Mountain cappuccinos are killers," I smirked. "That mound of high cholesterol cream . . ."

Gerry raised his eyes heavenward, Jason blew a derisive raspberry.

"A variation on Death by Chocolate," Jayne muttered. "Yes please." She reached down and retrieved the kazoo.

Scores evened.

"Time for serious business, guys," I said. "Millie's sudden disappearance has taken a sinister turn, I'm afraid. As I told you last night, all her possessions had gone from her room. It was only this morning that I realised that the door of the safe in the wardrobe had been shut and was reading *closed*. I went back to the Alhambra and asked the manager to open the safe. We found a pile of euros — and this." I fished in my pocket, brought out Millie's passport and dropped it on Gerry's desk.

All eyes focused on the maroon passport. No one said anything. There was no need. We all knew what it signified. A seasoned journalist doesn't take herself off into the wide blue yonder leaving passport and cash in the hotel safe.

After a long moment, Gerry sighed.

"Let me introduce Pilar who's been keeping tabs on the comings and goings of Millie Prentice."

A thin-faced girl standing beside the coffee machine stepped forward.

"Monday's report, if you please, Pilar."

"On Monday at 0800 the señora took a taxi to the harbour here. I follow her. She walk until she reach the boat of the name *Samarkand Princess*."

Vanheusen's yacht.

155

"In five minutes the boat leaves the harbour. I note the time, 0825. I wait. The boat comes back at 1215. I watch. I see Señor Vanheusen leave, but the señora she does not leave. I wait till it is dark and there are no lights on the boat, but still the señora does not leave."

Oh, Millie, Millie.

Another sigh from Gerry. "Difficult, probably impossible, to prove anything. He'd just say he landed her at Santa Cruz, where, no doubt, port records will have recorded his arrival."

Oh yes. Vanheusen would have covered his tracks all right. Cold-blooded bastard. I knew we'd never see Millie again.

"Thank you, Pilar. No need to stay. Off you go and enjoy the holiday."

The door closed behind her. Once again, Gerry's need-to-know policy was in action. What she didn't know couldn't be extorted.

After a moment, he said, "OK, I'll now bring you up to date on the late Rudyard Finbar Scott. I've a report here from forensics. It seems our man Ambrose has been quite a busy little bee."

The note of levity shocked me. Vanheusen wasn't the only cold-blooded bastard. At times Gerry ran him a close second. Millie had been a pain in the neck with those ill-timed investigations of hers, but he was brushing aside the fact that she was almost certainly *dead*.

"*Gerry*, I really think that's —" Then I caught his eye and realised he had been deliberately provocative in order to sidetrack us from gloom and restore morale.

"You mean he had something to do with Rudyard Scott's death *too*?" That death had looked natural enough to me, no evidence of a struggle, no sign of violence.

"We all know that when someone dies from what appears to be a heart attack, death can actually be due to drug overdose. So it will not surprise you that the toxicologist has found . . ." Gerry consulted a sheaf of papers, ". . . mono-acetylmorphine and morphine, a sure indication of the presence of heroin, also confirmed by . . ." He glanced down at the sheaf of papers again. ". . . pulmonary oedema, that's water in the lungs to us. Cause of death, a massive overdose of heroin aggravated by alcohol."

"Heroin? But when G and I —"

"Yes, eleven days ago you and the cat gave his room the all-clear for drugs, and so . . ." He tapped his teeth thoughtfully with his pen.

"Unless, of course, he had a stash of heroin in the safe?" I looked pointedly at Gerry.

"Nope," he said blandly.

From that answer it was clear to me that he'd ordered Scott's safe to be opened and the money removed, with the express purpose of precipitating a reaction from Vanheusen. But had he anticipated such a violent outcome? I could detect no trace of guilt, no sign of regret, so I'd have to pass on that.

"Are you with us, Deborah?"

Everyone was looking at me expectantly.

"Er, no, that is to say, yes," I said.

157

"I was inviting you to give us your ideas on Vanheusen's villa scam. When you're ready, Deborah." Reproof administered.

"I was just mulling over Scott overdosing on heroin, when he had shown no sign of using drugs, no sign at all."

"Brownie point there, Deborah." Reproof withdrawn. He'd wanted us to exercise our brains, and I had. "With that in mind, I asked them to look for the method of ingestion. Which turned out to be . . .?" A raised eyebrow invited us to exercise our brains again.

Injection? That seemed a bit too obvious for a "brain exercise". Everyone else must have been thinking on similar lines, for no one ventured an answer.

Gerry smiled. "My bet is that he was plied with spirits — alcohol and heroin are a lethal combination. When he was well boozed up, they went in for the kill. At the post-mortem they found a single injection site — in the right shoulder. He'd have had to be a bloody contortionist to have done it himself."

I hadn't much cared for the late Rudyard Finbar Scott, but all the same . . .

"Has that cleared things up, Deborah? OK, can we have those thoughts on how he works the villas?"

"It's definitely some kind of scam, but I haven't sussed it out yet, except it seems to involve the villa El Sueño. I visited it with Mrs Knight two days ago because she wants to buy, and I learnt this morning that her offer of £1.5 million has been rejected. If Vanheusen is blocking the sale of the property, the stakes must be *more* than £1.5 million."

"I think you could be on to something there." Gerry peered over the top of his gold rims. "Now, those files in Monique's office might throw some light . . ."

"As everyone's on holiday today, this would be the ideal opportunity to rake through them, but . . ." I chewed at my lip thoughtfully.

"But we don't want anyone to know you've been there, though it would be easy enough for you to get in with your pass. So . . .?"

Oh, oh. He was into brain workout mode again.

I couldn't resist a little Gerry-baiting. "So, while I lurk in the shadows, Jason will scale the wall, run through the high-security beam, wrestle with the pack of slavering dogs and have a starring role on their video surveillance cameras."

"Me superman, you Jayne . . ." Jason drummed a tattoo on his chest.

"No, she Deborah. *Me* Jayne." Jayne blew a soft raspberry on the kazoo.

Gerry didn't deign a reply. He twitched the party hat out of his pocket and proceeded to pluck methodically at the tissue paper. When the hat had been reduced to a mound of pink shreds, he looked up.

"So what we need," he stirred the mound with his forefinger, "is . . .?" Resumption, as if uninterrupted, of brain workout mode.

I sighed and capitulated. ". . . for me to get in without anyone knowing about it."

"Exactly." He leant back in his chair.

159

"And you're going to tell me how." I made it a statement, not a question. But he wasn't letting me off so easily.

"Now who could call at Vanheusen's house on New Year's Day without rousing suspicion?" He swivelled his chair to the right.

"Wine merchant? Caterer? Vet?" I hazarded.

He swivelled to the left, shook his head.

I was getting tired of this. "Oh, I don't know. Plumber, electrician, the man to read the meter."

"Getting warm." He rewarded me with an encouraging smile.

"Come *on*, Gerry. Nobody's going to come to read the meter on New Year's Day."

"Try one of your other suggestions, then."

If I'd had a party hat to shred . . . I tossed a mental coin. "Electrician."

"Exactly. Vanheusen is about to experience a massive outage."

"A complete failure of the electric power? How will that get me in? His security equipment is certain to have its own supply."

Gerry smiled. "Of course." He waited.

He didn't expect *me* to be the electrician, did he? We'd get things done in a fraction of the time if *only* we didn't have to go through this question-and-answer rigmarole *every* time.

"I've got it," I said brightly. "I act the electrician, put my hands in the main fuse box, bugger up his wiring, incinerate myself. And Jason, disguised as a paramedic, sneaks into Monique's office while my crisped body is being carried out."

A giggle from Jayne, a muffled snort from Jason. From Gerry nothing.

I broke the silence. "Correct me if I'm wrong."

He did. For five minutes he held forth on the error of my ways and the cardinal sin of Levity. An episode referred to later by a gleeful Jason as The Sermon on the Swivel Chair.

After which, Mr Burnside unfolded his master plan. "As I was saying, before that facetious interruption," he glanced reprovingly in my direction, "we will arrange a cut in electricity to the Vanheusen property. The estate must have either a dedicated supply from the local substation — it's big enough for that — or be fed through an overhead line. When Vanheusen phones the electricity company, it'll be easy enough to fix things to our advantage."

He punched in a number on his desk phone. "Tomás? We're going to need you tonight. How would you suggest we go about arranging a power cut to a large property without affecting anyone else? Mm . . . I see. OK. Hold yourself in readiness."

He put the phone down with a satisfied swivel of his chair. "It seems it's just a matter of pulling the fuse, either at the substation or on the pole carrying the line to the property. The pole would be more discreet. The fuse is enclosed in a plastic box. We remove the fuse and put the box back in position. The UNELCO lettering on the van will be our passport to invisibility.

161

No one will be the wiser, and Vanheusen will be completely in the dark."

Joke. I was off the hook. Gerry had recovered his good humour.

The white UNELCO van had been stopped for some minutes. Entombed in the tool-locker, I couldn't see or hear a thing. I was curled, sweating, knees to chin, in a space that was tiny, cramped and airless. I had an overpowering urge to straighten, stand up. Mind over matter, I told myself. Summon up the Alpha waves, divorce yourself from your surroundings, imagine yourself . . . Impossible. It was definitely a case of matter over mind. I'd have to stretch out my legs, just *have* to . . .

I released the bolts holding down the tool-locker lid and cautiously pushed it up. Total darkness. The hand I moved in front of my face was visible only where it broke the thin grey-black line marking the top and bottom of the van doors.

Through the thin metal walls, came a faint murmur of voices. *Click, click, clunk.* Keys rattled in the lock. Tomás was giving me as much warning as he could that he was about to throw open the van doors. I sank down, closing the lid quietly behind me and fumbled for the bolts. They slid into position with a soft *snick*.

Tomás's muffled voice: "There you are. Just the usual gear."

Yellow light filtered through the row of air holes in the base of the chest. The van lurched as someone heavy clambered in. Metal scraped as equipment was shifted aside. I heard the *thump thump* of cable and plastic tubs being moved.

A rough Spanish voice growled, "What's in there?"

"PPE. Personal protective equipment. Wet-weather clothes, boots, overalls."

"And here?" A hand slapped on the lid above my head.

An exasperated sigh from Tomás. "Gas bottles."

"Gas bottles? What d'you need *them* for, *hombre*?"

"Soldering joints. Heat-shrinking the PVC on cables." Tomás feigned impatience.

My box shuddered. Beside my ear, bolt sockets creaked under pressure as a hand tried to lift the lid.

Tomás again, "Locked. I keep that locked. There's stuff people want to steal in there — as well as the gas bottles, there's valuable apparatus for fault-tracing and that sort of thing. Got the keys in the front of the van if you want to waste your time and mine too. Hurry up, mate. Your boss'll be wanting the lights back on."

"Right, get them."

I think I stopped breathing.

The bluff hadn't worked. *Shit*. Operation Canary Creeper done for, binned.

"*Host-ia!* Bloody jobsworth." Tomás was cool and calm, at least on the surface. The driver's door slid open with a rumble. Rummaging noises, then, "They're here somewhere . . ." More rummaging. "Got 'em."

One of Gerry's strengths was that he took into account that things could go wrong, and planned accordingly. If the worst happened, my instructions were to take advantage of the element of surprise and use minimum violence. With luck, Vanheusen would simply regard the whole incident as an attempted burglary. Damage minimised.

It all depended on my not being recognised. I pulled the black silk balaclava over the lower part of my face. Inflicting violence on others is definitely not my scene, but one thing for sure, when the guard opened the lid, I wasn't just going to lie there a quivering jelly in my black outfit. He wouldn't *really* be expecting anything untoward, certainly not a belligerent jack-in-the-box. The element of surprise would be on my side. I'd knock him down and dodge into the bushes. In a brawl Tomás was well able to look after himself.

Keys jingled, very close.

"*Mierda!* It's not the right bunch. Must have left them back at the depot. Well, it'll take me *only* forty minutes, I suppose." A heavy sigh from Tomás, full of resignation. He should take up acting as a second career. "Just log my time of arrival so Mr Vanheusen will know the delay's not UNELCO's fault." When it came to improvisation and quick thinking, Tomás was on a par with Jayne.

A grudging growl from the guard, "Leave it, then."

The van lurched again. The doors clanged shut.

My whole body was shaking in the aftermath of an adrenalin rush. I sucked in a lungful of stale air and let it out slowly.

A *toot toot*, an amicable salute to the guard and a signal to me, a revving of the engine and we were on our way up the drive.

164

As we jolted slowly over traffic bumps, I reviewed the strategy for my entry to the house. A guard would be waiting, alerted by Security at the gate. He'd escort Tomás to the main consumer unit, allowing me to slip inside the building and make for Monique's office. Simple but effective. If things went according to plan.

They didn't, of course.

The engine was switched off. *Crunch crunch* of feet on gravel and Tomás calling, "One of you guys going to show me where the consumer unit is? Right, I'll just get my voltmeter and toolbox."

The van doors opened. Tomás whistled a few bars of "Tea for Two". Two guards. It was unlikely that both would go with Tomás. Problem. Big problem.

I heard, "If the fault lies at the substation or at the line pole leading into the property, I'll have to look for a fault there. But first let's go and check at your consumer unit."

The voices faded. I slid the bolt, and slowly . . . slowly . . . eased up the locker lid. As arranged, he'd left the van doors slightly ajar, activating a dim glow from the van's interior light. Also as arranged, he'd left a clear passage to the doors through all the equipment — wooden ladder propped against the three-tiered tool rack, T-bar sockets, giant wrenches and what appeared to be a couple of short-handled giant soup ladles, pushed to the side out of harm's way. When I made my exit, there'd be no giveaway clink of tools or rattle of latch.

I slithered over the edge of the tool-locker and lowered the lid back into position. It wouldn't do for a guard to take a look in the van and find a box, last seen closed, now with its lid open. I crouched there listening. The drone of a plane on its final approach to Reina Sofia airport . . . the distant hum of *autopista* traffic . . . from Vanheusen's lake the rhythmic *whurr whurr* of frogs, doubtless heavy-jowled thugs of the American bullfrog variety. And, close at hand, *scrunch scrunch*. Gravel, boots pacing on gravel. Approaching . . . receding . . .

I pushed gently on the van doors. A pity Gerry's powers hadn't extended to organising a blackout in the sky. The all-too-bright moonlight floodlit the strip of driveway and silvered the dark stems of a clump of giant bamboo. Bright moonlight generates very dark shadows. A shadow amid the shadows, I crept out of the van and peered round its side.

A hundred metres away the firefly glow of a cigarette cupped in a hand. I couldn't see the pale blob of a face, so the man's head must be turned away. It would take only seconds to cross from the van to the open door of the building. But could I risk those tantalisingly few paces? That guard's peripheral vision might well pick up movement, and then . . .

The trouble was, I couldn't afford to wait too long. The schedule laid down for me by Gerry was tight. At the briefing Tomás had been confident he could spin out the inspection of the consumer unit for ten minutes, perhaps a bit more. Precious minutes had already gone. I'd have to make my move very soon or abort the mission to break into Monique's office.

166

How could I distract Security's attention and give myself those vital seconds to get to the service stairs? I fumbled among the objects on the bottom tier of the tool rack. I needed something small. *Clink.* My hand closed on the bar of a socket holder. The socket heads must be . . . here, in a neat row. I grabbed a couple — I wasn't to know that the ones I selected were hellishly expensive *and* the most useful of the whole set, was I? — and lobbed one . . . then the other . . . into the exotic planting that screened the service area and office wing from rolling lawns, landscaped gardens and the house proper. My mini-decoys dropped through branches, caught, dropped again, with satisfyingly loud rustles that positively shrieked *investigate*.

The red arc of the cigarette end launched into darkness. As the probing beam of a powerful torch flitted over the bamboos and oleanders, I crossed the narrow gap between the van and the house and darted through the open door. No shout of alarm pursued me. At the bottom of the stairs to the basement I could see the reflected glow from Tomás's krypton spotlight. A murmur of voices drifted up.

The service stairs lay straight ahead, shadowy in the dim emergency lighting. He would draw a blank with the electrics downstairs and head off for the fictitious inspection of the substation and pole. I'd have precisely fifty minutes in Monique's office before he returned to reinspect the consumer unit and test the power.

I made my way up to the first floor. When she had shown me round after the job interview, Monique had pointed out the security camera positioned over the entrance to the office suite. Naïvely she hadn't treated it as a major security lapse to reveal that at thirty-second intervals it stored in its memory pictures of the corridor and, of course, of anyone passing. Tomás had warned it would still be active despite the power failure if it had a back-up battery.

I eased the service door open a crack. The corridor beyond was patched by moonlight shining through the floor-to-ceiling windows. No red light on the camera. I waited. Ten seconds . . . fifteen . . . red light. The light went out. According to Monique, the camera wouldn't be reactivated for another thirty seconds. Should I go now? Never take anything for granted. I started counting . . . twenty seconds . . . *light on*. Ten seconds early, perhaps she hadn't been so naïve, after all. The light went out. I had only twenty seconds, but it was time enough to dash the ten metres, key in the security code and close my office door behind me.

The office was not as dark as I'd expected. Moonlight through the half-closed blinds barred the walls and glinted on the chrome legs of the office furniture. There was no need to use my pencil torch to cross the room. The inner office door was secured by a simple mortise, an easy job for my picklocks. Five seconds and I was in.

I closed the door behind me and leant against it. Here in Monique's sanctum, the heavy curtains excluded most of the light, apart from a silvery-blue triangle up at the curtain track. Safe to use the torch. The narrow beam swept round the room, fingering the terracotta Teide mountain, lingering on the intricate locks on the door of Vanheusen's office, finally coming to rest on the filing cupboard.

In the cardboard boxes labelled *Members*, *Contracts*, and *Properties*, there was a good chance I'd find out why Vanheusen was so reluctant to sell El Sueño. Time was limited, so which box was most likely to yield results? I'd go for *Properties*.

I stepped forward, but I'd forgotten Monique's aping of that interior-designer fad, curtain-puddling. Why couldn't she have curtains of normal length like everybody else? One foot was trapped in the pools of curtain material spread across the floor. As I tried to free it, I clutched for support at the elegant spindly legged desk. A bad move, for it wobbled alarmingly, toppling one of the silver-framed photographs. The onyx calendar nudged towards the edge, heading to certain destruction on the marble floor. I dropped the torch on the table, lunged forward and rescued it in the nick of time at the cost of sweaty palms and thumping heart. If it had broken, I might as well have left a card announcing, *Intruder was here*.

I set about restoring the items to their positions on the desk. How had the calendar stood in relation to the photographs? Behind . . . no, in front. I drew it forward a couple of centimetres, and felt my arm brush against the torch. I watched helplessly as it rolled over the edge of the desk. It hit the ground. The beam flickered and died.

Shit, plunged into darkness. Without a torch, I couldn't read those files. Mission a failure. I dropped to my knees and crawled round the desk, making slow methodical sweeps with my hands. It was only a matter of time . . . sure to find it . . . keep calm. I felt for the corner of the desktop. If the torch fell off about there . . . It couldn't have rolled far. Got it! I snatched it up and flicked it on.

Were there any other nasty little surprises on the way to Monique's fancy filing cupboard? I sent the beam dancing ahead of me across the smooth white marble floor and thereby avoided the traps of a gilded wastepaper basket and another stagnant pool of green curtain.

I tackled the flimsy lock on the armoire. *Click click.* The levers yielded to my picklock. Nineteenth-century cupboards weren't designed to act as safes. Thirty-five minutes left . . . I pulled out the box marked *Properties.* I wedged the torch between two of the other boxes to free both hands for a proper rummage and began my search. I flipped through the first section — *Properties for Sale.* Nothing significant, only photos of El Sueño and other luxury villas, with ground plans and specifications.

Perhaps I'd be luckier with *Properties Sold.* More photos of expensive villas, all in the same architectural style as El Sueño, but with enough little differences to individualise them. Vanheusen knew what would appeal to the ultra-rich. If you have a winning formula, stick to it. At each front entrance, new owners smiled proudly. In one of the photos a rotund gent in pinstripe suit pointed possessively at the brass nameplate as if to boast, *Yes, it's mine!* Behind him, carved double doors stood invitingly ajar. Señor José Gálvez, with an address in Madrid, was now the proud owner of El Paraíso — a Spanish name for a Spanish owner. For Mrs Knight, would El Sueño have been anglicised to The Dream?

I thumbed quickly through the rest of the photos. El Paraíso, El Sueño, Elysium, La Paz, Mon Repos, Shangri-la, Spanish Idyll, Valhalla. Attractive names with a subliminal appeal to the prospective buyer.

My brain had been ticking away as I looked at those pictures and something wasn't right. Something important. Something . . . I flicked through the file pockets again. El Paraíso, El Sueño, Elysium, La Paz, Mon Repos, Shangri-la, Spanish Idyll, Valhalla . . .

I closed my eyes and emptied my mind. Like a bubble of gas rising to the surface of a black pool, a thought floated up from my subconscious, fleeting, half-formed . . . That photo of the proprietorial Señor Gálvez . . . I pulled it out of its plastic pocket and held it closer to the light. Those broad shoulders, hands like shovels . . . Without that bushy moustache he could be . . . I plucked a page from the file and held it at right angles to his face, covering the upper lip. *Steve*, chubby-faced crewman on *The Saucy Nancy*, stared up at me.

Well, well. If *one* of Vanheusen's property purchasers was phoney, that might mean that all the purchasers . . . No time to work it out now. I carried the *Properties Sold* folder over to Monique's desk, slipped the digital camera from my pocket and, carefully avoiding any entanglements with the onyx calendar and silver-framed photo, went to work.

Five minutes later I pushed the box back into its place in the cupboard. It might be advisable to copy the *Properties for Sale* folder as well . . . Finished. Twenty minutes left. I'd have to leave in fifteen. I surveyed the other files: *Brochures, Contracts, Members, Promotions*, and flipped quickly through *Contracts*. No significant info there — just legal forms. *Members*, however, should yield names that could be followed up by surveillance and interviews. I carried the contents over to the desk and took pictures of the lot.

By the time I'd tidied everything away and locked the cupboard, I'd overrun my time. I'd left myself only three minutes to get to the bottom of the stairs — barely enough. It took ten seconds to skirt Monique's antique table, carefully avoiding those ambushing curtains, and another few precious seconds to slowly, *slowly*, open the door a crack. I checked for the camera light. Off. Wait . . . *Wait* . . . It couldn't be more than another nineteen seconds, but when time was running out . . . Sixteen precious seconds lost before the red light winked on, another ten as the camera taped. Then I was off along the moonlit corridor, through the service door, and taking the stairs two at a time. Down. Down. Eyes focused on the next step. As each foot hit the centre of the tread, a whisper of sound. The last turn of the stairs, and I'd sixty seconds before Tomás finished fiddling in the innards of the consumer unit, turned the lights back on, and came up from the basement. I'd make it.

Sixty seconds to safety. One minute. I peered through the gap between the door edge and the jamb.

Standing with his back to me was a guard flicking ash from the top of his cigarette.

Bloody fool to have left things so late.

As I stood there, the lights on the stairs to the basement came on. I heard Tomás saying, "The fault *was* at pole. And now that's this end rechecked. You'll radio the gate to let me out?"

A grunt of assent and a shadow moved on the wall, coming up the basement steps. If I stayed where I was, discovery was imminent and I'd no way to get rid of my camera with its incriminating images. If I made a dash for the shrubbery, there might be an opportunity later to get into the van while they were searching the bushes . . . Not an option. If I escaped a bullet in the back, there were the dogs.

I nipped back up round the curve of the service stairs. And there I sat, listening to Tomás go out to the van, close the doors and with a cheerful "*Adíos, hombres*" and revving of engine, drive off. If they checked the stair . . . I rose to my feet. Fight or flight? I didn't fancy my chances either way.

A guard's voice, "That's put our schedule way out. We should have checked the building half an hour ago."

"*Mierda* to that! Just rerun the cameras and —" The heavy outside door banged shut.

Sitting on the stairs with the red-hot evidence of what I'd been up to burning a hole in my pocket, I wasn't *totally* desperate. I had to hand it to Gerry, Gerry Belt-and-Braces Burnside. Every operation had to have the fail-safe factor built in at the planning stage. So my present predicament had actually been catered for — if I didn't make it back to the van in time, he'd factored in another opportunity for me to get out. When Tomás discovered that I was not in the van, he would return. How long would I have to wait? It would take, say, five minutes for him to drive out of the grounds and check the van at a safe distance from the Vanheusen estate. He should be back in ten minutes. It's funny how time's relative. It whizzes along or creeps like a snail, passes in a flash or lasts a lifetime. The leaden minutes dragged on . . .

I spent them trying to figure out Vanheusen's property scam. It was easy to see how payments from phoney house purchasers could be used to launder drug profits. But these eight properties must have cost him a fortune, so why did he turn down Victoria's £1.5 million? And why was he so keen to sell to that mystery bidder for *less* than she was offering?

I was still tossing ideas to and fro when I heard the squeal of brakes. Tomás? I leapt up. This was my only chance and I mustn't blow it. I heard the outer door opening. Somebody flicked a switch and the stair was flooded with light.

Tomás's voice was loud and clear. "Like I said, I'd fixed the fault at the pole. But I've just had a radio message from HQ that a switch has tripped at the substation. I've got to check that there's not going to be an overload here. Sorry, guys, more than my job's worth if your boss is blacked out again tonight, eh?"

Ribald comment from one of the guards.

Tomás again, "Artificial surge, that's what we need. Then I'll know if the fuse I put in is heavy enough to withstand that fault at the substation. I'll need to check the consumer unit for something with a load, probably those security floods. So one of you head for your control panel, and if the other comes with me, he'll be able to radio what to switch on and off.

Boots scraped on the basement stairs, then silence. I crept down and peered out of the door. If either guard came back, I'd be in full view. The night air was cool on my face. Over to the right, frogs rasped softly. I could see the van just a couple of metres away, back doors invitingly ajar.

The security lights along the back of the building went out.

Two strides, and my hand was on the van, tugging at the doors. It took only seconds to scramble over the tailgate and pull the doors shut, but not completely shut. An observant guard might notice that, and anyway, I needed the interior light to pick my way over the jumble of equipment. I climbed into the tool-locker, sank down into my metal coffin, and lowered the lid with all the relief of an Unquiet Soul returning to its grave in the churchyard at the first glimmer of light in the sky.

CHAPTER
FOURTEEN

"So you see, G, it's all very fishy."

Gorgonzola's eyes narrowed. Up to now, she'd been showing very little interest in my account of Steve's translation from lowly deckhand to millionaire owner of El Paraíso.

"Of course," I added thoughtfully, "he *could* be a Spanish grandee who's lost all his cash at the casino, and be hiding from his creditors — masquerading as a cheerful Cockney chappie aboard *The Saucy Nancy*. Yes, it's all very fishy, don't you think?"

With a wide toothy yawn she jumped off the bed and stalked away in the direction of her food bowl, tail stiffly upright. G was bored with the subject, and she wasn't the only one.

I closed my eyes and pulled the sheet up over my head to shut out the sunlight that was poking intrusive fingers through the thin curtains. After that somewhat stressful nocturnal break-in at Exclusive's offices I'd come back home looking forward to a well-earned sleep, and I was going to have it. Gerry had my initial report and the photographs. Let him work it out.

Click . . . click . . . click of claws on a metal bowl. An empty bowl. *Click . . . click . . . click . . . click*, the feline equivalent of drumming fingers. It was my own fault. I shouldn't have used the word "fishy" in my ruminative chat to G. I scrunched the sheet more tightly round my head and wedged a finger in the ear not buried in the pillow.

Whump. A heavy body landed on the bed. A paw scraped gently but insistently. Through a gap in the sheet, I felt hot breath on my cheek.

"Gerr-off, G. I'm trying to sleep." Just a ritual protest, useless, of course. I knew it, she knew it. When it came to a battle of wills, G won nine times out of ten.

I made a last appeal. "I've had no sleep," I whined.

The paw paused. I waited . . . and waited . . . Psychological warfare.

Muttering, I gave in and threw back the sheet. I heard a soft thud as paws hit floor. I swung my feet to the cool tiles and saw she was in position beside her bowl, knife and fork poised, so to speak. I abandoned any further thought of a lie-in.

After I'd fed her, I was feeling a little peckish myself. At least I didn't have to call into Exclusive today. I'd make myself some breakfast, then snatch a couple of hours on the patio before the afternoon meeting with Gerry.

I've said before about best-laid plans . . . By the time I'd washed up the dishes, it was 9 a.m. and already the sun was hot. While I set up the sunbed under the shade of the pergola, G sat supervising on one of the remaining posts of Jesús's rickety fence. Then we both stretched out to digest. Above my head, the papery magenta bracts of bougainvillea stirred in a light breeze, a tiny wisp of fluffy cloud drifted by. Warm and relaxed in the dappled shade, I let my mind drift . . . My eyes closed . . .

. . . Vanheusen's tanned face smiled at me as he motioned Monique to open her black cylindrical handbag. "I think you'll find it's all there. £1 million for Persepolis Desert Sandstorm."

She snapped open the catch and emptied out the contents. A blizzard of notes floated down and settled in a huge drift on his desk. From behind the mound came his disembodied voice, "When Persepolis mates with Samarkand Black Prince, the offspring will be unique. The world will beat a path to my door."

I started stuffing the notes into my pocket.

"One moment, Ms Smith. We have to take into consideration the bill for the Reikimaster, have we not? Monique, the handbag."

With a soft whine the handbag morphed into a vacuum cleaner. Monique waved it over the pile of notes. *Shlooosh*. In a reverse motion replay, the drift of notes arched up and vanished into the black interior.

Perleep perleep perleep peep peep. Vanheusen eyed the ringing telephone. "That will be the new owner of El Sueño," he purred. "Why don't you answer the phone?" He reached for a stray note that had fluttered to the floor and placed it carefully in his wallet.

The identity of the mystery buyer was in my grasp. All I had to do was reach out — but my arm was held down as if by a heavy weight. I willed my hand to pick up the receiver. *Perleep perleep perleep peep peep*. Paralysed, I couldn't move. *Perleep perleep perleep peep peep*. I made a tremendous effort and wrenched my arm free . . .

With an indignant yowl Gorgonzola leapt off the sunbed. A faint *perleep perleep perleep peep peep* was coming through the open kitchen door.

I heard a discreet cough from the other side of the fence. Jesús's bright eyes peered at me over an armful of empty olive cans. "*El teléfono*, señora."

Only the Extreme Travel office knew my mobile number, and they'd only call if — I staggered up from my recumbent position. Rubbing my eyes, I ran to the kitchen and snatched up the phone from the kitchen table.

"Yes?"

"Hi, Debs. What kept you?" Jason's voice. "Care to come over to my pad? I've got something to show you."

"I was catching up on some sleep," I snarled. "This is not another of your variations on the theme of 'Come and see my etchings', is it? I've told you before, Jase, I don't want your attentions. I have never wanted your attentions. I *will* never want your attentions. Now bugger off." I ended the call and flung the phone onto a chair.

Perleep perleep perleep peep peep. My first impulse was to pick the damn thing up and hurl it across the room, but if I trashed the phone or switched it off, the office wouldn't be able to contact me. And Jason was quite capable of coming round and beating on my door.

I snatched up the phone again. "*Bugger* you, Jason," I howled. "Why don't —"

Miaow. That was unmistakably the sound of a cat. Then Jason pleading, "Don't hang up, Debs. Fact is, I need your help."

"Help?"

"Just listen." A piteous feline wailing sounded in my ear. "I've bought myself a kitten, Debs."

"Mmm," I said unenthusiastically. Feckless Jason with a cat was not a good idea.

"I find this very difficult, Debsy. I'm begging. I'm on my knees. I don't know how to look after it. *Please* come over."

In the background I could hear *miaow, mi-aaa-ow*. If it had been Jason wailing, I would have been immune. His pleas would have fallen on deaf ears. And he knew it. I hesitated.

Miaow, mi-aaa-ow.

I weakened. "Just what do you expect me to do, Jase?"

"Give me a few tips, that's all, over a cup of coffee. It will make all the difference to me — and Brunhilda."

"Brunhilda?" I squeaked.

"Yes. She's a sweet little thing. You'll love her."

A defenceless little kitten at the mercy of irresponsible Jason. How could I refuse a mission of mercy to a dumb animal? I refer, of course, to the cuddly kitten. And Gorgonzola loved a run in the car. I'd take her with me.

"Come on, G," I said, "let's go to the rescue of Brunhilda."

Jason's pad was in the nearby township of Adeje, only a short drive inland and upward from La Caleta. A few years ago it had been little more than an unremarkable village nestling in the foothills of Teide. Two twists of fate had plucked it from obscurity onto the tourist trail — first, the inhabitants' culinary speciality, roast chicken smothered in garlic; and secondly, its position guarding the entrance to that rockily scenic ravine, the Barranco del Infierno. Alas, Adeje had become a victim of its own fame. No more could you wander along the *barranco* on a whim. Now if you wanted to trudge the rocky ledges high above the dried-up river bed amid an unfolding panorama of rust-brown lava crags, it was pay up and numbers restricted. Booking essential too at Restaurante Otello to sample that to-die-for garlic chicken and the tiny wrinkled-skinned Canarian potatoes in piquant red mojo dip.

I'd asked Jason why he'd chosen to rent a pad in Adeje.

"The *barranco* and the chicken," he'd said with a grin. "After walking the one, I can dine on the other."

But I suspected the real reason was the fine choice of tapas bars and pavement cafés. Plastic furniture and red or green umbrellas sponsored by the manufacturers of soft drinks spilt out onto the pavement under the jacarandas that lined the main street. The cheap and cheerful plastic vied with shiny chrome tables and chairs in the more stylish and fashionable cafés. And for those with a preference for watering holes of a more traditional ambience, there were the wooden benches, high counters and dark smoky interiors of the working-men's bars. I'd a bet on with Jason that there were more bars, restaurants and cafés here than any

181

other kind of retail premises. When we'd nailed Vanheusen, perhaps we'd have time to stroll around to find out who was right.

Sandwiched between all those bars were shops, not one of them plate-glass superstores. Indeed, many of them didn't have windows at all. You had to poke your head through their grilled doorways to find out what was on sale. But the long steep slope of Adeje's high street held all the essentials of twenty-first-century life — furniture, spectacles, mobile phones, computer consumables, that sort of thing.

You can overlook the whole of Las Américas from the heights of Adeje. Gorgonzola and I sat for a moment on the low wall of the parking bay opposite his apartment, surveying the curve of the coastline with its fringe of beaches, the tall fingers of hotels, and the sun glinting on windscreens on the *autopista* below.

I scratched G's ear. "Are you staying here to have a snooze in the sun, or are you coming to say *buenos días* to Brunhilda?"

I was answered with a wide yawn.

"Does that mean yes, or no, or maybe just a maybe?"

After a moment of indecision, she braced her front legs, stretched and flopped down in a gingery heap on the warm stone.

"I'm disappointed in you, G," I said. "What about poor little Brunhilda? Where's your maternal instinct?"

She flicked her tail dismissively. Eyes closed. Subject closed.

The place where Jason laid his head — and if he could, his latest girlfriend — was a duplex apartment with a huge terrace screened from public view by thick hibiscus and oleander hedging. I'm a snooper by nature, so I couldn't resist applying an eye to a teeny gap where a branch had died. A white plastic lounger — wide enough for two — was unoccupied. On a small table was a glass of lager and a booklet, some sort of manual. There was no sign of either Brunhilda or Jason.

His head appeared at an upstairs window. "Front door's not locked, Debsy. Just let yourself in."

I sprang back guiltily and scurried along to the front door.

He flung it open. In one hand was a clump of mistletoe. "Happy New Year, Debs."

"Happy N —"

His lips closed on mine. I allowed him five seconds, then pulled away.

"*Feliz año*, Jason. Now, where's that dear little kitty?"

"She's through here. You'll love her. She's absolutely fantastic." He ushered me into his minimalist living room, a den of black leather and chrome furniture, spotlit alcoves and glass shelving.

Through the open French doors, sunshine streamed across the polished hardwood flooring. Where was Brunhilda? I'd expected her to be patting a ball of paper, digging tiny claws into the sofa, or dozing on one of the giant floor-cushions.

He burbled on, "If you could just help me out on how cats react —"

"Oh Jase," I interrupted, "you've not let her escape out into the garden, have you? If she gets through the hedge —"

"It's OK, Debs. Don't panic. I've got her trained and —"

"Don't be ridiculous," I snapped. "You can't train a kitten just like that."

"What d'you bet? I tell you what," he smiled complacently, "if you're wrong, you give me another kiss under the mistletoe, a proper one."

"If she comes the first time you call, I'll give you *two* kisses." I flung myself down on the sofa. "Right. I'm ready to be amazed." I folded my arms.

He took up position behind the sofa. "Here, Brunhilda-a-a." He gave a short whistle.

From the garden came a long-drawn-out *mi-aa-ow*. That didn't sound like a kitten to me, more like a full-grown cat.

"Here she comes," Jason crowed.

A shadow broke the shaft of sunlight at the French doors, a shadow with strangely distorted square head and stumpy ears. Funny the tricks light plays. You'd think —

Aaaaargh, I screamed, unable to help myself. I'd expected a cute little kitten, all big eyes and fluff, but framed in the doorway stood a hideous plastic and metal creature with huge blank Darth Vader eyes.

"Gotcha!" Jason chortled. "Say hi, Brunhilda."

The beast emitted a deep rolling purr and bounded forwards. I tried to spring up, but Jason's hand on my shoulder pressed me down.

"Just watch this demo, Debsy." He jabbed at buttons on a handheld remote control.

It sat. It lay down. It rolled over. It stood up, tail swishing gently from side to side.

"Realistic or what, eh? Sixteen built-in motors. Object sensors. Voice recognition," he drooled.

Pathetic. A grown man regressing to second childhood, playing with a gadget that was, despite its cyber wrapping, little more than a battery toy.

"Great, isn't she, Debs! What else would you like to see her do?"

Lie down and die, I was tempted to blurt out. But it *was* the season of goodwill, after all. He was like a child showing off his favourite Christmas present. I couldn't bring myself to crush him with a sour remark.

"We-e-ll," I said, "what about —" For the second time that day a feline shadow broke the sunlight path across the polished floor. Paused. Edged forward. Gorgonzola's gingery head was peering inquisitively round the frame of the French door. This was going to be interesting. "Well — what does she do if she meets another cat?"

Oblivious to the new arrival, Jason was studying the control unit. "I'm keeping her indoors so that's not likely to happen, but I think this would be the natural response."

He punched a couple of buttons. Brunhilda's head lowered, her back arched and her tail shot vertically up. He jabbed more buttons.

Tssssss. Brunhilda's angry spitting hiss was pretty convincing.

Gorgonzola obviously thought so too. There was an answering *Tsssss* from the direction of the French doors. G stood silhouetted against the sun, eyes narrowed, tufty coat bristling. *Tssssss*. Slowly, deliberately, she advanced, stiff-legged and menacing.

Jason was standing open-mouthed. I was the first to break the stunned silence.

"Gosh, look, Jase, it's like a rerun of the standoff in *High Noon*."

He rallied. "Better get hold of that mog of yours prontissimo, Debs. Brunhilda'll zap her one and polish her off."

He could be right. I'd half-risen when Gorgonzola sprang forward with an ear-piercing yowl. A blur of movement, a savage swipe of her paw, and Brunhilda clattered onto her side and slid along the floor. *Whirrrr*. There was an ominous grinding and the acrid smell of overheated circuit boards. The four metal legs waved feebly, and were still.

Another howl, this time from Jason. "That scruffy brute of yours has trashed Brunhilda." He jabbed desperately at buttons on the control. "I'll never forgive you, Debs."

I didn't think it politic to remind him that *he* had invited *me* over. An odd growling came from G's throat as she circled the prostrate heap of metal. I scooped up my still-spitting bundle of fur and fled. At least this little incident had erased from his memory that rash promise of mine.

"*Two* kisses. What an escape, G," I muttered into her moth-eaten ear.

Gerry's debriefing session was scheduled for 5p.m. I just had time to deposit Gorgonzola back home and make a quick call at Exclusive's offices to inform Monique about Rudyard Scott and Millie Prentice. Had Vanheusen confided in her? Was she in any way involved? Her reaction to the news should tell me.

"*Dead?*" There was no doubt that Monique's surprise was genuine.

"I'm afraid so," I said. "Mr Scott died of a heart attack, it seems. The maid found him in his room on New Year's Eve."

She crumpled up a piece of paper and tossed it into the bin. "Well, *really. Most* unfortunate."

It was unclear whether she was expressing regret for the untimely demise of a fellow human being, or for the loss to Exclusive's coffers from the considerable expenditure on discounted flights and hotel accommodation. I watched as she opened a file on the computer and deleted Rudyard Scott's name from the current list of clients.

I cleared my throat. "Er, I'm afraid there's more bad news."

She frowned irritably. "What *next?*"

"Millie Prentice has —"

"A born troublemaker!" she snapped. "Don't tell me she's upset Mr Wainwright with that pushy manner and those tiresome questions of hers?"

"She's packed her bags and gone."

"I *knew* she wasn't really interested in purchasing! Just in it for the free holiday. Some people have no scruples. No scruples at all."

Monique tapped savagely at the keyboard. Millie joined Rudyard Finbar Scott in the electronic graveyard of the recycle bin.

I timed my arrival at the Extreme Travel office precisely, not late for the follow-up briefing, but the last to arrive. That way I calculated that I could choose a chair as far as possible from any murderous glances cast by the owner of the deceased Brunhilda.

Gerry glanced pointedly at his watch. "There you are, Deborah. We're about to start."

"Sorry, Gerry. I had to get treatment for Gorgonzola." "Treatment" was sufficiently vague to cover all sorts of medical intervention on G's behalf — including the actual one of Jesús sitting amongst his geraniums wailing his soothing *madrelena*.

"Treatment?" He raised an eyebrow.

"She's out of sorts. Nervous prostration." I subsided into the only vacant chair.

A snort came from immediately behind me, and Jason's voice muttered in my ear, "Not as prostrated as Brunhilda. You owe me, DJ."

Did he mean the two kisses or the 2000 euros he'd no doubt paid for Robocat? Either way, tough. "No way, Jason!" I hissed. "What about G's therapy bills? She's still quite traumatised by that —"

"*If* I could have your attention?" Rebuke administered, Gerry powered up the computer. Steve's chubby face smiled out at us from the plasma screen. "I think we all know Steve Jenks of *The Saucy Nancy*." Dissolve to man in pinstripe suit pointing at the brass nameplate of the villa. "And now, Señor José Gálvez with an address in Madrid, proud owner of El Paraíso. Comments?"

There was a moment or two of silence before audience reaction on the lines of "Definitely the same guy".

Simultaneously, a whistle of surprise from Jason. "Hey, that's Jenks."

Gerry leant back in his chair. "I think we've established one spurious purchaser. And if one is a sham, I think we can assume there will be others." He jabbed the keyboard. In quick succession, up came the pics of El Sueño, Elysium, La Paz, Mon Repos, Shangri-la, Spanish Idyll and Valhalla, their owners smiling broadly for the camera. "Thoughts on any of these?"

General murmurs, but this time, no observations.

I mentally flicked through the photos. "Could you bring up Shangri-la again, Gerry."

In front of the villa stood a couple, the man's arm encircling the woman's shoulders as if claiming possession of her as well as the house. I stared at her face, trying to visualise it without the sunglasses. Most people take them off for a photo. Maybe she'd just forgotten, or perhaps she wanted to conceal her identity . . .

"I think . . ." I said slowly. "I'm not sure . . . but she *could* be . . . Monique's cousin, Ashley."

"Well, I think we are on the right lines there." Gerry made a note on his pad. "I'll get some mugshots made up. You'll find them in your pigeon-hole tomorrow,

189

Jason. Check them out against Vanheusen's known associates."

He tapped a key, and El Sueño materialised on the wall-screen. "Would you like to say something, Deborah?"

"Not much to add to my report, I'm afraid. I didn't find out anything more on my nocturnal visit to the office, but . . ." For the benefit of the others I recapped on the story of Mrs Knight and the Reservation Contract.

"I think we can assume there is no Reservation Contract. Now, what we have to ask ourselves is: why is it worth more than £1.5 million to keep this particular villa off the market?" Gerry's gaze swept our faces. "Any ideas?"

An invitation to exercise our brains. Much furrowing of brows, stroking of chins, chewing of lips.

Jayne cleared her throat. "Can we see the other properties again?"

El Paraíso, Elysium, La Paz, Mon Repos, Shangri-la, Spanish Idyll, Valhalla paraded before us once more.

She narrowed her eyes, appraising. "It's just struck me that all these photos are taken from *exactly* the same elevation and viewpoint. Reminds me of the backdrop of a photographic studio . . ." Her voice trailed off.

"Same place, just the props changed?" said a voice from behind me. "That urn of geraniums exchanged for the classical statue? The door colours and styles are different, but it's easy enough to replace a door."

190

"Even easier to alter things digitally." Jason always went for the high-tech angle.

I leant forward. "Zoom in on the nameplate, Gerry."

"We know *they're* different." Jason, still ruffled, was having a dig.

I ignored him. "That top screw on the right-hand side. The dome cap's missing. I caught my sleeve on it."

Flick to Elysium. Missing dome cap, same position.

Gerry pressed more keys. "We'll just check the other nameplates . . . Ye-es, conclusive, I think." He clasped his hands behind his head and stretched back in his chair. "Thank you everyone. A very productive session. We've just sussed out *how* he's laundering the money — by fictitious sales of the same villa. Now all we've got to do is to connect that money to drug trafficking."

As I prepared to leave the meeting I was on a high. My little piece of nightwork had moved things on considerably. Even Jason managed to summon up half-hearted congratulations before he rushed off — presumably to resurrect Robocat. The high lasted for all of thirty seconds. Just as I had my hand on the interconnecting door to the outer office, Gerry ambushed me.

"A moment, Deborah. You'll have the plans in place to gatecrash Mansell and Monique's little tête-à-tête at the barbecue on Saturday?"

Truth to tell, I was feeling quite nervous about the matter. It hadn't been easy to come up with a strategy to break through Vanheusen's tight security. Even a palm tree would have to present its invitation for scrutiny by hard-eyed men.

191

"Oh, yes. I've a *date* with Destiny," I said enigmatically.

With some pleasure I saw a tightening of his teeth on the plastic of his glasses. He liked to be the cryptic one. He chewed an earpiece thoughtfully. Then, "Action Plan to me by 10 a.m. Friday."

CHAPTER
FIFTEEN

Monique splayed out her fingers on the polished surface of her desk and studied the long, glittering nail extensions. "Good, aren't they?" she said. Little sparks of refracted light shimmered and danced with every movement of her fingers.

Well, whatever they were good for, it certainly wasn't for picking up telephone receivers or pressing buttons. Was that why I had been summoned from my desk in the outer office?

"Wow, they're wonderful," I said and meant it. "Flutter your fingers again." Silvery light twinkled and flashed. I must be careful not to betray any knowledge of the Snow Queen costume. "Is this something to do with your outfit for the barbecue tonight?"

This was greeted with a cagey smile. "You'll have to wait and see — oh, but of course, you won't be there."

Oh, but I *would*. Eavesdropping, hoping to find out why Vanheusen rated her assignation with Jonathan Mansell important enough to be kept under wraps. Perhaps too, I'd suss out how deeply Monique herself was involved in the money-laundering scheme. She was probably just a minor cog, as I was sure she'd been kept in the dark about this week's two murders. I hadn't made up my mind about Mansell, either. Innocent dupe of Vanheusen's mob, or fellow-criminal?

"Well, is it yes or no?" She was waiting impatiently with raised eyebrows for a reply to some question I hadn't heard.

"Er . . . yes," I hazarded.

She frowned. That hadn't been the right answer.

"I mean no. Definitely not."

"Well, you've taken it better than I expected." She sounded surprised. What *had* she said? What *had* I agreed to?

With a metaphorical bow and scrape in my tone, I asked, "Monique, could I possibly ask you to repeat —"

Buzz Buzz . . . Buzz Buzz . . .

Her icicled fingers hovered for a moment over the telephone on her desk. With a *tut* of annoyance, she motioned for me to press the loudspeaker button. "Mr Vanheusen's office."

The tinny whine was unmistakable. "I understand Mr Vanheusen is holding a costume barbecue tonight. I've checked with the desk clerk but no invite's been left under the name of Wainwright. I'm not one to bellyache, but it seems that somebody's goofed."

Her tone was soothing and sympathetic. "I'm *so* sorry, Mr Wainwright, if you've been misinformed." She shot me an acid glance. "You see, the barbecue is for employees and business associates only. It's Mr Vanheusen's expression of appreciation for the service they've given in the past year."

A spluttering bleat signalled Wainwright dissatisfaction.

"It's disappointing, I know, Mr Wainwright. I quite understand. I'll instruct Deborah to arrange a complimentary dinner with a bottle of cava. If you —"

A querulous, "Where?" spiralled from the handset.

"At an establishment of your choice, of course, Mr Wainwright." Again her tone was sweetness and light, her expression thunderous.

The Grouch grumbled acquiescence.

She disconnected and leant back in her chair. "I think I dealt with that screw-up of yours rather well, don't you?"

I nodded. Whoever had screwed-up it hadn't been me, but I certainly wasn't going to make things worse by arguing. "You handled that expertly, Monique." Praise where praise was due, after all.

Her frown of censure faded. I took advantage of the moment.

"Er, would you mind going over what we were discussing. It'll help me to understand it all a little better."

Instant frost descended. With the tip of one of the nail extensions, she flicked shut her desk diary and pushed back her chair.

"There's *nothing* to understand," she snapped. "To deal with any emergencies, you are on duty tonight *and* tomorrow. You had Christmas off so you can't expect the Three Kings festival as well. Especially as, when I asked you a moment ago, you said you had *definitely* not made any arrangements for that period." She seized her handbag. "So that's settled then. I don't expect to hear any more about it. Now, I'm off to have a bath.

195

Then it's the hairdresser. And I'll need *at least* an hour to fit my costume before the limousine comes." She swept out. "Don't forget that reservation for Mr Wainwright," drifted back along the corridor.

On duty tonight. Stuck here in the office.

How the hell could I do my little eavesdropping act if I was tied to my post for the duration of the Three Kings celebrations? I stared blankly at the empty doorway. As Shakespeare put it:

That is a step
On which I must fall down, or else o'er-leap
For in my way it lies . . .

I did as I was told. Virtuously I stayed on duty at my desk planning the next Outing. But only till 7 p.m. And I didn't forget about that reservation for The Grouch. In the end, he grudgingly took up my suggestion to dine at one of the small, exclusive and prohibitively expensive eating establishments in Las Américas.

At a few minutes to seven I finished setting up the answering machine and pressed Play. *I'm sorry. The Exclusive office is closed for the holiday. If your call is urgent, please telephone Carmella at Viajes Extreme, Las Américas 922 . . .*

Carmella, alias the resourceful Jayne. I'd have to erase that message before Monique arrived at the office in the morning or I'd be fired. And that would spell the end of Operation Canary Creeper.

Darkness was already falling as I shut the office door quietly behind me. Ten minutes later the yellow lights of the distant marina winked conspiratorially as I drew up in the darkest corner of the car park on the cliff-top promenade. No other cars were parked nearby as yet, but snatches of conversation and laughter drifted across from the brightly illuminated steps to the beach two hundred metres away.

I bundled the unwieldy palm tree costume under my arm and headed for an unlit path zigzagging steeply down to the beach. Even in the dark the start of this unofficial shortcut was easy enough to find, marked as it was by a clump of straggly bushes silhouetted against the paler night sky. I stopped and listened . . . Only the *frrusssh* of waves breaking gently on the beach below.

Vroo-oo vroo-oo-ooom. The hollow din of an engine with a holed exhaust blasted into fragments the peace of the warm night air. Misaligned headlights swept the arc of the sky, mini-searchlights probing for enemy stars. A vehicle was bumping across the uneven ground between the car park and the shortcut path. I threw myself flat among the euphorbia bushes and peered through the tangle of branches. With a crunch of gears and a metallic squeal, the car came to a halt. The doors opened and two figures scrambled out.

"I thought I saw someone over there, Jay." The voice was young, female and apprehensive.

A muttered, "Shhh, Cath. Just another freeloader like ourselves. C'mon, path's this way."

The two figures crossed the gritty volcanic soil towards me. I buried my face in the soft folds of my palm tree bundle. The crunching footsteps were very close now.

"What if we're rumbled, Jay?"

"God, Cath, what a wimp! There'll be hundreds mobbing the place. Just think of all that free booze."

Jason's voice. I should have remembered that Belt-and-Braces Gerry *always* had back-up for a plan. The fact that Jason was at the barbecue with the same mission as myself showed just how important Gerry thought it was to find out more about the link between Vanheusen and Mansell. Cautiously I moved a branch aside and risked a look. Silhouetted against the pale night sky were baggy trousers and clown-style wigs.

"Put your arm round me, Jay. I'm afraid of heights," Cath giggled.

The two figures morphed into one. I suppose Jason would call it "getting into the role".

I sniggered into the palm fronds. I'd pick my time and . . .

"Come on, Cath. Let's get down there and party." Scuffling and giggling, they disappeared from view.

Lugging my palm tree costume, I followed in their wake. Sliding one foot carefully in front of the other, I made my way slowly down. By the time I reached the beach, my fellow party-crashers were well ahead. I watched their silhouettes break into a lurching run. As they approached the nearest marquee, flares set on iron posts in the sand elongated their shadows into cavorting and capering Giacometti figures. I took a tighter grip of the fake palm tree costume and ducked into a clump of the Real McCoy handily close to the end of the path. It wouldn't do for someone to come along while I was transforming myself into a tree.

When I'd spotted the costume in the hire shop, I'd been sure it was perfect for my mission. And I was still sure, though it was a bit of a hassle to put on — as I'd already found in a trial run in front of my bedroom mirror. It had taken a good ten minutes to wriggle into the narrow tube of the trunk, pull up the long, concealed zip and arrange the realistic fronds. This time I didn't have Gorgonzola playfully using my trunk as a scratching post, but with my legs imprisoned in a cylinder of material tighter than the tightest hobble skirt, it was going to take God knows how long to shuffle the couple of hundred metres across the sand to the marquee area. *Shit. Shit. Shit.*

I'd just set out on my marathon shuffle, when a foot scraped against stone on the cliff path above. I inched back among the trees, one phoney trunk amid five genuine. Party-crashers? Security, judging from the flash of torches and no attempt at concealment. Two dark shapes loomed. *Keep going, guys.* But sod's law, they stopped a few metres away. A match scraped, a cigarette end glowed.

"Well, that's the path closed now," the bulkier shape grunted. "No drunken bum'll get past Felipe at the top. And quit bellyaching about being on duty on a holiday. The boss is paying us treble rates, isn't he?"

"Think he'll want us again on the 25th?"

"Sure to. *And* every night till then. Now that the arty-farty sculpture's finished, he wouldn't want anyone making off with it before The Big Do, would he?"

Silence. Then, "Beats me how anyone can go overboard like that for a cat. Spends thousands of euros on it. A nut case, that's what he is. Talks about it as if it's an effing human."

"Sodding right, Eduardo." A snort of derision. "Heard he's arranging a *wedding ceremony* for it."

At the earthy comments that followed, a more refined palm tree would have turned pink with embarrassment, but *palm tree vulgaris*, that's me. Anyway, I had more on my mind than maiden blushes. Vanheusen holding a wedding ceremony for his cat . . . I didn't like the sound of that at all.

Eduardo's radio emitted a tinny squawk.

"*Shit*. That's the last chance of a smoke we'll have till this thing's over."

A tossed butt came dangerously close to lodging in my floppy headgear. I flinched. My fronds rustled and swayed.

"Wind's got up." They moved off.

As I'd thought, it took me ages to shuffle across the couple of hundred metres of sand over which the clowns had so lightly skipped. I don't recommend palm tree attire in any situation where quick action might be on the agenda. At last I put down roots, strategically positioning myself in front of the marquee to waylay the waiter emerging with a tray of drinks.

"Excuse me." I whipped out a frond-covered arm and relieved him of a slim glass of bubbly cava.

As I sipped, I studied the surrounding throng. There were Father Christmases and clowns aplenty, and even a Christmas tree or two, but I could spot no other palm trees of the artificial kind. And no sign of the Snow Queen, or of Jonathan Mansell, either. Not a problem:

200

when the Snow Queen arrived, she'd home in on him like a bee to a honey pot.

"How do palms reproduce, Jay?" a female voice slurred behind me.

I feigned deafness. Jason could be a damn nuisance, but he *was* a professional. He'd never have come near me if Gerry had put him fully in the picture. Gerry and his *bloody* "need-to-know".

"They make a *date*, Cath."

Cath howled with mirth. I maintained a lofty silence and moved away.

Sticking to my repertoire of nod, grunt and glass clinking, I circulated. When I located the Snow Queen, I'd —

And there she was.

Thoroughly enjoying the sensation she was causing, Monique was shimmering down the steps from the car park, every movement sending forth flashes of cold, glittering light. She acknowledged the burst of spontaneous applause, her fingernails erupting in a burst of crystalline fireworks. I watched as Jonathan Mansell in the flowing white robes and corded headdress of a desert sheikh greeted her and ushered her to some tables set a little apart from the rest beside a clump of dwarf palms. Ideal for eavesdropping. Who'd notice one more tree, after all?

It took five minutes to get into position in the clump of palm trees. Rough bark snagged at my outfit as I parted fronds, not my own this time, to give me a clear view of their table. Her high-pitched laugh tinkled on the warm night breeze, but frustration, oh frustration, that's all I could hear. I hadn't bargained on the party buzz drowning out everything else. Without warning, they pushed their chairs back and rose to their feet. At a racing snail's pace I shuffled along in their wake.

The Snow Queen's tiara flashed from near the water's edge. There were fewer people in that direction but, unlike the barbecue area, that strip of beach was dark, illuminated only by the phosphorescence of the breaking waves — and that concealed my stealthy approach. Against the backdrop of moonlit sky and sea, Mansell was a ghostly shadow in his pale robes alongside the flashing, sparkling Monique. They strolled to and fro along the sand, an advertising copywriter's cliché — two figures silhouetted against a sea silvered by moonlight . . .

Each time they turned their backs I took the chance to shuffle forward a couple of metres. After my third shuffle, they passed within range of my eavesdropping fronds.

". . . I've one big reservation about that, Monique. Criminal elements could —"

"Oh, I don't think that'll be a problem. Ambrose will be in complete control. He's got a lot of experience in that field, and, of course, as you will be one of the directors, you'll . . ."

A loud burst of laughter from somewhere behind me drowned the rest. Then they were past, their words reduced to an indistinct murmur by the long *scrrr-unsssh* of pebbles dragging in the waves.

202

Just the info Gerry wanted. On their next approach perhaps I'd get a clue to what the business deal was. I waited.

". . . thing is, Las Américas already has a casino. Can't see them licensing another one."

Another tinkling laugh from Monique. "No problem there. Ambrose can guarantee . . ." Frustratingly, a gust of wind blew the rest of the sentence out to sea.

So Vanheusen had plans for a new casino — a much more efficient laundering-machine than property sales. The Alhambra would be an ideal front . . . No wonder he was so keen to persuade Mansell to become a business partner . . . Damn, damn, *damn*. If only they would stand still. They stopped and gazed out to sea as a particularly large wave crashed thunderously onto the shore. I leant forward, straining to hear more, but could make out nothing, only an indecipherable murmur.

They made their way back to mingle with the crowd. I'd learnt all I was going to learn. Time to go, but the cliff path was out because of the security guard now stationed at the top. I shuffled off towards the main steps on a course that would take me round the fringe of the party.

I'd just reached the steps when a chord from the band cut through the noise and Vanheusen's voice boomed through the speaker system. "Guys, I think you'll agree we've all enjoyed this celebration of the Feast of the Three Kings."

Whoops and cheers.

"Glad you enjoyed it. Now, let's draw it to a close in the traditional style for this time of year."

The band launched into the introductory bars of "Auld Lang Syne".

A kilted Scotsman seized my fronded arm. "C'mon, hen," he slurred in a cloud of alcoholic fumes. "I'll show you how we dae it in Scotland, darling."

"Yo, ho, ho, palm tree." A laughing pirate, complete with eyepatch and assorted blackened teeth, grabbed my other arm, and I was caught up in an exuberant circle of linked hands. There was nothing I could do. To resist would draw unwelcome attention.

"Should auld acquaintance be forgot . . ." The pirate and the Scotsman swung my fronded arms vigorously up and down. "An' never brought to mind . . ."

"Go easy on the swings, guys, for God's sake," I yelped. I might as well have kept my mouth shut.

"Should auld acquaintance be forgot . . ." My right arm was swung forward, my left jerked painfully back. "For the da-ays of auld lang syne."

The Scotsman and the pirate surged forward with the others in the circle, dragging me behind them. "Now gies a hand, my trusty friend . . ."

"Guys," I yelled, "I can't —" I teetered precariously, lost my balance and collapsed sideways on top of the pirate, pulling the unsteady Scotsman with me. By the time we had sorted ourselves out, the whole thing was more or less over.

Boom. Boom. Boom. Under the cover of an explosion of red and green maroons, I turned to shuffle quietly away. A crash of chords from the band and deafening cheers heralded another announcement but, intent on making my getaway, I wasn't paying much attention.

". . . Snow Queen." A roar of applause.

"What was that all about?" I shouted to the pirate above another roar of applause.

"Best costume. Nobody else stood a chance, did they?"

Everyone was watching Monique as she shimmered and glittered her way onto the platform to claim her prize. She clutched the microphone. "Thank you *so* much, Mr Vanheusen. This is *so* unexpected . . ."

I put a foot on the first step. "Keep talking, Monique," I muttered.

A burst of applause.

"In addition to the first prize," Vanheusen had taken the mike again, "the judges have decided to give an award for the most original costume . . . and so . . ."

I reached the fourth step.

". . . I'll ask the Snow Queen to announce their decision."

"I'm *so* honoured, Mr Vanheusen."

Six steps negotiated, only another eight to go.

"The winner of the most original costume is . . ." A dramatic pause, much rustling of paper and thumping of microphone. ". . . that adorable little palm tree."

Shit. Hell and Damnation.

"Whey hey! Thaar she goes." The pirate's halloo sank my last chance of sneaking away unnoticed.

Eager hands pulled me back down the steps, pushed me through the crowd and lifted me onto the platform.

Please, please, please, don't let them discover who I am.

"Congratulations to a worthy winner." Vanheusen held out an envelope.

"Thank you," I squeaked.

"Ah, I detect a palm tree of the female kind." He put an arm round my shoulder and drew me towards him. "As *my* prize, I claim a kiss from the winner."

Shit.

"Now, let's see whose pretty face is concealed behind all this greenery." He twitched the fronds aside.

"My God!" Monique shrieked. "It's *Deborah*!" She thrust her face close. "What are *you* doing here in that ridiculous costume? You're fired. Do you hear me? *Fired.*"

CHAPTER
SIXTEEN

"Fired." Gerry's tone was flat.

"Sacked, booted out, given my cards. However you like to put it, out on my ear." I was despondent, even though my unmasking had been due to sheer bad luck, not incompetence.

"Mustn't feel bad about it, kiddo. No use crying over spilt milk."

Kiddo, indeed. He was only a few years older than me. Still, I appreciated the attempt to make me feel better about this setback to Operation Canary Creeper.

He gave one of his thoughtful chews on the earpiece of his glasses. "That casino info is prime stuff. Now, is our friend Mansell going to throw in his lot with Vanheusen? And if so, does he realise the business won't be the right side of the law? That's what we'll have to find out." He was silent for a moment. "On a scale of one to ten, what are the chances of them taking you back?"

"Zero, Gerry," I sighed. "With the open microphone everyone heard Monique. And the jeers and catcalls of *We want the palm tree* — that sort of thing — made her madder than ever. They swept me away and carried me up the steps singing *Viva España* and *Viva The Palm Tree*. No, not a chance."

"So we've lost you as our eyes and ears . . ." He drummed his fingers thoughtfully on the desk. "But has it blown your cover?"

I shook my head. "I'm pretty sure that both Vanheusen and Monique assumed that I did it just to be part of the action. And talking about action, Jason seemed to be having a good time. Did *he* come up with anything?"

"Jason?"

That blank look didn't fool me for a minute. "A clown with an empty-headed girl in tow, that wouldn't have been Jason, would it?"

"A clown. A Jason look-a-like. Really?" He looked back at me blandly.

I narrowed my eyes. "Really. Not just looking like Jason, sounding like Jason, behaving like Jason. C'mon, Gerry. Level with me."

"Talking about Jason," he sidetracked expertly, "that bug he helped you plant on *The Saucy Nancy* has delivered the goods. A consignment's arriving, in . . ." he glanced at his watch, ". . . about twelve hours' time at the little cove below the village of Masca. At 0200 hours. Just the sort of romantic spot a courting couple from Los Gigantes might choose for a bit of privacy. I'll have Jason and a girl in the shadows among the rocks." He eyed me speculatively.

Jason given carte blanche to snog. There'd be no holding him back. *No way* was I going to spend even one second in a clinch with him. I opened my mouth to say so.

"No, I'm not going to ask *you*," said mind-reader Burnside. "The smooching's got to be for real. Can't have you jumping up and socking him one when he gets too familiar, can we?"

Well, that was a relief.

"He'll use his camera phone to show us what's going on," he added.

I sniggered.

"The hand-over, I mean." His tone was severe, but his mouth twitched.

"Who's the lucky girl, then?"

Silence.

"Sorry. Shouldn't have asked." I got up. "I'll let you know if I hear anything from Exclusive."

"Odds on you will, Deborah. That obsession of Vanheusen's with your cat could still be a lever to keep the connection going"

I paused halfway to the door. "That's just what I'm afraid of."

He raised an enquiring eyebrow.

"A hot tip from V's Security, something I overheard at the barbecue. It seems he's planning a wedding for Thug Prince." I frowned, trying to relive the moment. "And there's to be a Big Do on the 25th. I've a nasty feeling there's a connection."

"Slapped wrist, Deborah. I don't recall you mentioning that." He poised a finger over the tape machine's replay button.

"Sorry," I sighed. With all the drama of my unmasking, it had completely slipped my mind.

"The tiniest detail can be crucial, Deborah."

Oh dear, I'd screwed up again. I crept out.

One of Gorgonzola's endearing little traits is that she can tune in to my moods. She was there to meet me as soon as I let myself in, rubbing herself consolingly against my legs with tiny mews of commiseration. I scooped her up and pressed my cheek into her soft fur. "*Nobody knows the trouble I've seen . . .*" I crooned in her ear. Her rough tongue rasped my face. "What we both need, G, is comfort for the inner woman." I broke open a couple of tins of tuna. I had mine on toast, she had hers in a bowl.

Later we sat companionably under the pergola on my little patio. To be more precise, I was sitting, she was standing on my lap, arching and purring contentedly as I stroked the grooming brush down her back and over her sides.

"You gave Robocat her comeuppance all right, G, didn't you?"

A loud, rumbling purr of agreement.

"Do you know that Ambrose and Black Prince have designs on your body?"

A slow stre-e-tch of her forelegs, an unsheathing and sheathing of razor-sharp claws.

Perleep perleep perleep peep peep. I let my mobile ring. I'd left Extreme Travel only an hour ago so it was unlikely to be the office. It was probably only Jason moaning on about Brunhilda. *Perleep perleep perleep*

210

peep peep. Or Victoria Knight with an update on her meeting about El Sueño, but I really didn't feel up to soothing and consoling anyone just now. *Perleep perleep perleep peep peep*.

With a sigh I laid aside the brush. "Sorry, G, that phone's getting on my nerves. Gotta go." I gave her a light prod.

Cue for well-rehearsed battle manoeuvres. G stiffened her legs, claws emerging in readiness to clamp. I rose speedily to my feet, pausing long enough midway for her to abandon ship.

Perleep perlee . . .

"Hi, DJ." Jayne's voice. "You've a summons from Monique Devereux. I'll read it out. *Ms Smith has omitted to leave me the arrangements for the next Outing. Ask her to bring them to Exclusive's premises at 5p.m. today. Monies due to her will then be paid.* Hey, must be missing you already. Maybe a chance to get reinstated."

"Bit of luck, then, that I took my Outing notes home to work on. Thanks, Jayne."

I had till 5p.m. Plenty of time to re-establish relations with a somewhat peeved cat before venturing into the lion's den.

With the arrangements for the Sunset Outing clutched in my hand, I pushed open the etched glass doors of Exclusive's office suite. There were a couple of little details still to complete. Monique, or my successor, would have to see to those. Tough, *mala suerte*, as the Spaniards say. I clip-clipped across the expanse of polished marble towards the reception desk. My arrival had been radioed from the gate, so Miguel was expecting me, but there was no customary greeting of *Buenas tardes, guapita*. Instead, he kept his head lowered, ostensibly reading the Exclusive newsletter. Upside down.

I came to a halt in front of him. He didn't look up. I gave a little cough. "*Hola*, Miguel. I've an appointment with Señora Devereux."

"She is expecting you, señora. Please go up." Averted eyes, a faint flush along the cheekbones evidence of his embarrassment.

I turned away.

His soft whisper just carried. "They find your message on the answering machine. They go crazy." I felt his eyes on me as I made my way to the lift.

With all that fuss about gatecrashing the party, the message I'd left on the answering machine to divert last night's calls to Jayne had slipped my mind. Oh well, this didn't really add to my woes. Perhaps I could even turn it to my advantage, proof that I'd not been totally irresponsible.

The brushed-steel elevator doors opened silently onto the corridor. In the coming meeting with Monique, now that things were past redemption, should I be devil-may-care, or penitent and apologetic on the thousand-to-one chance that she might change her mind?

I pushed open the door to my ex-office and stopped in amazement. Less than twenty-four hours ago it had been decorated in modern minimalist style — white

212

walls, white ceiling, white marble floor, black leather furniture with shiny chrome tubular legs.

All gone. Goodbye the black and white minimalist style, the primary colours of the Mondrian painting. Hello, the heavy brocades, dark furniture and gloomy decor of seventeenth-century Spain.

Monique was standing near the window. "As you see, Cousin Ashley and I have made a few changes." An open-necked white shirt and pinstripe suit had replaced the Snow Queen's glittering gown, but the frost was still in her voice. The frost hardened into ice. "This is the Deborah Smith who took your job, Ashley." Pointedly, she didn't ask me to take a seat.

I looked over at the elegant woman sitting at my desk. Except for her elfin hairstyle she was a clone of Monique. She had the same large brown eyes and perfect facial bone structure, the same expertly pencilled eyebrows and enamelled nails.

It had been obvious all along that Monique had never reconciled herself to my appointment as her assistant. Unfortunately, when it came to the crunch Vanheusen had had other priorities in the shape of a gingery bride for Black Prince. Now that I'd blotted my copybook, she had seized her chance and lost no time moving Ashley in — stepping into the shoes of the departed while they were still warm, and all that.

Cousin Ashley, as the pseudo-owner of that villa named Shangri-la, was almost certainly an accomplice in his money-laundering scheme, involved right up to the tips of her shell-like ears. And while I was in cliché mode, this new broom had certainly swept clean. *A few*

213

changes, eh? There was nothing left of the old office, nothing at all.

"I can see you've made changes, but . . . but . . ." I floundered to a halt.

I'd hit the right note. They exchanged gratified smiles. Ashley crossed her elegant legs and sat back in the chair behind the desk, not my familiar tubular chrome and leather swivel but an ornately carved throne padded with velvet cushions.

"Isn't Monique *marvellous*." She made it a statement of fact, not a question. "These furnishings are *so* much more in keeping with the Exclusive image. And they give a real sense of place." She settled herself against the velvet cushions and gazed round appreciatively at the gloomy decor. "You *never* liked that modernistic scheme of his, did you, Nicky? Ambrose only needed the *teeniest* of prods and —" A warning look from Monique cut her short.

"Let's just say that I advised Mr Vanheusen that the modern look was cold and soulless," Monique was smoothly diplomatic. "Our clients have firm roots in the past."

That translated as fuddy-duddy, conservative and dull. It summed up rather nicely what I felt about this make-over of *theirs*.

"Now, if you'll just hand over the arrangements for the next Outing . . ." Ashley, overeager, half-rose from her seat.

There aren't many pluses to summary dismissal, but one was that I didn't have to be on duty in Exclusive's office at 8 a.m. I could lie in bed a little longer in the morning. To savour that pleasure in full, I left the alarm switched off. *Best-laid schemes of mice and men* and all that. I'd forgotten to communicate this decision to Gorgonzola. Dragged into consciousness by fishy breath on my face and a persistent twitch of the sheet, I levered open one eyelid. Pitch black, not even dawn, early even by feline standards.

"*Gerroff*, G." I dragged the sheet over my head, buried my face in the pillow and drifted down . . . down . . .

Thump thump thump. An infantry battalion plodded up and down my back, merciless, relentless. Only four feline feet, but it felt like forty. Eyes shut tight, I willed myself to stay asleep. Relax . . . *Relax* . . . Think of it as therapeutic foot massage in some expensive Asian spa resort.

It was no use. I flung back the sheet. "Can't I have *one* decent night's sleep?" I snarled. "It's not even *dawn*, for God's sake."

I heard the soft thump of feet on floor, followed by a faint piteous mew. Enormous copper eyes stared at me, plaintive, reproachful. All an act. I knew it. She knew it.

"OK, G, you win." I padded my way to the kitchen, wincing as my bare feet made contact with cold terracotta tiles. She scampered ahead, bushy tail a triumphant moth-eaten banner.

I retired back to bed, drew the sheet round me, closed my eyes and waited for sleep. And waited . . . And waited . . . An hour later I was staring at the ceiling, now faintly visible in the grey light of dawn. I

215

might as well get up . . . I was lying there, still contemplating action, when the phone call came from Jayne at the office.

"Hi-i-i, Jayne," I yawned. "You're the second female to disturb my beauty sleep this morning. Something come up?"

"We're going to have to make some modifications to today's trip to the north. Come in early, will you." None of the usual banter, an alarm signal that brought me wide awake in an instant.

"OK, Jayne." For the benefit of any listener on the line, I heaved a sigh. "See you."

Early was the Department code for *urgent*. From her subdued tones, I gathered that Jayne was signalling some sort of a setback. And it must be a big one for the bouncy, voluble Jayne to be reduced to a couple of sentences. All the way to the office I worried about it.

The cheerful rainbow logo on the plate-glass windows only served to deepen my sombre mood. No pot of gold, but something dark and disturbing, waited behind this rainbow, I was sure of it. The Department didn't issue alerts lightly. Whatever it was, I wanted to delay discovery — my fingers were fractionally slower unlocking the door, my traverse across the floor to the one-way mirror fractionally protracted, my smile in the one-way mirror forced. Behind me in the mirror, I could see Jayne's desk, papers precision stacked, computer covered, the only sign of life the red glow of the light on the answering machine. The levered locks

216

clicked softly. I could put this off no longer. I took a deep breath and pushed open the door.

"What's this all about, guys? Has —"The words died in my throat.

They were sitting there in silence, staring at the floor or the wall or the ceiling. Nobody met my eye.

Only Gerry looked up as I stood in the doorway. "Sit down, DJ."

He had never addressed me that way. My legs folded beneath me and I sank into the nearest chair.

The cough as Gerry cleared his throat sounded shockingly loud. "Now that we're all here —"

There was one seat still unoccupied.

"Aren't we going to wait for Jas —" I stuttered to a halt.

The look on every face, Gerry's expression, told me before he put it into words. "Jason's fighting for his life. Critical."

A voice behind me muttered, "And Juanita's dead."

I stared at Gerry. "What — ? How —?" My mouth was dry.

His lips were moving but somehow I wasn't taking in what he was saying.

Jason, smooth-talking, opinionated, brash, arrogant . . . In spite of all his faults and our little spats, I was rather fond of him.

". . . Jason and Juanita . . . attacked . . . knifed . . . sea . . ." Gerry's voice was coming and going. A strange effect, as if someone was turning on and off a switch.

I ran my tongue over dry lips. "I can't take it in."

Gerry got up and went over to the coffee machine. "It's been a bit of a shock for you — for all of us." He handed me a black coffee. "A fisherman, a guy called Joaquin Suárez, has a shack where the ravine from Masca widens into the cove. It seems that he'd hurt his back, so hadn't gone out fishing last night. He heard shouts and a scream, and when he looked out he saw two men scrambling into an inflatable that shot off in the direction of Los Gigantes. He's had trouble before with local tearaways damaging his boat, so he went to investigate. He found Jason face down among the rocks." A long pause. "At our end, we knew something was wrong. We alerted the police launch standing by at Los Gigantes. Their searchlights found Juanita."

I made myself ask, "What are Jason's injuries?"

"Massive blood loss from stab wounds to the back. Punctured lung." Another long pause. "Prognosis uncertain." He drained his coffee in one gulp. "Juanita didn't stand a chance." He stared into his empty cup. "It was her first assignment."

Juanita. I didn't know her, had never met her. Her first assignment, he'd said. She'd have been young, keyed up, thrilled to be working with Jason — he had that effect on girls. Why did it seem worse that the dead colleague was young, at the start of her career? A dead colleague is a dead colleague, old or young. It could have been me. *Would* have been me, if I hadn't drawn the line at Jason's wandering hands. *I* had turned down the assignment — and Juanita was dead.

With an effort I concentrated on what Gerry was saying. ". . . attack pre-planned. They knew our operatives would be close by, observing. Which leads, I'm afraid, to only one conclusion. They've detected the bug on *The Saucy Nancy*. The whole bloody thing's been a set-up."

I glimpsed the depth of anger behind the calm exterior. Gerry seldom let his feelings show.

"Yes, looks like it was pre-planned." Jayne sounded tired. "The men must have been landed hours earlier, or come down the track from Masca. But how could they be sure that Jason and Juanita were the right people to target?"

"They'd have made a hit on *anybody* who was lurking about, on the off chance they'd be lucky." Gerry tapped thoughtfully at his teeth with a pen. "But my guess is that they homed in on the signal from his mobile phone. He was reporting the arrival of the boat."

I gulped down a mouthful of lukewarm coffee. That would be it. Nowadays any self-respecting crook has the latest, most sophisticated tracking and eavesdropping devices at his fingertips. Even if Jason hadn't actually been making a call, radio signals from his switched-on mobile could have been used to pinpoint his position to within a few metres. Poor Jase. Poor Juanita.

Gerry leant forward, resting his interlocked fingers on the desk, the signal that he was about to launch into his what-I-am-about-to-say-is-disagreeable routine.

"We mustn't let this get to us. Forget Jason, it's time to move on."

Murmurs of protest.

He swept on, tone brisk, matter-of-fact. "The minuses of last night are obvious. Suggestions as to the plus points?"

Stunned silence.

"OK, I'll start." He leant back in his chair. "Jason's not been able to tell us anything, but the fisherman Suárez said the two men he'd seen were definitely black, dark-skinned. And that means . . .?"

We thought about it.

"It means," I said slowly, "that they weren't the crew of *The Saucy Nancy*, and so . . . and so . . . they wouldn't have recognised Jason."

"Good, Deborah. And that means . . .?"

Did he *have* to inflict his brain exercising on us at a time like this? I felt like screaming, *Just tell us, you silly bastard*.

I took a deep breath, pressed my lips firmly together, took another deep breath. "I *suppose* it means that I'm in the clear."

"Right." A twitch at the corners of his mouth registered and condoned that rebellious *suppose*.

Nobody else could come up with a plus point. Tactfully, Gerry didn't recap on the minus points. The meeting broke up shortly afterwards. All *I* wanted was to get away, get into my car and drive. Drive away from everything, everybody.

"Hold on a minute, Deborah."

What did Gerry want now? Reluctantly I turned to face him.

"It'll be some time before Jason will be returning to his pad." The words *if ever* hung unspoken in the air.

220

He slid a key over the desk. "I'd really appreciate it if you'd go there and clear out the fridge and get rid of anything perishable from the cupboards. Make a note of any portable items of value and I'll have them put into secure storage."

Clearing the deceased's house.

"Anything else?" My voice sounded brittle. Why was he asking *me* to do this? Why hadn't he asked Jayne? Sometimes I hated Gerry.

He didn't look at me, merely started doodling on a sheet of paper. "Oh, and perhaps you'd better turn off the water and switch off the electricity, so that'll mean emptying the freezer."

I got it now. It was his way of saying that he didn't think Jason would make it. Preparing me.

From the parking bay outside Jason's apartment, the distant tower blocks of Las Américas waded through a silvery haze, the hum from the busy *autopista* far below a reminder that everyday life goes on for those not caught up in tragic events. I stood there for — how long? I don't know. At last I took a deep breath. It wasn't that I felt an intruder while the owner was away, more that I couldn't shake off the feeling I was about to enter a dead man's apartment. I steeled myself to unlock the door and start erasing his presence.

Tentatively I pushed open the living room door. Jason wasn't dead yet. He still had a chance. Hot sunshine streamed across the polished flooring and ricocheted off the stark chrome furniture and modernist glass shelving. Laid out stiffly on one of the giant floor-cushions were the mortal remains of Robocat. Averting my eyes from this reminder of our last encounter, I flicked shut the vertical blinds.

In the kitchen, I set about emptying the fridge — milk down the drain, butter, cheese, eggs, a packet of bacon and half a loaf into a large black rubbish sack. I left the pack of San Miguel beers as a sort of talisman, amulet, rabbit's foot, an offering to the gods for his return. There was no freezer to unload, just the fridge icebox containing an opened packet of peas and a half-empty tray of ice cubes. The fridge more or less emptied, I switched it off at the wall and left the door ajar. There'd be no mould or nasty smells when — if — Jason came home.

I made a quick survey of the kitchen. Worktops clear, apart from a couple of cups upside down in their saucers. I put them in the crockery cupboard and lugged the rubbish sack into the living room.

A folded newspaper lay on the coffee table. I added it to the sack . . . With the blinds closed and the bright sunlight cut out, the minimalist decor seemed bleak and soulless. Jason really was — *is* — obsessively neat, I thought. Nothing else to tidy up here, but there'd be bedding and laundry upstairs.

I was about to close the door when I caught a glint of silver under the sofa. I reached under the heavy piece of furniture and pulled out a fish-shaped piece of metal with a faint, but unmistakably fishy, pong. The reverse was inscribed *A Robomeal for Robocat*. I laid it on the floor-cushion beside Brunhilda, gently closed the door behind me and made my way upstairs.

222

I'd never been in Jason's bedroom, though every time we met he'd tried to lure me there. I'd imagined a giant waterbed, mirrors, that sort of thing. But it was all disappointingly ordinary, minimalist with an oriental slant. Two floor-to-ceiling black and gold banners hung on each side of the bed. Not to my taste, but rather striking against the rich red of the wall behind them. The rest of the room, with its white walls, black sheets, black cotton spread, had the same stark look as downstairs.

I bundled the bed linen and the contents of the laundry basket into a sheet and tied a giant knot. In a tall glass vase on the window sill was an amazingly realistic single white orchid, Jason's seduction prop. I'd take it home with me as a reminder of our battles of wits.

I bumped the bulky laundry bundle down the stairs and left it in the hall ready for collection. All that was left to do was to dump that kitchen rubbish in the communal bin. I lugged the sack out to the front door and dropped it beside the services box. When it came to turning off the water and electricity, it felt horribly like switching off Jason's life support system.

In the hall I hesitated, then on impulse went back to the living room and scooped up Brunhilda and her fishy meal. I closed the front door and turned away. That was it then. Nothing more to do. I'd the feeling that I wouldn't be back.

CHAPTER
SEVENTEEN

My role in Operation Canary Creeper could very well be at an end now that I'd been cut off from my Trojan Horse role at Exclusive. An unsettling thought. The sun was hot on my back. I closed my eyes and let the stress and tension of the last two days seep away into the warm sand of the beach in front of the five-star Hotel Bahía del Duque. Masterly inactivity would be the order of the day . . . Here, no loud conversations in English, German or Russian, no tedious shouted discussions of last night's football match, no raucous purveyors of doughnuts, pineapples and coconuts. The Duque's five-star charges for sunbeds and umbrellas made sure of that. Here, the public beach had been groomed to meet the expectations of the super-rich. Shaded from the sun in blue-and-white tented pavilions, the Duque's guests reclined on white-cushioned mattresses twice the thickness of any found elsewhere.

It was free of charge to lie on the sand, though. I'd spread my towel beside the white-painted wooden pier that supported the Duque's beach-café — not a cheap and cheerful *chiringuito* bar, but resplendently

224

equipped with white tables and chairs and smartly uniformed waiters.

I let the sounds flow over me . . . distant cries of children playing in the waves . . . the clink of china from the café tables above my head . . .

Chairs scraped on the boards above me. A snippet of conversation drifted down ". . . wasn't *my* fault. I don't know why you keep going *on* about it. Yes, I *know* it was a bit of a disaster, but the trip wasn't *my* idea —"

Somebody was having a bad day.

"*Outing*, not trip. You can't even get the word right." The words were hissed *sotto voce*.

Outing. Like a drop of icy water on my back, the word jolted me wide awake.

"How was I to know it was Booze Cruise night? The Outing was planned by that girl you sacked. Probably did it deliberately —"

"Well, you *should* have known," snapped Monique's voice. "It was *you* that chose Tuesday *and* you should have checked with me before booking." I could tell she was in a towering rage. "Our clients were exposed to drunks and —"

I mustn't miss a word of this. I reached out for my T-shirt, wrapped it round my head and face as if to protect myself from the sun, and rolled over to prop myself up against a wooden pier-support directly below the speakers.

"The señoras wish to order?"

"Two coffees. Black." Monique snapped out the words.

"But, Nicky, you *know* I don't like —"

"Shut up, Ashley. You'll need your coffee black when you hear what I've got to tell you." Monique swept on. "As I was saying, I have something unpleasant to tell you." I adjusted the T-shirt to free an ear.

"Ambrose rang me this morning at my apartment. He was positively *incandescent* about that Sunset Outing fiasco of yours. I had to plead with him, Ashley, to let you stay on, to give you one last chance."

"*One* teeny complaint and the man —" Outrage in Ashley's every word.

"Not one complaint, two. *Both* our clients voiced their displeasure. Mr Wainwright was particularly upset. I believe he phoned Ambrose at some unearthly hour to tell him so. I have to say, Ashley, that this all reflects badly on *me*. I recommended you, after all."

"Anyone can make a mistake, Nicky. What about the time when *you* —" Her voice dropped to a low murmur.

A long silence, then the creak of wooden boards heralded the return of the waiter. "Your coffees, señoras."

I heard the soft *chink chink* of china.

Another lo-o-ng silence. "But I thought —" Ashley, on the defensive.

"At Exclusive, you're not being paid to think, Ashley, you're being paid to *know* — and if you don't know, you check. One more mistake, *one* more, and —"

With a sharp *chunk* cup forcibly hit saucer, the executioner's axe hitting the block.

226

How long before Ashley again blotted her copybook? Three days? A week? Perhaps, after all, there was a chance that I'd see my office again . . .

The phone call came two days later.

"I've got good news for you, Deborah. Mr Vanheusen has reconsidered your case, and is willing to reinstate you."

"Oh, Monique, that's wonderful. Thank —"

"You realise, of course, that I had to plead quite strongly on your behalf. Yes, quite strongly. In view of your cavalier attitude to following instructions on at least two occasions, it took some effort to convince him. However, he has agreed to give you one more chance. One more."

Ashley had obviously messed up *her* chance.

"Er . . . Ashley?" I ventured.

"Promotion." Monique moved smoothly and briskly on. "Before she left, Ashley was dealing with a somewhat unusual request from Mr Mansell. I'm up to my eyes in work so I'm delegating it to you. Come in this afternoon and I'll fill you in on the details . . ."

They were as hard as rocks, those velvet cushions on the over-carved chair, recently graced by Cousin A, so suddenly and mysteriously translated to higher things. For the second time I flipped through Exclusive's photo-library of scenic shots. Jonathan Mansell's requirements were *very* exacting — somewhere off the tourist track, somewhere special, somewhere the Alhambra could escort favoured guests. And the deadline was tomorrow. Had Ashley, unable to come up with a suggestion, thrown in the towel, or had a desperate Monique finally lost patience with her? I was getting pretty desperate myself. Seeking inspiration, I stared for a long time, chin on hand, at a picture of snow-capped Mount Teide . . . been there, done that . . . the reds and browns of the multi-hued caldera really did look like the surface of the moon . . .

I'd cracked it. The Lunar Landscape on the flank of Teide would be ideal _ a star attraction, but not easily accessible even by car, and so, definitely off the tourist track, and definitely special. The Paisaje Lunar fitted Mansell's requirements exactly. Those bizarre, wind-sculpted, creamy yellow columns would be a breathtaking sight against a blue sky. I'd drive him from Vilaflor to the small car park at the end of the Lomo Blanco, and from there we'd go on foot through the pine trees and lava fields to the site itself. On the way I'd do my utmost to find out Mansell's line on that proposed casino deal.

Vilaflor's long main street was deserted except for a stray dog and a workman painting a wall. Across a narrow *barranco* a huddle of whitewashed houses with faded pantiled roofs slumbered in the pale sunshine.

I drew up the 4×4 outside a pavement café-bar guarded by a gnarled almond tree, its bare black branches sprinkled with delicate white flowers. I'd had an ulterior motive for putting a café on the itinerary sheet. While we sat drinking our coffee and gazing over patches of garden planted with vegetables and orange

228

trees, I'd steer the conversation round to casinos. The opportunity came sooner than I dared hope.

Mansell looked up from his study of my Paisaje Lunar info sheet. "I laid it on the line to Vanheusen that I wasn't going to waste time on an uninspired wine tasting in Icod when I'd plenty of teething troubles to sort out at the hotel. If this trip lives up to your description, it'll be exactly what I had in mind, a day excursion to make the guests remember their stay at the Alhambra."

I saw my opening. "You'll need something special for evening entertainment, too, I suppose?"

"I've got something in mind for that, but it's still very much in the planning stage. Now, if the Paisaje Lunar is to be part of the Alhambra experience, how would you suggest . . ."

Casino subject closed. Stymied.

At the wooden sign *Lomo Blanco* we left the smooth tarmac to bump along a beaten earth track with the pine-covered slopes of Teide on the left, and a sheer drop to the valley floor on the right. The sun was burning down from the bluest of skies and the heady scent of pine wafted on the wind — all spirit-lifting stuff, but not for me, for I couldn't see any way of steering the conversation back to casinos in general, and the Alhambra's casino in particular.

As I'd promised it would be, the Paisaje Lunar was spectacular. The crème caramel-coloured columns, carved and chiselled by the honing wind into fairytale towers, pillars and buttresses were framed against a cobalt blue sky. Mind-boggling, awe-inspiring, sensational.

Mansell got out his camera. "Fits the bill exactly, Deborah. You've hit the jackpot for me with this."

But I hadn't as far as Gerry was concerned. I was back to square one. I'd found out nothing.

It just shows that you should never give up hope. Forty-five minutes later when we got back in sight of the car park, Mansell gave me just the opening I needed.

"Hope we don't find the car's been broken into."

"Oh, criminals are busy with *much* more lucrative things back in Las Américas," I laughed. "The real money's in drugs nowadays."

He gave me a quizzical look. "You're not speaking from experience, I hope?"

"Only hearsay from Ramón, the guy I go out with." I pressed the remote to unlock the car. "According to him, drug barons launder their profits through clubs, fake time-shares and casinos." As I turned the key in the ignition, I added, "It seems that casinos are the prime target for dirty money. Cash flows through, and it's impossible to check on where it comes from and where it goes. That's Ramón's job, to give businessmen advice on how to avoid being caught up in dodgy schemes."

I left it at that. If Mansell asked me to contact "Ramón", we'd know for sure that he was in the clear.

CHAPTER
EIGHTEEN

On the days that I didn't come home for lunch, Gorgonzola tended to be in a bad mood. She hated being "home alone" for a whole day, though she was quite able to come and go through the barred pantry window to access her water bowl and any morsel that remained from her breakfast. With this in mind, on the way back from the successful outing to the Paisaje Lunar I stopped at a supermarket and bought two tuna steaks, a large one for her and a smaller one for myself.

Tactics would be critical when G and I came face to face. Should I grovel with much wringing of hands? On the lines of, "Oh, my poor neglected and abandoned Gorgonzola. How can I make it up to you? As a token, please accept this large tuna steak — much bigger than the one I've bought for myself."

Or should I briskly brazen it out? "Don't be a wimp, G. It's time you dieted anyway. If you were hungry, why didn't you go out and catch yourself a mouse like any self-respecting cat?"

I inserted my key in the lock and tiptoed down the hall. As I eased the kitchen door open, I crooned a honeyed, "I'm back, *tresorita mía*."

Silence. No thump of paws landing on the tiled floor, no appeased purr or even a querulous yowl.

Perhaps an ingratiating, "*Cariñita, cielita mía*" would do the trick?

Nope.

Either I'd not grovelled enough, or, more likely, overdone it with "my little treasure, little darling, my little angel". G's ear for detecting insincerity was rivalled only by her nose for sniffing out drugs.

Time to get tough. I flung the door back on its hinges. "OK, G, quit sulking. Duty is duty. We all have to make sacrif —"

No cat.

Tap tap tap. Tap tap tap. It took me a moment to realise the sound was coming from the back door. *Tap tap tap*.

"Señora, you are there? I bring the cat."

I put the tuna steaks on the kitchen table, and turned the key. The door edged open, three centimetres, five, ten. Just above ankle level, a gingery face materialised, nose twitching. Before I could say, "Missed me, G?" furry shoulders forced their way through the widening gap and a furry body hurled itself through the air to make a precision landing on the table. In a blur of movement both tuna steaks, clamped in slavering jaws, disappeared into the setting sun.

"G!" I screeched.

"*Madre de Dios*." A startled Jesús stared after her. "She have the hunger." He lowered himself creakily onto a kitchen chair. "Señora, I have come to tell you that this afternoon I hear the noise of pans in your *cocina*. I know you not home, so I say to myself, they have come back, *los vándalos*. I look in your window. *Mío Dio!* What am I seeing?" Eyebrows raised, eyes round with astonishment, Jesús was not to be hurried. The telling of a story was all.

I played along, thumping a hand on my chest in a suitably theatrical gesture. "What are you seeing? Tell me, Jesús. This is giving me a heart attack just hearing of it."

"I am seeing *nothing*. Nothing, señora."

"Nothing?"

"I hear the sound of the pans, but I see nothing. No peoples going up and down in the *cocina*."

"But what . . . ?"

"I think they are making the fool. They are hiding and seeking, as you say. Quick as the lightning I unlock the door, and like this, I shout, 'AA-EEE.' The noise, it stop. Like *that*."

"And . . . ?" I breathed, entering into the spirit of things.

"And," Jesús narrowed his eyes, "I see who is doing this." He paused for maximum effect. "It is the cat," he cackled. "The cat, she is *los vándalos*. Heh, heh, heh!"

"The cat?" I echoed.

"She throw her plates round the *cocina*. It make much noise. She very hungry." Another cackle. "But I think she no hungry now."

I'd just sat down to a scrambled egg supper kindly supplied by Jesús, when my mobile's *perleep perleep perleep peep peep* stopped my fork halfway to my mouth. I hadn't been expecting the office to call. Perhaps tomorrow's debriefing session had been rescheduled.

"Jayne here. Sorry to disturb your evening, Deborah, but could you just nip in and sort out a couple of things that have to be in place by tomorrow?"

So it was something important, but not a crisis. I finished my emergency supper, then refilled G's water bowl, but left the food bowl empty as a pointed reminder that she'd had her supper — and mine.

Jayne wasn't at her desk in the outer office. Unusual. It suddenly occurred to me that this summons might mean that Jason ... I paused with my hand on the white door. I'd know by their faces if . . .

Gerry was on the phone. I picked up a briefing sheet and took a seat next to Tomás, flicking him a covert glance to see if there was bad news. He winked and gave me his usual, "*Hola, guapa.*"

That didn't fit in with bad news. It was safe to ask, "Have you heard how Jason's doing?"

Before he could reply, Gerry cut in. "OK, everyone. This meeting's to bring you up to date. We've a new member of the team, just flown in from London. Name's Charlie."

Jason's replacement. I made a tentative hand-raising movement. "Can I ask how Jason is doing?"

"No longer critical, but I'm afraid he'll be out of commission for some time. In the meantime, Charlie will . . ."

Not critical, so there was hope that once again he'd be wowing the girls with his fancy sports car and his designer shades.

". . . and if this leads to the breakthrough I'm hoping for," Gerry was saying, "things will be all wrapped up."

Damn it, I couldn't ask him to repeat. That *would* be putting my head on the block. I'd have to get the gist from Tomás later.

"Any questions about your role, Deborah?"

The bastard. He *knew* I hadn't been listening.

"We-ell, Gerry," I played for time, "I'm not *quite* clear about —"

"Yes, Deborah?" his expression was deadpan.

"I mean —" I floundered.

"Mmm?" Raised eyebrow. That translated as, "You've been rumbled, Deborah. Admit you weren't paying attention — and grovel."

A *bzzzz* from the outer office signalled that someone had just pushed open the door from the street. Saved by the bell, as it were. All eyes switched to the one-way mirror. We watched a female, white-blonde hair gelled into aggressive spikes, ring through one nostril, give a cursory glance round the empty office, then wobble on ridiculous high-heeled sandals towards the white door. We heard her call, "Hey, you guys, where is everybody? I've got an appointment." She stood in front of the mirror, head on one side, as if studying her reflection. A hitch-up of tight leather micro-skirt, a hitch-down of skimpy orange micro-top and a display of toothpaste-ad white teeth.

Behind me a chair scraped as Jayne rose to her feet. "Give me a couple of minutes. I'll deal with this."

"It's OK, Jayne." Gerry flicked a switch, the levered locks clicked open, and the twenty-first-century siren sashayed in. "Meet Charlie, everybody."

Jayne subsided heavily into her chair as if felled by a chop behind the knee from one of Charlie's spiky-heeled sandals. We'd all assumed that our new colleague was male. This had been Gerry's little joke, or, more likely, a reminder not to make assumptions and jump to conclusions.

Charlie smiled that perfect smile again. "Hi, guys."

"Take a seat, Charlie. I'll just recap to put you in the picture." Momentarily Gerry's eyes rested on me. "As yet, we've had no useful feedback from the bug in Monique Devereux's office, and after the regrettable *Saucy Nancy* episode, anything that did come in would be unreliable."

The room was silent while we all thought about Jason and the false information that had sent Juanita to her death.

He swivelled slowly in his chair. "Tomás, I want you to remove the office bug. The risk of blowing Deborah's cover is too high. We'll liaise about it later." He stopped abruptly, mid-swivel. "We've established *how* Vanheusen launders the money, but to prove that the source of the money is indeed drugs, new tactics are called for. What I'm banking on is that our pal Vanheusen is greedy for cash, wants results quickly — and people in a hurry make mistakes." He tapped the briefing sheet. "As I've said here, *The Saucy Nancy* was the last link in the

Vanheusen supply route, but is now useless to him because our planted bug shows that we're onto John Sinclair. Until he can reorganise, he will have to fall back on a primitive, but tried and tested method of transport, the human mule. Our colleagues in Tenerife have been keeping tabs on lone female tourists who stay only a couple of nights before jetting back to Europe. They've built up a dossier of women and hotels."

With a mark-up of up to a quarter of a million pounds sterling on a kilo of heroin, it wouldn't take many mules to keep things ticking over. Gerry was onto something there.

Abruptly, he leant forward, planted his elbows on the desk, fingers interlocked, chin supported on thumbs, always a sign of him getting down to the nitty-gritty. "The plan is to put tabs on females that fit the mule profile when they arrive at Reina Sofia or Los Rodeos airports. We let them through to see who contacts them. What Operation Canary Creeper needs is to link that person with Vanheusen. And that's where you ladies have a role."

Charlie gave me an exaggerated wink. She must guess what he had in mind, which was more than I could, thanks to not paying attention a few minutes ago. Was he going to play cat and mouse again with his questions?

I relaxed when he continued with, "Let me expand on this. We all know the problem with keeping tabs on mules."

Eager to be on the ball this time, I nodded brightly, as if mules and their problems were an open book.

"And the problem is, Deborah?"

The swine. I didn't have a clue. "To be sure that they're 'clean', they'll be under surveillance at the airport by their runners," I hazarded.

"Er . . . right." He didn't quite cover his surprise. "And there's the time factor. The pattern is that they stay, at most, a couple of nights, and once they get to their room, they hole up there till the exchange is made."

Charlie thrust an arm into the air and fluttered a hand for attention. The skimpy top parted company with the micro-skirt. The eyes of every man in the room targeted the gold ring glinting in her navel. "If they're holed up, how are we —"

Gerry cleared his throat. "I've every confidence you'll think of something, Charlie. As I was saying, if we knew *in advance* where they were booked in, we could have personnel," he glanced at Charlie and myself, "in place ready to strike up an acquaintance. But, till we get a breakthrough on one of those hotels —" He broke off as a light flashed on his desk console. "Call coming through on the outside line, Jayne. Better take it." He leant back, stretched. "OK, everyone. That's all for today. Right, Tomás, let's go over how you propose to remove that bug."

Jayne disappeared through the white door, and Tomás got up for his confab with Gerry.

I turned to Charlie. "Hi, I'm DJ. It's Deborah on formal occasions when Gerry wants to lord it over me." My eyes strayed to the nose ring. "Forgive me for being personal, but did it —"

"You're asking about the ring? Everybody does. No, didn't hurt a bit." She fiddled with it. "I'm seriously thinking of doing my lip next."

I winced. "Won't that make you somewhat memorable for undercover?"

"*Au contraire.* They remember the girl with the nose ring." The fiddling fingers tweaked. "Without it I'm just one of the crowd. *Voilà.*" She held up the ring.

I blinked. No hole, just a faint red mark on her nostril. Charlie the punk, now morphed into Charlie the modish teenager, all naïvety and innocence.

"One of those clip-on things." She gave it a quick polish on her skimpy top. "Goes anywhere." She popped it onto her lower lip. "See?"

Over at the desk, the low murmur of the bug-removal confab hesitated, then resumed.

"Wow!" My admiration was genuine. Charlie had hidden depths.

Jayne's voice came through the intercom. "Call for DJ. It's Jonathan Mansell."

With a thumbs-up to Charlie, I went out through the white door, and picked up the receiver.

"I was hoping you'd be in the office." I detected a hesitant note in his voice. "That friend of yours, that you mentioned this morning. I was wondering . . . that is . . . I was thinking that he and I should have a talk."

"Do you want me to give him a call?" I tried to inject the right degree of casualness into my voice. "You could meet at a bar."

"Great. Somewhere quiet, not too noisy."

I laughed. "He's not one for noise either. OK, I'll see if I can get hold of him." That shouldn't be too difficult. He wasn't too far away, sitting at his desk on the other side of the white door. "I'll call you back."

I was smiling when I rejoined the others. "I think we may have the breakthrough you were looking for, Gerry," I said.

CHAPTER
NINETEEN

Los Abrigos was only a thirty minute drive from Las Américas — but it could have been on another planet. No massed hotels, shopping centres and crowds, just half a dozen tiny fishing boats bobbing in the little harbour, its dark waters streaked silver and gold by the lights from the circle of fish restaurants lining the quay. No loud music blaring from bars, no busy hum of passing traffic, only the *slap slap* of water on the harbour rocks, children's cries from the narrow side streets, and in the warm night air the aroma of frying fish.

El Burro Perezoso, The Lazy Donkey, was an unpretentious bar tucked between two fish restaurants. It was the perfect place for a clandestine rendezvous: shadowy but not gloomy, busy but not crowded. Through the open doorway spilt out soft yellow lamplight, the murmur of voices and the deep dark chords of a guitar, lingering, dying . . .

A few weeks ago Jason had taken me there, hoping that I'd fall, first for the Canarian atmosphere of the place, then for him. And I had fallen — but only for the place, the ochre-washed walls, the dark beams, the simple wooden tables and the glazed tile floor. Wooden casks nestled on trestles behind the bar and golden-brown haunches of mummified ham hung on steel hooks from the low smoke-darkened ceiling.

I had an hour to savour all this with Gerry, alias Ramón, while waiting for Mansell. The cardinal rule for meetings of this kind is to arrive early, very early, and to keep a clear head. Another rule is to assume you're being watched. So, for that hour we sat in cosy tête-à-tête, toying with a drink. The casual observer would see a couple gazing dreamily into each other's eyes, whispering sweet nothings interspersed with long silences.

In reality we were playing a game of fiendish ingenuity devised by my drinking companion. Player one (decided on the discreet toss of a coin) quoted the first line of a poem. Player two had to provide the second line. Back to player one for the next line and so on till memory crashed. The fiendish part was that only the winner of the round was allowed to take a swallow of his (or her) drink. The occasional outbreak of a "lovers' tiff", when a dispute arose over the accuracy of a line, added an extra touch of authenticity for any observer.

Gerry's glass was still three-quarters full, whereas mine was nearly empty. I'm pretty good at this, I thought smugly.

I took a winner's sip of Rioja. "Your turn," I said, throwing my head back and laughing merrily, not just for the benefit of watching eyes.

He thought for a moment, then:

"A bunch of the boys were whooping it up in the Malamute saloon . . ."

Easy. Robert Service was one of my favourite poets. I'd let him think he'd got me on the run. To give the poor guy hope, I frowned, then recited haltingly, "The kid that handles the . . . the . . . music-box . . ." I paused as if searching for the words. ". . . was . . . was . . ."

He smiled, confident he'd got me. His hand closed round his glass in anticipation of victory.

". . . playing a ragtime tune," I finished. "Your turn."

Realising that I'd been stringing him along, he said through gritted teeth:

"Behind the bar, in a solo game —"

I pounced. "Mistake," I whispered in his ear. "It's not Behind the bar. It's Back of the bar." I drained my glass and pushed it forward for a fill up.

But he leant forward and said quietly, "No more game playing, Deborah. Back to business."

I looked up. Mansell was threading his way through the tables towards us. I waved a greeting. Top marks that he'd dressed in faded denim shirt and jeans. In a local bar such as this, a smart business suit would have drawn all eyes to him — and to us. I squeezed Gerry's hand affectionately and whispered, "The time has come, the walrus said, to talk of many things."

Mansell pulled up a chair at our table. "Sorry I'm a bit late. There was a tailback on the motorway for nearly a kilometre at the turn-off to Los Abrigos."

"It doesn't matter." I smiled. "Gave us a chance to catch up. I haven't seen Ramón for ages. Ramón Martinez, Jonathan Mansell."

Gerry nodded a greeting, "*Encantado*," and signalled the waiter to bring another glass.

Introductions over, I sat back. It was up to Gerry now.

Under cover of filling Mansell's glass, he leant across the table, voice low. "Señor, anything you need advice on, I'll be happy to help."

For some moments Mansell studied his wine. "It's nothing definite." He swirled the liquid round the glass, "More a gut feeling. And —" He looked up. "Something Deborah said set me thinking."

"Mmm?" Gerry ran a finger round a wine splash on the table.

"About a link between casinos and money-laundering . . ." He trailed off and resumed the close inspection of his wine.

"That is true, Señor Mansell." Gerry's English was lightly accented. "The link is very strong. Not, *claro*, in every case. Some casinos are, as you say, above board. But for the drug barons, what could be easier than to hide the incomings and outgoings of their money under the cover of a casino?" He gave a wry smile and shrugged his shoulders. "The more respectable the reputation of the casino, the better the cover."

Mansell sipped his wine thoughtfully. "Hmm."

A long silence.

Through the open door I watched a fishing boat leaving the harbour, its wake a silvery razor slash on the dark skin of the ocean. On the roof of its dog-kennel-sized cabin, sat three ball-floats, gigantic oranges ferried into the night. The wheelhouse light winked, then as it rounded the mass of the mole, was abruptly extinguished. The *putt putter* of the engine faded . . .

The silence dragged on.

Gerry broke it. "A successful businessman, like yourself, señor, has already shown judgement and instinct. Trust that instinct."

Mansell appeared to come to a decision. "You're right." He finished off his glass in two quick gulps. "As a matter of fact, I *have* been approached with the proposal of a joint venture — the opening of a new casino in Las Américas as part of the Alhambra. It would be very profitable for the hotel. Very tempting, but . . ."

Gerry's eyes held Mansell's. "But you have doubts about the honesty of this business partner?"

"Ye-es." A reluctant nod.

"May I ask the name of this man?"

"We-ell." His eyes flickered in my direction.

So he was embarrassed, or perhaps wary, about shopping Vanheusen in front of one of Vanheusen's staff. Time for a discreet withdrawal to the loo. I gathered up my bag and headed in the direction of the *señoras*.

While slowly counting up to a hundred, I gazed at my reflection in the mirror, renewed my make-up, combed my hair, adjusted an earring, examined my nails. Four minutes. Mansell might need longer, given his reluctance to take the final step and name names. Gerry wouldn't want to rush things. I leant against the tiles, stared at myself in the mirror again, and sought inspiration on how to pass the time. Got it! A dramatic rendition of *The Ballad of Dan M'Grew*, declaimed at full volume to take full advantage of the acoustics.

"*A bunch of the boys were whooping it up in the Malamute saloon.*" I tossed back several imaginary drinks, and slapped several imaginary backs.

"*The kid that handles the music box was playing a ragtime tune.*" My fingers fluttered and danced over the marble basin surround.

"*Back of the bar, in a solo game sat Dangerous Dan McGrew.*" Triumphantly I slapped down the winning ace. Spades.

"*And watching his luck, was his light-o'-love, the lady that's known as Lou.*" I struck a sultry pose, hand behind head, eyeing my reflection through lowered lids.

"*Were you ever out in the Great Alone, when the moon was awful clear.*" I gazed soulfully up at the bare round bulb of the ceiling light glowing softly above my head.

"*And the icy mountains hemmed you in with a silence you most could hear.*" I cupped a hand to my ear. Nothing. Not even the drip of a tap. The heavy door cut off all sounds from the bar. I was alone in my silent white world.

"With only the sound of the timber wolf . . . Aaaooooooooo . . ."

246

This went particularly well, the ululation echoing eerily round the tiles. So hauntingly atmospheric, indeed, that I threw back my head to let rip again.

"Aaaooo —"

There's only a certain amount of time you can spend in the Ladies before someone thinks you've passed out, or passed away, or are up to no good. A fierce, "*Qué pasa?*" cut through the echoes.

The howl died in my throat. Peering round the door was a leathery brown face, beneath the face, a faded black dress, wrinkled stockings, tired old shoes.

I clutched my heart. "*Madre de Dios!* Oh my God, it is the water pipes!" I pointed. "The pipes have frozen." *Las tuberías se han helado* was the only plumbing phrase I could summon up in this emergency.

Leaving the Lady of the Loo peering apprehensively at the piping, I swept up my bag and scuttled out. Had I given Gerry enough time? Surely by now he would have prised Vanheusen's name out of Mansell.

In my absence things seemed to have gone well. As I approached, Mansell pushed back his chair. "You've given me some useful advice, Ramón, and quite a lot to think about. I'll be in touch if there are any more developments."

"And you, señor, have told me much of interest." Gerry leant forward and draped an arm round my shoulders. "I think it better if we leave at different times, so Deborah and I will stay here. We've a little unfinished business of our own to attend to." He nuzzled my ear.

We watched him leave. "*Jackpot*," Gerry muttered.

Jackpot, eh? Sounded like it could be translated as *breakthrough*. On the strength of that, I went to the bar and ordered us two large gin and tonics — on expenses, of course.

I was right about the breakthrough. Gerry leant forward and murmured, "He told me all about Vanheusen's plans for a casino in the Alhambra. I thought that was all I was going to get." He was positively purring with satisfaction. "But then I struck gold. Mansell said, 'You've convinced me that Vanheusen's dealings are distinctly shady. That's set me wondering about a block reservation that Exclusive made a week ago.'" Gerry clinked my glass in a toast. "Four rooms booked at the Alhambra till further notice."

"I don't see why he'd think there was something odd about that," I said. After a glass of wine and the G&T, I was feeling pretty mellow. I thought I'd humour this drip drip of information.

"Even at the time, Mansell thought it was a bit odd that they were the *cheapest* rooms available, bearing in mind that Vanheusen's clients are rather well heeled." He waited.

I played along. "Well, could be Vanheusen was having a bit of a cash-flow problem."

"*And* that occupants of the rooms stayed only two days."

I sipped thoughtfully at my drink. "They didn't like the rooms?"

He winced. "You *do* like your little joke, Deborah."

"Oh come on, Gerry, hit me with it. I can't stand the suspense."

"*And* that they were all single women."

I couldn't resist. "What? Not one of them was *married*? No wedding rings, eh?"

He sighed and hastily rephrased. "They were all women on their own."

We clinked glasses again. The mules' stables had been located.

CHAPTER
TWENTY

I stared in fascination at Charlie's shirt, the front of which appeared to have been shredded by the claws of a hungry tiger. Her slim legs were encased in trousers of the finest pale blue suede, so tight she could have been poured into them. In a concession to the elegance of the marbled foyer of the Alhambra, she had transferred the gold rings from nose to ears. Gone the aggressively spiked hair, in its place the chicest of styles, a smooth blonde cap. She was lounging on a cushioned divan with a clear view of the front entrance, apparently engrossed in the screaming headlines of *The Sun*.

In contrast to this gorgeous creature, I felt like a dowdy sparrow in the smart casuals of my visiting-the-Alhambra-on-behalf-of-Exclusive gear. No cushioned divan for me. I was seated, rather less comfortably, on a carved wooden chair in the striped pavilion. Each of us, in our different ways, merged into the background scene.

I tapped my pen thoughtfully on my teeth. I'd been here an hour with another three to go. I might as well use the time profitably by finalising the details of Wednesday's Outing to Gomera. Victoria Knight and Herbert Wainwright would be going home in a few days' time, so what could I rustle up that would be completely different from the usual run-of-the-mill excursion? Idly I contemplated one of the Alhambra's gleaming brass urns, in its convex side a mini-reflection of the reception hall — intricate plasterwork, red carpet, Charlie on her sofa ... I'd already hired a catamaran but, to give Victoria a boost after her disappointment over El Sueño, I'd arrange for sparkling cava, tapas perhaps and a folk group of Gomeran singers and dancers — all courtesy of Exclusive. Then, on the island itself, a demonstration of the making of the powerful palm honey liqueur and a little bottle to take home as a souvenir. Yes, Victoria would like that. Herbie Wainwright might not, but very little pleased him anyway.

The camera phone in my pocket vibrated. I switched it on. Staring back at me from the screen was a thin face, dark shadows under the eyes, eyebrows mere smudges of colour against a sallow skin. The mule. I put the phone back in my pocket and shuffled the papers into a neat pile. Reflected in the Ali Baba urn, Charlie was putting down her paper and leisurely picking up her phone.

"Engineer an encounter," Gerry had said to both of us. "Then you'll be a familiar face for the lonely mule to latch onto when all and sundry are decanted from their rooms by an opportune fire alarm. With luck she'll let slip something of importance."

To engineer an encounter was easier said than done. One thing for sure, Charlie's approach would be entirely different from mine. I'd be hovering near the reception desk when the mule checked in, go up in the lift with her, get chatting. If she was an experienced mule, she'd be relaxed and more receptive. I'd play it by ear.

There she was. Just coming through the plate-glass doors into the lobby, wheeling a small trolley case. The stylish cream linen suit did nothing for that sallow skin. I scraped back my chair and half-rose. I'd have to get into position to intercept her.

A shadow fell over my table. An all too familiar querulous voice whined, "Can I have a word with you, ma'am? Right now!" The pinched features were flushed, the thick pebble lenses heliographing outrage.

Over Wainwright's shoulder, I saw the mule pause uncertainly and look around, then move towards the reception desk. Short of shouldering him aside, there was no way I could get past him. Out of the corner of my eye, I saw Charlie spring into action. In one fluid movement she jumped up, dropping the pages of *The Sun* at the mule's feet.

"It'll have to be stopped, I tell you." From his tone Herbert G Wainwright III meant business. He dragged a chair nearer the table and sat down. "*If* I could have your full attention, ma'am."

Reluctantly, I dragged my eyes away from Charlie's flustered attempts to gather up the scattered pages. Aided by the light breeze from the ceiling fans, she had successfully ensnared her quarry.

I turned in one ear to Charlie's giggled apologies and the mule's startled response, switched on a professional smile and assigned the other ear to the Wainwright whinge.

"All the way over here to Tenerife . . . about to spend good dollars on a luxury condo . . . a lot of dough involved . . ."

I polished my smile and let him drone on while I strained to hear Charlie's conversation with the mule.

"You're English!" Charlie's voice had acquired a nasal twang. "Don't tell me. Let me guess. Liverpool? You're from Liverpool? Which part?"

Mumbled reply.

"Fancy that. Lived there till I was ten. Bet it's changed . . ."

Wainwright was wittering on, ". . . and Los Cristianos seemed so . . . but nobody clued me in about . . ."

I assumed an "I'm all ears" expression, and focused on the scene in the foyer. Charlie rounded up the last wandering page and tucked it under her arm. "I'm staying here too. Name's Charlie. See you around . . ."

I had to hand it to her, Charlie was a real pro.

". . . prancing about butt naked." Wainwright stopped abruptly.

I wrenched my attention back. "*Naked*?"

He nodded slowly, "Yeah, bare." I must have looked blank, for he added, "Nude."

What *was* he talking about? "Nude," he'd said. Had there been cavortings in the plashing fountains of the Alhambra? Had a streaker accosted him in its splendid corridors? I played for safety. "Why that's . . . that's *terrible*. I really can't believe it."

He leant back in his chair. "Yeah, well, if Vanheusen thinks I'm into that kind of thing, he's goofed up. And you can tell him so."

"I'll certainly do that." I drew the writing pad towards me. "He likes serious complaints to be put in writing." I summoned up some soothing jargon. "So that it can be properly actioned." I poised my pen encouragingly. "So if you'll just go over it from the beginning . . . You were . . .?"

"In Los Cristianos, on the pier, waiting in line for a round-trip ticket to the little island out there. I wanted to see the place from where that guy Columbus made the trip to the US of A."

I wrote: *On the quayside at Los Cristianos en route to La Gomera*. What on earth had this to do with Vanheusen and Exclusive? "Yes, and . . .?"

"That quayside-wall billboard." He stopped.

Billboard? Quayside wall? He must mean the bright mural depicting fish — whale, dolphin, that kind of thing — and the huge multicoloured lettering *Los Cristianos Puerto de la Naturaleza*. Just like him to complain that it was gaudy, cheap-looking, an act of vandalism on age-old stone.

"Yes?" I prompted.

"I asked the guy next in line what the ad meant, and he told me —" He paused. "He told me that it said . . ." He leant confidingly over the table and lowered his voice. ". . . Los Cristianos opens the door to *nudism*. Seems that they're about to designate the main beach solely for the use of *naturists*."

254

Trust Wainwright to be standing next to a joker. What Los Cristianos was touting was the Environment. Nature, not naturists. Luckily he took my strangled gurgle of mirth as a cry of horror.

He nodded. "I see we're on the same wavelength. This sure changes things." The heliographs flashed annoyance. "I'd been seriously considering that penthouse condo, but looks like I'll have to pull out now."

My expression grave, I murmured, "I'm sure Mr Vanheusen will be *most* concerned. I'll report this to him immediately. He has a lot of influence behind the scenes, and pressure can be brought. You can definitely put your mind at rest."

The smoothing of Wainwright's ruffled feathers took several more minutes. By the time I had leisure to look around again, there was no sign of either Charlie or the mule.

At 9.05a.m. the next day, in accordance with Gerry's briefing, I was sitting in the Exclusive striped pavilion apparently browsing through assorted papers. Guests at the Alhambra tended to favour late breakfasts, so there wasn't much activity in the foyer — a small group waiting for their excursion bus, cameras and guidebooks at the ready, a family checking out and through the arched doorway leading to the Casablanca courtyard, an ear-phoned jogger making a slow circuit of the lake/pool, baseball cap shading eyes, slim brown legs powering a pair of designer trainers. In one minute's time the fire alarm, courtesy of Gerry, would shatter this five-star tranquillity. There was no sign of Charlie. She'd likely be holed up in her room, a few doors down the corridor from the mule, savouring the luxury of the Alhambra's crisp Sea Island cotton sheets, and sipping a cup of Earl Grey tea.

Twenty seconds to go.

Tweeeteeteeet tweeeteeteeet tweeeteeteeet. A strident twittering and chirping shattered the hush of the reception hall, as if thousands of invisible songbirds had burst out of the gilded cage in the Café Bar Oasis and were swooping and fluttering beneath the fretted arches and soaring ceilings. The staff switched smoothly into well-rehearsed fire-drill routine, interrupting the checkout and ushering the family and excursionists firmly towards the front entrance.

As they trooped out to the car park, I called over to the head of reception, "Check me off, Paco. I'm off to Muster Point D to reassure the Exclusive clients." I scooped up my papers and made for the fire assembly point.

If I hadn't known where Point D was, I'd have located it by Wainwright's whinging nasal drone, as hard on the ears as the twittering fire alarm. Pink skinny legs descending from the mass of soft terry towelling, long scrawny neck thrust belligerently forward, like an irate anaemic flamingo he was targeting the unfortunate employee in charge of the muster list.

"You hear what I say, mister? If a guy's liable to be dragged outta bed just after sun-up to hang about in a goddam parking lot, he expects to be issued with a decent robe."

The Grouch could take care of himself. My real objective was Muster Point E. I sidled discreetly round the back of a small group of guests, pausing only to have a quick word with Victoria Knight sitting placidly on one of the benches, face upturned to the warm sun.

Charlie should have latched onto the mule by now . . . And there was the mule, pale as ever, gazing nervously round as if the long arm of the law was about to reach out and seize her. But where *was* Charlie? Not among the twenty or thirty people gathered in small groups at Muster Point E, checking in their names or gazing speculatively at the windows of the Alhambra. Not among the late-risers coddled in Wainwright-maligned Alhambra bathrobes. Not beside the red-baseball-capped jogger, now sporting wraparound dark glasses, running on the spot to music on a CD player.

Well, it looked like it was up to me now. I took a step forward —

"*It's me, it's me, O Lord, jogging in the parking lot . . .*" sang the red-baseball-capped figure, trotting a nimble circle round me on those slim brown legs.

And indeed it was. Charlie had morphed again. Everything was under control. I allowed a couple of papers to flutter from my hand and chased them across the car park, catching them up at a nearby seat half-hidden by an almond-perfumed pink oleander. From there I could keep a discreet eye and ear on events.

"Hey there, Scouser. Met yesterday, remember?" Charlie's grin was open and friendly.

She received a guarded smile in return.

"Bit of a pain isn't it, this fire alarm." A slow-motion jog round the mule. "Hope you don't mind me nattering away like this." A fancy piece of jogging on the spot. Then, "I'm really cheesed off with all these false alarms. Same carry on last week from burnt toast in the kitchens. Somebody left a door open, the barman told me, and smoke drifted into the corridors." The jogging stopped as she fiddled with the CD player. "Bloody thing's stopped working! Supposed to be jog proof too . . ."

I sat back as Charlie set to work demolishing the mule's wall of reserve. By the time the *bomberos* arrived, she was on first-name terms with Lisa and they were engaged in animated discussion of pop bands and lead singers. As for me, I filled in the next half hour working on ideas for the Exclusive picnic.

The fire engine and its crew drove off. From Charlie an explosive, "At *last*! C'mon, Lisa, I'll stand you a tall latte." In heated debate about the latest pop idol, they strolled off towards the Café Bar Oasis.

"CU @ Harley's 20.30." The text message had come in from the office half an hour ago. Probably from Jayne. Must be something important if it couldn't wait till tomorrow's briefing. Had there been a sudden development re the mule?

I got there with ten minutes in hand. The big American cars — Dodge, Buick, Pontiac — icons of a world long gone, chrome fenders gleaming, paintwork polished to a mirror finish, were lined up in a last beauty parade outside the glass portals of Harley's restaurant/bar. Last in line, a battered military helicopter, dowdy Cinderella among these splendid dinosaurs, drooped its rotor blades sadly, as if cowed by the surrounding splendour. A chain and a couple of bouncers kept at bay a little group of gawkers, reinforcing the unwritten message: *Admire, but do not touch*.

Hands in pockets I strolled over to join the rubberneckers in front of a sage-green vintage two-seater with tiny rear window and Bonnie and Clyde-style upright boxy shape, all sharp lines and voluptuously rounded boot. To me, a car's a car, useful to get from one place to another and I've never been much interested in models and marques. But I have to admit I was fascinated by the huge round bowls of headlights, running boards wide enough to serve as comfortable picnic seats, and the long bonnet slashed with vertical gills like the body of a powerful fish. I was not so taken with the spindly wire-spoke wheels. *Two* spares, one strapped on each side of the bonnet, suggested all-too-frequent mishaps. And as for that flimsy bumper, elegant but oh, so useless . . .

Brakes screeched behind me. I swung round to see a taxi stalled in the middle of the road, the rear door half open.

"I *thought* it was you, dear." A cardigan-clad arm pushed the door fully open, a plump leg levered its owner out of the clutch of the pseudo-leather upholstery. "Just a *momento*, señor. I — come — back." Oblivious to the outbreak of hooting horns, Victoria stepped onto the pavement. "I saw you and just *had* to ask you *now*. You see, about El Sueño, I've decided there's nothing I can do . . ."

So she had finally given up her dream of El Sueño. Just as well. Little old lady versus all that Vanheusen clout, no contest.

". . . for a couple of weeks, that is. The Reservation Contract runs only till the end of the month. As you said, dear, there's always hope. So what do you think? Can I arrange with Mr Vanheusen to stay on at the Alhambra till then?"

"*Not* a good idea," I said quickly.

"Oh . . . I was so sure . . ." Her face crumpled, her shoulders sagged. Inside the woolly cardigan, the chubby body seemed to slump.

Damn. Urgent retrieval of situation required. "Not a good idea to *tell* Mr Vanheusen anything, I mean."

An all-terrain baby buggy was rapidly bearing down on us. I steered Victoria towards the next-in-line of Harley vehicles, an ugly Pontiac built like an armoured car, bulky metal visor reducing windscreen to a slit, bumper that would do credit to a bulldozer.

"In property matters, Victoria, you have to play things close to the chest, never reveal your hand to the opposition. If the contract *does* fall through, and they know you're out there waiting, they'll bump up the price."

I wasn't giving her false hopes or being kind now to be cruel later. The way Operation Canary Creeper was progressing, there was a good chance that Vanheusen would be behind bars before the month was out. The company's assets would take some time to sort out, but perhaps a way could be found to . . .

A slow smile lit up her face. "So you *do* think it's worth a try?"

"I think that if you return home without giving this a go, you'll *always* regret it. If you agree, we'll leave Mr Vanheusen out of it and I'll quietly arrange for you to stay on at the Alhambra."

"Nothing venture, nothing win. That's what my Jack always said. And . . ." a whisper so soft, I had to strain to hear above the roar of a passing Titsa bus, "one day he won the Big One."

She waved a hand in vague acknowledgement of another impatient *beep beep beeep* from her abandoned taxi. "*Momento, momento.*" Leisurely, refusing to be rushed, she fished in her handbag and held out Exclusive's invitation to the Farewell Cruise. "You'll want this back, then. I'd been so looking forward to it, but I'd be an impostor, wouldn't I?"

"Victoria," I said, "playing things close to the chest means exactly that. Don't change any arrangements that don't have to be changed. The cruise will be going ahead anyway, for Herbert. What's one more passenger to a man like Mr Vanheusen? I think he can afford the expense, don't you?"

Beeeeeeeeep from the taxi. The engine revved to a high scream. "You come or no come, señora?" Another ear-splitting rev.

"I come, I come." She stuffed the card back into her bag and scuttled across the road.

"Remember," I called after her, "say nothing — not even to Herbert."

Hand on the half-open door, she turned towards me. An eyelid drooped in a slow conspiratorial wink. "My lips are sealed, dear."

Eight-twenty-five. I'd go in now. If you've ever been to Harley's, you'll know that it's not exactly *quiet* — its cheerful bustle, conversation-drowning music and subdued lighting made it perfect for a clandestine rendezvous. I joined the small queue of those waiting to be shown to a table, giving me the chance to eyeball a monstrous, macho Harley Davidson on its circular dais, a sparkling chrome juggernaut, the very personification of power and speed aptly called The Beast.

"Hi there, I'm Suzy." A girl in a black T-shirt and black trousers rattled off the Harley greeting in an Australian twang. "Do you want to sit upstairs in the Sports Bar, or here in the restaurant? Smoking or non-smoking?"

"Restaurant, non-smoking and over at the back." It was darker there.

With a deft movement she fielded a black and white booklet from the stack and turned to scan the tables. "Nothing free over there at the moment. 'Fraid we're real busy tonight."

She steered me towards *Sunset Blvd*, an alcove to the right of a red neon sign flashing WC. Not as private as I'd hoped, considering it was adjacent to the flight path to the loo, but on second thoughts, possibly better —

those heading in that direction would have their gaze fixed on the sign and their mind on the objective.

"Why not have a lee-surely drink while you choose your meal?" She thrust the black and white booklet into my hands, switched on a practised smile, and swept off.

I'd been thinking of an unadventurous, bog-standard beer. I scanned the drinks on offer. Harley's Comfortable Screw, Benders Banshee, Bubblegum Shot, One Between the Sheets . . . Flaming Zombie, rum and fruit juice with a circle of flaming fire. Now that sounded intriguing. But regrettably, no. Nothing, alas, would be more likely to draw attention to my darkish corner than a circle of flaming fire.

"Mind if I sit here?" asked an American voice.

"Sorry," I said, continuing to study the multicoloured pages of the drinks' list, "seat's taken."

As if I hadn't spoken, the female pulled back the chair and flopped down.

"Excuse me! I just told you —" I registered the spiky hair, the nose ring, the eyebrow stud, the cheeky grin. I had to hand it to Charlie. Nobody would associate her now with the stylishly fashionable young woman lounging in the Alhambra foyer or this morning's baseball-capped young fitness freak. And she'd engineered the meeting perfectly.

Suzy returned, pencil poised.

"I'll have a small beer," I said.

Gold nose ring glinting, Charlie ran her finger down the drinks' list. "Make mine a Benders Banshee."

Suzy put the pencil to work, handed over two menus, and headed back to the door. New customer, same smile.

"Don't you just love the decor? That traffic sign over there is a scream." Charlie dissolved in a fit of giggles. "*Soft Shoulders. No standing at any time.*"

"Something come up, then?" I asked as we flipped open our menus.

Charlie got down to business. "You may have noticed that after the little excitement of the fire alarm, Lisa and I were quite buddy-buddy?"

I nodded.

"So, over a latte or two we shared confidences. I told her about my partner knocking me about and cheating on me with my best friend — and of how I got my revenge."

I raised an eyebrow.

Charlie returned my look. "Tell 'em what they want to know. She looks like the kind of poor sod that guys take advantage of in that way."

"Result?"

"Instant bonding. We cried on each other's shoulders and agreed to meet up again in the bar at Happy Hour. I wasn't sure if she'd turn up, but she did. I launched her on a hot chocolate and brandy — I'd told the barman to make hers double strength — and after the second, the oyster opened up."

"And a pearl was inside?"

"You bet. Gerry was like a cat with a dish of cream."

"Cats don't like cream," I said. "Anyway, it's bad for them."

264

"Figuratively speaking, pedant." She pretended to sulk. "You're tarnishing my golden moment."

"Oh come on, Charlie, get on with it."

Things were hotting up at Harley's, and so were the decibels. She leant forward so that her head was close to mine. "Her 'friend', as she calls him, said he'd meet her at the Alhambra, but there's been a change of plan. She's to meet him tomorrow over in Gomera at Valle Gran Rey."

"If we knew which ferry . . ." My plans for the Outing were fairly fluid. Places and times could be easily altered.

Charlie grinned triumphantly. "Found that out too. She's taking the 0900 catamaran. Gerry's instructions: you've to keep tabs on her, get as much as you can on the handover."

CHAPTER
TWENTY-ONE

Pale sunlight crept down the foothills of Teide, fingering dark outcrops and glinting off windows in the scattering of white houses high above the port. The *Hasta Luego* Outing to La Gomera was the final entertainment for Herbert Wainwright and Victoria before they flew home, with or without purchasing property from Exclusive. A lot of last-minute planning had been necessary to dovetail our itinerary with the mule's arrival at the remote harbour of Valle Gran Rey. The resulting changes meant I'd be in big trouble with Wainwright when he discovered that we wouldn't be making the scheduled visit to Columbus's house and "The Spring That Baptised America".

Talking of trouble, there he was, standing on the quay. With his Bermuda-length white shorts, thin hairless legs and knobbly knees, he reminded me of an ungainly stork dispossessed of its favourite chimney pot. He was looking pointedly from his wristwatch to the empty berth where our private-hire catamaran should have been tied up. Quite lost on Herbert G Wainwright that special early morning feel to the air, the tang of salt and fish and the picturesque charm of the red and blue fishing boats dancing in the ruffled waters of the harbour.

He marched up to me. "I guess we've got a no-show here."

"No need to worry, Mr Wainwright. There's our boat rounding the harbour mole. Now, about the — er, problem you brought to my attention on Monday." I cast a meaningful glance in the direction of the colourful *Puerto de la Naturaleza* mural on the harbour wall. "Mr Vanheusen has been updating me on how he's dealing with it." I launched into a long and entirely fictitious account of meetings with the mayor, ending with, "You have his assurance that he's making progress."

Wainwright compressed his lips into a thin line. "I sure hope so. Nothing's gonna be signed till I see results."

Dear me, it looked like Exclusive was going to lose out on another deal, but I felt I was doing Wainwright a favour. Once the Vanheusen empire began to crumble — sooner rather than later, if Operation Canary Creeper came off — things would get pretty sticky for any investor.

I looked round for Victoria. There she was, XXL-size handbag swinging from one arm ("for the shopping, dear"), cardigan tightly buttoned against morning chill, lining up the approaching catamaran in the viewfinder of her cheap-and-cheerful disposable camera.

Wainwright shaded his eyes against the pale rays of the rising sun and studied the approaching ship. "Not exactly the *Queen Elizabeth*, is it?"

The heavy seas that had delayed the catamaran ferry were all too apparent after we left the shelter of Tenerife. Uneasily I eyed the paper sick-bag as a wave slammed against the side, lashing the window with a sheet of spray. The ship swooped, checked abruptly, swooped again. Moments later the unmistakable sound of breaking glass came from the direction of the bar. I looked to see how my clients were coping. Herbert Wainwright was gazing out at the white-caps flecking the unbroken expanse of blue. Not a complaint or whinge to be heard. Victoria was immersed in an illustrated guide to Gomera, oblivious, it seemed, to the lurching motion of the ship. I was the only one who was suffering. *Splat* on the window. Perhaps if I imagined myself riding these waves on a windsurfer, leaning out on the harness, the wind in my hair, the water frothing under the board . . . I stood up, body relaxed, knees flexing to the motion transmitted through the soles of my feet. That was better.

A violent right-angled turn sent me staggering sideways to collapse back into my seat. With a stomach-churning sea-saw motion, the horizon tipped violently sideways . . . and righted itself. Swoop. Lurch.

Just as it looked like nothing could save me from an ignominious resort to the sick-bag, the rolling suddenly eased. With that sharp turn, the catamaran was now running parallel to the shore. Flat brown hazy land sharpened into cloud-capped mountains and the reddish brown cliffs and white cubed houses of San Sebastian.

Click. Click. Click. Captured for Victoria's album were the red and white fishing boats pulled up on the black sand. "That line of palm trees. Doesn't it remind you of Nice and the Promenade des Anglais?" *Click. Click. Click.*

Misery-guts Wainwright morosely studied the grey cloud-cap that hung low over the green mountainous interior, dispatching exploratory wispy tendrils down towards the little town. "Looks like rain."

A good moment for me to announce that change in the itinerary. "Luckily we're not stopping in San Sebastian. We're going round to the other side of the island."

"This here is San Sebastian and we're not stopping? We're *not* gonna be touring the Columbus house or the Spring? I've a bottle ready to fill."

"We'll be stopping on our way back," I soothed. "It'll be much quieter when all the other tours have gone."

As the boat was obviously not putting into port, he had to be content with that.

Forty minutes later we arrived at Valle Gran Rey. Engines throttled back, we slid into the small harbour crouched in the shelter of a towering red headland. At its foot the sea was tinged a vivid emerald green. A seagull soared, a white speck against the cliff's shadowy mass. But the scenery hardly registered. My mind was on the mule. I'd be free to keep tabs on her once Victoria and Wainwright were on their way to the premises of Palm Honey Gomera.

As soon as I'd waved them off, I picked up the keys for a previously arranged rental car and parked it near the gates to the port, wheels to follow wheels if she got into a car. If I had to trail her on foot, strolling tourists would provide cover. To one side of the harbour was a small patch of beach strategically placed to give me a view of the jetty. From this safe distance I'd be able to see her arrive on the slower car ferry. I spread out a beach towel, disguised myself behind a large pair of sunglasses, and waited . . .

Not many passengers disembarked. A family with a toddler in a pushchair, an old woman dressed in black, three hikers with backpacks, a smart-suited business-man with briefcase, a group of cyclists. The old woman hobbled slowly along the quay. The family bundled toddler and pushchair into a waiting taxi. The businessman sat on a chair at the little harbour-side café and talked into his mobile phone. The hikers consulted their map and strode purposefully off in the direction of the town. The cyclists mounted their bikes and rode off, weaving in and out of the little crowd of bystanders. There was no sign of the mule. My eyes scanned the jetty. Had she outsmarted us? Led Charlie up the garden path, created a smokescreen while she made contact somewhere else, sold us a pup? With a sigh, I concluded she had. I took off my floppy hat and started to fold up the towel. *There she was*, stepping onto the quay, a slight figure in white trousers, white shirt, carrying a pink shoulder bag. I crammed the towel into my bag, and by the time she approached the small café, I was sitting on the harbour wall two hundred metres away studying a guidebook. She passed

270

the café without a glance. The rendezvous was not there.

At the gate to the port she stood for a moment looking about her. I lowered my head into the book and waited for her to make her move. After that moment's hesitation, she set off briskly round the corner that led to the coast road, ignoring the narrow streets twisting upwards into the town. She'd have to be back to catch the last ferry at four o'clock, so the rendezvous would have to be within easy walking distance. That indicated somewhere on the coast road itself.

She was out of sight for the couple of minutes it took for me to get into the car and negotiate the light traffic and strolling pedestrians. If I lost her now . . . I relaxed. In the middle-distance the slim figure, that shocking-pink tote-bag swinging on shoulder, was striding along the wide pavement under a line of jaunty shuttlecock palms. Ahead, the coastal promenade stretched arrow-straight to Calela, the next village. She'd be in sight all the way. I drew into the kerb.

The sea was a mass of turbulent white-caps. Close to the shore, lines of surf creamed and a long surfers' wave swelled. I watched it rear, curl into a tube, and toss a mist of spindrift skywards before it thundered down onto the rocks in a flurry of foam. Moments later came the long roaring rumble of lava stones tumbling and dragging in the undertow.

She had almost reached the first houses of the village. It was time to make a move. I started up the engine and crept along as slowly as I dared, far enough back not to spook her, but close enough to see if she made a sudden dart into one of the premises she was passing. But she walked briskly on, straight through Calela, glancing neither to right nor left — nor behind. A woman with a mission.

I cut the engine. The road stretched ahead, the sea to the left, banana plantations and jagged mountains to the right. The rendezvous could only be at La Playa, that distant scatter of white buildings shining in the sun, a hamlet revamped as a mini-seaside resort where bronzed bodies and fishermen's boats competed for space on the black stony beach. I calculated it would take Lisa a good fifteen minutes. No shade for her, no cover for me. By the time she reached La Playa, she'd be hot, tired and dusty from dodging on-coming traffic. Her guard would be down. I'd go ahead of her and wait for her to arrive. She wouldn't be suspicious of anyone sitting on the sea wall as she passed, or in one of those cafés, making short work of a cool San Miguel.

And that was exactly what I was now doing, sitting in a café, glass in hand, guidebook and map spread out on table, tracking the pink speck of her bag as she trudged towards the village. Her pace was not so brisk now, more of a plod. As I'd thought, heat and distance were taking its toll.

The promenade was busy with tourists strolling, sitting on the sea wall, eating at café tables. Too early to say if anyone was taking an interest in that eye-catching bag, as good as a placard round her neck, the ID for her contact. He or she would make a move only at the last moment. And so would I. I'd already paid for my beer, so I could move quickly if they went off together. And

I'd chosen my table for its angle to the mirror that ran along the right-hand wall. If they came in here, I could do my Lady of Shalott act and watch them via the mirror. Be Prepared and Leave Options Open, as Gerry might say.

Lisa was closer now . . . But I still had a couple of minutes to fill with tourist-type action while I watched and waited. I pushed away the beer glass and flicked through the pages of the guidebook till I found the postcard I'd bought in the shop next door. *Having a wonderful time*, I scribbled, then, as if seeking inspiration, gazed thoughtfully out at the street.

Lisa had arrived. She was twenty metres away, her back to the beach, eyes darting to left and right. I chewed at the end of the pen and added, *here in Gomera*. I let my gaze travel aimlessly over the people in the street. Nobody had moved forward to greet her. She took a few hesitant steps to the right, then to the left. Inexperienced Lisa was attracting attention. I wrote a few more words on the postcard. *Spending the morning at La Playa*. She was still doing that little dance of indecision. I took a sip of beer and added, *Going to visit the pottery vill —*

I half-glimpsed a sudden movement among the idle spectators sitting with their backs to me, legs dangling over the sea wall as they sized up the talent on the beach. A thickset man in a check shirt had swivelled round and half-vaulted onto the promenade. *John Sinclair*.

I let the pen drop from my fingers and took cover by scrabbling for it under the table. I could see Lisa, or rather her white-trousered legs, one sandalled foot tapping the ground restlessly. A moment later, faded green trousers and black slip-ons came to a halt beside the sandals. A good vantage point this, but any longer down here would make *me* the focus of unwelcome attention.

I raised my head cautiously above the rim of the table. They were still talking, just outside the door. Seated again, head bowed, I applied the newly retrieved pen to postcard. *Going to visit the pottery village where plan is to buy a big pot for the garden.* Head propped on hand, I risked a quick glance through spread fingers. They'd choose somewhere less public than a crowded promenade for the exchange, so nothing would yet have been handed over. Once they moved off, I'd follow. I swept postcard and pen into my bag.

When I looked up, they were standing just inside the door looking round for an empty table. Would Sinclair recognise me as the silly girl who'd accompanied Jason on *The Saucy Nancy*? He'd seen me only briefly at the start and end of the trip. Apart from that unfortunate throwing-up in the oil drum episode, I'd spent the time flat on my back in the cabin clutching a sick-bag. He'd been up on the con tower most of the time, and he'd had no reason, no reason at all, to be suspicious of the hare-brained girlfriend. Contrary to what Jason thought, you can't fake that distinctive greenish pallor of seasickness. No, he wouldn't remember me. Neither would Lisa, who'd seen me only briefly at the fire muster point. Nevertheless, I whipped on my sunglasses. Hide your eyes, hide your interest.

Two tables were empty, one within earshot, slightly in front and to my left. Ideal. The other, across the room, was further away and behind me, but visible in the mirror. Not so ideal. And that, sod's law, was the one they chose. While their attention was on giving a waiter their order, I flipped open my camera phone, laid it on the table as if waiting for a call, and lined it up on the mirror to ensure I would capture the exchange. Then to blend in with the surroundings, I applied myself once more to the postcard. *Don't know how I'll get a big pot back in the plane though!* When he made the exchange, I'd be ready.

"The señora is finished?" said a voice at my shoulder. The waiter gathered up my empty glass and wiped the table as an indication that I was expected to leave. The *bête noire* of a busy café is the lone postcard-writing customer who blocks a table at busy times.

"Ah, señor, I've been trying to order." I flashed him a winning smile. "Would you bring me a coffee?" I slid a ten euro note over the table, adding the Spanish for "Keep the change" and another smile, conveying *mucho* gratitude.

"At once, señora." We'd come to an understanding. My observation post was safe.

But in these few vital moments, I'd almost missed the exchange. Sinclair was passing across a rolled-up magazine. Lisa's hand had stretched out to take it. I reached forward to press the *capture* button.

"The señora did not say if she wishes the coffee *con leche*."

275

Shit, shit, shit. The waiter was blocking the camera's view of the mirror. It was essential to obtain photographic evidence of the handover, and I wasn't going to get it. An apologetic, "Well you see, I was busy ordering coffee and chatting up the waiter," wouldn't go down too well with Gerry.

"*Si, con leche,*" I said and he moved aside.

The magazine had been withdrawn back onto Sinclair's lap while a waiter manoeuvred plates, saucers and beer glasses into position on the stylish but somewhat bijou table. Saved. To my rescue had come a deus ex machina in the shape of their lunch order. The tension of the thwarted exchange was reflected in Sinclair's set shoulders and Lisa's unnaturally stiff pose and clenched hands.

In the mirror I watched the waiter slip the bill under the menu holder, swing the tray under his arm and turn to another table. Sinclair's hand closed on the magazine. I reached forward and rested my finger lightly on the camera phone's shutter button. The magazine changed hands. *Click.* Digital capture.

Lisa fumbled in the pink tote bag and pulled out a video cassette box . . . *click* . . . and dropped it on the floor. Her fingers closed over the box . . . *click* . . . She was levering herself upright . . . She stretched out a hand to Sinclair . . . *click* . . . The cassette case with its cover pic of snow-capped Teide and red poinsettias was being slipped into a pocket in the leg of Sinclair's green trousers . . . *click.*

I punched a number into my mobile, texted, "*La Playa Caf Blu tbl 4*" and "*Go*".

276

My coffee arrived. I sipped it slowly. Lisa was forking the last piece of lettuce into her mouth when the unmarked car drew up outside. Seconds later four *Guardia Civil* officers sprinted through the open doorway and surrounded their table. No opportunity for Sinclair to get rid of that incriminating video case. No opportunity for Lisa to pocket the wad of banknotes and drop the magazine. It was one of the slickest snatches I've seen. In less than two minutes the *Guardia* scooped them up and drove off, blue flashing light now clamped to the car roof.

It seemed a pity to waste that postcard. I drew it towards me and added, *Gomera is very quiet. Nothing much ever happens here*, and addressed it to Jason.

My lunch with Victoria and Herbert G went rather well. Their evident overindulgence in palm honey liqueur, and my elation over this first real success for Operation Canary Creeper, cast a blissfully euphoric glow over our simple picnic on a secluded beach.

CHAPTER
TWENTY-TWO

Next morning I was still on a high; you know how it is, humming away to myself in the Exclusive office, all life's little difficulties surveyed through rose-tinted glasses. I could even find a touch of classical romanticism in the heavy brocades and ugly dark furniture inflicted by the late unlamented Cousin Ashley. Or view with equanimity this note from Monique. *Be a dear*, it cooed, *and dash off these invitations. Won't take you a minute.* Attached were four pages of addresses.

Rose-tinted glasses still perched on nose — at least I wasn't being asked to write them out by hand — I switched on the computer. While the mail-merge programme opened, I studied one of the invitations. Inscribed in gold lettering on red card were the words, *Ambrose Vanheusen invites you to the unveiling of the Art Work commissioned in honour of Samarkand Black Prince.*

"*Explain!*" The words rang out like a pistol shot.

My arm collided with the stack of invitations, scattering the blood-red cards over the floor like the splatter from some dreadful massacre. Hands on hips, eyes narrowed, face flushed, Monique stood framed in the doorway, in her black silk shirt and black designer trousers the epitome of an avenging gunslinger making his entrance to a Wild West saloon.

"I don't know what you . . ." I trailed off.

"I — think — you — do, Deborah." Each word was rasped out. She strode forward, melodramatically planting both hands on the desk, arms straight. "Allow me to aid your memory, my dear." Her eyes bored into mine. "*Nudes*."

It took a second or two to register that she was referring to Wainwright and the *Naturaleza* mural. I fought against an overpowering desire to giggle. Laughing would only make matters worse. Biting my lip, I gazed down at the desk.

"You understand me, I see," she stood up, arms folded.

I nodded. "Mr Wainwright has —"

"— has just told me he is not going to sign the contract for the luxury apartment in Los Cristianos. And when I asked him *why*," she took a deep breath, "he said something like, 'Can't take the risk of nudes on the beach in front of the condo' and said *you* knew all about it." The angry flush deepened. "*Well?*" She didn't pause for an answer. "I was right. Ambrose should *never* have hired you." Two fiery spots burnt in her cheeks. "You were unreliable from the outset. And when it came to following instructions, *totally* unreliable . . . the nerve of gatecrashing a private party . . . thanks to your meddling we've now lost another client . . ."

Unstoppable. I let it all flow over me. I was heading for dismissal again, and this time there'd be no hope of reinstatement.

The fiery spots burnt brighter. "A lot of money is involved . . . and now that the casino project's fallen through . . ."

I mustn't make eye contact, mustn't betray any interest in the casino.

". . . absolutely *central* to Ambrose's plans. Without it —"

"*Monique.*" Vanheusen stood in the doorway, in his tone and expression an unspoken warning.

The ensuing silence crackled with tension.

Chwunk. A car door closed in the courtyard below.

His suave mask slipped back into place. "Ah, Deborah, I see you're dealing with the invitations. Leave them for a moment, will you? Monique can handle it." A sharp glance in her direction. "There's something I've been meaning to discuss with you, Deborah. We'll have a little chat over coffee."

Her lips compressed in a thin, angry line. It would be guerrilla warfare in the office from now on, if I escaped being sacked, that is. But as I followed Vanheusen, I'd something more immediate on my mind. The subject of this little tête-à-tête could only be Persepolis Desert Sandstorm. And no matter how prettily packaged, it would be a demand, not a request. A demand for a mating with that thug of a cat of his, I was sure of it.

But during half an hour of pleasant chat about this and that, the subject wasn't brought up at all.

280

"Let's cut out all this formality, Deborah," he'd said. "It's Ambrose from now on." Liqueur bottle poised, his smile was warm. "A toast to The Prince and Persepolis?"

I left clutching my invitation to the Unveiling of the Art Work, an invitation personally presented by the manicured hand of Ambrose himself. Disturbingly there'd been no mention at all of mating our moggies. As I turned at the door to smile my farewell, he was sitting there, fingers interlaced, thumb thoughtfully stroking his upper lip, calculation in those pale eyes. That really set the alarm bells ringing.

It had, of course, been on the cards from the start of Operation Canary Creeper that Vanheusen might take too close an interest in Gorgonzola. That coffee tête-à-tête was definitely an amber alert.

The next day amber stepped up to red when Vanheusen made his move via a surprisingly cordial phone call from Monique.

It began with a warm, sisterly, "Ah, Deborah, so glad to have caught you." Yesterday it had been daggers drawn, today it was best buddies. "Just to let you know that the venue for the farewell reception has been changed from the Alhambra to *Samarkand Princess*. The limousine will collect you and our guests from the Alhambra tomorrow at 11 a.m. Return from the yacht will be at about four."

On the surface what she'd said seemed harmless enough. What alerted me was the sudden change of venue to Vanheusen's yacht. There must be a hidden agenda. Once out at sea I'd be safely out of the way. Using a passkey they'd slide into Calle Rafael Alberti numero 2 with that plump little Reikimaster in tow. And Gorgonzola would be at their mercy. That velvety voice, those caressing hands, would oh-so-expertly lure her into a carrier. I could visualise it all. I'd return to an empty house with no signs of forced entry. It would appear that G had strayed or wandered off. That would be their plan, or something like it.

It was time to set in motion the prearranged measures for Gorgonzola's early departure. I stared into her copper eyes and wondered how she would cope. She hated flying. Up to now I had always been there to pick her up within an hour of the plane landing, but this time . . . And then, accustomed as she was to home comforts, HMRC's kennels were no place for a cat, especially a cat of sensibilities . . . She stirred uneasily under my scrutiny, head lowered, pupils contracting to vertical slits.

If Vanheusen got his hands on her, he'd soon discover that she was no use for breeding. In a cold rage, he would turn his attention to me. He'd want information out of me, so there'd be no quick breaking of the neck or dashing out of brains for G — or for Deborah Smith. Those manicured hands would go to work on *her*. And he'd know just the way to do it. I would be forced to listen to her cries. Look into those pain-filled, pleading eyes while . . .

I picked up my mobile and rang Extreme Travel.

"Hi, Jayne. It's Debs. About the cheese I was delegated to buy for the party . . . I'll be tied up all day tomorrow at Exclusive's farewell reception. Could you collect it for me? Tomorrow, about ten? That's great. Owe you one." A prearranged coded message for G to be removed to safety and repatriated to the UK.

But I wasn't out of the woods yet. I'd have to concoct a story to explain her disappearance to Vanheusen. Lost, stolen, strayed? I stared thoughtfully at Gorgonzola. She could be run over while I was away all day on the yacht, the corpse collected by La Caleta Cleansing's Rapid Response squad. And I'd find it easy enough to act distraught. I'd only have to picture Vanheusen's torturing hands.

"C'mon, G," I said, gathering her up in my arms. "Last chance to listen to a *madrelena* from Jesús before you go."

Next morning, at ten o'clock, a white van bearing the logo *Electrodomésticos* drew up outside my door. Two burly men in green overalls heaved onto a trolley a large cardboard carton, contents one new under-worktop-size three-star refrigerator. The battered fridge they wheeled out five minutes later contained a wicker cat-carrier, contents one hopping-mad red Persian cat.

"Oooh." Victoria was wide-eyed, her mouth an O of astonishment. "When you said 'yacht', I thought you meant one of those little things with sails. I don't mind telling you, dear, that I thought it was all going to be a bit uncomfortable. Not to mention cold." She fingered the buttons of her cashmere cardigan. "I needn't have worried, need I, Herbie?"

A grunt from Wainwright. His eyes flicked from the white four-decker ship to the lavishly illustrated leaflet in his hand. "Nothing chintzy about this guy Vanheusen. Getta hold of this . . . *58,000-gallon fuel tank*. Seems it can barrel from the South Pole to the Arctic without gassing up."

"Why on earth would anyone want to do that, Herbie? All those shopping opportunities missed. Now *this* is more like it." Her finger stabbed down on the picture of an indoor pool decorated in Greek temple style. "This is what *I* call luxury. *A 12-seater spa pool with a hundred massage jets*. Oooh, lovely."

He didn't seem to have heard. "There's a tackle room with fifty fishing rods —"

"And for those who want to build up an appetite for lunch, a couple of jet skis and three sailboards," said Vanheusen's voice from above our heads. He was leaning on the rail, the very image of the millionaire playboy, tanned skin, glints of gold in his hair, casual white outfit no doubt costing the earth. His eyes rested on me. "Yours to try out, Deborah. You told me the other day you were into windsurfing."

Mr Affability himself. Well, why wouldn't he be? Once we set sail his men would swoop on G. By this evening Persepolis Desert Sandstorm would be his.

During coffee, held on the after-deck patio, we kept fairly close to the coast. Vanheusen pointed out landmarks and played Mine Genial Host to perfection, like all conmen, a master of psychology. Within quarter of an hour he'd subtly pinpointed our interests, smoothly playing each of us, reeling in and letting us run, till he'd hooked us all on some splendid offering on the yacht. Half an hour later, in the Spa Suite Jacuzzi, a hundred watery fingers were massaging a blissful Victoria. In the tackle room Herbert Wainwright was in his element sizing up each rod, assessing the balance — and finding a reason to reject.

As for me, I was now lolling on one of the white suede sofas, listening to the concealed hi-fi system softly playing Beethoven's *Romance No.2 in F*, surround-sound of course. Alone. Vanheusen had retreated to his cabin to take an urgent business call. I could make a pretty good guess as to who would be on the other end.

Lolling on the sofa, like Brer Rabbit I was "lying low and saying nothing" — but thinking a lot. Before I had experienced the sybaritic pleasures of *Samarkand Princess*, I'd always had it in my mind that a life on the ocean wave wasn't for me. I'd thought of it as cold, often wet, and all too frequently nausea-inducing, to be endured rather than enjoyed. Now here I was in a lounge stunning in its stark minimalism, sipping champagne, allowing myself one glass only, of course. An exploratory toe confirmed that the polished teak floor was the real thing, not laminate. The walls were a shadowy-white, sea-mist grey, I suppose you'd call it, if you wanted to keep the marine ambience. The soft white leather sofas were ever so stylish but impracticably low-backed. A Milky Way of downlighters sparkled on the ceiling. I'm a sucker for new technology — except, as you will have gathered, of the boys' toys kind — so I resisted for a full thirty seconds before stretching out a hand to the lighting touch-pad on the white marble coffee table, buttons variously labelled *fade up, fade down, moonlight blue, dawn pink, forest-glade green*. I pressed *forest-glade green*. Very restful . . . the crystalline-white petals of that ostentatiously extravagant planter of moth orchids were now a luminous aquamarine; that artistic plate of yellow lemons had magicked into a plate of limes. With all these lighting effects there'd be no need to change the decor or accessories. Maybe Tomás could fix me up something similar in Calle Rafael Alberti . . .

I closed my eyes and envisaged Vanheusen in his suite, hunched over a large-scale map of La Caleta, inching his Reiki-master marker ever closer to Calle Rafael Alberti, numero 2.

"Pleasant dreams?"

I opened my eyes. He was lounging on the sofa across from me, thumb thoughtfully stroking his upper lip in that strangely unsettling gesture.

"Mmm," I said, smiling inwardly at the thought of G's bowl of Cat Snax left prominently in the kitchen, and the thugs sitting there impatiently waiting for her. He'd be wondering why that "mission accomplished" call hadn't come. The smile reached my lips. "Just abandoning myself to the life of luxury, er . . . Ambrose."

He laughed. "Not much life in a one-day visit. A long weekend, now . . ." His eyes measured me for his bed.

I set the empty glass down on the side table. "You're forgetting I've a cat to look after. What would Persepolis do while . . . No, I couldn't leave her."

Perhaps that was a mistake. He'd be bound to offer G and me joint accommodation on board, *plus* a personal audience with Black Prince.

"I think you'll find that you won't —" He stopped. His turn for the secret smile? "Well, the offer stands. If you're ready, I'll show you the rest of the yacht. You'll see what you'll be missing . . ."

And, much as I disliked the man, I had to hand it to him. The modern furnishings were of the highest quality, nothing standard, or off even the most expensive peg. Everything had been specially commissioned, from flower vases to cushion covers, from carpets to bathroom taps. I would never, of course, admit to Gerry and Jason that I'd been impressed. In arguments with them I'd dismissed boats like this as no better than glorified floating caravans, cramped and hot. But Vanheusen's yacht was designer boutique, spa, private island hotel, all rolled into one — guest apartments and bathrooms to die for, and a state-of-the-art thalassotherapy suite, a marvel of mirrored ceilings and picture windows, sea-green tiling and miniature palms in terracotta pots. I'd have lingered, open-mouthed like some country yokel, but he whisked me through them all with an airy wave of his hand.

On deck once more, he stopped at the largest of the ship's three boats, a rakish three-decker power cruiser big enough to be a floating caravan in its own right. Black and menacing, it crouched in its cradle, a panther poised to hunt.

"A beauty, isn't she?" He ran his hand lovingly over the gleaming hull. "Top speed 30 knots, range 440 nautical miles, twin 440 diesels."

"Wow, it's one of those game-fishing boats." I tilted my head back and squinted against the glare of the sun. "What's that contraption on top, like a lifeguard platform?"

He shot me an amused glance. "It's a Global Transmitter. Safety gear. If we lose radio contact, *Samarkand Princess* can use GPS to track her."

Or to track floating packages. *Yes, that's how it was done.* A Global Positioning Transmitter signalling to a Global Tracking Device. A stealth vessel homing in on the target, dark packages bobbing in the vast expanse of the Atlantic . . .

To hide my excitement, I turned away. "I don't fancy taking a trip in that. I'm turning green at the thought — it's not envy, though. I'm a hopeless sailor if it's at all rough. Funny, I can windsurf in Force 5 and it doesn't bother me at all."

You know how it is when you're trying too hard to cover up something, you babble on, say something you later regret. Not that it would have made any difference. He'd have got me onto that sailboard somehow.

"Yes, you mentioned you were into water sports. On *Samarkand Princess* we've got jet skis, underwater scooters, scuba gear . . ." Exactly what he needed for collecting those packages. "And, of course, a couple of sailboards. How about working up a little appetite before lunch?"

Just like Millie, I made it easy for him. "I'd *love* to have a go on one of your sailboards. It's been weeks since there's been a good wind."

Just like Millie, I'd forgotten the kind of man I was dealing with. To be honest, I'd been so concerned with Vanheusen's designs on Gorgonzola, that I'd not given a thought to the possibility that I might also be in danger — not because I was under suspicion, but because if he got rid of me, Gorgonzola would be his.

"It's blowing a Force 4 to 5 today, judging from those white crests on the waves. Take that board there. I'll take this one." He pointed to a mean, lean, racing machine with fluorescent yellow footstraps. "I haven't had the chance to try it out since it was delivered last week. We'll put it through its paces."

Well, I couldn't resist the thought of skimming over those waves, leaning out, wind in the hair, all the time nursing that secret warm glow from outwitting his dastardly plans for G. So five minutes later I was changing into a wetsuit in a guest suite with one of those bathrooms to die for — wall mirrors, pale wood and creamy egg-shaped polished stone bath complete with gold-plated taps. I performed a fancy whirl in front of the angled corner mirrors, generating a chorus line of red-and-black neoprene-clad figures pirouetting to infinity. I waved and grinned. They waved and grinned back.

I sat on the edge of that wonderful bath and ran a hand over its sensuous curves. Should I? Yes. I swung my legs over and slid into its depths. I lay back and closed my eyes, imagining scented soapy suds, soft

289

music playing, lights romantically dim . . . Just the pampering I'd need when I returned from my whirl over — and no doubt occasionally under — the chilly waves. Mustn't keep Ambrose waiting, though. I clambered out and tugged on the neoprene boots.

He was standing on the boat-launch-cum-bathing deck, his suit a snazzily understated black and yellow. The slap of waves against hull had replaced the thrum of powerful engines as *Samarkand Princess* idled head-on to the run of the waves, ten or so miles off the Los Gigantes cliffs.

"Happy with that board, Deborah?"

I was indeed. It was not your usual hire board, battered and slightly dated. This should give that lean, mean racing board of his a bit of competition. And a nice touch, the red and black of my suit was an exact match for the sail.

"Like it, eh? That sail's a six metre. That do?"

"Fine," I said.

The wind tugged impatiently at the sail as he slid the board into the water. I stepped on, lifted the rig and clipped the harness onto my buoyancy aid. I leant out and powered across the waves. *Ya-hee-ee.* Arms braced against the pull of the sail, legs flexing to transmit the wind force to the board, I heard nothing but the water bubbling and hissing under the tail. I forgot everything, lost myself in watery combat against the elements. Forgot about Vanheusen and his plans for Gorgonzola, forgot about Victoria Knight and El Sueño, forgot Gerry and the office behind the white door. Forgot Millie Prentice and her fate.

290

Exhilaration. The board was a living thing beneath my feet, gathering speed, planing across the breaking crests of a picture-postcard blue sea. I looked up at the black cat logo on the red sail and hummed the opening bars of "The Ride of the Valkyrie". Alas, regardless of her doom, the foolish victim plays . . .

The shout came slightly behind and off to my right, words torn away by the wind. I turned my head and squinted across my shoulder. The yellow sail with its black cat logo was coming up fast, a welter of white foam beneath the raised nose of the board, the black-suited figure crouching to coax every knot of power from the rig. The wind seemed stronger now, but still within my capabilities. I'd make that new board of his work at it. I leant back and sheeted in.

Another shout, very close. Out of the corner of my eye, I glimpsed the nose of his board. Typical male, aggressively competitive, crowding me. I held my course. To obey the rules of the sea he'd have to veer away. He didn't. Our boards were now less than a metre apart, the sea boiling and frothing between them. His yellow sail blotted out the sky, blotted up the wind. My board was losing power, slowing. *Bastard*, this was foul play, deliberate sabotage —

Without warning, rig and board spun violently into the wind, whipping the board out from under my feet. Standing on water is not one of my accomplishments. In the slow-motion sequence of nightmare, I hung in mid-air for interminable seconds, then fell backwards, still hooked into the rig.

My brain screamed, *Punch at the harness release*. In an unstoppable chain reaction, the sail collapsed on top of me, I hit the water, the mast cracked hard, very hard, against my head. Darkness.

I choked as a small wave broke over my face, cold, shocking me awake. Dazedly I tried to remember what had happened. It seemed important . . . I'd been windsurfing . . . and something had gone wrong. What? I'd fallen off the board. At least I wasn't trapped under the sail. Concentrate, *concentrate*. Another wave reared, huge, towering, the white foam of its crest whipped off by the wind. *Find that board*. I kicked my way up the face of the wave, twisting round in a desperate attempt to spot the thin line of white board against all the white crests. Kick, twist, scan. *There*, a long way off, a glimpse of a big motor yacht.

As I sank down into the trough, memory returned — Vanheusen, the race, that rash manoeuvre of his, crowding me. Kick up to the top of the next wave, twist, scan. With a surge of relief I recognised the distinctive outline of *Samarkand Princess*. Where *was* testosterone man? Must have gone for the rescue boat. Down I went into the trough and back up again. The flat platform on the ship's stern was just visible through the spray. Yes, the bows were turning — but not towards me, turning *away*. Down . . . up. Down . . . up. Each time I reached the crest, *Samarkand Princess* seemed further off, but I didn't give up hope till it was only a black smudge on the horizon.

I bobbed up the waves and down the waves and took stock of my situation. Wishing wasn't going to get me anywhere. I had to face it, things looked bad — miles from land, wind strengthening to Force 6, water cold, board lost. The outlook was one hundred per cent black. Then I recalled Gerry's silver-lining speech. At that awful debriefing on Jason and Juanita he'd raised our morale when spirits were down. He'd spelt out the bleak facts — the bug on *Saucy Nancy* used against us, Juanita dead, Jason critical, fatal setback to Operation Canary Creeper. Everything as black as it could be. Then he'd fished in the top drawer of his desk and held up a black silk handkerchief.

"Sums up the situation, eh? As black as this?"

We'd nodded. He'd flexed the elbow of his anglepoise desk lamp, and *click*. The black square was no longer entirely black, but shot with threads of silver and grey. "Juanita's dead. That's the black. The grey? Though Jason's critical, he's not dead, and we're *aware* the opposition has discovered the bug on the boat. The silver is that now that we know how Vanheusen launders his cash, our tendrils will soon have a stranglehold on his little empire. Operation Canary Creeper is not in fact wilting, but alive and well. Endgame in sight."

Could I find a silver lining in my present situation? Well . . . I could see the brown cone of Teide and the rounded shoulders of the upper slopes. That meant I knew the direction of land, and therefore knew the direction to swim. And that Force 6 wind was onshore, pushing me *towards* the land. The water was cold, but I

293

was wearing a wetsuit, wasn't I? That would ward off hypothermia for some time. Board lost? I hadn't *really* looked, had I? I'd been too busy watching *Samarkand Princess* fleeing the scene.

On the crest of the next wave I lunged upwards like a basketball player aiming to score. Nothing ahead. Nothing, that is, but line after line of angry waves. Be systematic. Up the face of another roller. I swivelled a quarter-turn to the right. From the crest, another upward lunge. Nothing. Another quarter-turn. And another. 360°. I'd turned a full circle and hadn't caught even a glimpse of the board. But it *had* to be close. The drag of the rig in the water would act as a sea-anchor. It couldn't be far, *couldn't* be . . .

I suppose it was the mix of adrenalin and rage that gave me the strength to repeat that upward lunge four, five, six times, I lost count . . . eyes searching the waves for that solid horizontal line among the flying spume and spindrift. Then, as I slid down into yet another trough, I glimpsed a flick of red. Upwind, four wave crests away, twenty metres. Not *very* far.

Head down, I thrust forward in a frantic splashing crawl-stroke till exhausted muscles shrieked a halt. Maybe in the next trough. *No.* If anything, the board was further off, no doubt about it. Another wave passed beneath me. I bobbed like a cork into the trough. It was time to face facts. My flailing arms were making no headway against that silver-lining Force 6 onshore wind. Without my buoyancy aid there'd be less wind resistance. I'd be lower in the water and that would give me a *chance* of reaching the board. I fumbled with the release, then stopped. Without the buoyancy aid I'd drown. My fingers dropped away from the buckle. A catch-22 situation all right.

Top of a wave again. The board was definitely further off. I faced the unpalatable truth that by not making a decision, I was in fact making one. In a few minutes the board would be too far away. I'd be too cold and weak to reach it. *Stay with the board* is the windsurfers' maxim. Even if I couldn't get the sail up in this wind, it was my *only* chance of making it to shore. And my only chance of being seen by a passing boat.

My fingers were already stiffening. It was difficult to press and pull the release buckle. Press. Press. *Pull.* The straps loosened. I didn't feel the belt fall away, but the abrupt loss of buoyancy left me spluttering and coughing as my mouth filled with water.

Decision made, go for it. Head down, weary arms rising and falling, legs desperately kicking. On the wave crest, lift head to check direction, head down, slice through water, kick, kick, kick. Head up, head down, kick, kick, kick. Head up, head down, kick, kick, kick. Body a machine. No time to think. Every ounce of effort concentrated into action.

Pain jabbed through an arm as my hand smacked against something solid, but not hard enough to be the board. Treading water, I blinked to clear my eyes while the thinking part of my brain cranked slowly into gear. I'd bumped into the sail, still attached to the mast, semi-submerged, wallowing at an acute angle to the board. Well, my luck was in.

Next objective must be to hoist myself on board. I'd not much strength left, but leaning down on the mast would submerge it enough for me to float over it into the sail. I'd be halfway there . . . I put my hands on the mast, pushed down, wriggled forward. Success. I rolled over on my back and rested for a moment in the watery hammock formed by the sail. Halfway there . . . or halfway still to go. All a matter of perspective, really. The glass half-full is the glass half-empty. I stared up at the clouds scurrying across the sky, and debated this philosophical point. I've always been a sucker for oddball quotations like: *Distance doesn't matter. It's only the first step that is difficult.* Couldn't remember who said that, though . . .

A wave broke over my face. *Thspafh.* I spat out a mouthful of salt water. What was I doing, lying here as if I'd all the time in the world? Must be sliding into hypothermia. I rolled over. A lunge, a desperate half-scrabble, half-slither, and I lay breathless and panting, sprawled along the length of the board. I'd made it.

With the board see-sawing up and down, it was too risky to sit up, so I took a firm grip of the foot-straps and lay husbanding my strength. Was it wishful thinking, or had the wind dropped just that little bit? Possibly . . . Spray was no longer whipping from the crests. But the wind was still far too strong to raise the sail with the uphaul. And I was now too weak to attempt a water start. I'd just have to wait it out . . .

296

No warmth now in the sun hovering just above the horizon . . . no warmth in this neoprene wetsuit . . . shivering, shivering . . .

The huge orange ball of the setting sun hesitated on the horizon as if reluctant to slide into the dark waters on the edge of the world. In the Alhambra's Café Bar Oasis, the curved glass of the cupola flamed a molten copper, antiquing the fronds of the palms a dull mud-green. From the songbirds' gilded cage burst a crescendo of twittering, strident above the murmur of conversation and slow tinkling notes of the piano. In a quiet corner, Victoria Knight pensively turned the fragile stem of the sherry glass in her plump fingers.

From behind the sharply pleated blue-green fronds of a particularly fine dwarf fan palm, Charlie watched her once again raise the glass to her lips, once again hesitate and set the drink down untouched. Charlie's eyes narrowed. Never ignore placid middle-aged ladies behaving abnormally. Great oaks from little acorns grow. She owed her impressive record to picking up on little things like that. As if coming to a decision, Victoria reached down for her handbag and moved purposefully towards the foyer. Seconds later Charlie followed . . .

Two men and a woman in evening dress were standing near the lifts. An English voice, arrogantly self-assured trumpeted, "All set then?"

"Fiona's just coming. You know her. Takes a bloody hour to fix her hair." A loud braying laugh. "We'll be up the creek if the show starts on time."

297

Victoria Knight was standing beside the desk in the Exclusive pavilion tent, tugging at the locked drawer. Thwarted, her hand fell away. She straightened, looking around helplessly.

Get the approach right, Charlie thought, as she dodged round the southern counties threesome.

"Mrs Knight, isn't it?" She smiled reassuringly. "I'm a colleague of Deborah's. We work together at Extreme Travel. Waiting for her, are you?"

"That's just it. She *should* be here. I've been looking out for her for two hours." Her fingers plucked anxiously at the buttons of her cardigan. "That's why I thought if I could get hold of her travel agency's phone number . . . find out if she'd been held up there . . ." Her eyes scanned the foyer. "You see, today's Farewell Outing was a trip on *Samarkand Princess*. When she missed lunch, I asked where she was, and Mr Vanheusen said she had decided to windsurf back . . . and . . . and . . ." Her voice tailed off. "I'm *so* worried. You see, she'd *never* have gone off like that, without a word to Herbie and me."

Alarm bells rang. "Let me get this straight. Deborah went off windsurfing, abandoning you and — er, Herbie, on Vanheusen's yacht? Can you go over exactly what happened?"

Her plump fingers plucked at the soft wool of the cashmere cardigan. "Now, let's see. I was in the Grecian Temple Spa, trying out of one those state-of-the-art Jacuzzis with different programmes — just like a fancy washing machine. You get a wonderful view of the waves, you know, through these huge

298

windows, but they must take an awful lot of cleaning. Of course, I wasn't paying much attention to what was going on outside, but I do seem to remember seeing two sails dashing about."

"*Two* sails?"

"Yes, Deborah and Mr Vanheusen. Now let me get it right . . ." Victoria closed her eyes for a moment in concentration. "She didn't turn up for lunch, as I said. And when I asked where she was, he said they'd gone out together windsurfing, and she'd been enjoying herself so much that she'd decided to sail — I think that's the right word — all the way back to Los Cristianos. I assumed she'd be joining up with us again at the harbour, didn't think anything of it, until we arrived back, and she wasn't there to meet us. I said to Mr Vanheusen, 'Oh dear, perhaps she's had an accident', but he only laughed and said, 'No, no, of course not. With that wind behind her, she'll have got in hours ago, while we were still having lunch. Be back home now with her feet up. Anyway, she's wearing a transponder' — he explained it's a sort of radio device that sends out a distress signal — and *Samarkand Princess* would have picked it up if anything had happened."

Nice one, Ambrose. Charlie could recognise a tall story even in fancy packaging. She fished in her pocket for her mobile phone.

Victoria Knight dropped her voice still further. "Keep it between ourselves, dear, but Herbie's a touch self-centred. He moaned on about being left in the lurch, and hoping it wouldn't be the same dereliction of duty tomorrow when she was due to take him to the airport. And Mr Vanheusen clapped him on the shoulder and said not to worry, that Monique would be taking him."

Tying the bow on the fancy package, eh, Ambrose? It didn't look good for DJ. Charlie's fingers closed round the phone in her pocket.

"Well, that satisfied Herbie. But I know Deborah would never let him leave without a word. She'd be here by now to say goodbye. And then . . . and then . . . just a few minutes ago, I had this *awful* thought." Victoria subsided suddenly into the carved wooden chair. "*Clothes.*"

"Clothes?" Charlie frowned. Her fingers relaxed their grip and the phone slid back into her pocket. The woman had seemed rational, but . . .

As if sensing that Charlie was measuring her for a straitjacket, Victoria leant forward, her words tumbling over each other in an effort to convince. "She wouldn't have been windsurfing in that nice little outfit she was wearing, would she? She'd be wearing a swimming cozzie or one of these black rubbery suits. And she wouldn't go off home in *that*. She'd want to change back into her own clothes, so she'd have had to wait for us." Victoria put her hand on Charlie's arm, eyes pleading. "You do see what I mean, don't you, dear?"

Indeed Charlie did. She pulled the phone from her pocket. "I think you're right. But I'll try giving her a ring at home, just in case . . ."

She punched in the number . . . "No reply." She gnawed thoughtfully at her lip. "I'll try Extreme Travel

300

. . . Hi, Jayne, it's Charlie. I'm at the Alhambra. Deborah's not called in, has she? Hmm . . . I've a Mrs Knight here. She's been trying to get hold of Deborah for a couple of hours. They've been at a do on Vanheusen's yacht and she's a bit concerned. Seems Deborah went windsurfing with the boss man and hasn't come back . . . Apparently, the wind was so good that she decided to give the rest of the party a miss and return under her own steam . . . Mmm, I think so too. OK, see you."

She slipped the phone back into pocket. "Well, she's not at the office. They're a bit concerned too now, so they're going to alert the coastguard. They'll keep in touch and let me know as soon as there's any news." For Victoria's benefit she summoned up a reassuring smile. "Let's slope off to the Café Bar Oasis and fill in the time with a coffee — or something stronger — and you can tell me all about that yacht. I've heard it's absolutely fantastic inside . . ."

. . . I'd lost track of time. Trough, crest, trough, crest. Quite a soothing rhythm. From the top of the rollers land was visible, now purpled by dusk. The wind was less strong, the waves perceptibly smaller, but still too much for me to handle in my present state. Nothing else to do but lie here clutching the board and for the umpteenth time rerun that race with Vanheusen. Let's see . . . I'd been concentrating on keeping distance between us. Then rig and board had gone into that sudden uncontrollable spin. Had the board's long fin

301

perhaps collided with a semi-submerged object? No . . . I'd have felt the shock.

Gradually I came round to the idea that it had all been planned. But how? The board had been sailing hard, zipping through the waves, with the fin under a lot of pressure . . . The fin, he'd sabotaged the fin. If it broke, there'd be an uncontrollable sideways swerve. And that's *exactly* what had happened.

But *had* the fin broken? To find out one way or the other, I'd only have to reach down into the water. Keeping an arm in one of the foot-straps, I slid my fingers along the underside of the board. Instead of the long smooth profile of the fin, I felt a ragged, rough-edged stump. Stress failure or — ? Numb fingertips aren't the most sensitive of instruments. I stuck my fingers in my mouth for a couple of minutes to warm them up, and tried again. One edge was jaggedly uneven, the other rough but straight. Evidence that the fin had been sawn part-way through, just enough to weaken it if it came under stress — and Vanheusen's macho challenge had made sure of that.

What an idiot I'd been! All the while I was congratulating myself on how clever *I* had been spiriting away G, Vanheusen had been nurturing his own little scheme. Once he'd got his hands on Gorgonzola, he wouldn't want me around. Of course I'd have to be removed.

And slowly but surely, he'd nudged me into making the decisions he'd wanted. "You mentioned you were into water sports . . . How about working up a little appetite before lunch . . .? That board suit you,

Deborah . . .? We've got a rescue boat, so do you want to bother with a buoyancy aid? Slows you down . . ." Thank God I hadn't fallen for that one. But I had for the one that mattered — I'd surrendered to the exhilaration of speed, powered the board, stressed that fin. Bugger, bugger, *bugger*. It had taken a long time for the penny to drop.

Against the dark sky, the land was a denser black sprinkled with pinpricks of light. With the fin a stump, the board couldn't be sailed, even if I'd had the strength. I'd got rid of the mast-and-sail sea-anchor, hoping to accelerate my landward drift, but those shore lights were still a long way off. Overhead, a particularly bright star winked enigmatically as the moon glided from behind a bank of dark cloud, sending a silver pathway across the black water. So beautiful. The stimulus for another attempt at silver lining thoughts . . . He hadn't finished me off — yet. And the wind *was* still edging me in the right direction.

It was difficult to have silver lining thoughts, though. I'd just have to wait it out . . . So sleepy . . . Must stay awake, though, or I'd roll off the board. I slid my arms through the foot-straps, forcing them up past my elbows. I'd rest my head, just for a minute . . .

When I opened my eyes, it was to bitter disappointment. The shore lights seemed as far away as ever. Through lowering clouds, the moon was still cutting that bright narrow path across the water. I'd stopped shivering now, felt quite warm — one of the classic symptoms of hypothermia. That should have bothered me, but it didn't.

At one point as a wave carried me to its crest I heard the *putt-putt-putt* of an engine, saw a swaying mast light bobbing in and out of sight. A fishing boat was passing within a few hundred metres of me. I pulled my arms free of the foot-straps, struggled into a kneeling position, and screamed and waved frantically. Useless, of course. I hadn't a hope of being seen in the darkness, and the noisy beat of the diesel drowned my cries. But I continued to shout long after the engine's thrumming had died to a whisper, and it was the rawness of my throat rather than common sense that forced me to abandon that nonsense. I slumped face down on the board, the will to fight almost gone, draining away to a flicker . . .

I can't say how long I drifted after that. It could have been minutes, or hours . . . Gradually a new sound percolated, a regular muffled thud, as of waves pounding against rocks. I levered myself up on my elbows to peer ahead.

Without warning the board gathered itself, then hurtled forward and up, like a steeplechaser in the Grand National clearing one of those fearsome birch-twig fences. Crouched like a jockey on the horse's neck, I clung desperately to the foot-straps. *Crack.* The board smashed against a submerged rock. There was a moment of stillness before a powerful undertow sucked the board back, twisting, rotating. Ahead I glimpsed white water cascading off jagged black rock, heard the boom of waves. No time to work out survival strategies. The spinning board slammed viciously against another rock and split in two. A huge wave swept me forward.

Fingers locked round the foot-straps and legs trailing, as if cruising the rollers on a Cornish beach, I careered shoreward on my apology for a boogie-board.

Whumhsss. The wave broke, collapsed, crashing down in a thunderous welter of spray. A maelstrom of water flooded eyes, ears, lungs, totally disorientating me, making me fight for breath. Wrenched from the foot-straps, my fingers clutched gritty sand. Water frothed, surged past my face, receded. Another breaker smashed down. My fingers scrabbled for purchase. Limbs flopping like a rag doll, I tumbled and rolled in the back surge. Tumbling . . . tumbling . . . gulping air when I could . . .

A wave more powerful than the rest, that seventh wave phenomenon, flung me some way up the steeply shelving beach. *Whumhsss.* The next wave thundered down. I dug in fingers, elbows, knees, toes . . . dragged myself forward. Muscles protested, rebelled, weakened, but centimetre by centimetre I hauled myself a little further out of range. At last the waves plucked half-heartedly at my knees, as if acknowledging they had been cheated of their prey. With a final convulsive he-e-ave, I dragged my feet clear of the water and collapsed. Jiggered, knackered, pooped, bushed, whacked, shattered — put it any way you like, I was all of these and more. All in.

When I next opened my eyes, it was no longer dark. Slowly, painfully, I levered myself up on my elbows and took stock of my surroundings. It wasn't encouraging. The flat grey light between dawn and sunrise revealed that the "beach" was, in fact, merely a narrow wedge of sand fringing the foot of ragged basalt cliffs. In my present condition, in any condition, impossible to climb. Out of the frying pan into the fire . . .

At first I barely registered the muffled *thud, thud, thud* of a pile-driver excavating foundations for yet another new hotel. *THUD, THUD, THUD*. I stirred and opened my eyes. *THUD, THUD, THUD*. Crossly, I covered my ears with my hands. Sunrise was flushing the sand, the cliffs, the sea, a delicate rosy pink.

And, swooping low out of a huge red sun, *à la Apocalypse Now*, came the air-sea rescue helicopter.

CHAPTER
TWENTY-THREE

"Don't *fuss*," I snapped. "I'm perfectly all right."

Gerry raised an eyebrow, said nothing.

A long silence.

Then, "Hypothermia." He leant back, confident he'd served an ace.

"Mild," I returned.

"Concussion."

"Ditto, mild."

"Multiple lacerations and contusions."

"Pooh. C'mon now, that just means a few scratches and bruises — I've had worse from a scrummage in the January sales." I served *my* ace. "The hospital discharged me, didn't they?"

Gerry twirled a pencil clockwise between his fingers. He picked up a paper on his desk and read it silently, as if to refresh his memory. Who was he trying to kid? He never needed to read *anything* twice.

"Hmm. I'm quoting from the clinic's report, Deborah. *Released against medical advice. Patient discharged herself at* — Hmm, need I read more?" He put the paper down and peered at me over the rim of his glasses, another technique calculated to unsettle.

I gave in. "OK," I sighed. Dammit, I wasn't my usual armour-plated self, was I? "But I'm here, anyway. And I think I know now how they work the retrieval of packages dumped at sea."

He raised a sceptical eyebrow. "Very interesting, Deborah." I could tell he was just humouring me.

"They use a Global Positioning Transmitter signalling to a Global Tracking Device," I said triumphantly. Hah, that should get his attention.

"We'd already worked that one out," he said. Smug bastard. "They'll use an aquatic transmitter with a microcontroller programmable chip, probably the type used for tracking fish." He twirled the pencil anti-clockwise. "Activated on command. That way there'll be less chance of detection by anyone surfing for a signal."

"Oh," I said faintly. During my battle with the waves, the thought that I had this nugget of information to deliver had been one of the things that had kept me going. I swallowed my disappointment. "Well, anything new at this end?"

He tipped his chair back. "Just ask me what you want to know."

The Burnside drip-feed technique. Second nature.

I was stressed out, I admit it. Something snapped. "*Gerry*," I screeched, "for once in your life, just give a straight answer to a straight question." I reached over and brought the flat of my hand crashing down on his desk.

In the silence that followed, the hospital report fluttered face down to the floor at my feet. I reached to pick it up. Completely blank on both sides. *Bastard*. In my weakened condition, it was the last straw. I crumbled. First, a prickly pressure in my nose, then a constriction in the throat, finally, an involuntary sob I couldn't stifle and a couple of trickling tears, embarrassingly obvious.

It was the only time I've seen him discomfited. Silently, he passed me a handful of paper tissues. I'll draw a veil over the ensuing sodden-hanky scene. Suffice to say, Gerry made amends by being, for him, quite garrulous as regards future tactics.

"We'll let the next pick-up take place. And with *The Saucy Nancy* out of action, I'm counting on Vanheusen making it himself."

It seemed that while I'd been wallowing in the waves, courtesy of the said Vanheusen, electronic experts had hit pay dirt when they'd detected that *The Saucy Nancy*'s sophisticated GPS receiver had been set up to display target direction and distance. John Sinclair had been a tad careless — he'd not closed it down securely, enabling our white-coated brigade to hack into it. They'd be able to pick up the signal when it was activated.

"Now, how about a nice hot drink, Deborah?" Gerry took the damp wodge of paper hanky from me and dropped it into the waste bin.

When I nodded soggily, he went over to the coffee machine, punched a button, and came back with two mugs of soothing camomile tea. I'd forgotten that last week the coffee machine had had a brain transplant when overnight Gerry had become a convert to the life-enhancing properties of herbal tisanes. Lemon balm, camomile and peppermint teas were now dispensed under the labels of *Black coffee, White with sugar, White without sugar*. The resulting storm of protest had left him quite unmoved — according to him, it just proved his point that too much caffeine overstimulated the nervous system.

"As I said," he gulped down the vile brew, "we'll let the pick-up take place. He'll use *Samarkand Princess*, but that flashy ship of his will have to operate from Los Cristianos. It's the only local harbour big enough to take her." He drained the mug, laid it down, and leant forward. "She's a familiar sight there, won't attract attention. Once the signal from the beacon stops, we'll know he's made the pick-up, and when he comes into port with the goods —" He slammed a fist into his open palm. "*Gotcha*."

The beacon had ceased transmission an hour ago. In the powerful night-scope's eerie green glow, a distant ghostly shape powered through the waves under a midnight-black sky heavy with cloud. I lowered the scope and shifted from one buttock to another in a vain attempt to get into a more comfortable position, though comfort was relative, given the fact that I was sitting, knees to chin, on bare wooden planks that smelt strongly of fish and the sea. Piled over me was a tangle of scratchy, salty nets with hard little floats that snagged my hair with every pitch and yawl of the tiny fishing boat. Designed to carry one man, tonight it carried two — or to be more accurate, one man and a woman.

310

I'd *have to* straighten my legs, *have to*. This wooden tub was no bigger than . . . than . . . that polished stone bath of Vanheusen's that I'd so light-heartedly tried out only thirty-six hours ago. Perhaps if I did some of those anti-DVT exercises the airlines push at captive passengers . . . Circle foot clockwise, circle foot anti-clockwise . . . Lift heel from floor . . . No good. I pushed my feet hard against the side. The boat listed alarmingly, sending water sloshing over the low gunwale.

From the stern came a gruff, "Quit that, will you, wumman. You're shoogling the boat, dammit. This skiff's that unstable you'll have us cowped."

Expressive word, "shoogle". I suppose it conveyed shake and joggle, all in one. I peered through a gap in the heaped netting and made a rude gesture at Jock's bulky silhouette perched a few centimetres above the water. He'd not been at all happy to be confined to a spectator role. And, in addition, he'd been saddled with a gawping rubberneck, a female one at that. Observer status, I preferred to call it.

I'd pressurised a contrite Gerry into giving me a share in the coming action — even if it was just a grandstand seat a kilometre or so away. Not *just* a spectator role, though. We could provide timings, more accurate than would be possible from the shore, and give advance warning of any attempt by Vanheusen to slip out of the closing net in one of his smaller craft. So here I was in the aptly named *Berberecho*, a cockleshell of a boat if ever there was one, with only a couple of centimetres or so of freeboard, stern dredging the sea, uptilted bow trawling the stars.

A wave passed lazily beneath the boat, sending the masthead light arcing across the night sky. As the boat heeled, the dim glow from the packing-case-sized wheelhouse under-lit Jock's craggy face, two days' growth of stubble, cigarette drooping from scowling lips, flat fisherman's cap pulled low. Perfectionist Gerry was leaving nothing to chance. A jumpy Vanheusen would have *his* night-vision device trained on anything that moved between him and the shore, on the lookout for something not quite right, something not in the usual run of things.

There was no sign of the Taskforce hit squads. They'd wait till *Samarkand Princess* was committed to entering the harbour and was swinging round the mole, engines throttled back, before initiating their pincer movement to cut off escape. I poked the night-scope back through the nets and scanned the nearest building, a balconied and domed holiday complex, its sprinkle of lighted windows an indication of night owls returned from clubs, or holidaymakers cramming souvenirs into suitcases before an early flight. The top-floor apartments jumped into focus. All was dark there, only a gently swaying curtain in the black rectangle of an open balcony door, or the blank-eyed reflection of mirrored glass. But behind one of these windows lurked Gerry and his team. And, out of sight in the harbour, hidden behind the high wall, the assault Taskforce powerboats waited, engines slowly turning over.

Gerry was risking everything on this one throw of the dice. High stakes, rich prize. Vanheusen's presence on board when the package was located was the vital prerequisite for success. If he succeeded in slipping away, tables would be turned with a vengeance in the shape of high-powered lawyers, astronomical financial damages, international repercussions. And Gerry's career in shreds.

"Lights." A low mutter from Jock into the transmitter. "Ten minutes."

I applied an eye to a small aperture I'd made in the seaward-facing side of the nets. *Samarkand Princess*'s red port light and a string of cabin and deck lights now shone brightly where before there'd been only darkness. A casual watcher on shore, if he noticed anything at all, would think the yacht had emerged from a bank of sea mist. I pictured Vanheusen, drug packages safely stashed, feeding his thug of a cat a morsel of celebratory caviar, in his hand a tot of mind-blowingly expensive whisky.

I eased an aching hip, taking care not to shoogle the boat. *Samarkand Princess* drew closer every minute, her lights bigger, brighter. The whispered beat of her engines deepened to a growl.

"Four minutes." The cigarette tip glowed.

Now she was passing to starboard, white foam at bow and stern. I braced my feet against the gunwale in anticipation of the backwash.

Jock spoke into the transmitter. "Target turning. Two minutes." Then, for my ears, a muttered, "Brace."

I could feel us swinging round to meet the wake. I pressed my palms hard against the wooden side. *Slap.* The first wave hit. With our lack of freeboard, there was a real danger of being swamped. The little eggshell of a boat tilted its bow at an impossible angle towards the sky, tilted again. And again. Pitching, bobbing. I made a frantic grab for something to hold onto. There was nothing. My upper body tossed this way, that way, like laundry in an oscillating tumble drier. Involuntary gasps from me, stoic silence from Jock who was obviously made of sterner stuff. A particularly violent twisting lurch buried my face in salty nets. For a moment, just a moment, I regretted I'd used emotional blackmail on Gerry to let me be in at the kill.

Then Gerry made his move. Engines roared throatily at full throttle as powerboats surged from the harbour between *Samarkand Princess* and the shore, a swarm of angry hornets fanning out in attack mode from their byke, fanning out, encircling, cutting off all seaward escape. Now that our stomach-churning corkscrew motion had moderated to an irregular see-saw rocking, I managed to steady the night-scope and sweep the dark waters for any tell-tale splash of hastily jettisoned cargo. Seemingly oblivious to all the commotion, searchlights, loudhailers, shouts, *Samarkand Princess* sailed regally on and rounded the mole into the harbour. Snapping at her heels, the mini-flotilla scurried after.

I lowered the scope and fought my way out from under the scratchy embrace of the nets. My micro-nano role in Operation Softly-Softly was over. Now I was free

314

to goggle at the flurry of police activity, the blue flashing lights and wailing sirens, perhaps to revel in the spectacle of that bastard Vanheusen being led away in handcuffs . . .

Samarkand Princess glided to a halt and docked. Unfortunately, all I could see over the high harbour wall was the top of her superstructure, the navigation mast, radar dish and radio antennae, and the tantalising reflection of flashing blue lights on white paintwork. Abruptly the sirens fell silent. They'd be cordoning off the quayside, rushing the gangway, sprinting along the corridors and through those luxury saloons, probing, ferreting, rummaging in every nook and cranny. And I was missing it all.

"Let's get over there, Jock. I want to be in at the kill."

Not a twitch from his silhouette, not even an acknowledging grunt.

"C'mon, fella. Action!"

No response.

"Hi. Anybody there? You meditating, sleeping — dead?"

The silhouette stirred, straightened and gave utterance. "Whisht, lassie." He made a slow cutting motion, finger across throat. "Orders."

"Orders?" I squeaked.

Jock waxed loquacious. "You stay here till I get the signal."

He slumped back into suspend mode, and I knew it was no use arguing. I'd just be banging my head against a concrete block.

Sound of gritting teeth. Mine. Gerry had turned the tables, outwitted me once again.

CHAPTER
TWENTY-FOUR

Restlessly I tossed, turned and glowered at the triangular patch of sunlight edging across the ceiling above the bed . . .

. . . Fragile little lady had been kept safely out of harm's way by Jock The Minder. I'd gazed up at the dark sky, I'd stared at the sullen sea, I'd counted the twinkling lights of Los Cristianos. And then I'd done it all again. And again. All in teeth-gritting silence, you understand. I was missing out on the climax of Operation Softly-Softly, and there was nothing I could do about it, but I wasn't going to whine, or pester, or plead, and give him the satisfaction of rapping out another, "Whisht, wumman."

I endured another hour of bobbing about in that bloody boat before that bloody Scot sprang into life, if that can accurately describe a slow straightening of the back, flexing of shoulders and stretching of arms. At long last, the engine spluttered and fired.

I was sitting there, smugly giving myself a big pat on the back for all my iron self-control, when I realised that the distant harbour wall was slipping past from *left* to right, meaning that we were headed not for Los

Cristianos but for the marina at Las Américas. All self-control evaporated in a flash.

"Where the hell are we going?" I screeched above the clatter of the engine.

No reply.

I seized the scope and tapped it sharply on the wheelhouse roof. *That* got his attention. His head snapped up.

"Where are we going?" I yelled. "The harbour mouth's the *other* way."

To my fury, the dim glow from the binnacle betrayed an unmistakable upward twitch of his lips.

Shanghaied. There was no other word for it.

I'd only make a fool of myself by ranting and raving. It wouldn't get me anywhere. Better to feign nonchalance, give an impression of lofty insouciance. With an exaggerated shrug I laced my hands behind my head and leant back against the nets, outwardly calm, inwardly fuming that Gerry had pulled a fast one to keep me happy and let me think I'd persuaded *him*.

Well, I certainly wasn't happy now. Most definitely not. And as soon as Jock set me ashore, I'd whizz back in a taxi to Los Cristianos. *Samarkand Princess* would be cordoned off, but I'd sidle up to a familiar face and blag my way on board. I hadn't missed much, I consoled myself. They'd still be searching. Vanheusen didn't believe in half measures and taking chances. He'd have that package well hidden. Yes, that's what I'd do, blag my way on board. I could see, of course, that a confrontation between Vanheusen and myself wouldn't be a good idea, but by then he'd have been hustled away. In police HQ he'd be throwing his weight about and summoning his smart lawyers. Well, for once he wouldn't get his way. However high-powered his legal team was, they couldn't get him off the hook once we'd located that stash of drugs.

So, no tantrums from me when *Berberecho* nosed gently against the wooden pontoon in Las Américas marina. I merely smiled sweetly, dislodged a bit of cork wedged behind my ear, and untangled my boots from the tendril grip of the nets.

"Your carriage awaits, lassie." With a jerk of his thumb, Jock indicated a sporty yellow blob of a car on the quayside.

Gerry had relented and decided to give me a tiny piece of the action.

"Thank you, my man," I said loftily, grand lady to lowly coachman.

The car he'd sent was a squat Dinky toy of a car, ornamented on each side of the bonnet with impressive gill-like slits.

The driver's window slid smoothly down. Charlie's white-blonde hair gleamed from the dark interior. "Hi, there, DJ, just hop in."

"Nice set of wheels. Suits you," I said as I folded myself double and closed the door behind me with a clunk.

It might have suited the doll-like Charlie, but the interior was decidedly compact for anyone with long back or legs. In my dark green jeans and jacket, and with knees bent at an acute angle, I felt like an ungainly grasshopper.

I clicked the seat belt, "To the action, chauffeur mine."

"Not tonight, D-J-os-ephine. Straight home and to bed for you." She gunned the engine and drove off in the opposite direction from Los Cristianos.

Gerry had been one step ahead again.

"Oh come on, Charlie, we've just *got* to be there when they find the evidence to nail that bastard."

She crunched a gear. "I hear, but I do not obey."

"Gerry *owes* it to me after all I've been through," I whined in an appeal to her softer side. I should have known that she didn't have one.

"Mmmm mmmmmm mmmmmmmm," she hummed slowly, one hand off the wheel, arm sawing at imaginary violin. "Skip the sob stuff, Debs. You'll have my mascara running in a minute."

I lapsed into a huffy silence, and bided my time. Sooner or later she'd have to slow down, stop at an intersection, and when she did, I'd be ready, out and running before she could do anything about it. I edged a hand towards the door handle.

"Naughty, naughty! The door locks are on." I just hated that hint of a smirk in her voice. "Might as well accept what Gerry's decreed, DJ."

She was right. I slumped back in my seat, wearier than I cared to admit.

With the jarring lurch of an emergency stop, we pulled up outside my front door. "Doors to manual." Charlie deactivated the safety locks.

I climbed stiffly out. "Buzz off home now, Charlie. Escort duties over." I expressed my high dudgeon by slamming the car door.

The window slid down. "Not quite over, Debs. I'm on taxi-blocking patrol now." The window slid smoothly up. The engine cut out. Charlie and her yellow jalopy had taken root outside Calle Rafael Alberti, numero 2.

Stymied.

I flounced across the pavement. But to be absolutely truthful, after those hours crouched on hard wood and scratchy nets, a soft bed and pillow were suddenly very appealing.

Fretting and fuming over the events of the past few hours did nothing to induce slumber. So here I was, a couple of hours later, still restlessly tossing and turning. At last I dozed off, but I found no respite in sleep . . .

. . . I was at the wheel of Charlie's yellow jalopy, on the roof a sign, *Obedience School of Motoring*.

Gerry was sitting in the passenger seat with a large clipboard. "Take the next turn right."

I spun the wheel. The nose of the car turned left. A huge black cross appeared on the clipboard.

"Failed, Deborah."

Perleep perleep perleep peep peep. Perleep perleep perleep peep peep. I surfaced groggily, totally disorientated for a second or two. What time was it? I struggled up on one elbow and peered at the alarm clock. 8.30. I'd been asleep for only two hours, for God's sake. Across the room on the dresser my mobile *perleeped* again. It couldn't be urgent. Probably Charlie, checking to see if I was still at home. Let her sweat. I sank down again and pulled the sheet over my head . . .

320

. . . "Checkmate." Gerry plunked down his queen. "I'll give you . . ." He nibbled at an earpiece of his glasses. ". . . 0 out of 10 for reading my mind. Now let's try it again." He reset the board, slid his pawn to K4, and set the timer going. "You've got one hour to make your move . . ."

I fingered my pawn. The black hands of the timing-clock whizzed round. *Perleep perleep perleep peep peep*.

He shook his head sorrowfully. "Time up. Failed *again*, Deborah."

Perleep perleep perleep peep peep on and on and on.

I tried ignoring it, tried the previous tactic of pulling the sheet over my head, stuffing my fingers in my ears. Utterly useless. Charlie wasn't going to give up. I threw back the sheet. In three strides I crossed the room and snatched up the phone.

"Stop arsing about, you stupid pillock, and let — me — sleep. S-l-e-e-p. Sleep."

Jayne's calm voice said, "Take a grip, Deborah. We've a bit of an emergency here. I wouldn't have disturbed you otherwise. I'm afraid both Tom *and* Dick have called in sick. I know it's your day off, but we'd appreciate it if you *could* come in. We're really desperate."

Tom and Dick, the Department's panic button. The coded message was, *Report to the office prontissimo, asap, NOW*. Whatever was going on, it was something major.

"We-e-ll, just for you, Jayne," I said, now thoroughly awake. "But I'll have to call a taxi. I've no wheels at the moment." I'd left my car at the Alhambra on Friday on the way to the Farewell Cruise and hadn't had the chance to pick it up.

"It'll be quicker if I send someone, so don't bother with the taxi. I knew I could rely on you, Debs. Thanks, see you." She rang off.

There'd been an audible sigh of relief there. The unflappable Jayne losing her cool, I didn't like it one little bit.

I made a quick calculation — it would be fifteen minutes or so before my transport arrived. I'd just have time for a shower, a cup of tea, and —

Bzzzzzzzz bzz bzzzzzzzz bzzzzzzz. Someone was at the door punching out the Department code. Had Jayne dispatched that car before she phoned me? Through the fisheye lens of the security viewer I saw Charlie's blonde head, and in the background the Dinky toy yellow jalopy.

"Must be a bit of a flap on," I said as I edged open the door just enough to allow her to sidle in. It wouldn't do to startle any passing worthy of Calle Rafael Alberti with the way-out design of my psychedelic sleep-shirt.

"Too right." She eyed my shirt thoughtfully. "No offence, DJ, but mutton dressed as lamb, wouldn't you say?" She disappeared into the kitchen. Above the sound of the kettle filling up, she called, "Action stations, girl! You're needed. I know Gerry's not in your good books, but he'll be a guy up the creek without a paddle unless you can pull a rabbit out of the hat."

Effervescent Charlie spewing out tired old clichés was a sure sign of stress. Last night everything had seemed to be going nicely to plan. Whatever had thrown a spanner in the works, time was now obviously of the essence. Too bad about the shower — gone for a Burton in Charlie stress-speak — but at least by the sound of it, I'd be getting a nice strong cup of tea.

"Ready in a jiffy," I called from the bedroom, flinging off the scorned sleep-shirt and pulling on an old T-shirt and pair of jeans.

Charlie came in as I was sitting on the bed slipping my feet into canvas casuals. "Don't say I'm not waiting on you hand and foot." She handed me a mug. "This'll kick-start you, O Saviour of the Mission — not to mention of the Missionary."

I looked up at her blankly.

"I'll fill you in on the details on the way, but to wrap it up in a couple of sentences, we can't find the drugs. Unless Gorgonzola comes up trumps, Vanheusen gets off scot-free, and Gerry's for the high jump."

Beneath the chirpy exterior, she was pretty uptight. It was catching. I was tense myself now. I took a sip from the mug. Black coffee, not tea, but I gulped it down without protest.

I locked the front door and followed Charlie to the car.

"G's not been flown off the island yet?"

"No, no. You'll rendezvous with her at the yacht."

For the second time in less than five hours, I folded myself grasshopper-like into the front seat of the yellow jalopy. "Go easy on the gas, Charlie."

She didn't, of course. Shaken and stirred, I creaked out of the yellow hell-bubble and leant for support on the roof while I flexed my cramped legs.

"Hang on a minute." Charlie was rummaging in her little bumbag. "You'll need this." Solemn now, she thrust a police pass at me and jerked a thumb in the direction of *Samarkand Princess*. "You and Gorgonzola make a great team, DJ. You'll find that needle in the haystack, I know you will." A Victory V gesture of the fingers, a gunning of the engine and the yellow blob departed in a cloud of dust.

I didn't share her confidence. I knew that, for hours, dogs and specialist teams had searched the white floating palace that was Vanheusen's yacht, the four decks above the waterline, the spa complex, sun and sports areas, lounges, staterooms, bathrooms, crew quarters, galley kitchen, engine room — and hadn't found the drugs. No doubt about it, the Department was in deep *schtook*.

I found Gerry in the stunningly minimalist lounge. In time of stress he had resorted to the familiar, namely a swivel chair. As swivel chairs go, Vanheusen's white leather state-of-the-art model was in a class of its own, programmable by hand control for speed of swivel, angle of back, height of foot-rest and appearance/ disappearance of pop-out drinks tray. He brought me up to date on the progress of the search, or lack of it, absent-mindedly thumbing the control buttons like a set of worry beads.

"So you see, at the present moment we've got nothing on him — though Friday's little scheme to get rid of you might give us a useful holding charge, if necessary." He pressed a button and the chair swivelled slowly to the right. "Failure to report a distressed or endangered person to the coastguard, and/or go to help, is a breach of maritime regulations." Another button pressed, the chair swivelled left. "Even if we can't produce proof that he tampered with the fin and was responsible for engineering the 'accident', even if he denies boardsailing with you, one thing is irrefutable. You were his passenger, you set off from his ship and you failed to return." The foot-rest elevated itself to the horizontal.

"But this happened in Spanish waters —"

"Aha, *no problema* . . ." The chair back reclined to a comfortable angle.

I fought down a wave of irritation. He was one step ahead of me yet again, but this wasn't the time to bring up Jock and Charlie's minder roles to keep me away from last night's action. He popped out the drinks tray concealed in the armrest. "Yes, it's still an open-and-shut breach of regulations." The tray slid smoothly back into its slot. "Our Maritime and Coastguard Agency enforces regulations for British ships *anywhere in the world*. So Vanheusen can be charged with breach of a 1998 regulation, number 1691, to be exact."

"And the penalty's a whopping fine?" My eyes roamed round the vast expanse of teak flooring, the stylishly extravagant white leather upholstery, the bar's backlit shelves of connoisseur brands, the enormous plasma screen . . . not to mention that profligate forest of white orchids in the planter. "It would have to be pretty big to make a dent in the bastard's finances."

The swivel chair zoomed upright. "It's an indictable offence." He reached for the lighting control pad on the coffee table. "In the magistrates' court the maximum fine's £5000, chicken feed to a guy like Ambrose, but . . ." The Milky Way of downlighters blushed rosy pink. ". . . in serious cases — and we have attempted murder here, or if we can't prove that, *deliberate* abandonment of damsel in distress — it goes to Crown Court, and *there* . . ." Fade up sunset red. ". . . penalty's an unlimited fine, and/or two years in prison." Fade down to moonlight blue.

For a short moment we sat there, wearing the laurels of victory, celebratory drum rolls in our ears.

A tap at the door introduced grim reality in the shape of a uniformed policeman. "Señor Burnside, the second search with dogs has proved negative. Your orders?"

The curtain came down on the lighting effects. Gerry stood up and stretched. "OK, action time, Deborah. You've always claimed that Gorgonzola could out-sniff any dog. Now prove it. The stuff's got to be here."

Together we waited for Gorgonzola's arrival. Everything was at stake reputation-wise for both the Gs. I'm not usually given to nerves, but for a search to have any chance of success I'd need Gorgonzola's willing cooperation, and I suspected my reunion with her would be a little sticky. I was right. She made a point of registering her displeasure at being railroaded off in a fridge to be spoilt rotten by strangers. When I peered into the cat-carrier, she knew I was there, but all that was visible was a piqued ginger backside. A Bad Sign. Feathers definitely ruffled, so to speak. From past experience, I knew what was expected of me — self-abasement, pleading and coaxing and blatant bribery in the form of foodie inducements.

"I'm afraid Gorgonzola's in one of her moods, Gerry. She'll snap out of it, but it usually takes a little time. Maybe there's something in Ambrose's fridge that'll speed things up."

There might very well be. But what I really wanted was to be alone when I launched into the obligatory softening-up routine. G was well aware that I found uttering prissy terms of endearment excruciatingly embarrassing, so that is exactly what she demanded on those occasions when I overstepped the mark.

I'd better get it over before he came back. I unlatched the door of the cat-carrier. "I'm *so, so* sorry, G. You see . . ."

Thankfully I'd got through the required coaxing-and-pleading by the time Gerry returned bearing Black Prince's bone china bowl heaped high with the finest beluga caviar.

I held the bowl enticingly close to the twitching tail in the carrier. "Caviar — for you, *cariña mía*."

Up till then, apart from the occasional flick of her tail, I might as well have been speaking to one of those realistic furry sleeping-cat ornaments. Now the ginger rump heaved, leg muscles stre-e-e-tched, and in a flurry of movement the rump was replaced by narrowed copper eyes, twitching whiskers and drooling jaws. At a strategic distance I set the bowl on the floor, tactfully

327

but fatefully as it transpired, twitching it round to conceal the name of the owner, Black Prince. G emerged from the carrier and sat for a moment, eyes closed, nostrils scenting the air, like a wine buff nosing a glass of vintage rioja. It took her less than five minutes to polish off the lot. When she was sitting smugly washing her paws, I judged the time was right.

"She's ready now." I buckled on her working collar. "Where do you want us to start? In here?"

Gerry nodded. "Might as well, though a dog has been through here twice and drawn a blank."

"C'mon, G, search." I released my hold on the collar and pointed at the long white dining table with its guard-of-honour of white leather chairs.

She swished her tail in acknowledgement. Claws skittered across the teak flooring. She leapt effortlessly onto the highly polished table and gave a cursory sniff at the artistic centrepiece platter of lemons before descending to make a tunnelling run under the dining chairs. The bar received the same quick once-over, with a perfunctory glance upward at the illuminated shelves of bottles. No result.

When she showed considerable interest in the planter of orchids, I could sense Gerry's tension. An investigative paw created havoc among the fragile white blooms, but there was no follow-up crooning purr.

"She's not signalling a find," I said quickly, not wanting to build up hope. "I think Ambrose's floral display must be harbouring some kind of wildlife."

Proving me right, a large brown moth fluttered up, dislodged by a forehand swipe of her paw.

"Over there, G. Search." I pointed at the long white couches, the sofa-equivalent of stretch-limos. It wasn't likely that the dogs would have missed hollowed-out cushions or anything stuffed down between them, but on the off chance . . . We watched her scamper over the white leather, then head once more for Black Prince's empty bowl.

"That's the only thing she's interested in." Gerry's voice was flat with disappointment.

A snuffle, a petulant nudge of bowl with nose, a hopeful scour with the tongue for any missed morsel and she stared up at us, Gorgonzola transmogrified into Oliver Twist.

"Work, G," I said sharply, much mortified. Distraction from the search is ranked as a major shortcoming even in a trainee sniffer.

A tentative tap on the doorframe was followed by a hesitant cough. We turned to see a blue-uniformed, tubby *policía* officer holding up an expensive leather cat-carrier.

"*Problema, señor. Que vamos hacer con este gato?*"

Through the carrier's gold-gridded window, framed by a black halo of fur, glared the Brute of Samarkand's baleful orange eyes.

"Do with the cat?" Gerry was momentarily puzzled.

"Your first audience with Black Prince, Gerry." I hadn't realised the animal was on the yacht.

Cats can recognise their own bowls. The orange eyes narrowed, targeting G who was holding down the bowl with a paw, while her nose energetically hoovered the interior.

Behind me I heard a gasp and a grunt of, "*Hostia! Estáte quieto, cabrón!*" The Spanish equivalent of "Shit! Keep still, you bugger!"

I swung round. The sergeant's short far arms were struggling to encircle a cat-carrier that seemed to have developed a life of its own. I saw Gorgonzola look up, then unhurriedly sit back on her haunches ostentatiously licking her paw, a calculated pouring of oil on the flames, a deliberate goading beyond endurance of the owner of the bowl.

Gerry moved forward. "*Cuidado, hombre!*"

Too late. A snarling *tsssh* erupted from the carrier. It juddered and bounced. Tearing itself free from the *policía*'s arms, it thudded to the floor, the door-catch burst open and a spitting whirlwind of black fur rampaged out and rocketed towards the usurper.

I screamed. Gerry swore. The policeman's fingers instinctively clasped the butt of his gun. Only Gorgonzola remained unfazed. Macho neighbourhood moggies, uppity trainee sniffer-dogs, hi-tech Robocat, all in their turn had been flattened by a lightening uppercut from her ginger paw. One second that paw was peacefully performing her postprandial ablutions, the next it had metamorphosed into a razor-sharp Edward Scissorhands-cum-Joe Louis weapon of war.

THWACK. Ill-prepared by a pampered life of caviar and cushions for this Shock-and-Awe-style attack, Black Prince staggered back, murderous hellcat rampage abruptly terminated.

THWACK. Hit the enemy before he can recover. Hit the enemy while he's down. In the light breeze from the door, tufts of fine black fur wafted up like giant fluffy seeds from a freak dandelion.

"Do something, somebody!" I shrieked.

The sergeant shifted indecisively from foot to foot.

I grabbed the nearest thing to hand, one of the expensive orchids from the planter, and flung it at Black Prince. What I hadn't realised was that the roots were encased in a plastic pot full of bark chips. Halfway through the trajectory, pot and plant parted company. The orchid nosedived to the deck, dirty wet fragments of bark showered down on pristine white leather, and the empty pot hurtled onward with increased velocity to torpedo Gorgonzola who was crouched to deliver the *coup de grâce*.

Miaooow. She cast a reproachful look in my direction.

"Not too clever, Deborah. Whose side are you on?" In two strides, Gerry was at the bar and reaching for the water jug.

Ptshhh. Taking advantage of G's momentary lapse of attention, Black Prince pounced. Sharp teeth clamped down viciously on a moth-eaten ear.

With the fluid technique of a ten-pin bowler going for a strike, Gerry swung the litre jug with the full force of his arm. A mini curtain of water arced across the room.

Splattt.

In a trice, the menacing black puffball deflated to bedraggled black floor mop. For a couple of seconds Black Prince crouched dazed and dripping. Gorgonzola seized her chance. *Thwack. Thwack. Thwack.*

Gerry flourished the jug in a victory salute. "Atta girl!"

Hchwaaa-a-a. Ambrose's Treasure streaked for the open door.

"*Hostia!*" One second too late, the sergeant stuck out a boot to block Black Prince's exit.

"Shit!" One second too late, I made a grab for Gorgonzola.

In a blur of black and ginger, they'd skedaddled, vamoosed, hopped it, done a bunk. Gone.

I beat both men out into the corridor. The oiled teak floor and whisper-grey walls lit by a double row of runway-style lights stretched ahead with no sign of cats.

"That's all we need," said Gerry at my shoulder. "Vanheusen's prize moggie minus an eye, or panicked into jumping ship, 'missing, believed drowned'. The lawyers will certainly have a field day." He took off his glasses and polished them. "Well, you're the cat guru. How are we going to calm them down?"

"They went that way." I pointed at the spatter of drips on the teak floor. "Wherever they are, they won't be sitting quietly purring to each other, there'll be one hell of a racket. We'll track them down easily enough." I snatched up the cat-carrier and set off at a run. "If there's any of that caviar left in the fridge, bring a couple of plates." Given the choice — caviar, or murder and mayhem — there'd be no contest.

As I hesitated at a T-junction, I heard behind me the heavy pounding of police-issue boots and the laboured breathing of the decidedly unfit *policía*.

I pointed to the open glass doors leading to the sundeck. "You go that way, but get some help. It is *muy importante* that these cats are recovered safely."

He lumbered past, wafting the sharp tang of sweaty armpit.

To the left stretched a clone of the corridor where I was standing, the same teak floor, grey walls, runway-style double row of lights. As I ran past more doors, some ajar, I listened out for catty shouts and screams from within. No luck. I hesitated at the top of stairs with the arrowed notice *Boat Launch and Sea Bathing*. Had I heard a faint mew?

"Gorgonzola?" I called tentatively.

Only the low hum of air-conditioning, a muffled shout from out on deck, the slap of water on the hull.

But I was sure I hadn't been mistaken. I'd heard something. Time to show who was boss. "Here, G. That's an *order*."

Air-conditioning hum, water slapping . . .

I said, louder, "An *order*, G."

A mew, definitely a mew. Not the mew of a petulant, aggressive Black Prince. Not the *mia-oow* of G on the make, winsomely pleading I'm-a-poor-little-deserving-cat. But I'd heard something like it before . . . I couldn't quite place it . . .

The sound *must* have come from one of the open doors I'd just passed. I glanced back. Gerry was half-running towards me from the T-junction, balancing two heaped plates of caviar with the exaggerated care of a competitor in an egg-and-spoon race.

"Along here. I heard something, Gerry."

In two strides I was peering in the nearest door. An engraved brass plate read *Ambrose Vanheusen*. The salon-cum-office area was fitted out with maple wood panelling, a gentleman's-club-style desk, and green leather chairs and sofa — all very masculine. Across the room, through the half-open door, I could see more maple wood panelling and the foot of an oversized bed.

"Gorgonzola?"

From the bedroom issued a loud, rumbling *purrrrrr*. Long, smug and self-satisfied. It was the victory cry of a cat triumphant, signifying an enemy dealt with. Dealt with to the victor's satisfaction. *Purrrrrr*.

Again, just audible, I caught that weak mew. Sound triggers memories. Into my mind flashed the picture of four drowned kittens washed up against a riverbank, and a half-drowned Gorgonzola clinging desperately to the half-submerged log, a tiny mewing ball of ginger fur . . .

Through the hum of the air-conditioning, I heard a watery *splosh, splattsplosh*, followed a second later by that triumphant *purrrrrr*. Throat dry, heart pounding, I ran across to the open bedroom door. One glance took in ceiling spotlights blazing down on a rockery of small square pillows piled up on the oversized bed. Vanheusen seemed to be obsessed with brass. It was everywhere, gleaming against dark wood panelling: brass handles on drawers and side tables, brass covers on light switches, brass swivel arms on reading lights, more brass round the full-length mirror and on the picture-light over a portrait of Samarkand Black Prince sporting a flamboyant Champion of Champions rosette. Apart from a huge vase of flowers on a brass-bound chest, the whole ambience was, like the salon-cum-office, overpoweringly masculine.

No sign of either cat here, but from the en suite bathroom came an ominous *splash splash mia-ow. Purrrrrr*.

Behind me Gerry's shoes brush-scuffed on the salon carpet. "Got 'em cornered have you, Deborah?"

I flung myself across the bedroom and into the bathroom, all dark wood cabinets, gold-plated taps, green marble. And more lights. Lights in the ceiling, lights above the mirrors, lights trained on the huge teak bath with the upward swooping ends of a Viking longship. Under the lights its silky sides glowed in shades of cinnamon, mocha and peat-brown, the bath of a confirmed sybarite. Last night's raid must have rudely interrupted Vanheusen's relaxing soak, for the heavy spicy scent from half-burnt aromatherapy candles hung heavy in the air, and the bath was still half full of water. On its broad rim crouched a triumphant Gorgonzola, *couchant*.

She was safe and sound. I drew a long breath and sagged against the doorpost, legs weak with relief.

"What's —?" Gerry appeared at my shoulder in a whiff of fish.

From the depths of the bath came *Mwwww shptt glupp*. A sodden black blob was struggling to keep its nose and mouth above the surface, paws scrabbling ineffectually at the polished wooden sides. *My God*, Black Prince was drowning!

"No-o-o-o-o!" My shriek, magnified and distorted by all that marble, echoed round the room, feeding on itself as it bounced from wall to wall, an aural version of mirror-in-mirror reflections.

I hurled myself at the bath. Startled out of her *schadenfreude* spectator-role, Gorgonzola sprang down to the cream marble floor in perfect time to home in on the scatter of caviar jostled by my elbow from one of Gerry's plates as I pushed myself off the doorpost.

I made a grab for the scruff of Black Prince's neck as he sank and, in the role of deus ex machina, hoisted Ambrose's moggy from his watery grave. I heard the clink of porcelain on marble top as Gerry hastily deposited Ambrose's best china, and then he was swaddling Black Prince in a fluffy-towel straitjacket. He thrust the bundle into my arms. Two terrified orange eyes gazed into mine, a little black face enshawled in the expanse of white whimpered a mew. I rocked him gently and felt strangely maternal . . .

Gerry was studying the electronic touch-pad at the side of the bath. "Better get rid of all this water before the bugger dives in again. Let's see . . . *Spa jets, Whirlpool, Combination, Fill, Drain, Stop.*" He punched the *Drain* button. With a musical chord the bath waste-cover rose and the water flowed silently away to expose three rows of brass-mounted jets, at least thirty of them. With that lot powering away, the effect must be more of a maelstrom than whirlpool, not *my* idea of a relaxing soak.

He glanced at his watch and frowned. "All this has held us back. Time's —"

336

"I'm really sorry, Gerry. G knows when she's wearing her collar that she's on duty and focuses on the task. She's not easily distracted . . ."

Both of us eyed Gorgonzola, now crouched on the marble-topped unit, nose in one of the plates.

"I see what you mean." His tone was dry.

Miaow. My cradled bundle whined querulously.

"There, there, there," I crooned, "you're not such a big, bad cat after all."

Gerry glowered at me. "I don't have to remind you, do I, Deborah, that we've one hell of a crisis here? What we don't need is *another* lawsuit, and over an effing pedigree cat at that. Quit buggering around, playing the bloody nursemaid. What I need is you and that moth-eaten shock-trooper of yours to start work. *Right now.*"

I wasn't expecting him to lose his cool. That really got to me. Ignoring the slur on G, I looked round for somewhere to deposit my burden, somewhere secure. I made a rapid scan of the room . . . candelabra-stand of burnt-out aromatherapy candles . . . wicker towel basket. That would do. I turfed out most of the contents, replaced them with Black Prince, and fastened down the lid.

"I need *results.*" The crack in Gerry's composure was opening into a fissure. His finger stabbed down on the bath's electronic touch-pad, "And." *Stab.* "I need them." *Stab.* "Right now." *Stab.*

With a warning musical *ping* and a hum of motorised valves, the caps on the centre row of jets slid smoothly open. Gorgonzola paused in mid-munch, head raised enquiringly.

"There's no water in the bath, Gerry. You'll ruin —" I stopped. Tail high, G was stalking along the marble top, homing in on the quivering towel basket. "Gorgonzola! *No!*"

She really *was* trying to show me up. All office cred gone, I made a grab. Too slow and too late. With a soft thump she landed on the floor, sashayed nonchalantly round me, and sprang onto the edge of the bath. For a moment she balanced there, extending her claws experimentally, then leapt lightly down onto the rows of brass jets set in the bottom of the bath.

"*Can't* you keep her under control, Deborah? My God, she's treating the bath as a £20k teak scratch-post!"

In spite of her alley-cat appearance, G was a creature of taste and sensitivity — except in the face of extreme provocation, of course. No way would she commit such an act of vandalism. She was padding along the middle row of jets, claws carefully sheathed.

I sprang to her defence. "Well really, that's a bit —"

From her throat was coming a low crooning purr, the low crooning purr of the drug-detecting cat that has nosed out the Pot of Gold.

"Got'im, Gorgonzo-laaa!" I yelled.

Aaaaaaaaaa moaned back Ambrose's marble fittings.

Aooooooooo mourned the wicker towel basket.

CHAPTER
TWENTY-FIVE

The rays of the setting sun sidled through the curved glass cupola of the Café Bar Oasis bronzing the feathery tops of the palm trees, the signal for the songbirds in their gilded cage to jostle vociferously for position on the roosting perches. In the adjacent Marrakesh courtyard a white-kaftaned figure was lighting the pierced and fretted pottery oil lamps. The stuff of holiday brochures. I swirled the cava bubbles round my glass and for the first time in two months really relaxed.

This morning's drug find on *Samarkand Princess* had wrapped everything up nicely. Following Vanheusen's arrest, a vanload of papers had been seized from Exclusive's offices and after several hours of questioning, Monique and Cousin Ashley had been ordered to report daily to the nearest police office. Passports confiscated, of course.

Charlie refilled her glass from the bottle of inexpensive cava nestling in an ice bucket before us. "So . . ." She took a long swig that opened the sluice gates to a stream of clichés. ". . . when the chips were down, Gorgonzola came up trumps. Close run thing, though. Came within a whisker of —"

"Talking of whiskers, we should be toasting Black Prince," I said. "With all that scented bathwater and the aromatherapy fug, even G would have missed Vanheusen's little stash. Clever, you know. There's nothing suspicious about the smell of candles and bath oils in a bathroom."

"Anywhere else, and you'd have smelt a rat, eh?" Her *ha, ha* was followed by *ptschchchchh* as the cava bubbles took an unexpected re-route to her lungs.

"You sound like Black Prince going down for the last time, Charlie," I said. "Yes, we've got to hand it to Vanheusen. It was a masterstroke to fill the bath and make it look as if our raid had interrupted a long soak in that marvellous wooden tub."

"Jayne told me that the *Ministerio del Interior*'s phone was red hot with calls from Vanheusen's friends in high places. If it hadn't been for you and Gorgonzola," she reached forward to clink her glass with mine, "London would have put Gerry through the office shredder."

I leant forward lowering my voice. "I'll tell you this in confidence, Charlie. When he thought the drugs were too well hidden and it was all up for him, he quite lost his cool. He actually called G," I lowered my voice still more, "a *moth-eaten shock-trooper*."

I'm afraid this calumny was not treated with the horror it merited. Her *hahahahaha* ricocheted off the green glass cupola, momentarily silencing the songbirds and turning a few heads. Over her shoulder I saw the lamplighter light the last lamp and glide off towards the Casablanca courtyard.

"That levity's *quite* uncalled for," I growled. "You can go off people, you know. Anyway, Gerry made amends. He sent a messenger round with an icebox full of caviar, beluga, of course."

"Gosh, that must have cost him." I could tell that she was impressed.

I smiled. "I suspect he liberated it from the fridge of *Samarkand Princess*. Still, it's the thought that counts, isn't it?"

"Certainly is." Charlie swirled a finger round the inner circumference of her giant hoop earring. "Seriously though, DJ, I'm really going to miss Gorgonzola — and you, of course. I'm off tomorrow. Already packed. What about you?"

"I've a pile of paperwork this high on my desk that'll keep me here to the end of the week. It'll give me time to pop in and see Jason. I hear he's a bit down, so I've got something that will —"

Perleep perleep perleep peep peep.

I fished my mobile out of my bag. What now? Couldn't a girl have *some* time off?

"Deborah? Hello, dear. It's Victoria. I've been away all weekend, on a last tour round the island to see if there's anything to match El Sooeno. But you know how it is when you've set your heart on something. There was nothing, nothing at all." A wistful sigh whispered down the line.

"I really *am* sorry, Victoria." And I was. *It's so lonely without Jack*, she'd said. El Sueño had been her dream home, a place to find happiness again with grandchildren and a friend or two . . .

341

"Reception gave me your note, dear. I'm so glad everything's all right. And I'd just love to join you and your friend. I'll be right down."

"Looking forward to seeing you, Victoria." I stowed away my phone.

Charlie pursed her lips. "What's that little frown for, DJ? Something wrong?"

"Her heart's still set on El Sueño. I wish there was something I could do."

"I think you're on to a loser there." Charlie made little circles on the terracotta tiles with the toe of her Roman sandal, sending the tuft of fetchingly bizarre bird feathers that dangled from her pearl anklet fluttering and swooping as if in flight. "Vanheusen's busted. His assets will be frozen, so . . ."

I stared thoughtfully at the droplets of moisture beading the cava bottle. ". . . So once the law steps in, it'll be too late to do anything. Yes, tonight's the last chance for me to —" I stood up and waved. "Over here, Victoria."

While she settled herself on the wrought-iron chair and placed her handbag on the floor, I filled up her glass.

"I just wanted to say goodbye, Victoria, and thank you for telling Charlie that I was missing. A piece of my windsurfer broke off in the heavy seas, and if the coastguard hadn't turned up, it would have been very nasty. So I'm very grateful to you both." I raised my glass in a toast.

"Glad everything's turned out all right, dear." We clinked glasses. "Isn't it lucky that I got back in time for this little get-together. I would have been here earlier, but I called in at Exclusive's offices to see if that Reservation Contract, or whatever the term is, had timed itself out." She picked up her glass of cava, and put it down again. "Monique Devereux was there, doing some paperwork. She apologised for Mr Vanheusen not being available. In conference, she said."

"*Ptschchchchh*," Charlie spluttered, wiping her eyes. "Yes, he's in conference all right. In conference with the police. *Ptschchchchh*."

"The *police*?" Victoria's eyes widened. "Has there been a robbery?"

I leant over and thumped Charlie's back. "Something a bit more serious, I'm afraid. Exclusive's under investigation and Mr Vanheusen's been arrested. Financial matters, I understand."

"Mr Vanheusen's in prison? Oh dear." Victoria took a gulp from her glass and was silent for a long moment. Then, "This may sound a trifle selfish, Deborah, but does this mean that El Sooeno will come on the market again?"

I sighed. "I can't say, Victoria, but in these cases the assets are usually frozen. Financial matters can drag on and on, you know."

Charlie swirled her glass. "And if the case is proved, our Mr V will be out of circulation for a long, long time. I guess he'll find the accommodation Her Majesty provides is a bit more spartan than on that fancy yacht of his." She took a cautious sip. "I've heard prison meals can be quite good nowadays, but there'll be no more caviar for him."

"Or that thoroughly spoilt Persian cat of his," I added.

"A Persian? I've always wanted one of those, but Jack was allergic to long-haired cats . . ." A faraway look came into Victoria's eyes. "If Mr Vanheusen goes to prison, what will happen to the cat?"

I hadn't thought of that. "They don't have cat and dog homes here, but I think there's a couple of animal sanctuaries."

"It won't take kindly to a cage and consorting with common moggies, will it? The cat's a pedigree, and used to swanning round that villa and yacht of his." Egalitarian Charlie seemed quite unsympathetic.

"If it's lucky, someone might think to put it in a sanctuary. Otherwise . . ." I couldn't get out of my mind a trembling and bedraggled Black Prince looking up at me with huge frightened eyes. "C'mon, Charlie, he's a changed animal since he nearly drowned, quite timid and well . . . er . . . cuddly."

"Ha, ha." Charlie set down her glass with a thump. "Don't set me off again, DJ."

"Nearly drowned! The poor thing! And it'll be *so* missing its master." Victoria looked quite upset. "It's a pity I'm flying home on Friday. If only I'd been able to stay here in Tenerife, *I'd* have given it a home."

I didn't say anything. I didn't want to raise false hopes, but I was kicking an idea around in my head. There was just a chance . . .

The *Policía National* in Santa Cruz is situated on the stately Avenida Tres de Mayo, just up from the flowing white curves of Calatrava's auditorium and the modern three-level Titsa bus station. But unlike the *Policía Locale* opposite, which shouts its identity in a flourish of flags and letters nearly a metre tall, the National Police HQ lurks discreetly. No signs or notices advertise its presence. Only two storeys of a stone-block building peep over the three-metre-high roughcast wall; the lower windows are heavily grilled, the upper row protected by closed metal shutters. If Gerry hadn't given me precise directions, I'd have driven straight past.

"There's an underground car park with an entrance on the avenida, but the gate will be shut," he'd said. "You'll have to drive round the corner to the main gate."

What he hadn't said was that the main gate also shunned the limelight. It was set in high walls taking up the right-hand side of a narrow residential side street of bijou houses, each with its pillared porch and tiny, neat garden, each with its carefully chosen cactus, bougainvillea or agave plant.

After checking my papers at the barred gate with its Portakabin-style guardhouse, the uniformed guard admitted me to a central courtyard full of cars and unmarked vans. I'd anticipated some difficulty in arranging access to Vanheusen, but I'd told Gerry firmly that he owed it to me to pull a few strings, and he'd raised an eyebrow but no objections, so fifteen minutes after threading my way through the cars, I was face to face with Ambrose himself.

He looked up as I was ushered into a sparsely furnished room, very different from the sumptuous surroundings of *Samarkand Princess*. Beneath the slowly revolving blades of the ceiling fan, Exclusive's millionaire boss was sitting on a hard wooden chair drawn up to a cheap plastic-topped table. Santa Cruz Police HQ funds, it seemed, did not run to white leather state-of-the-art swivel chairs with pop-out drinks tray. The only things that swivelled were his eyes. After a quick glance at me, they slewed away and focused on the boots of the policeman standing beside the door.

I drew up a chair. "Hello, Ambrose. Monique wasn't allowed to come, so she asked me to find out if there's anything . . ."

He looked at me, thumb stroking his upper lip in that familiar gesture, eyes calculating, assessing. How was he going to play it?

"All this is a complete misunderstanding, Deborah." Said with a wry smile. "Some kind of stupid foul-up, but my lawyers are confident that they'll soon have me out of here."

He was polishing his brass neck, as Charlie would have put it. GRECO, the Spanish unit set up to combat major organised crime, had opposed bail, and HM Government would certainly be seeking his extradition.

"But enough of my temporary little difficulties." He flicked a hand as if brushing away an annoying insect, and leant back. "How did that board of mine handle on your run to Las Américas?" He certainly believed in polishing that brass neck.

346

I took my cue from him. "It handled wonderfully. Best board I've ever tried, but . . ." I inserted a wobble into my voice. "I don't know how to tell you this, but I had an accident and if a fishing boat hadn't come along . . . I don't remember much about it as I was a bit concussed, but I'm afraid your board's been lost at sea. I'm awfully sorry, Ambrose . . ." I trailed off with an embarrassed half-smile.

Relief flickered in the depths of those pale blue eyes. "You had an accident with the board? Well, I did say to you that it was a bit unwise to attempt a solo run to Los Cristianos." He reached across the table and patted my hand. "But there, there, don't you worry about that, Deborah. As long as you're safe, that's what *really* matters."

It's difficult to sound suitably grateful when someone who's tried to kill you expresses concern about your welfare, but I managed it. "That's *very* generous of you Ambrose. I feel bad about it, though. It was a really expensive board." I hesitated. Now to make my play. "I don't want to add to your worries when you're in a spot of bother but, as I said, Monique sent me. She's worried about Black Prince. If you're, er . . . detained for any length of time, she says he'll have to be put into an animal sanctuary."

"*No!*" The flat of his hand crashed down on the table.

I flinched. The policeman took a warning step forward. A silence fell. I let it draw out.

After a few moments I heaved an insincere sigh. "I do so wish I could look after him myself, but I've just heard that headquarters are sending me to South America. I'm quite looking forward to it, actually. I'll have similar accommodation arrangements to here, I believe, so I won't have to worry about Persepolis. It'll be absolutely marvellous to make short trips into the rain forest to see the rare gorgonzolias growing in the wild!" (Jayne would have been proud of me.) I flashed him an apologetic smile. "Oh dear, sorry for babbling on like this."

"Not at all," he said, his thoughts elsewhere.

It was time for my trump card. "Is there *nobody* you can trust to look after him? Somebody who breeds Persians, perhaps? But then you've got to be to be *so* careful that they don't take advantage, haven't you?" A strategic pause to let him work it out. "You know what I mean?" My raised eyebrow indicated the danger of unauthorised little Black Prince scions.

"It's worrying, yes." A tightening of his lips indicated that I'd hit my target.

"It's *such* a pity Victoria's flying home on Friday," I sighed. "She'd have been just the person . . . a cat lover, so motherly."

"Victoria?"

"Victoria Knight. She's the current client who was very keen to purchase El Sueño. She was so disappointed when she heard there was another buyer."

"Ah yes. I remember." His eyes flicked away.

"She could have looked after The Prince for you. He'd have felt so much at home in El Sueño. Just the other day she was telling me about the Persians she's cared for over the years." I was bending the truth a little. The only Persians she'd cared for, to be honest, were of the carpet variety. "They were just pets, of course. She's never had any contact with breeders. Such a pity she wasn't able to purchase the property."

"No contact with breeders . . . El Sueño . . ." He looked thoughtful.

I nudged things along a little. "When Monique heard that you'd . . . er . . . been taken here, her first thought was to collect Black Prince from the yacht, but for some reason the police wouldn't let her on board. They told her the cat had been dashing in a panic all over the ship and they'd put him in a cat-carrier. He's here now at HQ. I suppose you could say he's been arrested." The word "too" hung in the air between us.

He stared down at the scratched and scuffed surface of the table, muttering to himself, "El Sueño . . . have to be tonight."

"And Persian coats get so tangled, don't they? It's so painful for them if they're not groomed for a couple of days. I asked after him when I arrived here, and it seems," I sighed, "that The Prince is pining, not taking at all well to the cat-carrier." I let that sink in. "They're talking of sending him to an animal sanctuary — only till you're out and about again, of course."

I'd played all my cards. I waited. Overhead the fan performed slow gyrations, stirring the hair on the top of my head. In the silence I heard the creak of leather as the police guard shifted position.

"Let me see . . ." He pursed his lips. "I believe that the Reservation Contract on El Sueño expired yesterday afternoon. The chap said he'd other commitments now. So it *would* be available."

I piled on the pressure. "What a pity she didn't know that. On the rebound from her disappointment over El Sueño she's settled for a villa on the Costa del Sol. She's signed the Offer to Buy, and the Reservation Contract and all that. The only consolation, she said, was that she'd be paying £800,000 for that villa instead of £1.5 million for El Sueño." I pursed my lips. "She'll be saving such a lot of money that she'll probably not change her mind." A turn of the screw. "Especially as there'd be the contract cancellation costs too . . ."

Another little frown from Ambrose. Had I overplayed my hand?

Just when I thought I'd blown it, he capitulated. "If she agreed to take on the care of The Prince, Exclusive could match that price."

Neither of us commented on the implication that Black Prince's residence at El Sueño was going to be somewhat protracted.

Tomorrow's court order would freeze his assets. I'd have to make it easy for him to press me to act tonight. I pushed back my chair. "Well, I'll certainly put that to her on Thursday when I take her to the airport."

He stood up, sending his chair clattering to the floor. The guard took a couple of steps forward.

"The Prince means so much to me. He mustn't suffer a moment longer." He gripped the edge of the table. "If you've a pen and piece of paper handy, I'll write a note to Monique. That agreement *has* to be signed tonight, Deborah."

350

I almost felt sorry for him. "I'll see to it, Ambrose. I know just how you're feeling. I'd be the same with Persepolis. Tell you what, if you give me a note for the comandante, I'll take Black Prince away with me now."

When I phoned him, Gerry sighed and pulled a few more strings. And ten minutes after that, I was crossing the courtyard car park of *Policía National*, Santa Cruz. In my hand was the cat-carrier and its trembling occupant; in my pocket, Ambrose's handwritten note, the passport to happiness for Victoria.

Epilogue

I pushed open the door of Jason's room in the *clinica* and peered in. He was lying propped up on pillows, face pale, dark circles under his eyes. Over the worst, they'd said, but he had a long way to go. In Gerry's opinion, he needed cheering up, and here I was to do just that.

"Hi there, Jase," I said.

He raised a hand in greeting, his smile a shadow of the much-exercised playboy grin.

I perched on the edge of the bed. "Remember that bet we had? I'm here to deliver."

He frowned. "Bet?"

"I owed you two kisses, remember?"

"Ready when you are, Debs." I caught the gleam in his eye, the first sign of my old Don Juan Jason.

He wasn't exactly in prime fettle, so I didn't have to put up with too much of the lingering tongue-in-the-mouth stuff.

At length I broke away. "Not bad, Jase, for someone in a hospital bed." I gently removed a wandering hand. "And now —" I went to the door and opened it. "There's another lady outside waiting to meet you." I reached into my bag and pressed the remote control.

From the corridor came a long-drawn-out *mi-aa-oow*.

Framed in the doorway were the stumpy ears and grotesque square head of Robocat.

"Brunhilda!"

I squeezed another button on the remote control. The beast emitted a deep rolling *purrrr* and bounded forward.

The look on Jason's face more than compensated for that rather large sum of money I'd had to fork out to repair G's handiwork.

I spent the rest of the day cleaning Calle Rafael Alberti, numero 2 and disposing of perishables to Jesús and the rubbish bin.

A few more items and I'd have finished the packing. I held up a pair of faded jeans, a parting gift from Charlie. Slashed with horizontal slits all the way down the legs, I just couldn't see myself wearing them.

"They're the cutting-edge of fashion. Time you entered the twenty-first century, Debs," she'd giggled.

Maybe I *should* give them a try. I placed them in the case and closed down the lid.

It was almost time to go. I hauled out the cat-carrier from where I'd stowed it in the wardrobe, out of sight, out of the feline mind.

"You're not going to like this, G," I muttered, "but there's one more bit of packing to do. And it's you."

A well-established routine of Cajolery, Pleading and Bribery would be needed to persuade her into the cat-carrier. All three stages were a prerequisite. I'd asked Jesús to soften her up with the long-drawn-out quavering notes of his *madrelena*, and now, ready to cajole, cat-carrier in hand, I stepped out onto the patio.

Eeeee . . . aa . . . eee . . . Aaaah . . . aa . . . eeee . . . The undulating wails of the *madrelena* fretted the wall and zigzagged away into the night sky.

I'd miss Jesús, but not that droning off-key dirge. G would, though. She was lying on the bench under the papery bracts of the bougainvillea, paws limp, eyes half-closed. Smiling ingratiatingly, I put the cat-carrier down beside her.

She lazily stretched a leg and flexed her claws.

Eeeee . . . aa . . . eee . . . Aaaah . . . aa . . . eeee . . . Jesús was in fine voice tonight.

I unlatched the carrier. "Lovely soft blanket in here, G," I coaxed. "In you get."

She yawned sleepily and made no move to obey. To hell with all this craven buttering-up, I made a grab.

I was fast, but she was faster. A ginger blur arrowed its way to the top beam of the pergola. There, out of reach, she dug in her claws, literally and figuratively.

Impasse.

I flounced back indoors and unearthed her working collar from the suitcase.

"Collar, G." I dangled it hopefully in front of the carrier, then cooed with false heartiness, "Du-ty."

Her tail twitched as if in painful remembrance of The Snatching of the Hairs. She'd been caught that way before. Her back arched, her claws dug in more firmly.

This could take hours.

Behind me Jesús said, "I sing the *madrelena* and I hold the box. Then she come, señora. *No problema.*"

And there wasn't.

I secured the carrier door. "*Muchas, muchas grac —*"

I stared at Jesús. His lips weren't moving, but the *Eeeee . . . aa . . . eee . . . Aaaah . . . aa . . . eeee . . .* Notes of the *madrelena* were still spiralling up from his pots of geraniums like audible wisps of smoke.

"I make a *cinta,* a *cassetta,*" he confessed with a gummy grin. "When you go home, the cat every night she will hear the *madrelena* and she be happy."

I planted a kiss on each leathery cheek. "Jesús, you are a genius."

Number one priority, the purchase *prontissimo* of a set of heavy-duty earplugs.

Also available in ISIS Large Print:

Shafted

Mandasue Heller

Larry Logan is a small-time TV star with a mile-wide ego. Gutted when his latest show is axed, he's less than impressed when the only work he can get is fronting a fake game show — actually an undercover police sting to entrap criminals. His reluctance evaporates when the show rockets his career back to prime-time stardom. And when lovely, shy Stephanie enters his life, he thinks he finally has it made.

But then it all begins to go wrong. Larry is arrested, on-screen, for a shocking crime. He's shafted some dangerous men — is this their revenge?

ISBN 978-0-7531-8164-5 (hb)
ISBN 978-0-7531-8165-2 (pb)

The Twilight Time

Karen Campbell

Anna Cameron is a new Sergeant in the Flexi unit. On her first day in the new job she discovers she'll be working with her ex, Jamie, now married with a child. In at the deep end emotionally after many years without him, she's also plunged headlong into the underworld of Glasgow's notorious Drag — the haunt of working girls, drug dealers and sad, seedy men. Someone is carving up the faces of local prostitutes, an old man has been brutally killed and racist violence is on the rise. Anna must deal with all this, alongside tensions and backstabbing within her own team.

ISBN 978-0-7531-8072-3 (hb)
ISBN 978-0-7531-8073-0 (pb)

Where the Shadow Falls

Gillian Galbraith

An Alice Rice mystery

When the body of a retired sheriff is discovered in his grand house in the New Town of Edinburgh, Detective Sergeant Alice Rice finds herself hunting his killer. The search leads her to an unfamiliar world where wind-farm developers — with millions of pounds at stake — and protesters face each other with daggers drawn. Just as Alice thinks an answer is beginning to emerge, one of the suspects is killed in an apparent hit-and-run accident.

An unlikely coincidence or, as the search widens, is Alice now investigating a double murder?

ISBN 978-0-7531-8146-1 (hb)
ISBN 978-0-7531-8147-8 (pb)

Murder at Deviation Junction

Andrew Martin

December, 1909. A train hits a snowdrift in the frozen Cleveland Hills. In the process of clearing the line a body is discovered, and so begins a dangerous case for struggling railway detective Jim Stringer.

His new investigation takes him to the mighty blast furnaces of Ironopolis; to Fleet Street in the company of a cynical reporter from The Railway Rover; and to a nightmarish spot in the Highlands. Jim's faltering career in the railway police hangs on whether he can solve the murder — but before long, the pursuer becomes the pursued, and Jim finds himself fighting not just for his job, but for his very life . . .

ISBN 978-0-7531-8130-0 (hb)
ISBN 978-0-7531-8131-7 (pb)